THRILLING ADVENTURE
Yarns

EDITED BY ROBERT GREENBERGER

CRAZY 8 PRESS

Contents for Summer 2019

Thrilling Occult Yarns

Thrilling Sword & Sorcery Yarns

Cover Art by Alex Ronald

Logo by Jim Campbell
Illustrations by
Caio Cacau
Mike Collins
Karl Kesel
Peter Krause
Tom Mandrake
Jerry Ordway
Daniele Serra
Mark Wheatley

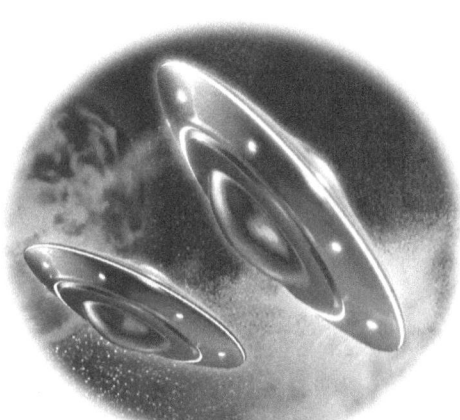

The Crazy Complicated Cat Caper

By WILL MURRAY

I DIDN'T think "cat," never mind cat's-paw, when the client first walked into my office. With his bristling eyebrows, needle mustaches and Malacca walking stick, he reminded me of another eccentric, namely Salvador Dali.

I eyed him up and down. "What can I do for you, Mr.—"

"Frasca. Felix Frasca." He didn't exactly purr his name, but he came darn close.

"Felix 'Catman' Frasca?" I asked. He beamed. "Precisely the same."

Now I'm no stickler for perfect grammar, but I would have liked him more if he had left off "the same." Or just skipped the precisely. Either would do.

"You have an estate in Castle Hills," I recounted. "You collect cat artifacts—"

"Feline statuary," the Catman corrected.

I don't like being corrected either, but I let it pass. Waving him to a seat, I asked, "What can I do for you, Mr. Frasca?"

"I would like to hire you," he said firmly. When he let the statement hang in the air as if that was all I needed to know, I repressed a growl of impatience.

"Most clients do," I said dryly. "Exactly what kind of caper do you have in mind?"

"Caper? Oh, I see. Levity." His teeth flashed beneath his quirky mustache. "Yes, I have arranged to purchase for a considerable, er, substantial consideration, a very valuable item that has by now arrived in Mexico. I would like you to pick it up and drive the prize back to Texas for me."

I could feel my eyebrows arching up. "Drive, not fly?"

"The object d'art would not tolerate the rigors of air travel, I fear."

"I see," I said, not seeing at all. "What is this object?"

"It is a bronze—a Corinthian jaguar, to be precise."

I smiled. I often do when I'm annoyed. "You can't fool me, Mr. Frasca. Corinth is in Greece and jaguars are native to South America. I should know. I own one. A jaguar, that is. Actually two, but one happens to be a sports car."

"Yes, I know all about your pet jaguar. That is the precise reason I hired you. We have cats in common. And you happen to be the infamous Kathy Delgado, the most successful and—dare I say it?—unorthodox private detective in San Antonio."

"I haven't exactly been hired yet," I allowed. "But let's skip over the incidental details and pounce on the prey. Why do you need a private eye to run an international errand?"

"An astute question, Miss Delgado." He drew in a deep breath. "When the city-state of Corinth was sacked in 146 B. C., the royal treasure stores were burnt to the ground. Among the ruins was found a new alloy—an admixture of gold, silver and copper subsequently dubbed Corinthian bronze. Apparently, the intense heat and other conditions smelted the ruler's treasures in a manner no modern metallurgist has ever been able to duplicate. As such, the resulting slag became more valuable than gold. No example of Corinthian bronze survives into the Twentieth Century, I might add."

Mr. Frasca paused as if I should be writing his little lecture down. When I failed to take up the challenge, he went on.

"Recently, a bronze work was discovered in an Inca mortuary tomb that appears to be of a similar alloy. A jaguar, as I indicated. If ancient Inca metallurgists independently fabricated Corinthian bronze, this example would be worth a fortune. I must have it for my collection, Miss Delgado. That is where you come into the picture."

"Why me?"

He smiled slightly, which quirked his eyebrows and needle points in unison.

"We are both cat fanciers. Experience has taught me that cat fanciers are the most trustworthy of persons. Which is why I turn to you to conduct the possibly priceless artifact into my possession." His smile widened. I thought of the Cheshire cat. I would have tugged on Mr. Frasca's tail if I thought it would erase that irritating grin, and if he had one—a tail, that is.

On the other hand, flattery is nice to hear. But that wasn't why I replied, "Where and when, Mr. Frasca?"

"Yes, in due course. But first there is the matter of the how much."

I quoted twice my going price and he didn't blink.

"It is a deal," Frasca purred. He really did purr that time. I have it on tape. My toe had triggered the hidden recorder at the first "precisely." A girl can't be too careful when dealing with clients with overcomplicated stories.

"Now," he continued, "you are to drive to El Paso and meet a Mr. Queztalcoatl, then take possession of the cat."

"What about U. S. customs? They're finicky about what comes over the border."

An envelope landed on my desk. "Here are your instructions, the receipt to be signed, and the proper papers. All are precisely in order. I will accept delivery at this very office."

"I'll need a retainer check, Mr. Frasca. Half up front."

Out from his blazer pocket came a check. It had already been filled out by the confident Mr. Frasca.

"This is more than half," I pointed out.

He smiled. "Precisely."

"No," I corrected. "Approximately."

Frasca shrugged nonchalantly as he rose to his feet. "I like to be efficient in my business dealings, so I took the liberty of writing a check in advance for what I determined to be a generous amount. We can settle the difference in due course."

I smiled him out of my office, saying, "In that case, I'll see you in a few days, Mr. Frasca. Give or take a fortnight."

I CALLED my rival P. I. and sometime confederate, Tony Blunt. We used to be partners, but Tony acquired ambition. His loss, as it turned out. I had outgrown the partnership, anyway.

"Tony. Kathy. I need to borrow your Volkswagen van for a couple of days."

His voice over the line winced with suspicion. Not that I can blame him, given our checkered history. "For what?"

"I just had a visit from the Catman," I volunteered.

"Is that anything like the Sandman?"

"Now that you mention it, I do feel as if I have some grit in my eyes. They could be second cousins, at that. But that's another story. Now how about that van?"

"Not without knowing the score, Kathy."

"It's a secret. But I have to drive to El Paso and pick up a certain something."

"El Paso? Is this on the level?"

"Probably not," I admitted. "But it's got my Irish up and I want to play it out to see how right I am."

"I didn't know you were Irish."

"I'm not. But I skipped last Saint Patrick's Day festivities, so I'm due to wear a little green."

Tony suddenly demanded, "What do you mean—to see how right you are?"

"No one's ever hired me to be cat's-paw before, and I want to see how it feels."

"No dice, Kathy. It smells dangerous." Tony sounded so concerned for my welfare that I decided to let him have his way for almost twenty minutes.

After the twenty minutes were up, he relented. "Okay, okay. But I'm riding shotgun."

"Imagine that we are shaking hands. Just remember whose case this is, Tony," I warned.

I made arrangements and we were on the road within two

hours. I filled Tony in around the edges, letting him smell the cream filling without knowing what was cooking.

"Sounds fishy to me," he growled. "Better turn this thing around right now, Kathy!"

"And return this fat retainer? No thanks!"

"Do you know how much time in the pokey goes with smuggling?"

"We're not smuggling anything," I snapped. "According to my instructions, the Corinthian jaguar is under glass and completely visible. Once I see the bronze, I'll wire Mr. Frasca and he will wire payment to Mr. Quetzalcoatl."

"That name sounds familiar," Tony muttered.

"Me, too. So I looked it up. It's the name of an Aztec god—the Feathered Serpent. Famous for being bloodthirsty and cruel. Doesn't sound like my type at all."

Tony moaned. "Is there anything about this that doesn't sound phony?"

"Yes, there is. Mr. Frasca's retainer check wasn't at all rubbery."

We took turns driving the bug until we crossed the border at El Paso. I batted my eyes and flashed my most disarming smile as I flirted with the customs officer at the crossing. He might not be on duty when I returned this way, and while a gal gets lucky when she least expects it, I like to make my own. Luck, that is.

I WAS expecting a curio shop. It was a dusty old pet shop, specializing in exotic birds. They set up a cacophony that rattled my ribs as we entered. I saw gray parrots and big-beaked toucans in dirty cages that would give Tigre, my pet jaguar, the shivers. The birds, not the cages.

Mr. Quetzalcoatl answered to the first name of Ramon. He got right down to bronze tacks. "I will show you the jaguar," he said, waving us into the back room.

Sitting uncovered on a table, it was bigger than I imagined. I've seen smaller television sets.

"The Maltese Falcon, this isn't," Tony breathed, echoing my own thought.

The jaguar was reddish-brown with gold glints. It looked too shiny to have been cached in an old Incan tomb for a thousand years or so. It lay coiled in a half ball as if cat-napping, its triangular ears perked up.

The casing was Plexiglas, and the whole ensemble was mounted on a perforated copper base that was almost as big as the display it supported.

"Why the holes?" I asked.

"Ventilation," said Mr. Q. "So the cat does not tarnish."

It sounded only half-plausible. But the look Tony gave me suggested he had swallowed it whole. He was never as bright as his mother imagined him to be.

While Tony went to find a Western Union office, I studied the jaguar. There was no question that it was a jaguar—although it looked nothing like my Tigre. Tigre was much more refined, but then she's a city cat. The workmanship was serviceable—nothing more. The rosette spots were etched into the skin, forming irregular outlines.

"How old do you suppose it is?" I asked Mr. Q.

Ramon shrugged as if he neither knew nor cared.

The door banged open. "Message sent," Tony reported. "Your bank will be calling."

It took nearly an hour, but this was Mexico. The phone rang, and Mr. Q fell into earnest Spanish converse with the caller. I caught enough of it to know that his bank account had grown by leaps and bounds.

After he hung up, we did a little paperwork, then Tony and Mr. Q loaded the bronze jaguar into the back of the Beetle. It took both of them. The display case was more clumsy than heavy, but it wasn't light either.

As Tony closed the rear doors, Mr. Q reminded us, "Do not forget to run the air conditioner. The cat is *muy* sensitive to heat and humidity."

"*Gracias*, Mr. Q," I said. We took off. I let Tony drive. He felt more in control that way, and would complain much less.

"Well?" I asked him.

"If there's any contraband concealed in the base," he growled, "I'll eat half, if you take the other half."

"No deal, Tony. I'm worried."

Tony slapped his forehead. "*Now* you're worried. For once, can't you worry *before* you take on a risky case?"

"Tony, I read up on Corinthian bronze before we left. It's not supposed to tarnish. That's one of its legendary advantages."

Worry picked at his sharp profile. "Maybe everyone's just being careful."

I turned to look at him. "Do you really believe that, Tony?"

"Not for a minute. But I got to tell myself something until this is all over…"

We reached the border crossing before we were ready. I pulled down the top of my peasant blouse as far as it would go—and then some.

At the checkpoint, Tony braked the van and rolled down his window.

The border guard was one of those no-nonsense types. He drilled Tony pretty thoroughly, and Tony gave it back straight and narrow, and without any guff. Sometimes he's useful that way.

"What's in back?" the guard asked.

I jumped into that opening with both feet. "Let me show him, Tony. I'm curious for a second opinion."

Ever the straight man, Tony said, "Sure, Kathy." He made it sound just like we were man and wife, which we are—in his dreams.

I stepped out of air-conditioned comfort into the dry afternoon heat, and reached the back before the guard. There, he got his first good look at me.

"Cat got your tongue?" I asked with a smile.

"You might want to fix that blouse," he muttered, turning crimson.

I made a project of it, and his face got redder. Then I flung open the rear doors.

"This is a rare Corinthian jaguar," I announced. "Maybe the only one in the world. I think we paid too much for it. What do you think?"

The guard splashed light from his flashlight, saw the gleaming golden cat, then spotted the holes perforating the copper base. He frowned. I'd swear he was even more suspicious than I was.

"To prevent tarnishing," I explained. "Here's the bill of sale, receipt, et cetera."

He glanced over the documents. "You'll have to take it out," he said sternly.

"Anything you say, officer." I started to clamber in, and right on cue, the right side of my blouse slipped down. The officer found that I was winking at him without employing my eyes. He couldn't help but stare.

"Everything okay back there, Kathy?" asked Tony impatiently.

I fixed my blouse and laid a finger in front of my lips. "Say nothing. He gets jealous. Insanely jealous."

This time the guard turned pale. I liked the speed at which he changed colors.

He also changed his mind pretty fast. Hopping in, he muscled the display case around, lifting one corner and then the other experimentally.

"It feels like there's something sliding around in the base," the guard said suspiciously.

"Oh, that," I said, thinking fast. "That's just the big old bag of charcoal to filter the circulating air. They use them in aquariums, you know."

The guard looked doubtful. He got down on his knees and using his flash ray, tried to peer in through the perforations.

"I see something that looks kinda like that," he said, climbing out.

I smiled and strung compliments with my words. "You have excellent eyes. I took a peek and couldn't make out a darn thing."

Clambering out, the guard said reluctantly, "You can go."

We went. After we were safety in El Paso, I turned to Tony, "Did you feel anything sliding around when you moved that thing?"

"Now that you mention it, maybe. It felt like ballast, though."

"Well, we got away with it—whatever *it* is."

"Don't count your chickens just yet, Kathy."

"It's not my chickens I'm confident about," I returned. "It's my cats."

THE next morning, we were back in San Antonio and going our separate ways. After dropping the bronze off at my apartment, I called the maid to let her know I was back, then drove to my office downtown. There were no messages. I phoned Felix Frasca first thing, but he didn't pick up. The second thing, I grabbed a newspaper and saw why he hadn't called. He couldn't.

The headline read:

CATMAN MAULED
TO DEATH
Castle Hills Art Collector Dies

The piece was brief. It seems that the precise Mr. Frasca was found on the exquisitely manicured grounds of his sumptuous estate, clawed to ribbons as if by a wild animal. But no such animal could be found.

I called my old friend, Daniel Drake of the Bexar County Sheriff's Department.

"Hello, Sheriff, what's this I hear about Felix Frasca?"

"If you read it in the papers," he said wearily, "you know as much as we do. It happened yesterday around 3 PM."

I made a quick calculation. That was an hour after the Catman wired his finder's fee to El Paso. I began to wonder how square that square border guard really was. Under the circumstances, he had been kind of a pushover.

"What killed him?"

"A cougar—maybe. We're hunting it now." Interest colored his routine tone of voice. "What's your stake in this?" he barked.

"Frasca is—was—a client."

He became firm. "Maybe you should come down to have a talk, Kathy."

"I will. Honest. But later. I just blew into town this minute."

"That gives you an alibi," Dan said dryly.

"Now, now, Sheriff Dan," I admonished. "Why would little ole me need an alibi?"

"Kathy, when did you ever *not* need an alibi? Don't keep me waiting too long."

"I wouldn't dream of it."

I HOPPED in the office shower to skim off the desert dust and heat. That took only ten minutes. During that time my office door was jimmied and an undetermined number of men entered and ransacked the place with an efficiency that was breathtaking. They might have been little mouse-footed packrats.

I stepped out naked as the proverbial jaybird, to behold the unhappy aftermath.

"Whoever they were," I muttered as I climbed into fresh clothes, "they didn't find what they wanted—and they didn't want me."

I checked the action on my snub-nosed .38 revolver and jumped back into my Jaguar XKE convertible. I headed home to Inwood. Fast.

Maybe I beat them to the punch, or maybe I had it figured all wrong, but my Papaya Arms apartment house looked sleepily normal when I pulled up.

I knocked on my own door before entering. A familiar growl replied. That was Tigre. My maid had been cat-sitting him while I was away. She must have dropped him off while I was at the office.

I keyed the door and stepped in, leading with my snub-nose. I dropped it when I saw that everything was in order.

Well, almost everything.

"Hello, Tigre. Tigre?"

For a jaguar, Tigre was tame. On second thought, tame might be a stretch. Half-feral was closer to the truth. She looked more like three-quarters feral as she slunk around the Corinthian bronze jaguar snoozing on the dining room table in its big display case.

"Why, Tigre!" I cried. "Don't tell me you're jealous!"

Tigre gave low growl in a way I never heard her growl before—it was not friendly, not playful. To tell the truth, it sounded positively weird.

"You're not in heat, are you? No, that can't be. You're fixed. Come over here, baby. Tell mama what's wrong."

But Tigre continued her nervous pacing, or stalking.

When I saw that she barely paid me any attention, I went into the kitchen to put on some coffee.

The percolator had only begun to bubble when a weird cry ripped through the apartment.

I raced in. "Tigre! What on earth—?"

The cry came again. I heard it distinctly. It was not Tigre. It sounded nothing like Tigre. I know every ripple in her vocal chords, and Tigre could never have managed such a screech. It belonged in the wild.

More to the point, Tigre's mouth was clamped shut when it came.

The vehemence of the cry took her by surprise. She recoiled from the display case and leapt atop the couch back, back arched, hackles raised, pacing back and forth. I'd never seen Tigre do that, either.

I crept up on the display case. The bronze jaguar was still curled in sleep. It had not come to life. For a crazy moment, I had wondered if it might have.

That left only the copper base with its sprinkling of perforations.

"Ventilation..." I undertoned. "But for what?"

I grabbed my tool kit and got down on the rug and began to work the retaining screws loose. Tigre paced like she was in a cage. The last time she acted like that there had been a rattlesnake loose in the apartment.

"Settle down," I told her. "I'm just going to take a peek."

Famous last words. I got one corner loose, and threw a beam from my penlight into the crack.

A yellow eye stared back at me. It reminded me of that rattler before I shot its head off. It gave me the identical goosebumps. Hurriedly, I squeezed the corner shut, and fumbled for the screws.

A screech like a barn owl shook me half out of my skin. Tigre pounced like a spotted fury, landing atop the display case. It came crashing off the coffee table.

So much for sealing the base. It broke open and something flashed out.

The next minute or three reminded me of one of those old movie cartoons where a dog and a cat turn into a spitting, shrieking ball of flying fur. It was hard to make out where one creature started and the other left off. All I could make out was tawny fur pinwheeling madly.

I got out of the way as fast as I could, and retreated to the kitchen, closing the connecting door to a crack.

Who was chasing whom I never did get straight. But if lightning in a bottle ever got loose, it got loose in my living room that day.

Round and around, they ran, spitting, snarling, screaming at one another. Fur flew. Claws swiped. No doubt fangs sank into furry flesh, but in the muscular whirlwind, it was hard to follow it all.

I know when I'm outclassed. I stayed out of it.

To this day, I don't know if Tigre cornered the creature, or it just happened to career into the coat closet. One moment all was fangs and fury, and the next Tigre was growling at my half-opened closet door.

That was my cue. I leaped in, slamming it shut. A low, surly growl came through the panel, then silence fell.

I looked around at the upset lamps and flood of magazines all over the fur-feathered rug and sighed.

"Well, it might have been worse."

Tigre was back on the couch, licking at a minor wound. Otherwise she seemed none the worse for wear.

I began picking up fur where I found it. Most of it was not from Tigre's dappled coat. This stuff was more coppery. A few fragments had dark patches, and I recalled catching glimpses of something that reminded me of a raccoon's ringed tail.

"That," I told Tigre, "was no raccoon."

Tigre regarded me without contradiction. Her feline expression was definitely reproachful, however.

I shrugged off the gathering guilt, grabbed the telephone and called a number I know by heart.

"Luis? I have a riddle for you: what screeches like an owl, sports a raccoon's ringed tail and a coat of coppery-red fur like a cougar?"

Aside from being a seasoned

reporter, Luis Serrano of the San Antonio *Express* was a walking encyclopedia of odd but handy facts.

"Sounds like a wildcat of some kind," he offered in his habitually absent-minded tone.

"No good, Luis. Wildcats are as common as squirrels. This creature is something special."

"What creature?"

"Never mind. Know any zoologists, by chance?"

"One or two. Here you go, doll. Grab a pencil."

I jotted down both numbers, thanked Luis before he could ask me out, and started dialing again.

But the seven digits of the phone number proved to be three digits too many.

My front door burst open and something hit me in the back, sharp and hard. The receiver fell from my hand, and my legs went out under me. Either the room began spinning, or I started turning like top. It felt like both. Counter-rotational forces quickly got the better of me.

I was clawing for my .38 when my chin hit the rug, and it was lights out, baby.

WHEN I came to, I was still alive. That counted for something.

Climbing to my feet, I almost made it. But my knees buckled. I gave it up and tried again. No go, Kathy.

There was a spot of blood on the rug where I had fallen. No enough to panic over, but a definite cause for concern.

I looked around, my eyes refusing to stay in focus. The Corinthian-Incan bronze was still there, half on the floor.

My closet door hung open. That meant the Tasmanian Devil was loose somewhere.

"Tigre...." I said weakly.

But Tigre didn't answer. Panic got me by the throat and I forced myself to crawl to the sofa. Climbing it was like scaling the Matterhorn. But I got on the cushions.

Working my way to a seated position, I took stock of the room. I didn't see Tigre. My heart sank. But I didn't see her beautiful tawny body, either.

Half an hour later, I was semi-ambulatory. A search of the apartment showed that Tigre had decamped.

When I had some strength back, I poured black coffee down my throat and shucked off my blouse and bra.

Standing before the full-length bathroom mirror, I examined my smarting back. And saw what looked like a puncture wound. Thin. Bruising had created an unlovely purple-black patch, and I knew I'd be a stranger to bikinis for at least a month.

A needle did that, I decided. Wait a minute. No, a tranquilizer gun! No wonder I felt hung over....

Knowing that I would be useless for a few hours more, I finished making that interrupted phone call.

"Hello, Dr. Shields? Kathy Delgado, private investigator. Oh, you've heard of me? How flattering, assuming your newspaper reading is selective. Yes, I do have a checkered reputation. Luis Serrano gave me your number. Listen, I am trying to identify a wild animal I caught a glimpse of..."

Dr. Shields was very patient with me. "You are describing no cougar or wildcat known in these parts," he said after I had sketched in the sketchy details.

"I think it was imported from somewhere else."

"Without more to go on, I'm afraid I can't help you, Miss Delgado."

"Call me Kathy. Wait. Try this line of reasoning. What would be the most valuable wild feline in or out of captivity?"'

Dr. Shields thought a long time. "There are ghost cats no one has ever captured."

"Excuse me, did you say ghost cats?"

"Merely a term used to categorize any unclassified feline reportedly spotted in the wild, but never captured or observed scientifically."

I thought of the phantom cat that did for Felix Frasca, and repressed a shiver.

"Tell me more, Doctor," I invited.

"Well, there are cats thought to be mythical that might have lived

at one time, but are now extinct."

"Name a few."

"The one that is most credible is *Felis silvestris cretensis*—the Cretan wildcat."

"Cretan, not Corinthian?" I shot back.

"I have never heard of a Corinthian wildcat," said Dr. Shields. "The Cretan wildcat is thought to have been a native of the island of Crete—assuming that it ever actually existed."

"Tell me, doctor—did it have a ringed tail?"

"It might have. No credible description has ever been given."

"If one were caught alive, how much would it be worth?"

"A small fortune, Miss Delgado. Any major zoo would pay handsomely to house the only specimen ever known in captivity."

I smiled my best smile of sincere gratitude, hoping that it communicated over the wire.

"You've been very helpful. Dr. Shields. Now I have to see about getting my shots."

"Pardon me?"

I hung up. I didn't have the energy to summon up a clever quip.

Next, I got Sheriff Drake on the line. "Hello, Dan? About that appointment we had. Something's come up. In fact, I want to report a catnapping. Tigre is missing. Forcibly abducted, by all the signs. I need to track her down before I could possibly think straight. Bye."

I got it all out in one long breath,

and the receiver back in its cradle before he got a word in. I was out the door before the phone started ringing.

Moments later, I was behind the wheel of my Jag, fishing into the glove compartment where I keep my bag of tricks—tear gas gun, midget camera, etc. It was looking pretty thin, so I brainstormed and stopped by a pet store to make a quick purchase.

"A pound of your most potent *Nepata cataria*," I requested.

The manager protested, "We don't sell it by the pound. I don't think we have an entire pound of the stuff in stock."

"Then sell me all you've got," I told him, slapping down my Diner's Club card.

EVENING had fallen as I pulled into Castle Hills. A few stars had appeared, but the moon was in hiding.

The estate of the late Felix Frasca was almost exactly as I pictured it—a white Colonial pile of sheer ostentation. I was surprised the town fathers had not bylawed it out of existence. Maybe they had tried, and failed.

It appeared to be moving day. There were big van trucks everywhere. Somehow, I didn't think it was the coroner's office combing the grounds.

I parked the Jag in a secluded spot, changed into my midnight-blue prowler suit, and slipped onto the grounds unseen.

I counted a half dozen men and they were taking empty cages into a huge detached building, and bringing them out again, draped in dark cloth.

One came out, and he recharged a pistol I assumed to be a tranquilizer gun.

I crept up on him, and stuck the cold barrel of my .38 against his stiffening spine.

"Turnabout is fair play," I hissed. "And I might add that this is real gun."

"Who?"

"Why don't you start the introductions," I suggested. "No? Then tell me where my pet jaguar is. Your spine will thank you for it."

"I can lead you there..." he said at last.

"You'd do that for little old me? How gallant of you."

He led, but I steered. In that fashion, we made our way to a truck with an open back.

He was nice enough to climb in and pull the wool blanket off Tigre's cage. Tigre was in a foul temper. I could tell by her beady little golden eyes.

I handed Mr. Tranquilizer a leash, which I had wrapped around my waist.

"You know what to do with this."

"Are you crazy?" he gulped. "He'll claw me to ribbons!"

"She, fraidy cat," I retorted. "Open the cage and I'll do it."

It went smoothly. I leashed Tigre

and escorted her out.

"Hold her a second, would you?" I asked. "She's too groggy to bite."

The catnapper took the leash in both hands, and I knocked him out cold with the butt of my .38.

"Serves you right," I said curtly.

With Tigre in tow, I stepped out into the moonlight.

"Jig's up!" I shouted.

Everyone froze.

It was a wonderful moment. Too bad it didn't last.

Somebody had a heavy barrel flashlight. He lifted it, hit the switch and dashed blinding light into my eyes. I flinched only a moment. A moment is all he needed.

The flashlight bounced off my noggin before I could react. I went down.

The next thing I knew I was at the bottom on a pig pile of attackers. I felt like a halfback who had been sacked by an entire football team. I got off a snap shot before someone disarmed me with a Judo hold. And I managed to do some impromptu dental work on another shadowy attacker with a sharp elbow. But I was outnumbered. And that's what counted.

They dragged me into the outbuilding, and I wasn't surprised by all the cages.

A few still had feral cats in them. They looked agitated.

"So," I said in a voice cooler than I felt. "The Catman also collected exotic cats—of the live variety. Now you boys are making off with the entire collection. Very slick."

"Only one really matters," said a man with wavy red hair and a thin mustache to match. I wondered if mustaches and cats always went together.

"The Cretan wildcat?" I suggested.

Redhead looked startled. "How did you—"

"Wild guess, I guess. Now what?"

He had Tigre by the leash. Tigre was taking things much more calmly than usual. I would have been disappointed in her, but I knew exactly why she was as docile as a Tabby cat.

Redhead said, "Mr. Frasca paid me nicely to superintend his private feline zoo. But I had my sights set on a richer life."

"So, when you learned he had scored a priceless wildcat, you set one of his own pets on the Catman?" I challenged.

"A fate that I am afraid lies in your immediate future, Miss Delgado."

"Call me Kathy," I said gamely. "Everybody does."

He threw Tigre's leash for me to catch and began backing out of the building under the cover of my own .38 snub-nose. "There's a master switch for the cages. Once I lock you in—"

"Pity poor me," I pouted.

The door closed and there was an electrical buzzing. Only four cages opened. That was plenty.

I counted a cougar, a mountain lion, and I don't know what the other two were. I never saw them before in my life.

I flung the leash away and said, "Scat, Tigre—and stay out of this."

Tigre seemed too dazed to do much of anything. But I forgave her.

Normally, I would omit the gory details. But there weren't any. Honest. Oh, the cougar came up and began licking my hand. One of the others sniffed at my feet and lay down, purring. In fact, they all tried to get snuggly.

Maybe it was because I have a way with cats, but I suppose it was the big bag of loose catnip I had rolled my catsuit in before putting it on.

I let them have their fun, collected Tigre and slipped out of there on the proverbial cat feet. No feline seemed to mind—especially after I flung some of the minty leaves from my brasserie catnip cache onto the floor for them to roll around in.

By the time I got Sheriff Drake on my auto phone, my heart had stopped pounding in my chest. I gave it to him as fast as before, finishing with, "There are three trucks. If you move fast, you can catch them. I'll race you to the finish line."

Of course, I had all the advantages. Tigre in the passenger seat, I peeled out and overhauled the cat caravan on the highway. Brakes screeching, I blocked the road.

They were not happy about it.

Redhead and two others came piling out of the lead cab. By that time, I had ignited two smudge pots I keep handy and flung them onto the road. You never saw such black smoke. No one could see a thing.

I'll give them points for trying. They came on anyway. In the swirling smoke, their headlights made splintery chinks of light. Enough to show me reaching hands. They were reaching for me. Thoughtful of them. I flipped the first one on his back, tripped the second, and wrenched a revolver from the third. It felt familiar, so I fired it into the air twice.

"Now that I have my gun back," I announced, "I'm placing you all in protective custody."

Redhead growled painfully, "From what?"

"From me. I'm madder than a wet puma."

Another voice asked, "You and what damn army?"

The sound of approaching sirens was nicely timed.

"Now that you mention it, I believe they wear blue…"

AFTER Sheriff Drake and his men had used up all the available handcuffs, I filled him in. Maybe it was the novelty of the case, but he wasn't as mad as he should have been.

"So, it was all over a wildcat," he was saying.

"A million-dollar wildcat, from the sound of it," I corrected.

Dan grunted. "That was pretty slick, the way you covered yourself with catnip before moving in on them."

"Not really, Sheriff," I admitted. "But it was the only ace I could think to slip up my sleeve under the circumstances."

He eyed me carefully. "What do you mean? It calmed them right down. Otherwise you'd have been ripped to shreds—beautiful shreds, but shreds nevertheless."

"That's just the thing, Sheriff. Catnip doesn't calm down *all* cats. Sometimes it enrages them. For all I knew, I *was* going to be torn to shreds...."

The look on his face was priceless. But he got over it quick.

"Maybe I should take *you* into protective custody," he threatened.

"From what?" I asked.

"From yourself!"

Opium Dreams

BY PAIGE DANIELS

ENRY Maloy's death came as quite a surprise to his family. Things like that didn't happen to prominent families in San Francisco. Henry was smart, strong, and capable of anything he put his mind to, and despite his mother's protests, he joined the Pinkertons on his twenty-first birthday. His mother and father thought it was just a phase and would soon come to his senses and run the family mining business, but in the fall of 1880, Henry never got a chance, he was gunned down by a cowardly soul from behind. No chance to fight back, no chance to see his enemy's face, just one pull of the trigger, and Henry's life was forfeit.

The roaring fire wasn't enough to stave off the cold of the damp fall night as the family gathered in the parlor of their modest Nob Hill mansion listening to the police relay the details of Henry's death.

A large man with a gray fluffy mustache wearing a dark blue woolen uniform cleared his throat and said, "We have the suspect in custody now, one Fan Shirong. Seems she was the proprietor of the opium den that..." the man trailed off and his gaze wondered to an odd red-headed girl staring into the fire. She couldn't have been more than eighteen. He cleared his throat and looked at Henry's parents. "Beggin' your pardon, Mister and Missus Maloy, should she really be hearing all of this?"

The stately woman wiped her eyes and barely gave the girl a glance. "Henry would regale Molly with stories from his duties as a Pinkerton all the time. It's nothing she hasn't heard before." She looked up and sniffed. "I told him it wasn't proper to..." She didn't finish the sentence, but instead sobbed.

The man standing next to her put his arm around his wife and nodded to the policeman to continue. The man took a deep breath and did so, "As I was saying. Henry was employed to clear an opium den on the employ of Mr. Wesley Masterston."

Molly's father added, "Yes, we know Wes very well. His son was a victim of those vile opium dens. It doesn't seem to matter a damn that laws were passed to rid our city of those abominations, they still claimed lives of promising young men like Wes's son..."

From the fire a tiny voice peeped, "No one made him do it, papa. He made his choices."

"Molly, dear, you're a young

Illustration by Peter Krause

lady you have no idea of how the world works around you. Just be still." Molly bit her lip and stared at her father. She dearly wanted to take him to task on this, but this was neither the time nor the place. This wasn't about her, but her brother. She gave a weak smile and nodded at her father. He patted her head and said, "That's a good girl." He looked to the policeman and said, "Are you at least taking down the den now they have shown you the heathens they are?"

"Oh yes, sir. I have a team on it now. With my team and the Pinkertons we should be able to take the den down by dawn. We're also questioning the proprietors on locations of other such establishments."

The woman patted her eyes, "Well, maybe it is of comfort that my Henry did not die in vain if these other establishments are destroyed."

The policeman started to speak but was interrupted by the sound of the door opening and a loud booming voice. "Mary. Homer. I came as soon as I heard. I can't tell you how sorry I am. If it wasn't for me..."

A tall lanky man took his bowler off his head and stood before the grieving parents. Homer put his hand on the man's shoulder and said, "Wes, you had no way of knowing. You were trying to do your part to make our community better." He gave the policeman a glare and said, "Something that

our local law enforcement doesn't seem to be able to do."

The policeman gave an uncomfortable clearing of his throat. Wes gave a sad smile and gave a quick comforting squeeze to the policeman's arm. "Now, Homer, it's not their fault. They haven't been allocated resources they need to get the job done. When I'm mayor things will change around here."

The police man seemed to be comforted by this a bit. He looked to Homer and Mary and said, "I think I've given you all the information that I have. I'll leave your family alone, but when we have more details, you'll be the first to know."

Mary replied, "Thank you, kind sir."

After the lawman closed the door Wes said to the family, "You cannot know how sorry I am about this. Henry was the best of all of us. He just wanted to make this city better. I set him on this mission. I...I... should have never done it." He sidled his way over to Molly sitting at the fire staring and put his hand on her fluffy red coif. "Molly, dear, how are you?"

Molly shrugged and barely a whisper escaped her mouth, "He was my best friend and now he's gone. He was good man and I don't think he'd ever go into a place of innocents and start causing mayhem. He always did his research before. He told me ninety percent of his job was just doing his research and talking the guilty into giving themselves up. There's something that's not right..."

Wes gave a knowing chuckle. She hated that chuckle. "Dear girl, I don't think you were privy to some of the more unsavory things your brother had to do. Let's just say the other ten percent of the time it wasn't pretty, but he did what needed to be done." Wes turned away from Molly and to her parents. "Mary. Homer. My deepest sympathies. If there is anything my family or I can do please do not hesitate to tell us." He put his bowler back on his head and went for the door. "I will call on you tomorrow. I am truly sorry."

As he opened the door to leave a brisk breeze flew in the parlor that chilled Molly to her core.

MOLLY didn't want to spend a second longer in that parlor. Being with her parents did little to comfort her. Like most occasions, they treated her like she didn't exist. She knew that Henry was their favorite. And why wouldn't he be? He was smart, chivalrous, handsome, everything that a parent wishes their son to be. But Molly, at eighteen, had no prospective suitors. Why would she? She had no traits that would attract anyone, her red hair was coarse and frizzy, she was short and little on the chubby side, and frankly she found mostly people to be a bore. She'd much rather spend time in her quiet room reading a good book or one of those scandalous dime store novels her brother would sneak to her over her mother's protest. Sometimes she'd even put a pen to paper and write her own adventures.

The tears came rushing forth thinking of her brother. He was the only one that understood her, that made living with their parents tolerable. Their childhood was spent playing in the backyard in imaginary worlds of dragons, steam contraptions, and wizards. As they grew older, Molly never seemed to grow out of her imaginary world, but Henry would always make time for her. Molly sighed and floated up the stairs to her bedroom, but before she reached her room, she passed Henry's room. She stopped and pushed his door and it opened with a creak. She quietly tiptoed and looked around the dark room. Mother and father would not be pleased if they were to find her in here.

The room still smelled like him, she inhaled deeply closing her eyes trying to commit her best friend's face to memory. She did not want to forget him, no she would never forget Henry. She opened her eyes and looked around. His room was very tidy, he had a very specific place for everything. It was a favorite game of Molly's to sneak in Henry's room and move a small object and see how long it took him to figure out that it was misplaced. Usually, it didn't take him long, that's what made him a great Pinkerton, his eye for detail.

She stopped at his writing desk and sat down flicking through his journal. Her fingers flitted over the ink stained pages only half reading the entries, more just wanting to be close to something that he touched. Then her eyes happened on it.

Oct 21 1870—Mr. Masterson has commissioned the Pinkerton's to rid Chinatown District of their opium dens after his son, Wesley Jr., was found dead in such an establishment. He feels this task is best taken on by a private company as the publicly funded lawmen have failed to get the situation under control. I, however, feel that Wes Junior was nothing more than lazy ratbag who never worked a day in his life, and his father, while well respected businessman in our circle, is a fulsome hornswoggler that I would no more trust than a common criminal.

Molly put her hand over her mouth to stifle a giggle. She was glad that she wasn't the only to feel this way about Mr. Materson and returned to reading.

But Mr. Materson has considerable influence in this community, mostly because of the money that he has, so I have no choice but to take this job. However, my gut is telling me that something isn't right about this job. I have done an initial surveillance of the den that we are to take down. All of the people were there of their own volition. While I do not condone the use of opium, the proprietors of the den did not seem to be thugs, but mere commoners just trying to make a living. I will do my best to fulfill my commitment, while trying to be as understanding to the proprietors as I can. This is not a job that I take on in zeal.

The entry ended and there was not another word scribbled on another page. Molly's shoulders slumped. She read the last two sentences over and over again. This did not sound like a job that should've ended like it did. She knew Henry was not one who took joy in tasks such as these and it did not sound like the proprietors would be the type to give in to such violence. There had to be something more to this case.

Molly paced trying to think of what to do next. She knew that her parents would not listen to her protests. But what could she do, she was just a.... She stopped herself from completing that thought. Henry would be very disappointed in her. He was always told Molly she was very smart, clever woman capable of doing anything she put her mind to, but she lacked the confidence to do so. Molly stared at the journal and pushed down a lump in her throat. Her palms began to sweat and her heart thumped in her chest when she realized what she needed to do. She needed to make this right. She needed to find her brother's real killer.

MOLLY looked down at her hands shaking and said firmly and quietly to herself, "That will be enough of that. There's no time to be cowardly. It's time to show your brother that you can be as brave as he thought you could be."

She took a deep breath and slowly opened the door to her brother's room and peeped out the hall to ensure she would not be spotted coming out of his room. Once she was sure that the coast was clear, she flitted down the hall to her room, and put on a heavy woolen coat over her cycling gown. Her mother hated when she wore this frock, and not something more befitting of a lady. However, the comfortable gown would serve her well in her journeys today. She found a sensible hat and fastened it on her head. Before she started out, she took a calming breath and whispered, "Henry, if you can hear me where you are please know that I'm going to make this right."

Escaping the house was not a hard task. Everyone was in their assorted rooms not paying much attention to the goings on around the house. Molly knew that she could find a few clues and be back home before anyone was wise to her leaving. The clicking of her boots echoed along the wet street. Molly wasn't sure where she was going, but she knew she had to get away from the house before she was spotted outside so walked and thought. Then a sort of morbid curiosity came over her. She had to see it, she had to see Chinatown where her brother drew his final breath. It wasn't really that far from here. She was in good health and walking briskly she could make it twenty minutes or less. Then she would go to her brother's office, which was on the way back home, and see what kind of information she could suss out there. But first she had to see Chinatown.

As she walked the mansions and houses with their well-manicured lawns started to give way to streets that were more narrow and cluttered. The drab brown and gray buildings were a stark contrast to the brilliantly painted houses in her neighborhood. The sidewalks started to become strewn with refuse and other things she did not want to think about. There was a heavy unpleasant smell in the air and unlike her quiet street there seemed to be constant noises. Molly's stomach churned with unease. She knew she did not belong here. She stopped walking a looked around taking in the sights and sounds. Then a noise that came above the din of city streets caught her attention. She strained her ears to hear where the noise was coming from, but it was gone. She sighed and closed her eyes and she heard it again. In the distance there seemed to be cries of distress and anger. She remembered what the police officer said about having the den cleaned out by the morning and she scrambled to the noise.

The noise took Molly through a series of narrow dark alleyways. As she scrambled to the scene, the hairs on the back of her neck rose and her stomach tossed and turned. She should not be in this area. She had overheard many stories her brother told about the horrors that happened to people in this section of town. Before she had time to rethink her decision, the whole scene unfolded before her. She slunk behind a building and peered around the corner to take it all in.

There were large men dressed in black woolen suits and bowler hats. The men gathered around a shoddy boarded up build-ing adorned with various signs adorned with gold and red Chi-nese calligraphy. The men's faces were ominous glowing in the barely there orange of the gas-lamps. The door to the building was wide open and all manner of refuse was ejected out. Peri-odically, the men in black would walk out strong-arming people, mostly men, protesting loudly. A few of the Chinese men were being roughed up and thrown in the back of a police carrier. Some of the more recalcitrant white men were also being thrown in, but the more subdued white men were just given a stern talking to then told to go on their way. A stray tear fell down Molly's cheek, this is not what Henry would've wanted. He was not a vengeful man, he knew the inherent dangers in his jobs. He would be the first to decry these actions.

Molly balled up her fist and took a deep breath. This scene gave her more fuel for finding out the real story and bringing it to light. She turned to go and then she was face to face with man. He grabbed her shoulders and growled, "What are you doing here?"

Molly looked the man up and down, this was not one of the policemen, but he was a young man, maybe about Molly's age, and he was Chinese. He wore a loose-fitting jacket with a straight collar and loose pants and had his hair pulled back in a long braid.

He growled again, "Did you think it would be fun to watch my friends and family being brutal-ized? All in a night's fun for your rich girls. Right? Was this a dare?"

Molly squeaked out, "N...N... No, I just wanted to see for myself—"

"See what? The heathens and their opium dens? The pagan joss houses? You shouldn't be here, you'll get hurt."

Molly said in a harsh whisper, "NO! This is where my brother was killed tonight. I wanted to see for myself. I know there has to be more to the story than they're tell-ing me. No one will listen." She turned away from the man, "It's not like you'll be any different. No one listens to me. I'm going to find what the real story is. Not that it will make a difference."

In an instant he jumped in front of her to block her. His tone was much softer now, "Did you say that your brother was killed here tonight?"

Molly forced a lump down her throat and nodded. "Yes, they said someone named Fan Shirong was responsible, but I don't know. It's just not right."

"That's my mother. She didn't do it though. She saw him go down and she was trying to help him, but she didn't do it. She doesn't even know how to fire a gun. They just assumed that she did it because she was next to the body."

"It seems that we both lost someone special to us tonight." She straightened her skirt and pushed passed the man as she said, "If you'll excuse me, I need to be on my way."

He gently grabbed her shoulder and said, "You're not going alone. I need to find some way to help my mother and you're the only person who can help."

MOLLY couldn't tell him no. She silently nodded and quickly walked away from the scene with the man following closely behind. As soon as they were away from the melee she stopped in the street and said to him. "Before we go any further, I need to know your name."

He bowed slightly. "Fan Bo."

She knitted her eyebrows. "Fan? So, your first name is the same as your mother's?"

He chuckled a bit. "No, we place our surnames first. You can call me Bo."

"It's very nice to make your acquittance, kind sir," she said as she smiled and courtesied. Her smile faded as she said, "I am awfully sorry that all this has happened to you and yours. I know that Henry, that's my brother, wouldn't have wanted to see any of this happen. But I'm not sure how much I can do to help your mother. The only thing I have to go on is my intuition and few scribblings. Maybe it's a mistake for you to go with me."

"Trust your instinct to the end, though you can render no reason."

She looked at him wide eyed. "That's Ralph Waldo Emerson. He was one of my brother's favorites along with Mark Twain, Sir Author Conan Doyle, and..." she stopped herself and blushed. "I tend to be a bit of a flibbertigibbet when it comes to reading. I'm sorry. But it just surprised me that—"

"That I can read?" His look wasn't one of disgust more of teasing.

"Well, if I'm to be perfectly frank, yes. And I'll add that your English is impeccable."

He shrugged and said, "Well, I was born here. And as for reading, my mother insisted that I learn to read. So, I picked up bit here and there. I love to read, especially the penny dreadfuls."

Her eyes lit up. "Me too! My

mother thinks a lady shouldn't be reading them, but I'm far from what you'd call a proper lady." This exchange left her more comfortable with her new acquaintance. "Okay, Mr. Fan, I think the best course of action is to go to my brother's office. It isn't that far from here. It's on the edge of business district and -"

She stopped at the sound of shouting behind her, behind her and there were two men in black barreling toward her and Bo. Bo started running and said, "Follow me, I know a short cut."

Without thinking Molly followed Bo into the dark streets. As they ran the yelling of the men behind them grew quieter and the sound of their feet hitting the pavement became all encompassing. Molly's chest felt like it was on fire and her feet were pinched and blistered. She was not accustomed to running so fast or so long. She pushed herself to go a few more blocks but finally her body gave in and she had to stop.

She cried out with a wheeze and huff, "Bo, I... I can't go one more step."

Bo was a good distance in front of her and screeched to a halt then sauntered back to Molly. He smiled and said, "I guess you don't have to run for your life a lot."

Molly coughed as she laughed and wiped sweat off her brow. "Dear me, no. I do have to say that I've never felt so alive." She took a few deep breaths and composed herself then looked around. "I think we're in the clear. They probably have more important things to worry about than us. I think we can take a more civilized gait now."

Bo nodded and let Molly lead the way. Despite the circumstances, Molly was quite enjoying the adventure she was on. It reminded her of a time when she was allowed to have fun without the constant nagging of her mother to be a proper lady. She looked at Bo and he didn't look like he was enjoying himself at all. She wasn't very good with people, but she felt she needed to ask after him. "Uh, Bo, are you okay?"

He shrugged. "My mother was my only family. My father sent for her and she was pregnant with me when she came over. By the time she made it here my father was dead. No one would tell her how it happened."

Molly bit her lip, "Oh my, that is terribly sad. So, what did she do?"

"Well, she tried to get back home, but that's a lot of money she didn't have. A group called the Tongs took her under their wing offering her a job and place to stay. Really, she had no choice. After I was born, I knew the things she had to do so we could survive..." he stopped in his tracks to compose himself. Molly put her hand on his shoulder to show her support. He continued, "I did not judge her. She did what she had to. I knew she was lonely and missed home. But at least we had each other, but now I don't even have that. She's a good woman. I know she would never kill anyone like that."

Molly and Bo continued walking and after a few moments of silence Molly offered, "Your mother sounds like a good person, like my brother. Society makes people into what they want to see, what's easiest to understand, but sometimes when we're really lucky we get to see the true marrow of a person."

"Miss Molly, I do believe that you're much more than you give yourself credit for."

Molly blushed and stopped and looked up at red brick building and said, "Here it is. This where my brother kept his office. If we're going to find anything it'll be in here. Are you still willing to go in? If we get caught..."

"I understand, but I need to do this for my mother."

"Well then follow me."

MOLLY made quick work of picking the lock on the front door, she would often pester her brother to teach her some of the Pinkerton skills. Truth be known, it didn't take much convincing for Henry to teacher her, it was kind of like they were young and playing in their imaginary world all over again. The wooden staircase creaked under the weight of Molly and Bo's footsteps. The narrow windows on the side of the staircase let in the barest hint of light just enough for the two to navigate the narrow stairs.

Once at the top of the landing, Molly silently pointed to a door down the hall and they crept to it. Again, Molly picked the lock and the door swung open and the two proceeded to a cramped office with a few heavy wooden desks and plaster walls with a few lopsided pictures on them. Molly looked at the dark room in silence. She had been to this office a few times visiting her brother. She always loved her visits here. Henry's co-workers treated her like their own sister. Oftentimes, they would tell her of their cases, challenging her to find clues, and to their amazement she would. But those days were over, Molly doubted the men would welcome her without her brother there.

She waved Bo in the direction to the desk in the corner. "This way. I know he keeps the drawers unlocked. I'm sure we can find something that will exonerate your mother."

As they walked Bo asked, "Won't your parents be looking for you?"

She shrugged. "I doubt it. They don't pay me much attention. I'm not really worth their while. Henry was always the shining star: handsome, smart, chivalrous. Me? I can't even get a single gentlemen caller to come my way. Most think I'm peculiar since I love to read and write. Most except Henry." She heaved a heavy sigh and continued, "I'll probably live the rest of my life under my parents' roof as an old maid."

"So why don't you set out on your own? See the world?"

Molly stifled a chuckle, "Mr. Bo, you are rich. How would I ever make it in the world?"

"I don't know, you snuck out of your parents' house undetected, made it through Chinatown unscathed, and were able to pick locks to get into here. I'd say that you can take care of yourself pretty well. I'd imagine your parents paid very handsomely for your education, so you're not stupid. Write stories for those penny dreadfuls you love so much, write about your travels."

A smile involuntarily came to Molly's face, and she fought it back. The thought was very tempting, but the only thing she wanted think about now was to find out the truth behind her brother's death. She stopped at an oak desk that was as neat as the desk in her brother's room. She gave an inward laugh at the symmetry and order of his desk. She brushed her fingers along the perfectly aligned notes and pens on the desk.

"Well then, I supposed we need to get on with it."

She picked up his notes and started to meticulously go through his papers on his desk and she found nothing more than humdrum notes on his cases, nothing remarkable. She moved to the drawers and her searched turned

up fruitless there too. Defeated she slumped in the chair and gave a heavy sigh then looked at Bo. "I'm afraid I'm useless. I just know there had to be something here, but I can't see anything. I don't know."

"If he did find something important, would he have kept it in plain sight? Did everyone know he kept his drawers unlocked? If so, would he have kept important things in there?"

She narrowed her eyes. "Well, I know he trusted everyone here and didn't have any cause to think anyone would meddle in his investigations." She stopped for a moment to think, then continued, "But if he did find something very controversial, he might have wanted to keep it safe. Where would it be though?"

Molly's eyes took in every detail of the desk while her fingers flitted around for anything that didn't conform to the surface of the desk, then she felt it. Her eyes went wide as her fingers happened on a tiny notch. "Mr. Bo, I think I might've found something."

They carefully cleared off the items from atop Henry's desk and Molly pulled at the notch revealing a secret compartment. Inside there was a leather-bound journal and a map of what looked to be Chinatown with various shops marked with either an 'X' or check mark. Molly carefully picked up the journal and sat back in the chair as she started to leaf through the ink stained pages. It seemed this wasn't just a journal, but a ledger with accounts paid and debts owed. The names on the ledger seemed to be Chinese. She showed the book to Bo. "Are any of these names familiar to you?"

Bo had the map in his hand and looked at the ledger, "Yes, they are all managers of businesses in Chinatown. A lot of the men don't own the buildings they have businesses in they rent from either the Tongs, Chinese Consolidated Benevolent Association, or even white men. No one really does fair business with the little guy." He showed her the map. "It looks like the businesses in this ledger correspond to the business on this map with a check, and as you can see our business had a check by it too. Whomever had this ledger was really hitting these small businesses hard. It looks like your brother found it important enough to hide. I wonder who it could've belong to?"

She turned the journal to the front page and embossed on the inside cover: W. Masterson.

She put her hand on mouth and said, "Lands... This isn't good. Put it back, Bo. We need to get out of here."

"I don't understand. Did you see who it belongs to?"

"I did and we're fighting a losing battle. Put it back and pretend you never saw it."

"But..."

Bo didn't get a chance to finish his thought, a group of men in black marched in the office along with two familiar faces.

Molly shrieked, "Papa!"

"Molly! Are you okay?" He stared down Bo and said, "What has this heathen made you do, Molly? Let's go home while they deal with that one."

She looked at Bo who was being roughed up by a few of the men. Off to the side was Mr. Masterson gathering up the journal and map from the desk. Molly did not know what to say. What could she do, she was just a— No! She could do better than that. It's time she stood up to all of them.

"No!"

Molly's father's face turned bright red. "What did you say?"

"I said, no. Bo didn't do anything, but help me. He's a good friend. I told you something wasn't right about the case. Look at the ledger and the map. Mr. Masterson owns many properties in Chinatown and is taking poor people for a lot of money. Henry had the ledgers hidden in his desk."

Mr. Masterson sauntered over to Molly and her father and gave his sickening smile. "Molly, dear, you're a young girl given to fanciful flights of the imagination. I am trying to rid this town of the savages such as that one," he said as he pointed to Bo, "I don't think you understood what you saw. Just leave this to the men."

Her head ached and she felt anger that she never felt before, "No! Listen to me. Look at the journal you'll see he even owns that opium den that his son died in. I'm sure that wouldn't look very good for someone running for election. I'm sure it's something you might even be willing to kill for."

The men in black stopped struggling with Bo and walked over to the exchange. "Is there something we need to know?" asked a tall man with handlebar mustache.

She had tears in her eyes, "I know he had something to do with my brother's death. I just know it. Check the journals."

The man in black gave Molly a sad look and said, "Dear, we can't check another's property without probable cause."

"It's not fair a woman is going to be tried and probably convicted for a crime she didn't commit." She looked at a forlorn Bo and added, "And I'm sure you'll charge him with some nonsense too. It's not right."

The man answered, "If it makes you feel better, there really isn't much evidence against the woman and the public is rather squeamish about putting women to death. More than likely she and her son will be deported back to where they came from. Away from causing any trouble here."

Molly's father took her arm and said, "Come now, let's go home.

You've had enough excitement for today."

She looked at the men then to Bo. Bo gave a sad smile then said, "To be yourself in a world that is constantly trying to make you something else is the greatest accomplishment."

She wiped a tear from her eye, "Ralph Waldo Emerson."

Bo continued, "Mother will be very happy to go home. This is the best option. Go write those stories. I'll be fine. Just remember you're stronger than they think you are."

Molly's father growled and pulled his daughter along. "Why are you talking to him? Let's go."

Molly followed her father out the door sobbing and shaking. Bo was right, it was the best option. If they ran, the whole city would be on them in minutes and then Bos would be convicted of trying to kidnap her other such nonsense. No, it was best that she go with her father. But Molly's restless mind knew that she'd never be the same.

T HE train rocked in rhythm with the clacking of the tracks. Out the window, the velvet grass coated the endless rolling hills. Molly looked out the window and smiled. Much like the other countries she visited, Ireland was even more beautiful than any of the books she read depicted. She looked down at the empty piece of paper and started to put her

thoughts into reality. She didn't
have much time before this man-
uscript was due, and if she used
her time wisely, she could get a
good bit done while on this train
ride.

*The intrepid heroine, Henrietta
Belle, and her companion Bo was
summoned for another adventure.
This time they had to solve the mystery of who was poisoning the town's
watering hole...*

The Legend of Hammer Jack Curry

By RUSS COLCHAMIRO

BURT "Hammer Jack" Curry strutted down the gangplank. For a mercenary, the great American warrior-for-hire, the years leading up to 1910 had been fruitful indeed.

Along the Eastern Chinese coastline, south of Qingdao, was the tiny port village of Xiahai. Salt water blew in off the ocean. The crew, twenty-five strong, sung in his honor:

I am the mighty Hammer Jack
Cur-ry!
Rea-dy to battle, to kill in a
hur-ry!
On land or sea or battalion on
the field
Hammer Jack conquers...
Never does he YIELD!

"Now look at that, boys," said Hammer Jack, who at six-foot-three was rugged, broad shouldered, and always ready to fight. The contingent of Chinese locals, most of them women, were pint-sized in comparison. "No wonder these Chinamen... these China dolls... called upon ole Hammer Jack Curry. You want to win, you need men on your side. Real men. Size, strength, and American might."

Xiahai, loosely translated as "going down to the sea," was practically hidden, engulfed by low-lying mountains to the west, a high ridge followed by a steep valley to the north, and a spindling of gullies, ravines, and soy farms to the south.

His ship, *The Jack Hammer*, docked at one of the village's five boat slips, fitting between a cluster of sampans, the villagers' long, flat-bottomed fishing boats.

Through his mustached lips Hammer Jack spit a wad of brown chaw over the side. The salt and pepper hair above his upper lip matched the wavy locks on his head, with a groomed patch from his bottom lip down to his chin. He peacocked himself in a black vest, maroon shirt, and a bundle of pendants dangling from his neck, including a miniature, silver-plated skull.

Xiahai was laid out before them. The villagers gathered at a respectful distance.

"Now," Hammer Jack said, taking the plank in long, thunderous strides. The skull tips on his black boots rattled with each step. His left hip sported a holstered 1903 Colt six-shooter with counter-clockwise revolving chamber. On his right, a single-edged Chinese

Illustration by Mark Wheatley

Dao sword, curved and razor sharp. "Where's the lady of the house? I believe there's a payment coming my way. Half on arrival, which is now, and the other half, well... when we wipe your enemies off this stinking Earth."

Hammer Jack's crew bellowed hearty, boisterous laughs.

Dark-haired, bowl-faced, and dressed in a beige tunic and sandals, Bai Cao met him on the dock. She bowed. Her voice was gentle and wispy, her demeanor deferential. "Greetings, Mr. Curry." For the China doll that she was, even with the slurred 'r' accent, her English enunciation was surprisingly clear. "You must be grateful to touch solid ground after your long journey. I trust your travels were without incident."

Foul-smelling from the long voyage from San Francisco, Hammer Jack looked back at his trusted vessel. "Poseidon tossed his trident our way, but *The Jack Hammer*'s a helluva ship. Best money could buy. We're focused and ready and armed to the hilts. But first... we need hot baths, warm ale, and clean beds." He winked at his crew. "And some female companions to break in the pillows."

His equally rancid crew laughed like jackals. Their voices carried through the village. In Shanghai and Nanjing, the cities blossomed with concrete buildings and dense urban thoroughfares. But Xiahai was still finding its way, a collection of gardens, terraces, streams,

and a pavilion, mixed with swaths of brush, reeds, and dirt dry as paste. Clustered along the village's western edge were tiny huts constructed of pounded earth foundations and timber frames, with walls and floors made of brick, earth, and wood.

"Yes, of course." Bai Cao seemed unperturbed by this. "We have quarters prepared for you, and there's ample company, if you so choose. It is a great honor to receive you. Your payment awaits."

HAMMER Jack did not lack in confidence. If anything, his surety of self oozed from his pores, his pheromones rumored to be so powerful they scared off attackers from miles away.

"I have to admit," Hammer Jack said to Bai Cao as he inspected the village. An experienced warrior, he was looking for tactical advantages and potential weaknesses. There were many keys to military success. He picked up some of those tactics—including well-timed diversions, or theatre, what the Chinese called "war magic"—from the very people he was now commissioned to lead and protect from invading forces. "I never thought I'd hear from you. Especially to act as your private army. I thought Chinamen despised Westerners. I learned that lesson first hand." He pointed to the jagged scar leading from the outside of his left eye all the way down to his neck. "I got this one during the Boxer Rebellion. Up in Weifang."

"You are correct." Bai Cao nodded quickly, then rattled off an order in Mandarin. Carrying a bamboo staff, the young female warrior two steps behind her nodded in acknowledgment then scurried off. "As you can see, most of our men were killed in battle. We have spent years rebuilding. The enclave helps keep us isolated from outside forces, although not well enough. But you have history with my father. He spoke of you, the great Hammer Jack Curry, fiercest American of them all. Master of the Rifle, Demon with a Fist, Disciple of Kung Fu. He said you were a committed student, your skill surpassing our most highly-trained warriors."

Hammer Jack breathed in compliments—even when cloying and obvious—as if they were the magic elixir to life itself. So much so that he ignored the faint tinge of gunpowder that wafted in on the breeze. An elder woman nudged several children toward higher ground.

"Yes," he said, unable to hold back a gaudy smile. He ran his forefinger across his mustache. *She doesn't know*, he told himself. *They never will.* "Your father was a good man. A born railroad man. We met in San Francisco. He led a work crew with discipline. Efficiency. A shame what happened to him."

As if his past transgressions rang out like a copper bell, without warning an explosion erupted, not substantial, but enough to destroy a storage hut. The villagers ducked, scattered, and drew their weapons, fearing an attack had already begun.

"Boys!" Hammer Jack commanded. "Recon. Now!" Five of his crew shuttled off toward the burning shack, rifles at the ready. "Looks like the party's started. I hope you're ready to—"

A dirty-faced villager with a long, razor-thin beard rampaged toward him. The attacker howled a war cry, wielding a sharp sword, much like the one fastened to Hammer Jack's hilt.

Instinctively Hammer Jack pushed Bai Cao aside, withdrew his own sword, and pivoted into a defensive position. His filthy attacker swung his sword at Hammer Jack, in a cross-body angle, at his mid-section.

Hammer Jack parried, using his own sword to thwart his much shorter attacker, requiring him to sidestep and then spin 360 degrees. Hammer Jack traded three slices, blade against blade, feet shuffling in the dirt. Calling upon his Kung Fu training, he planted his hips, then barreled his left leg into his attacker's mid-section.

The force of impact broke several ribs, dropping his assailant to the ground. Hammer Jack lifted his sword, and with vengeance in his heart, sought to decapitate the wounded man. Hammer Jack caught his reflection in the blade.

"No!" Bai Cao said, demanding her people focus on what was most important. "He is of the old world, loyal to my father, to our village. To our ways. He has had... trouble... accepting my decision to retain your services. We will discipline him, in time. But for now, we require every able body to fight our true enemies."

Adrenaline coursing, Hammer Jack fought his instincts to brutalize the injured man lying at his boots. But he looked upon Bai Cao and the rest of her village, seeing them as the collective damsels in distress that they were.

Two generations descended from the great Nian rebellion, the Sons of the Nianfei had settled in a tiny village to the west. They had risen again, laying claim to Xiahai, a tactical location given its access to the port. Hammer Jack and his crew were hired, at an enormous sum, to help fight off the Sons once and for all. Hammer Jack would fulfill his contract. He would save this village from certain defeat.

"It's all right, boys," he said, and re-sheathed his sword. He extended his hand. "It's all right. A lot of tension around here. Bound to happen. We sailed the globe because we're a force like no other, and the villagers need our help." He breathed in through his nose. The stench of high summer made his eyes water. *Maybe they suspect*, he thought. *I don't see how.*

But even if they do, they need me. "So... let's help."

"**B**OSS!" His first officer, Stephen Friedt, ran toward him. "You need to see this."

Well rested, and well serviced by multiple young consorts, Hammer Jack rolled his heavily muscled neck. He gazed up at the morning sky stretched out over the little China village, with their little China people, who despite their ancient ways and unique style of combat, did not understand the might of modern warfare. True nobility comes from winning the battle. There is no glory in defeat.

He envisioned Bai Cao's enemies, the Sons of the Nianfei, making their assault. And the look of dread on their faces upon realizing they'd taken up arms against superior forces.

Hammer Jack craved that divine moment. When reality breaks through the dualistic fog of fear and confidence. When terror washes over his foes. The moment of defeat.

How many men had he killed in battle? Hundreds? Thousands? No matter. He wasn't a maniac. He didn't kill for sport. He was a warrior in need of a war, a savior in need of the weak.

For a price.

He was a mercenary, after all. And mercenaries don't work for free. The Cao family had already lined his pockets, in gold and blood. More was yet to come.

"What do you got?" he asked Stephen Friedt, who was scanning the terrain through a retractable wood and cooper telescope.

Atop the north ridge they surveyed the hills below and the valley in between. Cloud cover rolled in, a wet mist clinging from the Yellow Sea. Bai Cao appeared from a hidden bunker. The village sat behind them, and below.

"Oh, I see," Hammer Jack said. "Camouflage. Good. What forces do they have?"

Elbows hunched, Bai Cao lay on her stomach between a chipped boulder and a thicket of reeds.

"The Sons of the Nianfei are savage fighters," she said. "They come in waves, fifty strong. Our scouts say they have two hundred total, possibly more. They are not the largest clan in the region, but the most deadly. Our families have lived in Xiahai for a thousand years, have fought off many invaders. We want to preserve our village and build for the future. But the Sons want to expand, to build an empire, and do so on our bones." She drank from a pouch of water. "Treat them as wild animals. Fear them, too. They are relentless. They will not withdraw, retreat, or surrender until they claim victory. Or die trying."

Hammer Jack breathed in again, inhaling the fumes from centuries past, the restless souls who died for a nation that had seen its finest days pass it by. They were living in America's shadow now. They all

were. He unsheathed his sword, admiring the blade. He stepped into striking position. He cut through the air.

"Die trying, huh Steph?"

Wiry and heavily tattooed, Stephen Friedt squinted through the telescope. He spit chaw. "That's what she said."

Hammer Jack sliced the air once more, his eyes drawn into a death stare. "Then we'll just have to make sure."

STEPHEN Friedt directed the rest of Hammer Jack's warriors, assigning them strategic positions around the valley. They were experienced fighters all, well-armed, fit with a cache of pistols, rifles, swords, bows and arrows, and grenades.

"Your men are all much... larger than I anticipated." From a dirt landing beneath the upper ridge, Bai Cao looked over her shoulder, at her own warriors, most of them women, the tallest of them a half foot shorter than Hammer Jack's shortest fighter. "We will need"— she smiled so fiercely it was almost a grimace— "all of their bravery and strength."

"You are right to be afraid," Hammer Jack said. "I've been watching your fighters. Competent and determined, but this is a man's war. Not that women can't fight. Oh, I've come across women stronger than bears, more lethal a pride of lions. But you? Them? No, my little lotus blossom. You have done well—as well as you could—to keep hold of what you have. But those days are numbered."

"That is why I called upon you," Bai Cao said, eliciting a faint smile from Hammer Jack. "Before he died, my father wrote to me that you had learned our ways, expert in Kung Fu. As you have studied our warriors, I have studied you. Your forms are precise. It takes even the most dedicated student decades of training to reach the level you have mastered so quickly."

Never one to pass up a moment, to demonstrate his prowess, Hammer Jack immediately took to the first form. Yes, Kung Fu evolved to protect against opponents and disable them quickly with strikes. But he liked to show off. He couldn't help it. He beamed with each skillful motion, drinking in applause only he could hear.

"Here." Bai Cao tapped the inside of Hammer Jack's left wrist, the blocking wrist. His palm faced out, extended past his forehead. "This is a most difficult position to hold. Your arms are thick, like an elephant's tusk, yet you move like a flower on the breeze. It takes incredible discipline, to control such movements."

"Yes, it does." Hammer Jack returned to a resting stance, his hand draped along his holstered pistol. Again, in his mind's eye, he saw their assailants rage over the hill, his way of preparing for battle. "But it's not my discipline I'm concerned about. You

say your villagers can hold their own. Show me. Bring them to the south ridge, away from prying eyes. I need to challenge them. Let's see how they do."

CONVINCED that Bai Cao's warriors were at least competent in battle—not front-line material, but skilled enough as a second wave—Hammer Jack spent the rest of the afternoon and into the evening finalizing their strategy.

He stood in his quarters, leaning on the wood table, a map of the region scrolled out. An oil lamp offered subdued light, the flame flickering behind glass. It threw shadows on the parchment.

"You're certain? Your information is correct?" He raised his eyebrows, staring down at Bai Cao. His bed was unmade. "They're attacking at dusk?"

"As certain as one can be," she assured him, "when knowing the thoughts of another. The spirit does not always ride the back of the dragon. Sometimes the dragon rides you."

Bai Cao nodded.

"Y-yes," Hammer Jack said, unnerved by her metaphor. Yet he couldn't allow himself to be perceived as unsure. "The dragon is fierce. I've battled it before."

"My father wrote to me of your journeys. He said you have the dragon's eye, the sight of the golden hammer," she said, her gaze momentarily distant. "Able to anticipate your opponents' movements, to counteract their tactics. But of course, your legend had already grown by then. Your role in the Boxer Rebellion. It is not a simple thing for us, to ignore the blades you struck here on our soil. You fought against the Society of the Righteous and Harmonious Fists. They were noble in pursuit. They fought against the influence of Westerners, who wished to eradicate our culture. And now here we are, engaged with such a Westerner, to fight other Chinese. These are difficult times for us, confusing. But as my father taught me, we do as me must."

"Your father was a good man," Hammer Jack said. "A wise man." *Only not wise enough to answer when opportunity knocks.* "When I reached these shores a decade ago, I had never seen Kung Fu. Graceful as a swan, lethal as a mongoose. I studied, while I could, and when I returned to America, in San Francisco, I sought a teacher. That's how I met your father. He trained me. He was relentless, exacting. He'd never met an American who appreciated martial arts. Your father taught me well. It was a horrible thing, the explosion. It took his legs. Infection did the rest."

There was more to the story, but Hammer Jack had no interest in telling it. The benefit of being separated by thousands of miles.

Information was difficult to come by. Misinformation, however, was a more readily available substitute, and the easiest to exploit.

Before Hammer Jack could continue, Stephen Friedt barged into his quarters. "The winds have shifted." He glanced suspiciously at Bai Cao, then whispered with the heightened look of a man whose survival instinct was calling him into focus. "We can smell their herds. They're coming. Now."

Hammer Jack slugged down a tin of whiskey. Droplets glistened on his mustache. "They know we're here. They've stepped up their attack." The oil lamp flickered. His heart shuddered. "It's time."

A CRESCENT moon, yellow, hung low in the China sky. They gathered along a dirt path behind the village square.

Hammer Jack had fought in moonlight before. Been victorious time and again. But were Bai Cao's forces prepared for black-sky warfare? Did these non-Americans, these tiny women with their tiny hands, have the strength, stamina, and exactitude to defend themselves? To survive the monstrosity of battle?

No, of course they didn't. That's why Bai Cao had requested Hammer Jack from halfway around the world.

The Sons of the Nianfei were far too motivated, skilled, and unpredictable—and therefore intensely dangerous—for Bai Cao's villagers. They could serve as nothing more than distractions, field nurses, and, only if it came to it, a last line of defense.

Hammer Jack and his mercenaries, the real warriors, would have to lead this battle. Conquer the enemy. He intended to walk away from the pending violence, and with all of his limbs attached. That wasn't going to happen with Bai Cao on the front lines.

"Steph!" Hammer Jack barked in a rough whisper. "Get Strock and Cordoza up on the northwest ridge. Have 'em take five men each. Same again with Lansco and Fitch on the northeast. Then send two squads around the bend and into the low valley beneath. If they can find a path behind them, even better. We can completely box 'em in."

"Already on it." Bristled in the moonlight, Stephen Friedt nodded behind him, to Bai Cao's forces. "What about them?"

"Line 'em along the ridges, a dozen feet behind our men. They're decent archers. Not the best, but they should provide enough cover. Besides," Hammer Jack said, and patted a satchel, "I brought enough grenades to blow holes all across the valley. Draw the Sons of the Nianfei into range, and they won't stand a chance. And for those who manage to get close and personal"—Hammer Jack ran his thumb along the sword secured to his thigh—"I'll show 'em how we do things back in the god damn U.S. of A. With a touch of China, so they feel at home."

Stephen Friedt checked the cherry-wood stock on his rifle. "And then? When we take the valley?"

Hammer Jack squinted, narrowing his focus beneath the moonlight. "Survey the damage, get the rest of our money... then pick your favorite from the ladies of Xiahai. They're gonna owe us a helluva lot more than a sack of gold."

PERCHED with his rifle in the brush, Hammer Jack studied the Sons of the Nianfei creeping through the valley. There were more of them than he expected, a hundred Chinamen at least, but they were sitting ducks, waltzing into slaughter.

"You seem confident," Bai Cao whispered, stalking up behind him. "Even with so many."

"A man who cannot tolerate small misfortunes can never accomplish great things," Hammer Jack whispered back.

Bai Cao smiled. "An ancient Chinese proverb."

"If you know the enemy and know yourself, you need not fear the result of a hundred battles," Hammer Jack said, quoting China's greatest military thinker, Sun Tzu. "If you know yourself but not the enemy, for every victory gained you will also suffer a defeat. If you know neither the enemy nor yourself, you will succumb in every battle."

"Your insights will serve us well," she said, visibly eager for the battle to begin. "We will most certainly need them."

Hammer Jack spit chaw through his front teeth. "It's a damn good thing then that I know myself. And what I know, little lotus blossom, is that I ain't never lost my life in battle." He produced his revolver, checked the cylinder, and returned the battle-tested weapon to his holster. "And I don't intend to start now."

THE energy shifted then, a quieting. A pause. The reeds settled. Crickets silenced. Hammer Jack surveyed the terrain. His men froze in place. Bai Cao's warriors were formless as shadows. Not a single blade of grass dared rustle.

Hammer Jack had survived enough battles to know that silence—especially sudden silence, when the wind itself holds its breath, terrified to even whisper— was a portent of danger. Imminent.

With a depression the width of a butterfly's wings, the insole of his thumb flexed against the rifle's trigger. It was a reflexive gesture, a response to the scent. Vague. Faint. Distant.

He inhaled through his nose, searching for the stench's source. Bitter? Salty? Pungent, for certain. One he knew. Maple syrup? And... discharge from a kerosene lamp?

No, not quite, but also a stench of urine, feces, mud, and wet fur, all fermented.

The odor intensified, a nasty stench.

And then it came.

A war cry. A squeal.

From the distance, on the opposing downslope of the valley. Beneath the crescent moon a ball of flame bloomed in the thick grass, glowing orange in the night. The squeal grew louder, more acute. A series of high-pitched Hell cries, as if a wild boar had been set on fire, screaming as the flames melted the flesh from its curdling body.

Which is exactly what happened.

Another squealing ball of flame. Then another and another. The wild, flaming boars appeared all across the valley. Two dozen at least, they rampaged in the darkness.

Hammer Jack peered down the scope of his rifle. He had a flaming boar in his sights. He curled his finger around the trigger when— *thwip!* Less than five feet away an arrow tore the face off one of his men, who toppled into the valley. *Thwip-thwip!* Two more went down.

Arrows flew. Gunshots rang out.

Hammer Jack's blood coursed. His breaths tightened.

There was no turning back.

THE battle descended into madness.

Hammer Jack's secret squadron,

the men he'd sent around the valley's edges to infiltrate the Sons' forces from behind, got caught up in the stampede of flaming boars. Their screams echoed through the valley.

Confronted with the harsh reality that he had underestimated the Sons, that he had mistaken his own might for effectiveness, Hammer Jack stared in terror, consumed with panic.

An arrow whizzed by—or was it a bullet?—catching him on the tip of his left ear, taking the lobe clear off.

He reached for the wound, his hand smeared with his own blood. The pain was intense, but it spiked his adrenaline, a jolt to the system activating his inner savage, his trained warrior self. The crescent moon shone bright, a glowing yellow sliver, but all Hammer Jack saw was red. Glint in the dragon's eye.

He ripped off one rifle shot after another, taking out one, two, three Sons of the Nianfei. But the more he fired into the melee the more they powered toward him, following the flaming boars into warfare.

Beside him Bai Cao unleashed a series of arrows—*thwip-thwip-thwip*—clearing a path into the valley. She ducked behind an old tree stump. Enemy arrows pierced the night—and four more of Hammer Jack's men.

His heart lurched for his fallen warriors, confused and unprepared for the Sons' savagery and skill.

Run, his inner voice commanded. *Live.*

Bai Cao commanded otherwise.

"Head into the valley," she said, determined to keep him on task. "The difference between who you are and who you want to be... is what you do."

Hammer Jack recoiled, pulling his shoulders back. Reading his trepidation, Bai Cao darted her neck, the movement short, intense, precise. Her eyes shifted with even greater swiftness.

Who he was: Hammer Jack Curry. Who he wanted to be: a man smart and cunning enough to see another sunrise.

Bai Cao made a sound—*wsht-wsht*—cutting through the chaos, signaling her warriors. As if materializing from the ether, in one synchronized wave they were all in position. Together, Hammer Jack realized, they had formed a wall of lethal archers, atop the ridge from end to end, bowstrings drawn.

"We will fill the night with arrows," Bai Cao said, shedding the image of a meek, frightened little villager like a snake sheds its skin. "Pierce the heart... the body will fall."

"Wait!" Hammer Jack felt himself losing control, terrified as his men dove deeper into battle. "*You* are going to cover *us?*"

Never before had Hammer Jack felt such impotence. Humiliation. Not because Bai Cao had made a strategic decision, but because he had misjudged her, overlooking that she was a shrewd woman and an expert warrior, leading a lethal army.

"You can remain here, hiding, on the ridge—a coward, without honor—and watch your men cut down like those flaming boars." With the skill of a true master, she launched an arrow into the bedlam, slicing the air, as if she had willed the projectile to obey her very command. It took out a Son, penetrating his throat. "Demonstrate that you have mastered Kung Fu, that you can master the yellow man. Unless," she said, and smirked at him, "Hammer Jack Curry... the great American warrior... is not up to the task."

THE air wouldn't come. Hammer Jack's diaphragm constricted. He was boxed in, a prison of his own making, fueled now by fear, anger, and humiliation. Bai Cao was goading him, taunting him, daring him to run headlong into the insanity of war. But what choice did he have?

The only choice he could make.

Fight like hell. Like an American. Like a man.

And show these Chinese bastards what happens when you take on Burt "Hammer Jack" Curry, the greatest warrior money can buy.

Like a mountain come to life, Hammer Jack stood tall, aimed his riffle, and fired. Trigger squeeze—head shot. Trigger squeeze—head shot. One after another he took out the rampaging Sons as his own men fought and died in battle.

Bai Cao's arrows rained down on the moonlit carnage, her army of warriors picking off the Sons.

His own ammunition gone, Hammer Jack stampeded into the valley. He extended his sword with a right-handed swipe, front-kicking the now headless Son into a charging boar. He whipped his massive hips counterclockwise, using a roundhouse kick to pummel another Son in the chest, literally crushing his heart.

The battle raged until dusk.

THE valley was awash with smoke and blood, the air thick with charred flesh. And death.

Hammer Jack stood amid the carnage, chest heaving, arms limp. Exhausted, he dropped his sword in the mud. Near him, gurgling, choking on his own blood, was Stephen Friedt. His fallen comrade stared into the sky, in a faraway trance, as the morning sun sparkled over the ridge.

Hammer Jack started to kneel—*thwip!* An arrow pierced Stephen Friedt's heart.

The shock jolted Hammer Jack, but there was nothing he could do for Stephen. So he did all he could actually do, which was fall to his knees.

Thwip! Like a burning skewer another arrow punctured his left shoulder, putting Hammer Jack on his back. He whimpered in pain, too weak to howl. *Thwip!*

A second arrow pierced his right shoulder, staking Hammer Jack to the ground.

He rolled his head back and forth, his body smeared in sweat, hair, piss, and blood. Hammer Jack pried open one eye, then the other.

Bai Cao stood over him, shouting in Mandarin. Her warriors encircled. One of them put an arrow in his left thigh. *Thwip!* Then the right. He writhed in pain.

Not a damsel in distress, Bai Cao was a cobra after all. "Did you really think that you... the mighty American...Hammer Jack Curry...could in a few short years master our traditions and conquer us? With our own skills and forms, techniques that have sustained our culture for a thousand years? Is your arrogance that profound?"

Thwip!

A fresh arrow punctured his abdomen. Hammer Jack groaned, white sparks before his eyes. He didn't hear it, but another arrow pierced his liver. His breaths drew quick. The faces, the women of Xaihai, blurred together.

Bai Cao encroached, stalking him. "The Sons of the Nianfei were going to attack us, sooner or later. So we paraded you around, to spur them into action. Our valley was the setting. You and your men...were the bait."

"N-no," Hammer Jack wheezed. "You c-c-can't..." He couldn't summon the words. *Nobody sets up*

Hammer Jack Curry. Except that Bai Cao had done just that.

"My father treated you like a son," she said. "He taught you the ancient ways. Honor. Dignity. Respect. But greed is your guiding star. He found gold in those railroad tunnels, and you saw a fortune for yourself. He did not die in a mining accident. You had him killed."

Hammer Jack retreated within, as if his soul—as if the lifeforce within him even was a soul—oozed into the mud. He had always fought for money. A fair transaction. A straight trade. But he stole, once. He murdered. It was only fitting then that it would come back on him. Here. Now.

"A boy from our village," Bai Cao said as the sun continued to rise over the valley. "He worked with my father on the railroad. In America. He saw what you did, setting the dynamite. You should have heeded the lessons my father taught you: 'If you must play, decide upon three things at the start: the rules of the game, the stakes... and the quitting time.'"

Hammer Jack whimpered as Bai Cao lorded over him, her legs spread apart, on either side of his torso. From his broken, fallow state she seemed as enormous as the Great Wall of China, as imposing as Death itself. She notched an arrow and pulled back her bowstring. Her warriors did the same.

"Now...for you...it is quitting time. We thank you for your

sacrifice. Your men, your weapons. And distracting the enemy. We now have their territory... your ship... and our money. My father would be proud."

A hawk circled overhead. Its screech pierced the morning light.

Bai Cao and her warriors extended their arms. Their aim was true. Hammer Jack's fighting song whispered on the wind as the bundle of arrows, one at a time, punctured his heart:

> *I am the mighty Hammer Jack*
> *   Cur-ry!*
> *Rea-dy to battle, to kill in a*
> *   hur-ry!*
> *On land or sea or battalion on*
> *   the field*
> *Hammer Jack conquers...*
> *Never does he YIELD!*

The Juggernauts of El Dorado

By ROBERT JESCHONEK

FROM the sound of the heavy footfalls in the jungle, I thought we must be under attack by at least twenty Spaniards. Immediately, I swung my musket up and aimed in the direction of the racket.

"Prepare to fight!" My father, beside me, had drawn his sword. He cut an imposing figure, clad in his ornate golden armor, swinging his golden blade overhead.

He looked every bit the legendary explorer, warrior, and nobleman known the world over as Sir Walter Raleigh.

"Stand your ground!" shouted father. "We are too close to our goal to be driven back now! The fabled city of El Dorado surely awaits beyond those very trees!"

As he said those words, the source of the heavy footfalls stomped ever closer, then burst from the foliage not thirty yards away. In that moment we could see how wrong we'd been about what had been causing that din.

No Spaniards leaped from that thicket, ready to keep us from our prize. Francisco Pizarro (nephew of the notorious conqueror of the same name, scourge of Peru and the Andes) and his army had been dogging our forces ever since the Orinoco River, but they hadn't gotten ahead of us here.

Rather, what was storming out of the forest was something I'd never seen before. It was a veritable juggernaut, a behemoth of gleaming black metal twelve feet high, its body studded with what looked like gun barrels. To my eyes, it clearly looked to be a weapon, a heavily armed monstrosity designed for battle.

More than that, it was *proof*—proof that we had finally found the lost city we sought. *El Dorado, the City of Machines.*

Father, I knew, realized this, too. "Hold!" he ordered. "Perhaps this is but an emissary sent to escort us to the city gate."

Gouts of steam hissed out of the twin smokestacks mounted on the juggernaut's upper back. Its torso rotated smoothly to face my father, and the two big gun barrels mounted on its shoulders swung around to point in his direction.

I heard a low rumble from its body, but I was already in motion. Dropping my musket, I raced toward my father, my gold-plated armor clanking as I ran.

There was a loud thump behind

Illustration by Karl Kesel

me, as of something being ejected from a tube. I launched myself at father, slamming him back and down to the ground, knocking the breath out of both of us.

As we landed, a projectile whizzed past overhead. The juggernaut's first shot had missed, thanks to me.

No sooner had it done so than father called out to his force of thirty-five men. "Attack!"

Muskets boomed around us in quick succession. Looking back, I saw they did no visible damage; every ball bounced off the juggernaut's black metal skin like birdseed off a windowpane.

It was incredible to behold. If the rest of the city contained mechanical wonders of a like nature, this El Dorado we sought was indeed a place of miracles, unlike any we had witnessed before.

But, would they be a match for the wonders of alchemy that we had at our disposal? That remained to be seen.

Hastily, I got to my feet and hauled father up to his. Then, without waiting for further instruction, I unclipped one of the glass grenades from the bandolier across my chest and took a step toward the juggernaut.

By then, the machine's torso had rotated to face other members of our party. Again, I heard a loud thumping noise, followed by the firing of a projectile toward one of our men. After its release, steam hissed out of the barrels and stacks behind it.

This time, the missile struck its target: Jack Lafferty, a stalwart among father's longtime loyalists. Jack was firing his musket when the juggernaut's shell punched through his belly in a spray of red. To his credit, he didn't scream when he went down.

Cursing the behemoth, I raised my grenade—a glass sphere filled with glittering gold liquid—then pulled back and threw it forward. I followed through on the swing of my arm, trying to focus on striking the target before it could do any more damage to our group.

God was with me. The grenade hit the upper quadrant of the juggernaut's broad torso, shattering into a thousand tiny shards. The contents of the capsule splattered the great machine's body, the golden liquid running over its ebony skin.

I experienced a terrible moment of doubt then. What if the juggernaut's body was molded from some alloy that resisted the grenade's transmutative properties?

But I quickly saw that my fears were for naught. Before my eyes, the compound from the grenade did its work, converting the juggernaut's skin from whatever base metal composed it to another metal of my choosing.

The black metal encasing the juggernaut turned gleaming silver—and then oozed down all around, melting away from the inner structure. It resembled actual silver in color only; in all other properties, there was nothing argent about it.

For it was the liquefied metal, *mercury*, that had replaced the monstrosity's impenetrable exterior. Centuries of alchemical study, one breakthrough after another, had led European civilization to this mastery. We had attained the *magnum opus*, the power to recreate the philosopher's stone, and that had enabled us to transmute metals at will.

As well as giving us other powers that had changed the world forever, of course.

"Well done, Wat!" father insisted on calling me by my family nickname, which I found annoying. "Move in, men!"

Father and the rest of us converged on the melting mechanical shell. Now that the skin was mostly gone, we could see a single being inside it—a brown-skinned little man sitting in a metal cage. He had short, glossy black hair and was wearing gray coveralls trimmed with red piping. A canopy of some kind of translucent sheeting—a non-metallic substance, apparently, that resisted our alchemical transmutation—had protected him from the oozing mercury.

Father barked out orders to us as we closed in around the device and its passenger. "Do not shoot or otherwise resort to the use of force, unless I say so!"

As we drew closer, the juggernaut's pilot scowled and raised his hands. He did not appear to possess a blade or sidearm; perhaps, in the belly of that once-mighty mechanism, he had not felt the need for further defensive measures.

"Good sir!" said father. "As you can see, we are quite capable of defending ourselves. But we come in peace!"

The pilot narrowed his eyes and rattled off something in a language I didn't recognize.

Father sheathed his sword in the golden scabbard at his waist and spread his arms wide. "We have come in search of the city of El Dorado. We wish only to explore the possibilities for an exchange of knowledge between our peoples."

The pilot rattled off a stream of words in yet another language, but this time I recognized it as Spanish.

So did father. Instantly, he shifted from English to fluent Spanish in addressing the pilot. "You say you don't know this El Dorado whereof I speak? Your magnificent contraption says otherwise."

The pilot switched from Spanish to English without missing a beat. Apparently, his people had made contact with ours at some point, as well as with the Spaniards. "*What* contraption?" He grinned at the puddle of mercury spreading out from the juggernaut's base.

"Touché." father laughed. "Then

I hope, since you are without the protection of such a device, that you will allow us to escort you safely through the wilderness." He walked to the edge of the puddle and extended a hand.

The pilot glared, then sighed and took the hand. "What did you say your name was?"

"Sir Walter Raleigh." Father turned and nodded in my direction. "This is my son, Wat. And your name, sir?"

"Ganix," said the pilot as father helped him step free of the metal framework. "Call me Ganix."

WE heard no further mechanical activity as we proceeded into the jungle along the trail of broken limbs and crushed underbrush left by the juggernaut. Nevertheless, we were all on guard, anticipating fresh threats at any moment from the forces of El Dorado or Francisco Pizarro.

Moving at the head of our phalanx, I kept my musket in hand and my grenades at the ready. My heart hammered in my chest and sweat rolled down my sides and back, soaking the goldthread tunic under my armor.

From the beginning, when we'd set sail from England, this had been the most important expedition of our lives. Father and I had so much to prove—him near the end of his career, and me at the start of my own. But now that we'd met the juggernaut, the stakes had risen. For we now knew that father

had been right all along—the voices back home that had called him stupid or crazy had been wrong.

And we didn't dare make a mistake now, or all we'd learned could be lost forever or stolen by the Spaniards.

"How much farther?" I asked Ganix as we plodded through a tangle of undergrowth.

"Hard to say." Ganix wriggled his arms, which I had bound behind his back. "Perhaps, if you untied me, it would restore my circulation and jog my memory."

"Not just yet," said father. "I've heard that a sudden rush of blood to the head can be unhealthy."

The heat of the jungle could likewise be unhealthy and represented a danger all its own. Checking the sun through the canopy, I could see we were barely an hour away from noon, at which time the day's highest heat would settle upon us. How much longer could we continue our march without losing momentum?

If it were up to father, we would never slow or stop, of course. Where the rest of us had grown more cautious, he seemed only to have become reenergized. Though weighted with armor and armaments in the jungle heat, and aged not a day under sixty, he walked with a spring in his step, as if on the way to a merry picnic in the English countryside.

And he never stopped talking for long. "I assure you, I am a great friend of El Dorado," he told Ganix. "I have been here before, to Guyana, in search of it."

"Why bother?" Ganix nodded at Father's armor. "You would seem to have all the wealth you could ever need."

"Wealth?"

"Everything you wear and carry appears to be solid gold or gold-plated," said Ganix. "I can't imagine where you found so much of that precious metal."

"Oh, this?" Father patted his golden breastplate, which was molded with his coat of arms—five diamonds arranged in a descending diagonal line from left to right. "We can *make* all the gold we like. We've been able to do so for *decades*. Haven't you heard of *alchemy*, dear fellow?"

"You can change the properties of metals?" said Ganix. "As you did with my…contraption?"

"Metals—and *other* substances. Solids, liquids, and gases are equally at our command." Father grinned and squeezed Ganix's shoulder. "You see? A relationship between our peoples *can* be beneficial, after all."

IT must have been noon, at least, when I noticed a change in the air—a thickening, as of greater humidity. I had to wipe the sweat from my brow with increasing frequency; the golden garments under my armor grew thoroughly soaked.

Then, amid the constant chatter and screeching of jungle insects and animals, I heard the keening cry of a gull. The bird's message was clear.

There was a body of water nearby.

Picking up my pace, I surged ahead of the others, heedless of any possible danger. The presence of a large body of water here in the uncharted mountains of Guyana—at the end of a mechanical juggernaut's trail, no less—could mean only one thing.

No one from the expedition called out or tried to stop me. As the foliage started to thin, I broke into a run, sprinting like a deer in spite of the armor and midday heat.

Suddenly, I broke through the tree line, emerging into the full brightness of the unfiltered sun. The blinding light, I'll wager, was rivaled by my own enormous grin at what I saw before me.

A vast curtain of dazzling blue spread out over an enormous basin ringed by rugged mountain peaks. More gulls wheeled in the sky overhead, gliding among the clouds.

But not all the clouds were the product of Nature.

Off in the distance, on the far side of this massive lake, giant plumes of white vapor puffed skyward. When I saw their common source, when I glimpsed it for the very first time, I gasped.

Father did the same when he drew up beside me. "Dear God." I felt his hand fall onto my shoulder and perch there, softly as a bird. "It's Lake Parime."

For a long moment, the two of us stood there alone, gaping at the sight across the lake.

To say that moment was the culmination of decades of struggle and sacrifice would not have been an exaggeration in the slightest. He had poured his heart and soul into this quest, and his dream had been contagious, passed along to me. He had come to this part of the world once before and failed, but I had come back with him years later to make it right. On this journey, we had had our differences, a hundred little strifes—but neither of us had ceased to believe in the object of our search.

Now here it was.

Along that far shore, at the base of a mountain blanketed in emerald jungle, sprawled a city of iron-gray and gleaming chrome. Even from a distance, I could see that its structures were ever in motion, pumping and turning and swinging with the regular rhythm of mechanical equipment. From end to end, huge smokestacks yawned out billows of whiteness.

Even then, watching from so far away, I knew it would be so much greater than I'd ever imagined when we saw it up close.

"El Dorado." Father said it in a hushed voice and squeezed my shoulder. "The legendary lost city of machines."

"Lost no more." I nodded slowly.

"Now comes the hard part."

He let go of my shoulder and slapped my back. "The *best* part, you mean. Striding those hallowed streets, basking in the wisdom of the great machinists."

"Do you think they'll welcome us?"

"One way or another." Father laughed. "I, for one, have no intention of coming all this distance only to be turned away."

"Or killed," I added.

"We need not fear that outcome," said Father, "as long as you follow my lead in all things. As ever."

With that, he walked away, already beginning his transit of the lakeshore.

And the magic of the moment of discovery and kinship between us was gone, up in smoke. We were back to our usual strained relationship, the one I had known ever since childhood: he loved me without limit but trusted only himself in things of a practical nature.

WITH Father in the lead and myself close behind, our party set off along the shore. El Dorado beckoned in the distance, rippling with the afternoon's heat like some desert mirage.

We probably would have benefited from waiting out the worst of that heat, but none of us suggested it. With El Dorado in sight, and father marching toward it with renewed vigor, how could any of us do otherwise?

Only Ganix dared speak his own mind on the subject. "Would it kill you to take a break for five minutes? Or at least walk in the shade of the jungle?" He blew out his breath in frustration. "If humane treatment of your prisoner isn't reason enough, I suspect it would make more sense not to approach the city out in the open, strategically speaking."

"If I wanted to *attack* it, perhaps," said father. "But I only wish to *visit* it in peace. We have nothing to hide here."

"I wonder if the inhabitants will accept your good intentions at face value," said Ganix.

Father ignored the comment. "I have *dreamed* of visiting this place. A civilization founded primarily on *mechanical* principals, rather than *alchemical* ones."

"And *I* have dreamed of dropping dead from *heat exhaustion*," said Ganix. "I wonder whose dream will come true first?"

"Most of Europe does not believe this place even exists," said father. "And if it does exist, they do not care. I have been called variously a lunatic, an opportunist, and an idiot for espousing my unwavering belief in it."

"Then you must feel right at home," said Ganix, "for I think of you in exactly the same way."

Again, father ignored his comments. "Our society has grown dependent on the works of alchemy, unwilling to consider the value of any but the most limited applications of the mechanical arts. But I know better. I realize that for all our transmutations and transformations, true advancement lies in the manipulation of the physical world by mechanical means."

With that, Ganix turned to me with an exaggerated pleading expression. "*Please*, good sir, won't you untie my hands so I may hold them over my ears and *block out* this endless yammering?"

I just smiled and shook my head.

"Perhaps that is just the thing for us," Father stopped suddenly in his tracks to cast a meaningful gaze at Ganix. "Perhaps we should do exactly as he suggests."

"Oh, good," said Ganix. "Oh, yes, please."

"Father?" I frowned with concern.

"If we free him and send him ahead, perhaps his people will see it as a sign of goodwill," said father. "A demonstration of our peaceful good intentions."

"Oh, certainly." Ganix nodded energetically. "That's exactly how they would see it."

"Or they might consider it ample *warning* to galvanize their defenses against us!" I said. "Do you really think it wise to give up the element of surprise?"

"Look at that place." Father gestured at El Dorado as it rippled in the distance. "Do you really think they cannot mount a most significant defense if they so choose, whether warned in advance or not?"

"All the more reason to consider his value as a *hostage*," I said. "This man might be the only leverage we will have against a superior force."

"Or the act of using him as a bargaining chip might bring about the very end we seek to avoid." Father shook his head. "A poor strategy by any measure." Walking around behind Ganix, he undid the bonds around his wrists. "Short-sightedness will not gain us the keys to paradise, Wat."

I felt my face flush. Great man that he was, Father tended to forget how much his offhanded remarks could burn those in his command—or in his family.

"Now then." Father tossed me the cords he'd just untied and stood before Ganix with his hands on his hips. "There are conditions on your freedom."

Ganix rubbed his wrists. "Is that so?"

"I expect you to tell them we chose not to hurt you."

"'Them?'" Ganix raised an eyebrow.

"Your people," said Father. "Tell them also what we did to your juggernaut, and that we could do much worse if confronted."

Ganix shrugged. "Can I go now?"

Father reached out and poked him in the chest with one gold-gauntleted finger. "Tell them also that we bring them a very great gift—and a stern warning of great dangers in store."

"Don't worry," said Ganix. "I will make it very clear how dangerous you are."

"*Other* dangers," snapped Father. "And let there be no doubt, Francisco Pizarro would *not* have set you free as I now do." With that, he stepped aside and gestured for Ganix to leave. "Until we meet again, good Ganix."

Ganix frowned and hesitated, as if uncertain he should leave. Then he shrugged. "Raleigh," he said, just before he ran off along the shore and disappeared around the bend of a high-banked cove.

AS we continued on course toward El Dorado, I picked up grumblings from the men. As loyal as they were to father, there were questions about his decision to release the prisoner. There were doubts, and I shared them.

He seemed to have had very logical reasons for setting Ganix free, but I wasn't sure I would have made the same choice. It was a situation that recurred quite often in those days, in his old age. In years gone by, I never would have doubted him...but now I had to wonder if his faculties were intact. Once in a while, I would catch him forgetting something, or misspeaking, or making a mistake, and I would wonder. Was the great Sir Walter Raleigh still as great as he once had been?

I was all too aware of the irony. Father didn't fully trust me because I was young, in my early twenties, and I didn't fully trust him because he was old.

THE first juggernauts showed up two hours later, when we were less than a mile from the city.

Until then, I'd dared hope we might complete our journey unmolested. After Ganix's disappearance, we had seen no sign of opposition or even habitation on the shore or in the tree line along it. Our biggest obstacles were the heat and the rocky terrain, which slowed our progress.

Then, with the city so close, looming just ahead, I felt the ground rumble underfoot. The shaking swiftly increased in intensity, making my glass grenades rattle on their golden bandolier.

"To arms!" shouted father. "Prepare to defend yourselves!"

As the words left his lips, the ground pushed upward some twenty yards ahead of us. The hump rose quickly, shedding sand and pebbles to reveal gleaming black armor underneath—the familiar form of a juggernaut like the one that had attacked us earlier.

As the first juggernaut reached its full twelve-foot height, two more thrust up on either side of it. When the rumbling ended, our path to the city was blocked by three black juggernauts with gun barrels pointed in our direction.

Father raised an arm and shouted so we all could hear. "Don't waste your bullets, men! We already know they won't pierce that armor! Grenades and spray-guns only!"

As one, we swung back our muskets, holstered our pistols, and reached for the weapons he'd asked for. Heart racing, I grabbed a grenade with each hand, tensing as I selected my targets.

I wondered, as I heard a familiar rumble from the juggernauts, what part of Father's message had disturbed the machinists of El Dorado to the point of ordering an attack. Perhaps we'd never had a chance of making peace with them at all; I had to admit, if I were in their shoes, I might have made the same move. Why risk everything by admitting unknown elements to your mechanical utopia?

"Stand fast, men!" said father. "If we perish, we do so in the cause of peace and knowledge!"

Mouth parched, stomach twisting, sweat flowing, I waited in the hot sun for the first shot to fly. The temptation was strong to get the jump on the juggernauts and apply an alchemical grenade to thin their ranks, but I held back, though I knew it might cost us dearly. Until the first exchange of fire, there was still a chance, however unlikely, that the standoff might be defused.

Or maybe that chance wasn't so slight, after all: suddenly, the middle juggernaut released jets of steam from the smokestacks on its back and lowered its guns. The other two juggernauts did the same.

No member of our expedition gave up his grip on his own weapons, though. Any outcome was still possible at this point.

"Hello?" Father waved at the juggernauts. "I am Sir Walter Raleigh of the British Empire. Perhaps your man, Ganix, has told you of me."

Steam hissed from vents at the base of the middle juggernaut's head. An obsidian plate slid up into the cowling atop the head, revealing a human face staring out at us.

A *familiar* face.

Ganix's face. "Yes, my man has told me of you," he said. "Though he *did* say you tend to talk too much, which could be a problem."

Father laughed. "For what reason, friend Ganix?"

"Because we have not a moment to waste." Ganix looked dead serious. "We desperately need your help."

Burning with curiosity, I spoke up. "Why is that?"

"El Dorado has fallen to Pizarro," said Ganix. "And we need your alchemical wizardry to help us regain it."

FROM above, none of us had realized there was a network of tunnels running beneath our feet. But that soon changed when Ganix took us underground.

We had agreed to go with him when we were satisfied with his sincerity and the veracity of the threat to El Dorado. Moments later, our party gathered around him and the other two juggernauts, filling a rectangular section of beach that turned out to be a moving platform.

Powered by steam pressure (like so many of El Dorado's innovations), the platform lowered us into the earth. As soon as our heads were below ground level, a door slid shut above us, concealing the opening into which we had descended.

After dropping dozens of feet, our platform came to rest in a dimly lit tunnel. Following Ganix's example, we stepped clear of the conveyance, which then ascended back up toward the surface.

Wandering, I spotted a pair of parallel metal rails laid along the tunnel floor, stretching off into the dark distance. Some kind of transportation system, perhaps.

"These tunnels were built for emergency evacuations of the city." Ganix's voice echoed when he spoke. "Unfortunately, few citizens thought to use them today until it was too late."

"Yet *you* managed to escape," I said. "And these others." I gestured at his companion juggernauts, who stood nearby like ebony monoliths, occasionally venting steam.

"When I entered El Dorado and saw the Spanish forces in control, I fled underground," said Ganix. "My friends, and certain others, were already below, preparing to retake the city."

"I did warn you about Pizarro," said father. "He is every bit the conquering savage that his father, Hernando, and his uncles were. Perhaps more so."

"We have had some small experience with Spaniards," said Ganix. "But they were monks, not conquerors. They taught us their language but never *harmed* us."

Father glared. "How many of your people has Pizarro killed so far?"

"Twenty, at last count," said Ganix. "Based on what I've heard, he is more interested in turning the city into a manufacturing center for war materials and utilizing the populace as a captive work force."

"So he can carve out his own empire in the Americas, no doubt." Father shook his head in disgust. "Perhaps he wishes to redeem his rather lackluster military career to date."

"Tell us about his forces," I said. "How many men?"

"Between eighty and a hundred," said Ganix. "Reports vary. All of them carry firearms and alchemical weapons similar to yours—grenades and sprays capable of transmuting metals."

I nodded thoughtfully. "And what of *your* remaining forces?"

"Five juggernauts, armed as you have seen." Ganix gestured at his two companions, who stood behind him. "A dozen men and women, three of whom possess some degree of military training.

Two dozen personal projectile launchers, intended for use by infantry." He raised an eyebrow and grinned. "Oh, and *flying machines*."

"Flying machines?" I asked.

"Two of those." Ganix nodded. "Prototypes of an experimental design."

"*Flying machines.*" Father said it in a stunned whisper.

"Sounds to me as if you have the makings of an excellent retaliatory force," I said.

"Except, perhaps, for the lack of military experience," added Father.

"And the lack of an adequate defense against European alchemy," said Ganix.

"Lucky for you, we have plenty of both." Suddenly, I felt a surge of will and conviction, a burst of inspiration. Though I was accustomed to letting Father, legend that he was, take the lead in all things, something came over me. Turning to the men of our expedition, I raised my fists in the air. "What say you, warriors? Shall we lend our sweat and blood to this cause? Shall we work hand-in-hand with these noble machinists to liberate legendary El Dorado?"

To a man, everyone in our party raised their fists and let loose a fierce *Yes*! (Even father, though he looked surprised and joined the chorus a few beats later than the others.)

I whirled from them to face Ganix in his juggernaut armor.

"You shall have the force you need! Now let us make preparations for what is certain to be a historic battle! Let us merge England and El Dorado, alchemy and steam, for a war the likes of which this world has never seen!"

Everyone cheered at that—this time led by Father, whose voice was the fiercest of all.

GANIX climbed out of his juggernaut and led us to the armory—the next chamber up the line—and showed us the cache of weapons. Meanwhile, refugees from El Dorado filtered in from side tunnels, eyeing us warily.

As I looked at the stock of projectile weapons and juggernauts, I was both impressed by the craftsmanship that had gone into them and uncertain they would be enough to carry the day. Would this smattering of mechanical arms, deployed in conjunction with our own alchemical weaponry, provide the level of force needed to stop a hundred Spaniards toting muskets and alchemical bombs?

"No." I said it aloud, interrupting Ganix's discourse on the virtues of machine-driven weaponry. "It won't be enough."

All eyes turned to me. The floor was mine.

"We do not possess overwhelming force," I said, loud enough for everyone in the armory to hear. "We must devise a new tactic, something that will confer the element of surprise in our favor."

Father, with his hands on his hips, nodded in agreement. "What do you suggest?"

Gazing around the armory, I considered the question. The devices at our disposal—I had never seen anything quite like them. Instead of relying on transmutation, as our alchemy did, they transferred energy into physical effects, be they related to destruction or mobility. If only we had these marvels at home, we could perform miracles; change the very fabric of civilization. And, if we ever *merged* these machines with our alchemical wonders, *then* we might truly be onto something.

Suddenly, an idea flashed through me like my own personal Pentecost. I knew what we needed to do, what might gain us the advantage in a conflict with Pizarro's forces.

And it was all right there in that room around us.

With a snap of my fingers, I wheeled to face Ganix. "Your people. Only three have military experience. But what of mechanical expertise?"

Ganix smiled. "*All* of them, of course. They are inhabitants of El Dorado, are they not?"

"Excellent," I said, clapping my hands together. "Then let us put them to work, shall we?"

"On what?" asked Ganix.

"On a project. A *special* project," I told him. "A *collaborative* project."

IN the hours that followed, the members of our expedition worked side by side with the refugee machinists, combining their weapons with ours.

The underground armory was filled with a flurry of activity and noise. People hurried in all directions, rushing from one task to another. The chatter of voices mingled with the clanging and crashing of tools and parts.

But one voice, as always, stood out to me above all others.

"Wat?" Father spoke up from behind me as I filled a metal basket with transmutation grenades. "How long until we're ready, do you think?"

I placed the last of the grenades in the basket and shut the lid. "Four hours, at most." Looking around, I quickly scanned the progress of the other workers. "Perhaps three."

"Good," said father. "The less time Pizarro has to toy with El Dorado, the better."

"Hear, hear." I nodded and reached for a wrench.

Which was exactly when father caught my wrist in his grip and squeezed it tight. "Whatever happens, Wat, I want you to know— I'm proud of the way you stepped forward. You were most...*commanding.*"

My heart beat faster with the marvel of it. Father so rarely complimented me in such a direct fashion. More often than not, his comments carried an undercurrent of at least mild condescension.

Now here he was, saying something I had given up hope of ever hearing him say, and the only undercurrent was one of paternal affection.

"Thank you, father," I told him in a casual way, trying not to show how deeply his words had affected me. "I appreciate your support."

Father squeezed my wrist tighter, then let it go. "As I have appreciated yours for all these years, though I have never spoken of it."

Then, without another word, he walked away, leaving me to continue my labors.

AN hour before sunrise the next morning, we left the tunnels at strategic points. Contacts on the outside had sent us intelligence on enemy troop positions via a remarkable device—a communication system that transmitted voices over airwaves. It was yet another invention undreamt of by European civilization, yet another reason to fight this battle for the future of El Dorado.

The time was right to attack: still dark, with many of the Spaniards still asleep. Ample sentries patrolled the streets and walls, but the number of alert and prepared soldiers was much lower than what it would be after sunrise.

At the end of a shared countdown over the communication device, the entirety of our forces poured out of the tunnels with weapons activated. Mixed teams of Englishmen and El Doradoans raced through the streets, brandishing steam-powered projectile launchers loaded with alchemical pellets. The pellets, when fired, had a much greater range than hand-thrown grenades; they allowed our men and women to fire alchemical potions from a greater distance. When the pellets hit, they transmuted Spanish gold armor to a greenish gas that sent the wearer into uncontrollable coughing fits, leaving them less difficult to subdue.

The five juggernauts, meanwhile, applied their own hybrid weapons to broader effect. Their converted guns sprayed alchemical concoctions in far-reaching streams, spraying Spanish artillery and ammunition stockpiles as enemy musket balls pinged harmlessly off their armor. While the Spaniards screamed and scrambled, their cannons, muskets, and armor turned to useless mercury or toxic gas. They hurled their own alchemical grenades but lacked the range of our steam-powered mechanical launchers. One juggernaut went down, its armor turned to crumpling tin by a grenade lobbed from a second-story window, but the other four continued their rampage, supported by our men and women on foot.

The Spaniards might have managed one successful attack from above, but the true advantage when it came to altitude was all ours. Our two flying machines swooped through the air above the city with ease, one piloted by Ganix, the other by me.

These machines consisted of a single seat suspended inside a lightweight framework with a broad wing on either side. All this hung from a steam-powered engine that turned an upthrust axle at a high rate of speed. When the axle turned, it spun four metal paddles that somehow lifted the entire device up into the air. Once there, the pilot steered the contraption by means of levers controlling the angle of the wings and a rearward rudder.

I didn't exactly understand all the mechanics of it, but I *loved* flying. It required some getting used to at first, but I took to it like a bird and put it to use against our enemies.

Soaring above the city walls, I dropped alchemical bombs on the Spanish sentries there, transmuting their weapons into useless mists and fluids. Swooping over the central plaza, I pelted the enemy ranks with grenades, sending them reeling. When a Spaniard tried again to bomb a juggernaut from a high window, I cruised past and fired alchemical bullets from a launcher through his window, rendering him weaponless.

With Ganix and me wreaking havoc from above, and our ground forces doing the same below, we were able to rout the Spaniards—but then they mounted a counterattack. Spanish reinforcements charged out of buildings where they must have been barracked for the night. Dozens of enemy troops swarmed out of side streets, attacking our forces in the plaza from the rear.

This time, our men and women were caught between the Spaniards they'd been fighting in the middle of the plaza and the fresh troops striking from behind. As I rushed to lend air support, I saw loyal English soldiers and El Dorado irregulars fall before the reinforced Spanish forces. The Spaniards hammered our people with a combination of alchemical grenades and gunfire—turning armor into liquid or gas with grenade strikes, then firing musket balls into newly exposed chests and guts, blasting apart organs with brutal efficiency.

Learning from their past mistakes, the Spaniards also swarmed the juggernauts, attacking from all directions. A juggernaut might lash out in one direction, but Spaniards attacking on other sides managed to pelt it with alchemical grenades, dissolving its armor. Soon, only two juggernauts of the original five remained in the fight. In a matter of moments, the Spaniards had gained ground; they might very well have driven back our challenge.

This, I could not let stand. I could not allow them to ruin Father's dream—*our* dream.

Circling overhead, I gave Ganix a hand signal; I would come in from one corner of the plaza, and he would follow close behind. Then, working the levers and stepping on a foot pedal to increase paddle rotation speed, and the speed of the flying machine's forward propulsion, I angled downward and dove for the Spaniards.

Musket balls leaped toward me as I came in fast and low; one punched through a wing, but the damage didn't bring me down.

Spaniards pitched grenades without making contact. Ironically, the wobble caused by the hole in my wing from the musket ball made my aircraft harder to hit.

It also made it harder to aim as I fired alchemical bullets from the projectile launcher—but my targets, the Spaniards, were clustered together, improving my chances of hitting *something* with my erratic strafing fire. I saw Spanish armor melt and turn to gas throughout the crowd, more than enough to break the troops' solidarity and soften them up for Ganix.

When I passed, he zoomed in behind me and emptied his basket of grenades, creating a cloud of alchemical fumes that fanned over the Spanish formation. Instead of affecting one or two soldiers at a time, as individual grenades would, the cloud swept over a mass of them, liquefying or evaporating their armor and weapons.

Which opened them up to the

muskets of the English and El Doradoans, and the projectile guns of one of the remaining juggernauts, who shot them full of holes the second the fumes had cleared enough to let musket balls through.

With one half of the Spanish pincer broken, Ganix and I repeated our maneuver on the other side of the plaza. This time he went first, softening the Spaniards with a hail of alchemical bullets, and I followed, emptying my basket of grenades.

The results were equally punishing for the Spaniards. Our ground forces blasted them ruthlessly as soon as the fumes had flushed away their armor and weapons and dispersed. The other remaining juggernaut waded in, firing steam-propelled projectiles from its guns.

At this point, the battle had swung firmly back in our favor.

As groups of Spaniards surrendered, kneeling on the cobblestones at the mercy of our troops—and other citizens of El Dorado emerged from hiding places and imprisonment during the battle—our dominance was evident. The strategic lesson was obvious: alchemy alone could not withstand the might of hybrid alchemical-mechanical warfighting techniques. The end of an era was at hand, and we were watching it happen in El Dorado.

Unfortunately, not all the old ways had lost their bite. As we were in the final stages of crushing the opposition, I saw a flurry of motion at the edge of the central plaza. Swooping in that direction, I saw an all-too-familiar scene play out below.

One of the Spaniards had taken a hostage—a dark-haired young woman of El Dorado in a gray smock. The Spaniard was holding a sword at her throat and shouting something to a group of our fighters: a demand for safe passage, no doubt, or a desperate call for surrender.

When I got closer, I saw he wasn't some low-ranking nobody but the most well-known of all the occupiers. None other than Francisco Pizarro—son of Hernando and nephew of Francisco the elder, conqueror of Peru—was holding that woman hostage.

How far he had fallen, and how fast. In the space of an hour, he had gone from conquering legendary El Dorado and seizing its steam-powered miracle machines to hiding behind one woman with a sword at her throat.

Suddenly, a lone figure darted out from a doorway and raced toward Pizzaro. As I circled overhead, I glimpsed a flash of metal—a sword in the rescuer's hand.

Pizarro must have heard his approach at the last second, as he let go of the woman and spun to face his opponent. Pizarro's sword swung up barely in time to stop the stroke of his enemy, but I knew his reprieve would not last. Because I recognized the form of the swash-buckler who'd challenged him as one of the great swordsmen of our age.

The man crossing swords with Francisco Pizarro was none other than my father, Sir Walter Raleigh.

For a moment, I felt a pang of fear. Pizarro unleashed a brutal sequence of sword strokes, driving father back a full three steps. Father seemed to falter, respond-ing with a half-hearted series of parries, and I worried he might not be able to fend off Pizarro.

Heart racing, I prepared to dive down and intervene. I wasn't about to let father die at the hands of Pizarro.

But I should have known better than to doubt the great Raleigh. In his old age, I'd lost trust in him, but it turned out he hadn't lost a step.

As I watched, Pizarro mounted another charge, whipping his sword through a complex pattern of slashes. One grazed Father's gold breastplate, pushing him back...and father stumbled.

Stumbling left and back, Father ducked a hacking blow coming in from the right—then delivered a low jab on the left that slipped between the gaps in Pizarro's armor, penetrating his upper right thigh.

Father drove the sword point deep and wrenched it around hard, slicing through flesh and arteries. Then he pulled it free and leaped away, though he needn't have worried.

Pizarro fell and let his sword clatter to the cobblestones beside him. Squirming and screaming, he clutched at the wound in his leg as his life's blood spurted from it, emptying out of the once-feared body that had caused so much suf-fering.

Pizarro the Conqueror had been conquered. El Dorado was saved.

Looking up at me, Father grinned and waved his bloody sword, signaling victory. If I had been down on the ground, I might have told him I was proud of what he'd done, as he'd told me earlier.

But I settled for flashing him a thumbs-up on my way past, instead.

THAT evening, long after the smoke of battle had cleared, father, Ganix, and I stood on a balcony and watched the sun set over Lake Parime.

Pizarro was dead and the city retaken. Instead of the roar of war, we heard the chugging and whir-ring and hissing of the machines of El Dorado, ever in motion all around us.

"We did it, my friends." Father, between Ganix and me, leaned on the balcony rail as the wind ruffled his silver hair. "We joined forces to defeat our common foe."

"And usher in a new era of

cooperation between alchemy and steam." I cast a meaningful look in Ganix's direction. "If you'll have us."

Ganix shrugged. "I can't deny we worked well together today."

"You should consider the benefits of alignment," said father. "We have much more to offer than simple transmutation of the elements."

"Alchemy, like your machines, has provided numerous advancements," I added. "A universal cure for all ailments, for example."

"And eternal life." Father looked back over his shoulder at Ganix and grinned. "What would you say if I told you we could give you *that*, friend Ganix?"

"I would say you have my attention." Ganix chuckled. "Yet your alchemy seems not to have provided a cure for *all* human ills, has it? Greed and hatred, for example? Cruelty and violence?"

Father turned back to the setting sun. "The human heart remains the human heart, with all its potential for evil—and good. It encourages us to make mistakes, to lose faith." He looked over at me, his weathered face glowing with red and golden light. "And to regain it."

For a moment, none of us spoke.

Then Ganix nodded. "If my people were to express interest in further collaboration with yours, how would we proceed? What would our next step be?"

"You'll have to talk to our ambassador about that," said Father.

Ganix frowned. "And that would be...?"

"Him." Father hiked a thumb at me. "Ambassador Wat Raleigh."

He winked at me then, and I smiled. We had come a long way, he and I. Gone were the days when we'd failed to trust each other, when we'd kept a dark distance between us at all times.

It was the start of a new era, indeed.

"Thank you, Father." I squeezed his shoulder. "But what about you?"

"I'll be marching the captured Spaniards off to jail," said Father. "Then launching another expedition, actually." His smile widened, as he stared off into the sunset. "I've heard tell of another lost city, deep in the jungles of Honduras. *Ciudad Blanca*, they call it."

I felt a surge of warmth toward him then, a wave of love and recognition. There would always be another lost city for him, another mountain to climb, another obstacle to conquer. Always another dream for the great Sir Walter Raleigh.

It was a way of looking at the world I knew all too well, from myself as well as him. Like father, like son.

Until now, at least.

"Though perhaps I've been hasty in naming you ambassador here," said Father. "Would you like to come with me instead to Ciudad Blanca?"

Until now, when I no longer needed to tailor my life toward impressing him, no longer needed to prove myself worthy of his love.

"No, thanks." I smiled and shook my head. "I think I'll have challenge enough right here."

"I know you'll do well." Father stood away from the railing and shook my hand, then pulled me into a hug. "You're the right man for the job, Wat."

Because I knew I finally had all the proof I needed.

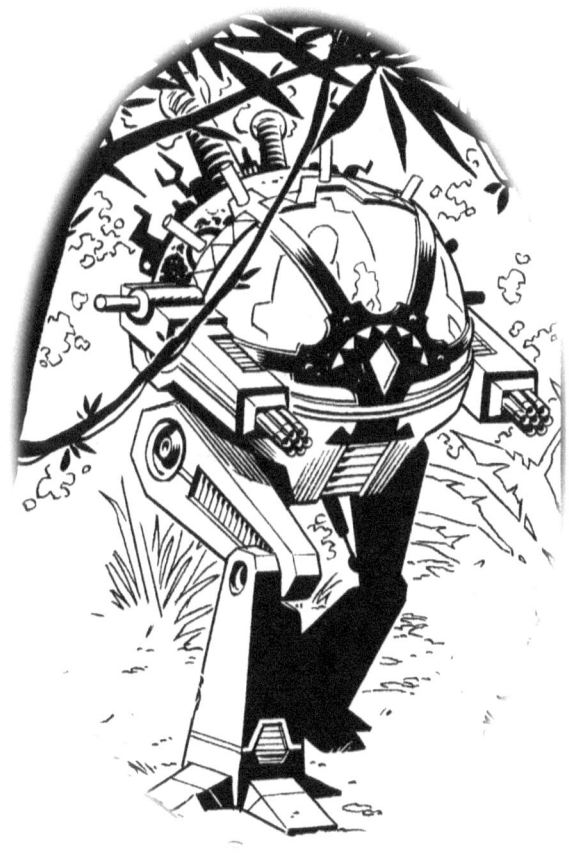

Professor Ironheart and the Führerbunker

By PETER DAVID

"THIS used to be so beautiful. This garden…now blown to hell and gone. So beautiful."

Hitler gazed around the shattered remains of the Chancellery Garden and slowly shook his head. He wished that he could remove the memories from his mind and insert them into Eva's mind whole, so that she could fully appreciate what he was seeing in his own thoughts. Eva was obviously doing her best, looking around and nodding and trying to appreciate whatever she thought he was seeing, but she wasn't terribly good at it. Knowing what you are supposed to do and actually accomplishing it are two entirely different things.

His dog, Blondi, was finishing attending to her business and now she scampered back over to him and nestled at her ankle. In the distance he could hear the roar of airplanes, the sounds of bombs being dropped non-stop on Berlin. He took personal offense at it, never even considering that he had inflicted identical punishment on other cities in Europe such as London.

Eva stroked the top of his hand. "We're not going to make it, are we."

"We'll make it," he said.

"You'll die rather than be captured."

"I'm not going to be captured, nor will you."

"Are you…" Her voice dropped to a whisper. "Are you going to kill yourself?"

"Of course not," he said. He glanced right and left, as if to make sure no one was listening. Then he lowered his voice as well. "I have it all arranged."

"What's all arranged?"

"New identities. A new place to live. All the papers are in my office."

"New identities?"

"Yes. You're going to be Mary Anne MacLeod."

"But I can't affect a Scots brogue!"

"Dinna worry, lassie. Ah can. Yuh married inta th' name."

A smile broke across her face. "That's…that's amazing! I had no idea you had such…" Then she gasped and pointed.

Hitler's head snapped around

Illustration by Caio Cacau

and he was stunned to see a young boy standing not ten feet away from him.

He appeared to be in his mid-teens. His clothes were shabby; he appeared to be a street urchin. His brown hair was sticking out from beneath the grey cap he was wearing. In his right hand he was holding a rose, and he was extending it toward Eva.

"Who are you?" demanded Hitler.

"No one," said the teen. "Just giving a gift to a beautiful lady."

Eva glanced at Hitler for permission. He nodded brusquely and she walked over to the lad and took the flower. She sniffed it. "It's beautiful," she said. She turned back toward him and said, "Adolf, look how—"

He had extracted his luger from its holster, taken aim and fired off a shot before she could complete the sentence. It struck the boy squarely in the chest and knocked him off his feet. The boy tumbled like a marionette that had had its strings severed. He lay on the ground, unbreathing, unmoving.

"Adolf, how could you?" said Eva despairingly, clutching the rose to her bosom. "He was just a boy."

"He could have been a spy," Adolf said briskly. "Some random urchin making his way to the garden, a short distance from the bunker? We cannot take the chance. I will arrange to have the body disposed of."

She looked as if she were about to start arguing again, but quickly she realized there would be no point to it. The boy was dead and even if she could convince Hitler that he had acted precipitously, it wasn't going to bring him back.

Hitler saw several birds descending toward the boy. That was good. Let them call their friends and devour him. One less thing to worry about.

He didn't see the birds swirl away a few moments later.

H E pulled the drawer open in his private office and removed two large envelops filled with documents. He extended one to Eva and she opened it tentatively. She slid the papers out, examining them in wonderment. "So much detail," she said, unable to keep the amazement from her voice.

"Absolutely," he said with a touch of pride. "Nothing has been left to chance." He paused and then said, "We are going to lose the war, Eva. There's no stopping the allies at this point."

"Are you sure?"

"Positive," he said. "It was the fault of my Generals. They were unable to accomplish even the simplest of their instructions. The next time…"

"Next time?" Her voice quavered slightly. She was not exactly enamored of the notion of Adolf launching a third World War.

"Next time we do it differently. No camps for the world to see. To hell with the Jews. I never should have bothered with them. It served a short-term purpose but long term lost us more than we gained. We should have just walled them off in a ghetto and forgotten about them. Trust me, I would not make the same mistakes. But...listen to me," and he took her by the hand. "In case something should happen to me, there's a man I want you to go to. His name is Fred. He works for me undercover in America."

"Wait, what do you mean, if something happens to you? What will happen to you?"

"My face is far better known than yours, Eva. The world is filled with people who want to dispose of me. Fred's contact information is in your envelope. Promise me you will—"

That was when an explosive noise from the hallway jolted both of them. Loud voices were shouting, *"Who is that?" "Get him!" "How did he get down here?"* But accompanying the shouting were quick wisps, gusts of air, and bodies were hitting the ground one after the other.

"We are under attack!" whispered Hitler. "Quiet! Get down behind the desk! Don't move. This is my secret office. Whoever it is, they likely don't even know about—"

The door burst open and a slender but powerful figure crashed through. Hitler fired off a shot and it missed, the target hitting the floor and rolling away. It sprang to its feet and Hitler swung his gun,

but knew he was going to be too late. His assailant was much too fast moving.

"No!" screamed Eva and she leaped in from the side, throwing her arms wide, her eyes frightened but determined.

The gun went off and nailed her in the chest.

Eva cried out and slumped forward, and Adolf, with a sob of horror, dropped his gun and grabbed her before she fell. "No, no, no," he kept whispering, and then his gaze shifted to the assailant. *"Sie bastard,"* he snarled, and then his eyes narrowed. "You. The boy from the garden."

"Not a boy," he said. "I'm Professor Ironheart."

"No. No, that is impossible." Hitler naturally knew Ironheart. He worked for the United States, had done so for years. He battled evil doers, mad scientists, insane men who created monsters. Hitler had known a number of them. They had spoken of Ironheart in low whispers of fear, and one by one they had disappeared.

But Ironheart had existed for decades. He couldn't be this...this callow youth...

"It's not impossible," said Ironheart softly. "Seventy years ago, my father and I were searching for the Fountain of Youth. We found it. So did pirates. They killed my father and I fell in. Now I'm immortal. Short of being shot in the head— or at least, so I assume—I cannot die."

"This is nonsense!"

"And yet you shot me, but here I am."

"How did you find me?"

"A tracing device in the rose I gave to your fiancée."

"Of course." Slowly Hitler eased her to the floor and stood up straight. "So now what? I know that the famed Professor Ironheart does not kill. So how are you going to extract me from the bunker? Get me out of Berlin in one piece? I am sure you have an entire plan."

Slowly Ironheart shook his head. "No. No such plan. My orders were very specific. They want you dead." He leveled the gun at Hitler's face. "I very much did not want to do this. For what it is worth, I am sorry it has come to this."

"Wait!" shouted Hitler, throwing his hands up defensively. "There is something I need to tell you!"

Ironheart fired. The bullet drilled through Hitler's forehead and the dictator stumbled back into his chair. He fell heavily, his eyes staring at nothing.

"Tell me next time," said Ironheart.

He heard the sounds of footsteps sprinting toward him and decided that it would be too much trouble to go out the way he had come in. Fortunately, there was an air vent directly above the desk. He clambered up onto the desk, slid into it and drew it closed behind him. He started slithering down the duct,

listening to the tumult behind him as Hitler's men entered the office and found the devastation he'd left in his wake.

He pulled his walkie talkie from his hip pocket. "Howler. You reading me?"

"Right here, Prof."

"Bring the prop top in to the bunker roof. I'll be there in five."

"Mission accomplished?"

Prof hesitated and then he said, "Yes. He's dead. Her too."

There was a brief pause and then Howler said, *"Sorry, Prof. I know you're not happy about it, but it had to be done."*

"Just meet me," said Prof, no longer having any desire to discuss the matter.

He scrambled through the duct, pausing briefly when he heard feet running on the floor below him. He was moving so quietly that he was relatively sure they wouldn't hear him even if he kept moving. But there was no point in not being cautious.

Finally, his crawlspace came to an end. There was a grating directly in front of him, and Prof attempted to lift it carefully off. But he had no luck. The damned thing seemed welded down. Deciding that he had no time to waste, and taking a chance that the noise would not summon anyone else, the Prof slammed down on the grating and knocked it to the ground. The sound echoed up and down the hallway as Prof dropped to the ground, glancing right and left.

There was a stairway to his right, but the sounds of feet were coming from all around him. There was no time to wait. He sprinted toward the stairs just as he saw two guards coming down. He charged shoulder first into the leading one, flipping him over in a judo toss, and then slammed a fist into the gut of the one behind him. The guard doubled over and Prof drove a spear hand to his throat. The guard gasped, choked, and Prof didn't wait any longer, throwing him on top of the first guard and effectively blocking the stairwell. By the time more guards arrived at the base of the steps, Prof was already halfway up the stairs.

Hurry up, hurry up, he thought desperately as he continued to sprint up the stairway. No one was getting in his way, and he considered that a benefit. For once something was going easily.

There was a door at the top of the stairs. It was not labeled, but Prof hoped that it would lead out onto the rooftop. Howler was going to be there within a minute and he had no desire to hang him up.

He burst through the door and sure enough, there was the roof. Even better, the prop top was hurtling downward from the sky. It was a two-man flying vehicle, a large blade whirling atop it, and it was utterly silent.

Howler Hanson was steering it. The battery was doing its job, propelling it through the air as its lack of noise deftly avoided anyone picking up on the prop top's approach.

The propeller over his head was whipping Howler's abundant black hair all over the place. It didn't seem to deter him, though; he never lost sight of the Prof no matter how much hair got in his face. "*PROF!*" he shouted, his bellow actually audible even though he was a distance away. Howler could make himself heard down the length of a football stadium. His ability to project his voice so loudly, along with the thick black beard and body hair that he sported so proudly, had earned him the nickname "Howler Monkey" Hanson in the service, generally shortened simply to "Howler" among his friends, of which he had very few. "*I SEE YA!*"

Professor Ironheart waved to him and ran toward the area of the rooftop where the prop top seemed to be landing. That was when a bullet cracked through the air, missing the Prof by bare inches.

He didn't even bother to glance over his shoulder. He knew that guards had caught up with him and now it was only a matter of seconds.

Realizing that landing on the roof was no longer an option, Howler tossed down a length of rope. It brushed against the roof as Prof sped toward it. He knew he was running as fast as he could, which meant he was pretty much faster than any other human on

Earth, but the rope still seemed to be an infinite distance from him.

Then a bullet slammed through his shoulder and he staggered, gasping. Another shot took him in the upper thigh and now he could barely walk, sinking to one knee.

Howler let out an infuriated bellow and the rope sped toward the Prof. He grabbed it, looping it around his left wrist, and the rope yanked him straight up. More bullets cracked past him. Had he been on the roof, he'd have been shot again, but the prop top hauled him toward the sky and the bullets flew under him.

Howler cut hard right and more shots whizzed right past the Prof. Astoundingly, Howler clasped the joystick between his knees, continuing to operate the vehicle as he hauled Prof up hand over hand. "*HANG ON!*" he shouted. Prof managed to nod, even as his head was beginning to whirl. He was having serious trouble remaining conscious.

Two, three more yanks and then he was staring into Howler's gruesome but lovable face. "Hey Prof. Good to see ya!" Once upon a time he would have yelled the words into the Prof's face, but he'd been working on moderating his conversational voice. He still spoke loudly, but it wasn't so bad under the circumstances. Howler hauled the rope into the prop top and Prof tumbled into the seat next to him.

"Get us out of here, Howler,"

said the Prof, and he coughed violently. Blood spat out from his lips and landed on the dashboard.

"You need a hospital?" said Howler, concerned.

"No, I'll be okay," said the Prof. He had pulled away his light jacket and now tore aside the shredded cloth to reveal the blood bubbling for it. "Just need a minute."

Slowly, deliberately, the skin began to close up. The blood slowed to a trickle and then stopped. Most remarkably, a small bullet pushed its way up through the skin and popped out into the Prof's waiting hand. He squeezed it tightly once and then slid it into his pants pocket.

Howler shook his head. "No matter how many times I see that, it always gets me."

"Me, too," said the Prof. "Get us home, Howler."

"Right away," said Howler, and the prop top angled away from Berlin as quickly as it could go.

ALI "Spotlight" Kokmen knocked on the door to the Prof's room, his combination laboratory and bedroom. Calling it a bedroom was something of an exaggeration, really. About ninety five percent of it was dedicated to the lab; the rest of it was a single bed and a dresser with clothes that were shoved in in seemingly random order. The Prof didn't set much priority by it. Then again, it made sense. Even though he was decades older than his companions, he remained effectively a teenage boy. His intellect was superb, his ability to engage in physical combat place him at wizard level, but there was still much of the teen within him.

Kokmen had only just recently arrived back at their headquarters on the 68th floor of the Chrysler Building. Howler had informed him that he should return as soon as possible, and that was unusual for Howler who preferred to think of himself as Prof's main man. Of all the furious five, Howler certainly seemed to have the most consistent relationship with Prof. Kokmen enjoyed claiming that it was because Howler was scarcely above being a teenager himself, but the fact was that Howler was typically a good listener, and that was oftentimes what the Prof needed.

Kokmen was a tall and elegant man, a respected judge in the New York Circuit Court. His decisions were said to be read by the Supreme Court itself for guidance on issues that were brought before them. His voice was deep and mellifluous; he sounded as if he were standing on a stage, declaiming to an audience, which was how he had picked up the name "Spotlight." He was carrying an elegant umbrella even though there was no hint of rain on the horizon.

"Prof?" he said, in this instance choosing to speak in a low, soothing voice. "Are you ever going to come out of here?"

"I'm putting the final touches on my bio-scanner," said the Prof, tinkering with a machine on the nearest table. "Gives thorough bio-readouts on anyone who enters. Helps us scan out anyone who isn't human but a disguised robot."

"A disguised robot? Seriously? I thought only we had cracked that technology."

"Just because we have doesn't mean no one else can." He turned in his chair to face Kokmen. "Besides, I haven't been here that long. A few days."

"Two weeks," Kokmen corrected him.

The Professor looked up in mild surprise. "That long?"

"Ever since you got back from Germany. Prof, you should be proud. You've effectively ended the War. You've saved thousands of lives that would have been lost if Hitler had managed to escape."

"I killed him, Spotlight," he said, as if speaking from very far away. "I did the thing I swore I would never do, after witnessing firsthand the brutality of the pirates…after I saw what they did to my father. I swore I would never do such a thing and now look. I'm no better than any of them—"

"That's not true, Prof, and you know it," Kokmen said, strolling into the room and shutting the door behind him. "Pirates loved to kill. It's what they did, whether it was called for or not. Anyone they didn't kill, they ransomed and sometimes even then killed them. You were under orders from the United States Government. You had no choice."

"One always has a choice, Spotlight," the Prof countered. "If I'd managed to get them out of there, do you think the government would have turned up its nose at him? Of course not. I killed him because for once I allowed my rage to overcome my morality. He was a thoroughly evil man, and yet..."

"And yet what?"

The Prof drew in a breath and let it out slowly. "And yet Eva Braun sacrificed her life for his. Did you know a new story is already making the rounds? That Hitler killed himself and she drank poison. The powers that be wish to keep quiet their involvement."

"You're upset because you didn't get the credit?"

"Don't be absurd," said the Prof. "Braun sacrificed herself. She loved him so much that she attempted to intercede, to avoid his being killed. Even Hitler was loved by someone who was willing to sacrifice her life for him. What does that say about him, Spotlight?"

"That people can make mistakes," replied Kokmen.

THE elevator doors slid open and the black clad woman strode onto the 68th floor. The lobby was empty except for a large desk and a woman seated behind it. She seemed quite bright and cheery, her fingers interlaced on the desk. "Hello," she said happily. "May I help you?"

"I wish to see Professor Ironheart," said the woman.

"Is this matter an emergency, since he isn't really seeing anyone right now."

"It's related to the war effort."

"How so, may I ask?"

There were two elevators. The one next to the one through which she had entered dinged and the doors slid open.

"Revenge," said the woman.

Five men also clothed in black, wielding machine guns, stepped out into the lobby and one of them opened fire on the receptionist.

The receptionist blew up. Her head flew one way, her arms tumbled off her shoulders. Springs appeared from her neck where her head had previously been.

"What the hell?" said one of the men.

"She's a robot. A damned robot," said the woman. She glanced around and then pointed at a large pair of double doors behind the receptionist. "There. Through there."

The leader of the men strode forward first. He was easily the largest of them, his head shaved bald and intricate tattoos etched on his scalp. He swung his machine gun up and said, "Stay behind me, Anne."

"Right behind you."

He stepped up to the door and kicked it open.

Howler was right there.

Howler's large hands leaped forward and he grabbed the machine gun out of his hands. "Shouldn't play with guns," he snarled and slammed it forward, the barrel crashing into the man's chin. A loud cracking of bone erupted; Howler had shattered his jaw.

Howler yanked the gun out of his grasp, swung it around, and opened fire. The team's leader was blown off his feet. Howler dropped into a crouch and opened fire on the other men.

It was exactly what Anne had been expecting. Her sharp eyes had already spotted an alternative exit into the offices. It was a hidden door, disguised to look like just another large portion of the wall. She slammed into it with her shoulder and the door swung open. It figured that Professor Ironheart wouldn't bother with a lock—

That was the last thing she thought before she discovered that there was no floor on the other side. There only appeared to be a pit for her to fall into, which she was in the process of doing.

Her hands lanced out and she just barely snagged the edge of the pit. She realized there must have been some hidden combination lock that, when triggered, caused the floor to slide into place so that anyone authorized would be able to walk in easily.

Anne dangled there for a moment, and then smoothly hauled herself up. She rolled up and out just as the floor slid back into place. Had she not managed to extricate herself, she would have been sealed in the pit, stuck there until Ironheart chose to let her out, assuming he ever did.

She sprinted forward, determined to find her target.

THE bodies of three of the men were lying on the ground, bleeding out into the lobby. The other two were hiding on the other side of the desk, crouched, with their guns ready to fire.

Howler was positioned with his back against one of the open doors. His mind raced as he tried to decide what to do. Then the simple answer occurred to him.

He threw himself to the floor, lying flat on his belly, and opened fire on the area along the bottom of the desk. There was nothing special about the desk; it was just ordinary wood and certainly not bullet proof.

The bullets from Howler's machine gun ripped through the desk's bottom, and he heard screams of agony as they chopped up the desk and laced into the feet and ankles of the guys on the other side. Howler smiled grimly to himself. The Prof would hate the use of such violent means in defending himself. He was much more inclined to use mercy bullets. Howler, on the other hand, never hesitated to use lethal weapons whenever necessary. Oftentimes the Prof would scold him, but never took any action beyond that.

Howler sped forward and leaped over the desk. The bastards were shrieking like stuck pigs, and Howler kicked both of them in the heads, knocking them cold. Then he glanced around. The woman was gone. He yanked out his walkie talkie and snapped, "Spotlight! You there?"

Normally Kokmen would have responded with some jaded comment, as was typical of the way they usually verbally sparred with each other. But the concern in Howler's voice immediately focused Kokmen on the gravity of the situation. *"I'm here. What's wrong?"*

"Some chick just tried to break in here with a five-member machine gun toting back-up. Three of 'em are dead, the other two unconscious. But the woman's missing."

"Could she have just gone back downstairs?"

"Someone who breaks in with a five-man back-up isn't gonna retreat when things get rough."

"You're probably right. We'll keep an eye out for her. Any idea who she is?"

"Goes by the name of Anne. Beyond that, I got nothin'."

THE Prof was crossing the lab toward Kokmen. "What is it, Spots?"

"Security breach," Kokmen said dismissively. "Nothing to worry about. I'm just going to scout around the area. You stay put."

He swung open the door and a black clad woman was standing, her gun raised and pointed straight at Kokmen's face.

Kokmen immediately dropped to his knees as a bullet flew over his head. He brought the umbrella up and around and snapped it open. She fired several shots directly at it, but the bullets ricocheted harmlessly off the umbrella's bullet-proof surface. He then twisted the umbrella's handle and fired a mercy bullet, guaranteed to knock its target on her ass.

Except astoundingly Kokmen missed. She leaped forward just as the bullet fired and somersaulted over the umbrella, landing behind him. She swung her gun around and this time there was nothing to prevent her from putting a bullet squarely into his chest.

That was when something flew through the air and crashed to the floor directly in front of her. Instantly the air was filled with smoke and Anne was blinded. She leaped to the right just in time to avoid another mercy bullet from Kokmen, who cursed to himself. The umbrella only fired two shots and he didn't have time to reload.

Anne spun and endeavored to shield her eyes, to spot the Prof who had created the smoke and blinded her. She stumbled forward, banged into a lab table and set things on the counter skittering forward. Gripping the table, she clambered atop it, trying to make it above the smoke so that she could properly see her target.

Suddenly a pair of arms with cabled muscle lifted her off the table. "Shouldn't stand there. There's some dangerous things up there," said the Prof as he slung her over his shoulder, sending her crashing to the floor.

She tried to scramble to her feet, but she was too slow. The Prof was already there. His hands moved so quickly that she couldn't even follow it. All she knew was that one moment she had her gun in her hand, and the next she was empty handed. The Prof calmly emptied her gun of its bullets; he even ejected the one in the chamber. Then, as the smoke began to dissipate, he stared at her as if seeing her for the first time. His eyes widened in surprise.

"Eva?" he said, his voice filled with incredulity.

"Eva?" said Kokmen from a few feet away. "Eva who...? Wait. Eva *Braun?* She's dead. You said she was dead. Sacrificed herself to save Hitler."

"She did. I saw it." He tossed the gun onto the countertop.

"And yet here she is," said Kokmen.

"First of all, the name isn't Eva," she said. Her voice no longer sounded German. If anything, she sounded Irish. "It's Anne. Anne Bonny."

"The same name as the pirate," said Kokmen.

She looked at him pityingly. "More than that."

"No," said Kokmen after a moment. "That's...that's ridiculous. You can't be..."

"What, did you think that your precious Professor Ironheart was the only person to find the fountain of youth?" she said contemptuously. "Eva Braun. Anne Bonny. The names are close enough."

"I suppose it makes sense," said the Prof. "Only a famed Irish pirate could ever feel anything like love for Hitler and his twisted country."

"The great Professor Ironheart, so smug in his superiority," said Anne. "You think your country is so superior? With entire Klans dedicated to killing negros. Irish being banished from restaurants or places of business. You may not have camps here, but your Jews don't get any better treatment. Your country is no different than ours. With the right leader, this country could *be* ours."

"Never," said the Prof. "You know nothing of the United States."

"So you say. But I know something that you do not."

"Really. And that is?"

Her hand moved so quickly that neither Prof nor Spotlight was able to react in time. She leveled her hand at him and a single shot derringer flew from her sleeve into her hand. "I'm armed," she said and fired the gun's single shot.

It struck the Prof squarely in

the forehead. His eyes rolled up and he pitched back, grasping for support against the table and then losing his grip, tumbling heavily to the floor.

"No!" screamed Kokmen just as Howler ran in and gasped at what he saw on the floor. "Prof! Prof!"

Howler charged forward and slammed into Anne, knocking her to the floor. It was not difficult for him to do so. She put up no fight. The gun tumbled out of her hand and she made no attempt to grab for it, first because it was empty and second because she had clearly done what she had to do.

"Your precious Professor is dead," she snarled, and then spat in Howler's face. Howler did not even bother to wipe out the spit that was dripping from his forehead. Instead his oversized hands clamped onto her throat.

"Should I break it?" he asked Kokmen.

"There's no point," said Kokmen. "She's like the Prof. She'll just heal."

"I don't think so," replied Howler. "Not when I rip her head off her body."

"Would your Professor approve of that?" she asked. "His men killing a helpless woman?" She didn't appear concerned over her proposed fate. Indeed, she seemed to welcome it.

"We'll never know," said Kokmen, "because you killed him, you—"

That was when a hesitant cough from the floor startled all of them.

"No," gasped Anne. *"No!"*

Slowly Professor Ironheart sat up. A bullet tumbled out of his forehead and he caught it.

"You said a bullet to the head would kill you!" she howled.

"I said I *assumed* it would. Seems I was wrong. Apparently, I do not get off that easily." He stood and stared at the bullet. "Another one for the collection," he said and tucked it in his pocket. Then he got to his feet.

"What do we do with her, Prof?" said Kokmen. "Howler suggested decapitating her. That would certainly solve the problem."

"Yes, I very much doubt the fountain's influence would allow her to regrow a head."

"Do it," said Anne. "You thought you killed me. You took my man from me. Certainly one more death on your hands would be a light enough burden for you. Kill me, damn you. I have nothing to live for anyway."

"We could just turn her over to the government," Howler pointed out. "They wanted Hitler dead. They won't mind attending to her."

"Yes," he said slowly. "They could toss her in a cell and she could remain there for the rest of her life. Which means forever. Not much of a life for anybody, is it."

"Oh, no," said Kokmen.

"What?" said Howler.

"He's going to let her go. You are, aren't you," and he stabbed a finger at the Prof. "You're going to let her go. I can see it in your eyes. You're still carrying all that damned guilt about killing Hitler. Prof, you can't…"

"Fairly sure that I can," said the Prof. "Howler, release her."

Howler didn't let her up so much as yank her to her feet. She gasped and stumbled slightly, but then caught herself.

The Prof stepped in close to her. "Eva…Anne…it is a good country. Better than you give it credit for. I want you to go out there, find a job. Find a career. Find a life. I am going to spare you in the hope that you will take this as an opportunity to go out and do some good with your eternal life, just as I have endeavored to do with mine."

She shook loose of Howler's grasp and stared at the Prof. "You're hoping that your good intentions will turn me around. Cause me to walk a better path?"

"That's exactly right."

"Prof, this is a mistake," said Kokmen.

"Perhaps. But I have to believe in the innate goodness of mankind. Because if I don't, then I'm fighting for nothing. We all are."

Spotlight looked at Howler for reinforcement, but Howler simply shrugged. Kokmen knew why. When the Prof was like this, there was no reasoning with him. He realized his umbrella was open and he snapped it closed.

"Get out of here," said the Prof.

Anne stared at him. "Not going to force me to promise I'll do better?"

"No. Get going."

She nodded, turned and left the laboratory.

"How could you do that?" asked Howler. "I mean, I know you're always looking for the best in people, but…"

"She was pregnant," said the Prof.

They gaped at him. "How could you possibly know that?" said Kokmen.

"My bio-scanner. She was the first one who I tested with it." He pointed upward toward a small scanning device that was mounted on the ceiling.

Howler could scarcely find the words. "She's pregnant…with Hitler's baby?"

"I doubt she cheated on him, if that's what you're asking."

"But Prof," said Howler. "What if it's another Hitler?"

"Assuming she stays in the United States?" Professor Ironheart shook his head. "In the heart of democracy? I'm hoping that he or she grows up to accomplish great things. At least that's my hope. And if not," and he shrugged, "then we'll stop him, too."

EVA'S head slumped back on the pillow, her forehead thick with sweat. The midwife had finally calmed the child's crying and swaddled him in a blanket. "He's very healthy," she said as she lay the child on Eva's chest. The child evidently heard her heart beating and took comfort from it.

"He should be. He's got a lot to do."

"Should I send your husband in?"

"Absolutely."

The truth was that Fred had been a perfectly good husband. He was already quite wealthy, in the midst of building a profitable real estate empire. He had high hopes for the future, and he did not hesitate to consider Eva...or, as she now called herself, Mary Anne (keeping her actual first name as her middle name) ...to be a true partner in his life. Adolf had chosen him well.

Fred entered. He had dark, thinning hair and a thick moustache that was nowhere quite as memorable as Adolf's, but quite complimentary nonetheless. "Is it a boy? A girl?" he said excitedly.

"A boy," said Mary Anne. "A fine son who will do you proud."

Frederick stood next to his wife and ran his fingers through her hair. "He's beautiful," he said. "What should we name him?"

Mary Anne touched her son's cheek. "Donald," she said.

He frowned. "Like the duck? No one will take him seriously if he's named after a duck."

"Yes, I know," she said. "No one at all will take him seriously. And so, they will always underestimate him. That, my love, is how he's going to follow in his father's footsteps. And he will learn what America really is, and appeal to all the same people his father appealed to." She sighed deeply. "It will be glorious."

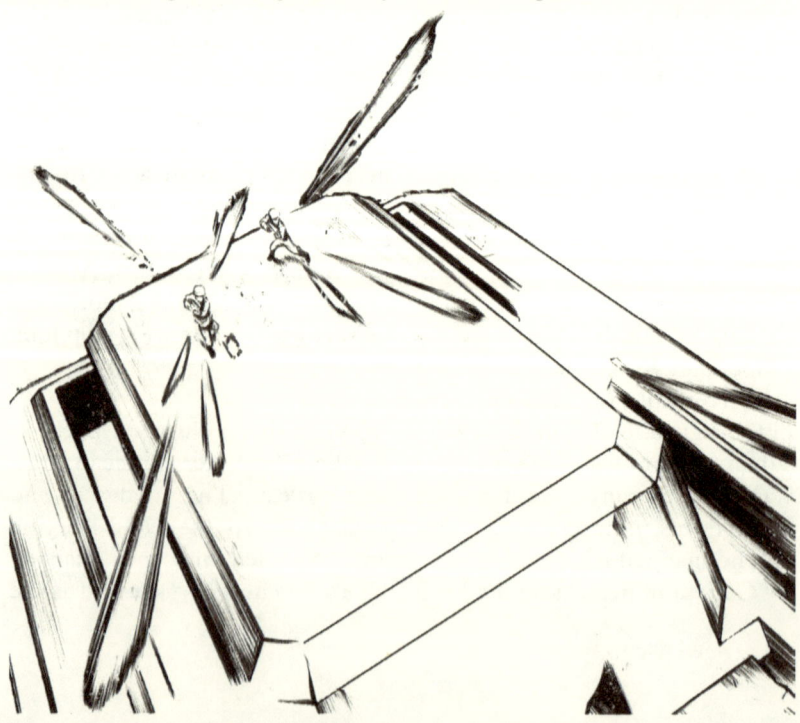

Masks

By MICHAEL JAN FRIEDMAN

IT had been a long time since Rita Cunningham let anyone tell her what to do. So when the thug holding a gun on a couple of elderly ladies told her to get lost, she declined to take his advice.

"You hear me?" he growled, his voice echoing in the benighted brick confines of the deserted factory street. "Take a powder before I plug you one."

Then Rita stepped out of the shadows and into the unencumbered glow of a streetlight, and the thug with the gun got a better look at her.

Even before he could get the words out, his eyes widened and he took a step back. Then he stammered, "Blue M-mask...?"

There was fear in his voice, genuine and undisguised. And for good reason.

In the last year and a half, Blue Mask had scoured New York's back alleys of crime and dirty dealing, giving criminals notice of a new set of rules in town: *You play, you pay.*

The police couldn't always be depended on to apprehend those who needed apprehending—especially when corruption ran rampant on the force. But Blue Mask appeared to be everywhere, giving crime the black eye it deserved.

Of course, there was always some low-life who figured he could fall between the cracks.

He'll learn, Rita thought.

Her first order of business was relieving her adversary of his weapon. Capitalizing on his surprise, she took a couple of quick steps and launched herself at him feet first. Before he could get a shot off, Rita kicked out with her heel and flattened his nose.

The impact sent him reeling into an overstuffed trash can, his gun flying out of his hand. But it was Rita's second kick—this one to the side of the fellow's head—that drove him to the ground face-first, the contents of the trash can cascading all over him.

Shandian ti, she thought with satisfaction. It wasn't as well-known as ju-jitsu but for her money it was more effective.

Stunned as the crook was, he planted his palms on the ground and tried to push himself up. Rita stopped him by planting her boot sole on his back and pushing him down again.

"Lemme go," he pleaded as best he could with his face pressed against the concrete.

"Not likely," she said, whipping out a tightly woven rayon cord

Illustration by Caio Cacau

and using it to hog-tie the crook's wrists.

By then, of course, the two elderly ladies had made their way down to the avenue. Rita hoped they found a more populated route on their way home.

"Lemme go," the crook groaned from under Rita's boot, "and I'll tell you something. That's how the cops work, right? I'll tell you something that'll help you nab somebody bigger."

In her experience, such tips often turned out to be useless. But she had nothing to lose by listening. "All right. I'm waiting."

"It's like this," the hold-up man said. And he told Rita what would help her nab somebody bigger. *Much* bigger. So big, in fact, that she couldn't help but be skeptical.

"How do you know this?" she asked.

He told her that too.

Rita frowned. It wasn't just that his source was a relatively plausible one. It was that the information *fit*.

"Thanks," she said, and attended to the rope that held the crook. But she didn't loosen it. She *tightened* it.

"Hey...wait a minute!" he shrilled. "You said you'd lemme go!"

"Not me," she said as she produced another strip of rayon and tied the fellow's ankles together. Then she retrieved her adversary's gun and slipped it into her pocket for disposal later on.

The crook struggled to free himself, albeit to no avail. "But the cops—"

Rita smoothed the front of her suit with her blue-gloved hands. "Sorry," she said, "I'm no cop." And she made her way out of the alley.

*I*t *isn't fair*, Rita thought as a server walked by with a silver tray full of canapes. Mere months ago, it would have been a platter full of champagne glasses. But Prohibition had put a damper on such luxuries.

Rita had spent her whole college career—four years at Barnard—waiting to drink a cocktail in public. *Then Congress goes and makes it a crime.*

She could still drink at home. Drink all she wanted, in fact. But where was the fun in that?

Then again, Rita wasn't there at the Waldorf Astoria, awash in the cheerful strains of a twelve-piece band, just to get spifflicated. She had a much more important objective in mind, if her informant's tip was to be believed.

She scanned the crowd for a particular face, for which she'd been searching since she arrived. To that point, she had been unsuccessful. However, the evening was still young, and the grand hotel's lavishly decorated Louis XIV ballroom was an expansive venue with room for hundreds of guests. One of them was bound to be the fellow she sought.

As it happened, Rita had never

met the object of her search. But, like most everyone else in haute society, she knew *of* him.

Rita was so intent on finding the fellow that she almost ran into someone else—literally. Before she knew it, a gentleman was face to face with her, looking every bit as surprised as she was.

Surprised and quite *handsome*, she couldn't help but notice.

The fellow had auburn hair with a tight wave to it, piercing green eyes, and a clean—one might even say heroic—jawline. Not a big man by any means—no taller than she was, Rita estimated, maybe even an inch shorter—but well-built for all that.

And nice ears. Not too big or too small, laid close to the skull. Rita had always appreciated a well-shaped ear.

In short, he was the kind of man you glimpsed once and found yourself wishing for a second look. He smiled in apology for the unexpectedness of their intimacy.

"I beg your pardon," he said, his voice a rich baritone.

Rita was about to tell him there was no need for an apology. After all, crowds had their ebbs and flows, and sometimes they thrust people into unintended places. But before she could open her mouth, someone threw an arm over the fellow's shoulder, and he was swept away into another part of the gathering.

Rita watched him go—until she heard a feminine voice in her ear:

"Forget it, honey. That Peter Janssen is an irredeemable gadabout."

Rita turned and saw the tight, sparkling smile of Glenda Deveraux, whom she had known since her first day at The Manning West Side Elementary School. "A gadabout. Really?"

"Yes, ma'am," said Glenda. "He's spent the last two years in Paris wasting Daddy's money on girls and booze instead of applying himself on Wall Street like his brothers."

"Do tell," said Rita.

"He only came back to the States to attend his grandmother's funeral. Then he's off again to wreak havoc on the Rive Gauche."

"Yet he's here at this fundraiser."

"Daddy must have demanded it. He who holds the purse strings is due a certain degree of filial piety."

Rita chuckled. "How well we know that law."

Not that she had to worry about obeying her father any longer. Thanks to a bank robber's bullet three years earlier, she was an orphan.

It was her misery in the wake of her father's shooting that had compelled Rita to keep such tragedies from befalling others—that had sent her off to the Orient in search of the methods she would need to survive that kind of endeavor.

"Well," said Glenda, "I'm off on a hunting expedition."

"Before all the good ones are taken?" Rita suggested.

"My dear, the good ones are

already taken. We're talking about the second tier now. For instance," said Glenda, pointing to a tall, sandy-haired fellow Rita recognized as Dan Audrey Bell, whose family owned a string of coalmines in West Virginia, "*there's* a fellow you can depend on. In fact, I'm going to depend on him right now."

Rita smiled at her friend's antics. "Good luck."

But Glenda's timing was poor, as it turned out, because Noah Fieldstone, the banking mogul who had hosted the fundraiser, just then took his place at the lectern upon the stage.

Seeing him, the band fell silent. And a few moments later, so did the crowd.

"Ladies and gentlemen," Fieldstone said in his booming voice, which echoed so insistently throughout the ballroom that the immense chandelier above it seemed ready to shatter, "I find myself in the felicitous position of introducing a man who requires no introduction. Still, I shall remind you that he holds the office of Secretary of Commerce under our esteemed President Harding, who is off to a brilliant start in this, the first of his two terms in office."

The crowd, mostly Republican of course, chuckled at the quip. Rita, whose politics ran in a different direction, did not.

Besides, she had other matters on her mind. Like continuing to scan the crowd for the man she was looking for.

"And when Mr. Harding steps down," Fieldstone continued, "the gentlemen who will speak to you now would be a most capable replacement. Without further ado, I give you...Herbert Clark Hoover."

Hoover, a husky fellow with straight brown hair and ample, cherry-red cheeks, shook Fieldstone's hand and took his place at the lectern. As he waited for the applause to die down, he slipped a paper from inside his jacket—his prepared remarks, no doubt—and laid it out before him.

Rita had seen Hoover before. A dour fellow from the cornfields of Iowa who had studied engineering at Stanford, he had visited New York a year earlier raising money for Harding's campaign.

Rita's father, a lifelong Democrat, would have hated both Harding and Hoover. But, in this crowd, he would have been in the minority.

As the ballroom fell silent, Hoover said, "Thank you all for coming." His voice wasn't as loud or as expressive as Fieldstone's but he could be heard well enough. "As you know, the Russian people are in a bad way these days. I am not speaking of their leaders, who have made the curious choice of pursuing the philosophies of Marx and Engel—philosophies that we here in the United States have roundly rejected. Rather, I speak of the general populace, who had no say in what kind of economic system they adopted after the fall of their Czar. A populace dying by the millions, I'm afraid, starved to death by the terrible famine that has swept their country. Forgive me, ladies, but I must paint an awful picture for you this evening—a picture of corpses piling up in the streets of little Russian villages because the ground is too frozen to allow for burials."

Hoover paused while expressions of outrage and dismay arose from his audience. But then, how could such an image not elicit a reaction from civilized people?

"We cannot stand by," said the secretary, "and watch them perish. Not if we have hearts in our bodies. Even now, a Russian Famine Relief Act is in the works in Washington. However, we should not allow the government to shoulder the entire burden of Christian charity. Those of us who have been blessed by God with prosperity must do our part as well. It is in this spirit that I ask you—no, beseech you—to dig deep and give what you can to save Russian men, women, and children who have nothing at all."

Hoover had demonstrated his customary shortcoming as a speaker, rarely lifting his eyes from his text. Nonetheless, he had made his point if the nods exchanged here and there throughout the room were any indication. But then, Rita mused, the rich liked nothing better than to be reminded of how rich they were, especially in contrast to the abject poor.

In any case, Hoover seemed to have accomplished what he came for. But Rita had not. She still hadn't spotted the man she sought.

Then her chance arrived—as, predictably, Hoover was joined on the stage by Douglas W. Renshaw.

Renshaw was one of the most charitable men in the city, always good for a high-profile contribution to a worthwhile cause, be it an orphanage, a settlement house, or a veterans' hospital. He had told the papers once it was a matter of family honor for him to give back to the society that had treated his ancestors so kindly.

Which was another way of saying they had grown rich as Croesus operating a string of fortuitously placed sawmills along the Hudson.

Renshaw was just as Rita remembered him: Very tall, blade-thin, with a long, bony face and a shock of unruly grey hair.

"Many of you know me," he said in his rather thin, high-pitched voice. "If you do, you know I don't take a back seat to anyone when it comes to supporting the needy—and no one these days is needier than the poor Russians."

The crowd cheered the sentiment. Hoover put his arm around Renshaw, who was several inches taller than the commerce secretary was. "And tell me, my friend...how much will you be giving from that *front* seat?"

Renshaw hesitated for a second. Then, perhaps carried away by the magnitude of the moment, he exclaimed: "Twenty thousand dollars!"

The crowd gasped. Not even the Rockefellers were *that* generous.

Rita was shocked as well. But it didn't change the task ahead of her. It only raised the stakes.

She would have tried to talk to Renshaw, tried to dissuade him from following through on his pledge. But she knew her plea would fall on deaf ears. Besides, who was she—an innocent young woman barely out of university and alone in the world—to know how Renshaw planned to make good on that pledge, or what kind of trap awaited him as a result?

Hoover made a few more remarks. Then he and Renshaw stepped down and Fieldstone, the banker, returned to the lectern and addressed the crowd again, his apparent intention to use Renshaw's example in order to squeeze everyone on behalf of the famine victims.

Rita never heard his pitch, however. She was too focused on Renshaw, who was surrounded by admirers as soon as he stepped off the stage.

This, after all, was the benefit of his rousing display of charity. Renshaw loved being the center of attention, much as others did. The difference was that with his name and estate, he could become what he loved.

Not that there's any crime in it, Rita mused. The crime was someone else's—and what she had attended the fundraiser that night to prevent.

Just as she thought that, her evening-long efforts were rewarded. There, on the outskirts of the circle that had formed around Renshaw, listening along with everyone else, was the man she sought: Tolliver Brindlebury. And, for her purposes, she could not have found him in a more promising position.

That Brindlebury, a stocky, bullet-headed man, was present at the fundraiser was hardly a surprise. He was, after all, the Chief of Police, responsible for the safety and security of all such galas in the City of New York.

That he was standing there hanging on Renshaw's words with such apparent curiosity...that was another matter entirely. Because if Rita's informant had been correct, Brindlebury's interest in Renshaw's pledge far exceeded the limits of his office as police chief.

In hopes of testing that theory, she moved closer to Brindlebury—not so close that one of the two uniformed men on either side of him would notice, but close enough to examine his expression.

After all, she had studied more in the Orient than just *shandian ti*. As well, she had learned the map of the human visage, one that yielded a storehouse of information to the devoted student of its geographical features.

In Brindlebury's visage, she saw greed. Sometimes it was difficult to spot, but not so in this case. It was unmistakable in the fellow's incipient smile, in the narrowing of his eyes. And where were those eyes trained...but on the unsuspecting countenance of Douglas W. Renshaw.

That crook was telling the truth, Rita thought.

She would have studied Brindlebury further, but Renshaw and his circle moved away, and the police chief declined to move with them. Whatever he needed to know, he'd already gleaned it from the rich man's conversation.

Rita too had learned what she needed to learn. And as she meant to spend the balance of the evening pursuing lawbreakers on the streets, she decided to call it a night.

She had already left the ballroom, gotten her wrap, and made her way outside to wait for her driver when a large figure moved to block her way. Looking up, she found herself confronted with the all-too-familiar countenance of "Cad" Cadwallader.

His real name was Chad. When he and Rita were six, he tried to look up her dress at school. Repeatedly. It was an all-day marathon that left her rattled and exhausted.

When they were nine, he tackled her and sat on her chest, pinning her with his considerable weight and refusing to let her up until she said a word that described a man's genitalia. She still remembered the feeling of helplessness as she tried to push him off her to no avail.

Rita never relented and said the word Cad required.

However, other girls did. As she found out later, she wasn't the only nine-year-old Cad had imposed himself on. Nor did his manners improve as he got older, in ways even more traumatic for his victims.

Eventually, his misadventures were brought to the attention of the courts. Had Cad come from humbler beginnings, he would certainly have spent time in a reform school. As it was, his father cut a deal: Cad would go to military school instead.

Not that he benefited from the discipline espoused by the Thomas Fearon Academy. In fact, it was there that he received the nickname "Cad" for the way he treated his dates.

Rita might have gone the rest of her life without seeing the lout. Unfortunately, that wasn't the way the Fates had woven her skein.

Cad grinned. "It's little Rita Cunningham."

She remained silent, hoping that he would be distracted by something, or get the message that she wasn't interested in speaking to him. It didn't work.

"You've grown up," said Cad, "haven't you?" He reached for her hand and she withdrew it. "Listen," he said, undaunted, "come have a drink with me. I know a little speakeasy on South Street that stays open all night."

Rita gave him the stoniest glare she could muster. "I don't think so." Then, as quickly as she could, she circumvented him and headed for the curb.

"Hey," said Cad, grabbing her by the shoulder and spinning her around, "don't act so high and mighty. I knew you when you were an ugly little thing."

Rita brushed his hand off her shoulder. "What a perfectly lovely remembrance."

He squeezed her wrist and moved closer to her, emphasizing the difference in their heights. Rita was tall for a woman but Cad still had her by a head.

"I invited you to have a drink with me," Cad grated, "and that's what you'll do."

She almost laid the bastard out. *Almost.* Only with a supreme exertion of will did she stop herself.

Were she wearing the Blue Mask, she would have sent him to Dreamland before he had any idea what was happening.

But at the moment, she wasn't wearing the Mask. She was Rita Cunningham, and she was surrounded by onlookers—which meant she couldn't give Cad what he deserved without people wondering what had gotten into her.

Yet she couldn't let him continue to squeeze her wrist like that. His very touch made her skin want to crawl off her bones.

It was a dilemma.

She was looking around for an acceptable way out of it when someone went barreling into her captor like a linebacker, narrowly missing Rita herself. As she watched, the newcomer sent Cad crashing into the side of the building. *Hard.*

Suddenly Cad was writhing on the ground, clutching his shoulder. "My shoulder!" he snarled. "My goddamned shoulder!" Rita's benefactor, meanwhile, got to his feet and straightened out his black bowtie, which had gone awry. As luck would have it, it was...what name had Glenda provided?

Janssen. Peter Janssen.

Unlike Cad, Mr. Janssen looked none the worse for wear. Unless, of course, one counted the bleary look in his eyes. But, that had less to do with the collision and more with the consumption of alcohol, it seemed to Rita.

She looked for the subtle outline of a flask on Janssen's person and found it in a pocket of his jacket. *Yes,* she thought, *definitely the consumption of alcohol.*

Of course, Prohibition didn't stop *everyone* from imbibing. Those who were determined to do so still found a way.

As a couple of Cad's friends helped him to his feet, Rita took Janssen's arm and led him away from the hotel entrance. She had to steady him, she found, as his condition prevented him from walking a straight line.

"Thanks," she said.

"Sure thing," Janssen replied with a drunken grin on his face.

Just then, Derek drove up with her car. A large Asian who had worked for Rita's family since she was six, he looked more than a little concerned when he noticed Janssen's arm around his employer.

What's more, Janssen *noticed* that he noticed. "That fellow's giving me the stink eye," he told Rita.

"That fellow," she said, "is Derek Ho, my driver. My very *protective* driver."

"Ah," said Janssen.

With an exaggerated gesture, he disentangled his arm from Rita's. Then he hiccupped, staggered, and spiraled to the ground.

Rita knelt beside him and—just to be certain—leaned close enough to smell his breath. Fortunately, it was laced with the scent of alcohol and nothing more nefarious.

She looked around, asking silently if anyone knew Janssen well enough to claim him. No one piped up. More than likely, members of Janssen's family had attended the fundraiser. However, none of them appeared to be in evidence.

Rita couldn't just leave him there. The man had done her a kindness, after all. And even if he hadn't, she would have been loath to subject him or his family to unnecessary embarrassment.

She turned to Derek and said, "Put him in the car, please."

Her driver looked skeptical.

"Are you certain that's a good idea, Miss?"

"I'm certain it's *not*," she admitted. "Be a dear and do it anyway."

Derek sighed. "As you wish."

Fortunately, Rita's driver wasn't just big. He was also in terrific shape for a fellow his age. He had no trouble lifting Janssen off the sidewalk or placing him in the back seat of Rita's car.

"I'll ride up front with you," she told Derek.

"Yes, ma'am," said the driver.

Moments later, they were headed uptown. But Rita soon stopped thinking about the handsome interloper behind her.

She was too engaged in the notion of saving Douglas Renshaw from his own generosity.

MORNING brought to Rita's tiny, second-floor garden a brave if tentative sunshine.

It had begun to rain rather hard on the way home from the fundraiser the night before, a situation for which Rita was grateful, to say the least. The criminals she hunted seldom ventured out in such a rain, after all.

It was after nine when her guest made his way down to the breakfast room, his hair still wet from the shower. He was wearing the robe Derek had left hanging on the door for him—Rita's father's robe, or one of them.

Angus Cunningham had been taller than Janssen, with broader shoulders. It was from him that

Rita got her athletic build, not to mention her unrelenting resolve to come out on top, no matter how formidable the adversary.

Of course, her father had competed in the arena of stocks and bonds, not the battleground of night-shrouded alleys.

Janssen smiled a sheepish smile as he stood there. His eyes were clear, untainted by his libations of the night before.

"Thanks for the robe," he said. "It's rather handsome, actually."

"It was my father's," said Rita.

"Really?"

"Hence the tartan. Our family colors."

Janssen considered the robe, then smiled again. "I envy you Scots."

"Before you ask," said Rita, "Derek undressed you. I couldn't very well let you sleep in the clothes you wore last night."

Janssen's smile faded. "I embarrassed myself, did I?"

"A bit. But not before you knocked a fellow who was bothering me off his pins."

"I see." His expression said he didn't remember the event.

"For which," she said, "I'm unutterably grateful. Coffee?"

"God, yes," said Janssen. He pulled out the chair opposite Rita's and sat down. "Black, please."

"Black it is." She picked up the coffeepot and poured for him. "Toast?"

"That would be lovely."

"Jam?"

"More than I deserve."

"We might disagree about that. You were quite the Johnny on the Spot."

Janssen's brow creased. "If you don't mind my asking...in what way was the fellow making himself a nuisance?"

"He grabbed my wrist." She pulled up her sleeve and showed her guest the resultant bruises. "It was unpleasant, to say the least."

Janssen's gaze sobered. "It must have been. I'm glad I was there to intervene."

"So was I."

"Even if I don't recall doing so." He sighed. "I don't imagine my father will be very happy."

"That you came to my rescue?"

"That I made a scene at such an august gathering."

"If you'd like to call him," said Rita, "let him know you're all right..."

Janssen waved away the suggestion. "He's accustomed to my disappearances. This is just another in a long list."

"I see," said Rita, not really seeing at all.

Was it Janssen's drinking that had him staying out all night? Or something of a more romantic nature? She had to admit that she had more than a casual interest in the answer.

In the next moment, Janssen solved the mystery unprovoked: "My father doesn't approve of my imbibing. Or of me in general. I'm not the son he wanted, I'm afraid."

Rita recalled her friend Glenda's remark about Janssen's antics in Paris. "Not everyone treads the well-worn path."

"In my case, it's less a path than a trackless waste." His eyes glazed over for a moment, as if he were thinking of something far away. Then they regained their focus. "Well," he said, smiling again, "I've imposed on your hospitality quite enough. If I can get my clothes back, I'll be going."

"Back to Paris?" Rita inquired.

He tilted his head as he absorbed the question. "You seem to know more about me than you've let on."

"Just what I heard last night. Women talk, you know."

"I suppose so. In any event, I intend to stay in New York a couple more days. I so seldom get back here anymore. Besides, I have some business to which I must attend."

Janssen didn't seem like the business type. But then, "business" could mean so many things.

"Well," said Rita, "good luck with it."

"Thanks." Her guest got up. "And thanks as well for the accommodations. It's not often I drink myself silly and wind up in such delightful company."

For a moment, Rita thought he would suggest their meeting again some time. But the invitation failed to materialize.

Still, she wasn't the sort of girl to stick with convention. If Janssen wasn't going to ask *her* out, she would ask *him*.

Even if he drank a little, and even if he was given to strange, solemn moments—both of which suggested some dark, internal struggle. But, in a way, that only made him more attractive to her.

"You know," Rita said, "if you're going to be in town a while... breakfast was so engaging, perhaps we can try *lunch* this time."

Janssen gazed at her for a moment—rather seriously, she thought, as if he were looking into a tomb. Then he said: "I'd like that."

"Lovely." Rita gave him her number.

"I know just the place," he said. "Have you ever been to Reuben's Delicatessen?"

"I can't say I have—though I'm partial to delicatessens in general."

"There's a sandwich there that will knock your socks off. Say, tomorrow at noon?"

"It's a deal," she said.

RITA was still thinking about Janssen that night as she descended into the dimly lit basement of her townhouse.

In a storage area only she frequented, she found and donned the man's suit she had removed from her father's closet after his death—the suit she had taken in with the sewing skills her father had insisted she learn as a girl.

Then the hat, and the gloves. And finally, the dark blue mask.

Rita considered herself in a mirror she had propped against the naked bricks of the wall. In good light, she would never have passed for a man. Her features were too fine, her lashes too luxurious. But in the shadows, no one suspected.

After all, could a woman fight the way she fought? Most people would have said it was impossible.

Satisfied with her appearance—that of a denizen of the urban night—she snuck out of the basement through the door she had discovered long ago, which gave access to the city's sprawling sewer system.

It was Rita's practice to emerge from underground through one of three other basements—all of them in Hell's Kitchen—thereby foiling the possibility of someone's tracing Blue Mask to her residence. However, her goal this night was barely three blocks away, in a neighborhood even more prosperous than her own—the neighborhood in which stood Douglas Renshaw's stately, white-columned mansion.

It was there that she expected to find a couple of crooks lurking in the shadows, waiting to take advantage of Renshaw's generosity. After all, Renshaw had pledged the princely sum of twenty thousand greenbacks to Hoover's famine relief campaign.

The problem was that Renshaw didn't *have* twenty thousand greenbacks. He had mismanaged his family's considerable fortune over the years, wasting it on dead-end investments, to the point that it paled beside its reputation.

The only way Renshaw could come up with the money he'd pledged was to sell some of his very prestigious art collection—which was what he had done in similar circumstances in the past. But he didn't want it to be known that he was doing so, for the sake of appearances, so he carried out the necessary transactions at night.

And for cash.

The buyer in this case, from what Rita had gleaned, was a reputable one—a Massachusetts textile manufacturer named Sutherland. However, it wasn't the buyer from whom Rita expected shenanigans. It was the unsavory types who had gotten word of the deal.

Whose mastermind was none other than the city's chief of police.

All she had to do, she figured, was catch one of the thieves—a cop, certainly—in the act, and turn him over to Harlan Pettigrew, the police commissioner. Pettigrew had months earlier put the word out that he wanted to root out the corruption in his department. If he was serious, this would be a way to get into the problem.

And if he wasn't... *Well*, Rita thought, as she made her way through the tunnels beneath the streets of New York, *even Blue Mask can only do what she can do.*

WHEN Rita wore the blue mask, she didn't like staying

in one place for too long. There was too much of a chance that she would be spotted by passersby. However, she made an exception in this case and planted herself in a narrow alley opposite Renshaw's place, between a music conservatory and the Estonian consulate— neither of which was open at the moment.

No one would see her there unless they came looking for her. And it was difficult to imagine why anyone would do so.

Rita had barely begun to hunker down in the embrace of the alley, preparing herself for what might be a long wait, when she heard a faint scraping sound behind her. It was at that moment that her reflexes took over and she whirled—just in time to ward off a blow from a shadowy assailant.

Whoever it was launched a second blow. She ducked and lashed out with her heel in response, but managed to only graze her half-seen target.

He's fast, Rita thought.

As her adversary went after her anew, he stepped into a thin bar of moonlight—and she gasped. She knew his face. After all, she'd sat across from it at her breakfast table.

It was Peter Janssen!

What's he doing here? Rita wondered as she turned sideways and avoided Janssen's attack.

Before he could pull his weight back, she drove her gloved knuckles into his ribs. But her follow-up punch struck nothing but air, her opponent having removed himself from harm's way.

Damn, she thought. *He can fight.*

Unlike the other night, Janssen wasn't careening drunkenly into a boor who hadn't seen him coming. His moves were quick, powerful, precise—the product of some serious training.

She searched the darkness, just in time saw him come at her again. She deflected his jab and struck underneath it. But her blow was turned away just as his had been.

Rita swore beneath her breath. For the first time in her adult life, she found herself pitted against someone she couldn't dismantle with a few kicks and jabs.

But she couldn't let this pas de deux go on—not when Janssen could ruin her effort to help Renshaw. *I've got to put an end to this*, she thought.

Then Janssen moved into the bar of moonlight again, and she got her chance. Balancing on one foot, she shot her foot at her adversary's dimly illuminated face.

What landed was more than a glancing blow, but not the finale Rita had hoped for. And as she pulled her leg back to strike again, she felt Janssen return her attack with equal ferocity.

She turned her face away in time to save herself some of the impact. However, there was still enough of it to send her spinning into a wall.

It was as Rita gathered herself for Janssen's follow-up assault that she realized she was missing something. She reached for her face and, with a shoot of horror, confirmed it.

My mask...

It had been torn away from her. Worse, she was standing in that single fateful bar of moonlight, her identity exposed for all the world to see.

Instinctively, she covered her face with her sleeve. But it was too late. Janssen's eyes had opened wide. He had seen who she was.

He *knew*.

"You...?" he whispered, his voice stretched thin with surprise.

Rita dropped her hand. "Me," she whispered back.

What now? she wondered.

In the blink of an eye, her world had crumbled beneath her, sending her spiraling down into a dark and uncharted abyss. She recalled something her father had said once: *A secret between two people is no longer a secret.*

Suddenly, Rita heard the purr of a car engine. Over Janssen's shoulder, she could see a Silver Ghost pull up in front of Renshaw's place. *Sutherland*, she thought.

The driver got out and opened the back door, whereupon a short man in a camel topcoat emerged. The two of them exchanged a couple of words and then the man in the coat made his way up the steps to Renshaw's front door.

Rita eyed Janssen. She couldn't see enough of his face to apply the tricks she had learned in the

Orient and divine his intentions.

Nor had she done so that morning. As her teachers had pointed out, it was wrong to use one's abilities for trivial purposes. It demeaned both the practitioner and the traditions he or she had inherited.

Still, Rita had had breakfast with the man. If he'd been a crook, she would have known it—wouldn't she?

"Tell me you're not working for Brindlebury," she said.

Janssen breathed what appeared to be a sign of relief. "I take it you're not either?"

"Not by a long shot," she said.

He knelt and picked up her mask, then handed it to her. "Then why *this*?"

She took the mask from him and slipped it back on. "Why?" she echoed.

Before she could answer, another car pulled up behind the Ghost. This one was black, menacing looking somehow. Even before it quite came to a stop, its doors flew open and a half dozen armed men spilled out.

Rita cursed beneath her breath. She was accustomed to fighting a single armed adversary, sometimes two at a time. But so many?

"Come on," said Janssen.

Before Rita could ask what he had in mind, he darted out of the alley, a .38 Special in his fist spitting bullets. He managed to hit one of the gunmen as the fellow climbed the steps to Renshaw's front door, but two others stopped and returned fire.

Janssen got as far as the hoods' empty car before he had to take cover behind it. His back to the vehicle, he reloaded his gun—no doubt in preparation for a charge at the two on the steps.

But he was outnumbered five to one. Eventually he would catch a bullet and that would be the end of him.

Rita didn't know why Janssen had made this his fight, but she knew why it was *hers*, and she would be damned if she let him fight it all alone. In the space of a heartbeat, she came up with a plan. First, she waited until she saw Janssen was done reloading. Then she bolted for the Ghost.

He waved for her to go back, no doubt misinterpreting her intent. But she ignored the bullets sent her way by Brindlebury's hoods, spanned the street at full gallop, and swung open the car's driver's-side door.

Sutherland's chauffeur was lying across the front seat, his hands clasped in prayer. Unfortunately, Rita thought, he would soon have that much *more* to pray about.

Slamming the car into reverse, she wrenched the steering wheel to the left as hard as she could. Then she gunned the engine, sending the back of the Ghost swerving toward the alley she had come from.

The gunmen didn't know what she was up to, but that didn't stop them from firing at her. Her windshield spider-webbed as one bullet and then another smashed through it. Fortunately, neither of them struck her—leaving her free to bang the car into drive again, dig her heel into the gas pedal, and send the Ghost trundling up the steps of Renshaw's mansion like a great, smoking beast.

It was the last thing the hoods had expected.

One froze in place and tried desperately—though unsuccessfully—to nail the car's driver. The other, who had more presence of mind, turned and ran for the house's open door.

Neither of them got very far. The one who ran took a bullet from Janssen's revolver while the other one got pinned between the wall and the Ghost's front bumper.

Bolting from the car, Rita made her way through the door ahead of Janssen. As she invaded Renshaw's imperially vaulted, gold-laced foyer, she took in the pertinent details at a glance: The three remaining crooks...Renshaw and Sutherland with their hands held high...an open suitcase full of money on a small wooden table...a pastoral painting on a large, bronze easel.

Unfortunately, Rita's unorthodox use of Sutherland's auto had attracted everyone's attention. As the gunmen unleashed a barrage at her, she had only one option: To slide beneath their line of fire.

In that manner, she took the feet

out from one of the crooks, flipping him like a shortstop in the way of a hurtling base runner. And as the hoodlum fell, he took a couple of bullets meant for Rita.

However, she wouldn't have him as a shield forever. Seeing his revolver was within reach, she snatched it up and pitched it at one of her adversaries. As she hoped, he stumbled as he took the brunt of the oncoming missile—giving her time to gain her feet, cross the foyer, and launch a kick at his head.

Please, she thought in a silent appeal to Janssen, *be behind me.*

Rita heard the crack of gunfire just as she snapped her target's head back, sending him careening into the staircase. However, she didn't know from whose gun the report had come.

Not until she found the last remaining crook and saw him crumble to the floor. A moment later, Janssen was by her side.

"Are you all right?" he asked, his voice full of concern.

"Fine," Rita said.

Sutherland and Renshaw were standing there open-mouthed beside their painting and their money, no doubt trying to divine what had happened to them. Before they could get too good a look at her, Rita darted for the door, and the night.

But she was certain she hadn't seen the last of Peter Janssen.

A S it turned out, Janssen was right. The special sandwich at Reuben's Delicatessen was the bee's knees.

"Scrumptious," Rita said. She wiped her chin with a napkin. "Absolutely *scrumptious*."

"I'm glad you like it," said Janssen, his enjoyment of *her* enjoyment clear to her even without her Oriental mind-tricks.

She looked around. Their table was in the corner of the otherwise noisy restaurant, away from the other luncheon patrons, just as Janssen had requested of the management.

"So," Rita continued in a voice a bit too low for anyone but her lunch partner to hear, "you work for the Commissioner?"

"On occasion," Janssen replied in the same *sotto voce*. "His younger brother and I were in ONI together."

"The Office of Naval Intelligence?"

"The same."

"Is that where you learned your hand-to-hand?" she asked.

He smiled. "There and elsewhere. I don't spend *all* my time abroad guzzling spirits, you know."

"Just some of it?"

"We've all got our...demons. So," Janssen said, changing the subject, "at Renshaw's place... you were following the same trail I was."

"Apparently. Except I got my lead from a street crook, not from Harlan Pettigrew."

"Who, by the way, tells me he'll have everything he needs on Brindlebury by end of business today. In his experience, dirty cops crumble faster than a month-old crouton."

And the men who'd try to rob Renshaw had all been dirty cops. "Good to hear," said Rita.

"Also," said Janssen, "you were a lot braver than I was. I had a half-dozen operatives on their way to join me, and you were going to go it alone."

"Ah," said Rita, "but I had a mask."

Janssen laughed. "You did indeed."

"That is, until you knocked it off me. You'll have to teach me that move some time."

"Of course." He grew serious again. "I trust you'll keep my... secret. It makes me more effective as an operative if people think I'm a good-for-nothing."

"Even your family?"

"Unfortunate, but necessary. Someday, I'll tell them the truth. But not today."

"While we're keeping secrets..." said Rita.

Janssen seemed to understand. "You've nothing to fear, I assure you. The Blue Mask will remain an urban legend. As it happens, I admire your abilities—as well as your approach. It's brilliant, really."

"What is?" she had to ask.

"That you dress as a man. No doubt, your adversaries would be less frightened of you if they knew you were a woman."

Rita shook her head. "That's not the reason I dress as I do."

"No?"

"It's because I *like* it."

He looked at her askance. "You...*like* it?"

She didn't know why she was baring her soul there in a corner of Reuben's Delicatessen. However, she felt a bond with Janssen, one she had never felt with anyone else.

"I always have," Rita admitted, "as far back as I can remember."

"You...like dressing as a *man*?"

The way he said it made her feel diminished, and she didn't like being diminished. *Maybe*, she thought, *I made a mistake confiding in him.*

"So what?" she asked stiffly. "Does that make me less of a woman in your eyes?"

Janssen regarded her for a moment. Then he said, "Not in the least."

Was he as sincere as he seemed? "Really?" Rita prodded.

"Everybody's got a little quirk. Even if you can't tell just looking at them."

Just to be certain, she asked: "You mean that?"

He nodded. "Sure."

Rita felt herself drawn to Janssen as she had never been drawn to anyone before. To find a man she liked who had no problem with her...what had he called it?

A quirk.

Her whole life, she'd had to pretend she was someone she wasn't. She couldn't tell anyone, not even her father.

But someone knew now. And it was all right with him. He was gorgeous and exciting and smart, and he didn't mind how she liked to dress.

She wanted to cry.

"I have just one request," Janssen said.

An alarm went off in her head. *He wants me to stop being Blue Mask.*

But that wasn't it. "I want to help you," he said.

Rita started to ask how. Then she saw the look on his face, and she knew. It was the look she'd seen in the mirror the day she decided to become Blue Mask.

She shook her head. "I work alone."

Then she remembered the way they had coordinated their efforts at Renshaw's place. Flawlessly, as if they had worked together all their lives. And Janssen *had* demonstrated an expertise in hand-to-hand combat that rivaled her own.

"You don't understand," he said, and explained what made their teaming up so important to him.

Rita sat back in her chair. Her mouth, she realized was open. She closed it. "You're not kidding, are you?"

"I'm not," he confirmed.

She considered the situation for a moment. A *long* moment. Then she said, "All right. Let's do it."

"**R**EMEMBER," Rita said, "I'm in charge."

"No argument here," said Janssen, who was considering his appearance in her basement mirror. "Besides, everyone will think that anyway. You're dressed as a man, after all."

It was a good point.

He turned to her. "So how do I look?"

She looked him up and down. "Skirt's a little short."

Janssen smoothed out that part of his outfit. "You think so?"

"I do."

For a moment, Rita thought her newfound partner would give her an argument. Then he smiled. "Whatever you say. You're the boss."

She had to admit that she felt odd standing there with him, dressed as he was. But it felt good to have someone to watch her back on the streets.

Besides, if he could accept *her* quirk...how could she fail to accept *his*?

Belle of the Ball

By Aaron Rosenberg

"SHIP ahoy!" the young lad in the crow's nest of *Nature's Grace* shouted, his voice cracking with excitement—and fear. "Ship ahoy!"

"What?" The ship's captain, a fair-minded man named Galib Kawaja, came charging out of his cabin, buckling on his sword belt as he went. The sun had not yet risen above the horizon, and he had been sound asleep, as had most of the crew. "Where away?"

"Hard to starboard," the lookout replied from up above, "and heading right for us!"

Racing to the starboard rail, Kawaja stared out over the water—and his face paled at the sight of the tall, angular ship speeding toward them ahead of the just burgeoning dawn. Its full white sails caught the wind, bellying out as the ship rushed forward, seeming to almost skim across the waves, but it was the smaller, darker shape fluttering by the prow that held his attention.

It was a black flag, with a skull and crossbones displayed in white. Only this one, he saw as it drew ever closer, bore a pair of cannons instead of the usual bones. And that could only mean one thing.

"To arms!" Kawaja shouted, even though he knew it was most likely futile. "All men, to arms!"

Nature's Grace was a flurry of motion as groggy sailors emerged from the hammocks belowdecks and raced to the railings and the riggings, cutlasses and belaying pins at their belts, knives in their boots. Kawaja himself checked that his sword was loose in its scabbard, then began to load his pistol. But the shot fell from his hand, the cast-iron ball rolling away across the deck, as something smashed through the railing not two paces to his right, careened across, and then shattered the portside railing as it made its exit.

There was no mistaking what had just happened.

"Ahoy, the ship!" a voice shouted from the approaching vessel, which had lowered its sails, letting its dying momentum carry it the rest of the way until its prow nudged up against their rail—right where there was now a gaping hole. "Toss down your weapons and surrender, or the next one won't just crease your deck, it'll split her in two!" The voice was a woman's, and might have been sweet if not for the sharp tone and the harsh words.

Kawaja growled, hand reflexively going for his sword, but his common sense soon got the better

Illustration by Caio Cacau

of him and instead of drawing steel he unbuckled and let the still-scabbarded weapon fall at his feet. His pistol, still unloaded, clattered to the ground beside it. "Do as she says, men," he called out. "There's nothing else for it now."

Every one of them knew that it was certain death to go up against the pirate captain known as "Cannon Belle."

"**A**NOTHER fine haul, Cap'n," Quince declared, holding up a heavy crystal decanter. "And look, I secured the best o' the lot for you!" He was a sour man with golden hair, hence the name, but he was an able first mate and loyal as the day was long.

"Thank you, Quince," "Cannon" Belle Pearcy told him, accepting the decanter and a matching goblet and pouring a measure of ruby-red wine from the one to the other, then raising it in his direction. "To your health." Her own thick mane of hair was black as sable and hung in a heavy plait nearly to the small of her back, swaying as she shifted with the ship, adjusting to keep her balance as naturally as breathing. The black tri-corner captain's hat atop her head was wide enough to keep her face shaded even though the sun was now casting its golden rays across the *Deadshot*'s deck, but her bright blue eyes still glittered as if generating a light of their own.

"And to yours," he answered, hoisting a similar goblet and taking a long swig. Belle took a sip of hers as well, the rich, velvety liquid sliding down her throat, then forced herself to take another, longer swallow. With honor satisfied, she placed the crystal set on a nearby barrel and moved to the railing so she could supervise the transfer of *Nature's Grace*'s goods to their own hold. The ship's crew was all behaving, which was wise—her men had by now all been trained up to be a surprisingly well-mannered lot as long as things went their way and everyone did as they were told, but all it took was one hothead taking a swing at someone and the whole scene would spin out of control.

Singling out the ship's captain from the crowd of sailors who had been brought over to the *Deadshot* for safekeeping, Belle approached him. He was a short, sturdy man with plain but strong features, and she was impressed by how carefully he was holding himself and his crew together.

"Thank you for being so reasonable about all this," she told him, stopping a few feet away. "Once we finish securing your goods we'll be on our way and then you can be on yours." She favored him with a sharp smile. "We will be securing your cannon, of course. Wouldn't want you to get any ideas about shooting us from behind and reclaiming your cargo."

He acknowledged her with a short nod. "Thank you for not overstaying your welcome," he replied. "And for keeping your men in check. Wanton looting we could not have stood for. This, this is far more . . ."

"Civilized?" she supplied, and Kawaja smiled.

"Indeed."

Belle smiled back. "I see no reason why piracy must equate to barbarism," she explained, exactly as she'd told her crew many a time. "Nor why pride should overpower sense."

He studied her, though he had the decency to do so without staring, and to linger more on her face than on the figure so clearly displayed in her black velvet pants, fitted white silk shirt, and red leather vest. "You are not what I had expected," he stated finally. "I thought . . ."

"That I'd be bloodthirsty and cruel?" She laughed, then sobered. "I am—when I'm crossed. If you and your men had resisted, I'd have slaughtered every last one of you." She sniffed. "But why throw lives away, whether yours or mine? That would be a waste, and I abhor wastefulness."

Back on *Nature's Grace*, her steward, Dan Bell, waved. That was the all-clear—the ship had been stripped of its valuables, and its cannons emptied, any powder removed. "It seems our business is concluded," she told Kawaja, "which means it is time for you and your men to be on your way." She doffed her hat and swept into a low bow, as if to royalty. "Captain."

He bowed back, and though shallower it was still that of a man to his equal. "Captain." Then, turning on his heel, he gestured for his men to follow him and led them back aboard their ship. Soon lines were cast off and the two ships parted ways, men on both sides using long poles to separate the two vessels.

"Where to now, Cap'n?" Quince asked, joining her near where Gregor manned the wheel.

"Home," Belle replied, her gaze already fixed across the waters. "Back home." She flashed a quick grin at her first mate. "Time to spend some of these ill-gotten gains."

He grinned back. "Aye, aye!" he agreed with relish.

They both laughed, but Belle was barely paying attention. In truth her mind had already wandered toward home, and the scene that awaited her there.

It almost made her decide to stay at sea a while longer. But she knew she could not. There were obligations to attend, and attend them she would. Despite any desires to the contrary.

"ISABELLA? Isabella!" A pale shape suddenly flickered in front of her face, mere inches from her eyes and nose, and Bella flinched back, instinctively raising a hand to catch the offending item. The sound of her name trailed off in a gasp, and she realized that Abigail was standing there staring at her even her mind registered the delicate silk and wood and ivory clasped between her fingers. Carefully Bella opened her hand, releasing the carved and painted fan she had captured and offering it back to her friend.

"Goodness!" Abigail stated, snatching back the accessory and clutching it to her chest. "I thought sure you'd mangled it beyond repair! What has gotten into you lately?"

"I'm so sorry," Bella managed. "I— my thoughts were elsewhere, and you startled me."

"I should say so! And does your startlement often result in violence?" her friend pressed, huffing a bit. Most of that indignation was feigned, Bella knew. Abigail did enjoy a good scene.

"It . . ." Bella trailed off, fighting to hide the smile that threatened to grace her face, and to swallow the laughter that struggled to burst forth. Did her startlement often result in violence? Yes, indeed, and typically of the pistol and cutlass variety! She pictured herself slicing Abigail's fan to bits, and could no longer conceal her amusement.

"Oh, you will be the death of me, Isabella Parsons," Abigail exclaimed, but her own lips quirked up. "Or at least the death of my fans!" Then she laughed. Bella was relieved. She had not truly meant to upset her friend. But her mind had wandered, and for an instant she had forgotten which world she was in just now.

And that was a mistake she dared not make.

Obligingly, she focused upon her surroundings once more. They were at Barrage Hall, the meeting place and entertainment venue of their county, and all around them were their peers, the landed gentry, dressed in their finest and dancing, singing, playing, eating, and conversing with one another amid the music and the frequent to and fro of servants bearing lovely food and drink. It was a party, after all, the first ball of the season, and Bella had promised Abigail months ago that she would be back in time for them to attend it together.

Only, now that she was here, she could not help but wish that she were elsewhere. Specifically, back on the *Deadshot*, her legs clad in close-fitted velvet pants rather than layers of ruffles, her sword and pistol at her side.

That was a different life, however, and Bella forced herself to remember where she was—*who* she was—right now. Which is why she put on a smile, patted the seat beside her, and said, "Come now, Abigail. Sit beside me and tell me what's transpired since I left. I can only imagine what has occurred in my absence."

Fortunately, her friend needed no additional coaxing. "Well," she declared, dropping onto the bench in a flurry of silk and lace and ribbon, "you will never guess! Mary Winstead, you remember how she was pining for that merchant's son she'd met back in London? So she . . ."

Bella did her best to listen attentively, but only a very small portion of her truly cared that Mary had eloped with her merchant boy, or that Brian Fried had returned from his time overseas with a laughable mustache but an impressive limp, or that Constance and Beatrice were not speaking to each other—again—because they had both taken an interest in the same man—again. How had she ever found such things to be of any interest, she wondered. Because surely she had. She did not recall being so persistently, terribly bored in the past.

But she certainly was now.

Her eyes darted about the room even as she listened, taking in the tall, leaded-glass windows and the heavy, oak-paneled doors and the candles in their sconces lined up evenly on both sides to illuminate where the glow from the massive overhead chandeliers failed to reach. Her peers were busy mingling, laughing and carrying on, but Bella realized that she much preferred the bawdy sea chanties of her crew and the roar of the waves, the whistle of the wind as it filled her sails.

That was a party!

Movement across the room captured her attention, and Bella focused on it just in time to see a broad back disappear through an arch into the adjoining room. And who had *that* been? Cutting into her friend's rambling discourse, she asked, "Abby, is there someone new about? Someone tall, dark, and well-formed?"

That set Abigail tittering, any imagined outrage at being interrupted cast aside in favor of conspiratorial giggling. "Ah, you noticed him, have you? I might have known! Barely back a day and already setting her sights on the finest man I've ever seen!"

"Abigail." Bella tapped a finger on her friend's knee, stopping her mid-torrent. "Who. Is. He?"

"Oh, well, that would be Commander Reid," Abigail answered with only a brief, feigned pout. "Newly arrived from London, no less! A fine figure of a man, and a complete gentleman—meaning, of course, that he seems far too preoccupied to pay proper attention to any of the young ladies residing here." The way she stated that last bit made it clear that this was truly a crime beyond any other, and should be punished accordingly. Abigail, like Bella herself, was a young lady possessed of at least moderate fortune. Unlike Bella, however, her friend had little else to occupy her time beyond occasionally visiting other ladies of her acquaintance, doing needlework, planning social engagements, and shopping for a suitable husband. There were few enough here to choose from, which was why any newcomer—particularly a handsome one—would of course pique her interest.

Bella, on the other hand, had more than enough to occupy her time without such frivolous pursuits.

"**G**EOFFREY!" she called out the next morning while seated at the breakfast table. The tall, stooped figure of the family butler appeared in the doorway almost instantly.

"Yes, milady?" he inquired. "More tea?" He scooped up the teapot as he approached, the delicate china almost disappearing between his enormous hands.

"Oh, well, perhaps a touch," Bella agreed, extending her cup. "But that is not why I called." She indicated the heavy ledger that lay open beside her place. "What is this here? A hundred pounds for oranges?"

"Ah, yes." Geoffrey looked apologetic, wringing his hands together now that he had restored the teapot to its customary place. "Your father was desirous of them, and as you know they are deuced hard to come by, especially at this time of year. It was necessary to procure them from a merchant down in Derbyshire, and I am afraid the shipping fees were rather steep."

"A hundred pounds? I should say so!" She sighed, then sipped at her tea to cover it. She could not be too angry at Geoffrey. He did his best when she was away, but of course he was still only staff despite his many years of loyal service. If her father insisted

upon a purchase, Geoffrey could hardly gainsay it. Only she could do that—when she was in residence. Which had been less and less often, of late.

Well, that ended now. "I will deal with any such extravagances in future," she insisted, and Geoffrey bowed. She could not mistake the relief on his face. Now he would not have to struggle with balancing his master's cravings and demands with the practicalities of maintaining their household. That was Bella's job.

Fortunately, it was one she was more than capable of handling— and had been, even before her recently acquired career.

As if summoned by her thoughts, a second figure emerged through the door, this one as hunched as Geoffrey but far shorter and far thinner, a small, frail figure whose wisps of white hair and puzzled expression suggested he had just awakened from a bad dream.

Bella only wished that were the case.

Good morning, father," she said dutifully, rising from her seat to cross the room and embrace him. But gently—Sir William Parsons, Lord Roderick had never been a robust man but in recent years he had grown nearly skeletal, a shadow of his former self. "Would you care for some breakfast?" She escorted him to his seat across from her and then poured him tea.

"Ah, yes, thank you, my dear."

He beamed up at her. "How kind." Reaching for the sugar, he dumped several teaspoons of it into his tea in rapid succession, stirring rapidly, then took a sip. Isabella could not imagine how his mouth did not pucker at such cloying sweetness, but he merely nodded and sipped again. At least he seemed content. She returned to her own seat and went back to perusing the household accounts while nibbling at toast, having her tea, and keeping an eye upon her father.

"Are there any oranges, by chance?" Sir William asked. He looked up at Geoffrey with childish glee. "I do love oranges!" Bella had to stop herself from barking at him for throwing away money on such foolishness.

Commanding a pirate ship was almost a relief after this!

A FTER breakfast Bella changed to a walking-about dress of soft blue-gray that nicely offset her trim blond curls and drew attention to her eyes. As she set a hat atop her head, she recalled how her best friend had shrieked upon seeing her last night. "Your hair!" Abigail had cried, gloved hands nearly going to Bella's head but then retreating to her own chest instead. "What happened to all your long, lovely curls?"

"I grew tired of them," Bella had replied airily. "I feel worlds lighter now." She twirled for effect. In truth, she had hated to cut her hair after growing it long for all those years. But fitting it beneath her sable wig had proven next to impossible, and she had been more concerned about protecting her identity—and therefore her life—than soothing her vanity. Besides, she did like the way they looked now. And it saved so much time in preparation!

"Well, it is rather fetching," Abigail had agreed, then laughed. "Leave it to you, Isabella—you go away on holiday and come back practically a different person!"

More than you know, Bella had thought, a little sad at the fact that she had to keep such a secret from her oldest and dearest friend. But there was nothing for it—Abigail was a notorious gossip, utterly unable to keep a secret. Even one that could put lives at risk.

Pushing all that from her mind, Bella gathered up her purse. "Daniel!" she called, and the family coachman appeared. "Please collect the trunk in the hall for me," she instructed. "I am conveying it to Mr. Klein." He bowed and departed at once to see to it. A few minutes later he returned to escort her to and into the waiting carriage.

The family solicitor, Sascha Klein, had a handsomely appointed office on the second floor of one of the buildings in town, just above a tailor's. Daniel pulled the carriage up by the door and helped Bella out, then she waited as he unstrapped the trunk, hefted it down, and carried it inside and up the stairs. Once at the top she knocked twice and, upon hearing "Come in!", pushed the door open and gestured for Daniel to set the trunk inside.

"Thank you, Daniel," she told him. "You may return to the carriage. I shan't be too long, I think."

"Ah, Ms. Parsons!" Mr. Klein had risen from behind his desk and crossed the thick rug to greet her. "How lovely to see you, as always!" He took her hand in both of his and clasped it warmly. Bella smiled in return. She had known him her whole life, and considered him almost an uncle—which was why she did her best to ignore the way his gaze had changed as she had grown older, or how he held her hand perhaps a second too long.

"Always a pleasure, Mr. Klein," she said instead, gently extracting her hand and gliding to the nearer of the two chairs before his desk. Taking the hint, he returned to his own seat, though he continued to regard her fondly—and slightly hungrily—once they were both seated. "I have brought some additional funds to add to the family account." She indicated the chest, which sat behind them where Daniel had left it.

"Oh, yes? Very good." The solicitor leaned forward. "I do not mind telling you, Ms. Parsons, in all confidence, that some of your father's recent expenditures have been . . . peculiar, to say the least.

And ill-advised, but that is the limits of what I may accomplish, to advise against it."

"Of course. Rest assured, now that I am returned you will see an immediate cessation to such purchases," she promised. "In the meantime, that should be more than sufficient to clear any recent debts and cover expenses for some time." It had better be—the trunk contained the bulk of her captain's share from the *Deadshot*'s many successful raids, and was full of coin and jewelry and items like candlesticks and goblets and dueling pistols. Nothing that could be readily identified, however. She had made sure of that.

"I am sure. You are an excellent steward to your father's interests." It was clear that Mr. Klein was bursting to ask where such newfound wealth had come from, but as a gentleman he could not. And as the family's confidante, even if he had asked—and even if she had answered truthfully—he would have been honor-bound to keep her secret.

Bella was not about to trust her life to his honor, however.

Instead she rose to her feet. "Thank you, as always, Mr. Klein," she stated as she moved back toward the door. "I am grateful that my father and I can continue to rely upon you."

She was gone before he could catch hold of her hand for another lingering good-bye.

At least that is settled, Bella

thought as she relaxed back into the carriage and listened to the crack of Daniel's whip ordering the horses into motion again. Her family's estates were enough to provide a comfortable living, especially for such a small household as theirs—provided they did not indulge in extravagances like hundred-pound shipments of oranges! This additional money would take care of that, and allow them to continue with a greater sense of security than before. Besides which, she would keep a tighter grip on the purse strings from now on, so that her father could not make any more wild purchases. Their home and estates were once again secure.

Which meant the need behind her recent foray into piracy was now at an end. For some reason, that made Bella almost want to weep. She concentrated on staring out the carriage window instead, studying the town and how it quickly gave to countryside as they headed for home.

"WHY, Isabella!" The high, shrill voice made Bella wince, but she managed to smooth that expression away even as she turned. "How lovely to see you again!"

"And you, Constance," Bella replied, leaning in to brush cheeks with the other young woman, and then with her sister and companion. "And dear Beatrice. How are you both?"

"Oh, we are fine, just fine," Constance answered quickly, holding both of Bella's hands and leaning back. "Now let me take you in! My, you did get some color, didn't you? Such a sight! And your hair! Where did you holiday again, that they thought shorn scalps were in fashion?" Beatrice tittered, the sisters' dark eyes glittering with malice, and Bella gritted her teeth as beside her Abigail grumbled just loud enough for her to hear.

"It was an island in the Caribbean," Bella replied after extricating herself. "A lovely place, warm and sunny." She shuddered slightly, and only partially for effect. "Coming back to the damp and cold and fog was quite a shock, I can tell you! And of course such weather does horrors to one's complexion, not to mention digestion—but I'm sure you don't need me to tell you that!"

The tittering turned to gasps, both girls' eyes flying wide as the rapid succession of insults sank in. "Well, I never!" Constance declared, gathering her skirts and flouncing off, Beatrice right behind her.

"That may well be the problem!" Bella called after them. "A little fresh fruit would work wonders!" The sisters did not give any indication that they had heard.

Abigail, however, burst into laughter. "Oh, you are wicked!" she exclaimed, face still red from humor. "But they deserved that!"

"They always did," Bella agreed,

trying and failing to tamp down her own grin. It was true—the Tremont sisters were vain, nasty, grasping creatures, always ready to find fault with others in order to make themselves look better. As some of the only other young women in their circle, Bella and Abigail had been forced to tolerate the pair, at least in public. Now Bella found she simply couldn't be bothered to pretend any longer.

Accordingly, she turned to her friend. "Abby, I'm afraid I must dash," she said. "Some of my father's affairs—well, it appears I may need to settle them in person. Abroad."

"Oh, no!" Abigail clutched her hands. "You cannot leave again! You've only just returned!"

"I know, and I shall again, and soon," Bella promised. "But for now, it's urgent I go."

A gleam came to her friend's eye. "And what about Commander Reid?" she asked slyly. "Rumor has it he is looking for you, with the intent of asking you to dance."

Bella smiled. "Perhaps some other time." She pressed her cheek to Abigail's, hugged her briefly, then turned away. "Keep a weather eye out for me," she suggested, and then strode from the ballroom as swiftly as her gown would allow, leaving her friend to puzzle over that last phrase in her wake.

"WHITHER away, Cap'n?" Quince asked. She was in her customary place just to the side and a pace or two behind Gregory, where she could watch the ship sail without disturbing his view of the waters ahead.

"I'm not certain yet, Mister Quince," she admitted, then laughed. "But there is a whole wide world out there for us to explore, and plenty of ships upon the sea for us to capture. I think it's high time we found a few of those."

"Sounds good to me," her first mate admitted. "Besides, the men were starting to get fat and lazy sitting around spending all their wealth. Time to whip 'em back into shape again." He turned serious for a moment. "Didja hear about the new Naval officer, though? Sent down from London, straight from Her Majesty, with orders to hunt us down. A Commander Reid, I think."

"Indeed." Belle considered that, then smiled, hands going to her hips just to the sides of her sword and pistol. "Sounds like we'd best be ready for him, then."

This time it was Quince who laughed. "Oh, I'll make sure the lads are ready," he promised, and marched off, already bellowing orders.

Belle observed as her crew leapt about, dancing to the first mate's tune, and the *Deadshot* sped across the waves like the deadly predator it was. For now they seemed alone on the high seas, but she knew that would not last—nor did she want it to. After all, where was the thrill in a chase with no one to chase—or be chased by?

"Very well, Commander Reid," she said softly, glancing back toward the retreating shores of home before turning to face forward again. "I believe I'm ready for that dance now."

She hoped he would not be disappointed by her choice of venue, or her calling the tune. But she had decided that she had no intention in letting someone else dictate such choices to her.

This was who she was. Cannon Belle, captain of the *Deadshot*, Terror of the High Seas.

And she had never felt more alive.

Girl Running from House

By JIM & BECKY BEARD

"AND now the mazurka, Susannah. Remember: happy mind, sad heart. A mazurka should be played with both qualities."

MY name is Andrew Conway. When I first read the classified in *The Plain Dealer* calling for a piano teacher on Lonely Island it seemed too good to be true. Now that I'd been here for the better part of a month, I suspected I should have followed my initial instincts.

Room, board, and plenty of free time to work on my symphony, in addition to the stipend I'd receive for giving lessons five days a week, was an offer I hated to refuse; so it was that I found myself speeding across the bay in a small motorboat piloted by one Weatherling, a crusty sort who probably didn't know Bach from Beethoven.

My student, sixteen-year-old Susannah Saxon, was pretty, and she knew it. If her big blue eyes and bouncy blonde hair were a temptation, however, her guardian and sister, Karen Thorne, was a hovering spectre that kept me in check. There was no softness in that lady, and there were no attractions that I could see. The pair were as different as summer and winter.

"ANDREW?"

"Mr. Conway," I corrected. She pouted prettily.

"Mr. Conway, do you recall that painting I mentioned the other day? The one that—"

"We are studying Chopin, not Mussorgsky. Enough about pictures. Now, *da capo*."

THAT evening's meal was a far from pleasant affair. As usual, the food was palatable if not exactly mouthwatering. Then there was the chill atmosphere of the dining room, which had nothing to do with the gusts rattling the windowpanes. I took a stab at conversation.

"This painting you've lost, Susannah. Your father's, you say?" Susannah's late father was none other than David Saxon, the "Great Lakes Gauguin," a fact I'd learned shortly after my arrival.

"*I* didn't lose it, Andrew."

"Susannah!" snapped her guardian. Susannah giggled behind her napkin.

"I didn't lose it, *Mr. Conway*," she said. "But it's lost all the same.

I only saw it once. When I was a little girl. At a party. It was a picture of me running from the house."

A clank of cutlery drew my attention to Karen Thorne, who sat glaring at her sister.

"You know very well, Susannah, that this is not something we discuss."

"But why? The painting is mine! It's mine! Why won't you just give it to me?"

"Susannah, go to your room." Susannah sat for a moment, mouth open, then stood and flung her napkin onto the table in rage. Even in the dim light I could see the flush that covered her fair skin almost to her ears as she exited.

"Was that really necessary? If the painting's hers why not just—"

"I do not wish to discuss this, Mr. Conway," she interrupted, her words measured. We stared at each other across the table.

"I apologize if I have offended you, Miss Thorne." I rose, bowed stiffly, and left the room.

I FOUND myself walking along the shore to cool my head. Miss Thorne had been unduly harsh to Susannah at supper, I thought. If the painting belonged to the girl, why not let her have it? I wondered, not for the first time, if I should resign my position here. The symphony I had hoped to compose was progressing slowly. As for my student, her talent was somewhat precocious, but she didn't seem interested in applying herself. It was frustrating. Added to these things was the prospect of listening to the spirited Susannah and her spinsterish sister bicker til spring. I all but made up my mind to quit. They could find another teacher.

As I headed back to the house, I chanced to look up at a lighted window, Susannah's, no doubt, as she was standing there on the balcony. Backlit by the lamp in her room, her figure was clearly outlined thru her nightdress, which was entirely too sheer for the weather. She waved at me before disappearing inside.

She was nearly at the bottom of the staircase as I entered the foyer. She'd donned a peignoir of the same fabric as her gown. On her feet was a pair of maribou-trimmed mules. The pigtails framing her face were at odds with the rest of her ensemble. My heart lurched at the effect. She was playing at being a woman, but she was still very much a child.

"Tell me about the picture, Susannah." She put her finger to her lips to silence me and led the way into the drawing room.

"It was beautiful," she said, after carefully closing the doors and leaning back against them. "All moonlight and shadows..." It was apparent from her faraway look that she was viewing the painting in her mind's eye.

"We're not really sisters, you know, Karen and I."

"Yes, I know, you're stepsisters.

Karen told me. She said that your father and her mother were married when you were five and she was thirteen.

"Why do you suppose she becomes so angry when you mention the painting?"

"I don't know," Susannah said emphatically. "Jealousy, probably. She goes just crazy when I look for it." She bit her bottom lip and frowned.

"Why is the painting so important to you, Susannah?"

"Because it's the only thing left that was my father's."

"But what about the self-portrait?"

"You were in my father's studio?"

"Was that his studio? The only thing in there is the portrait."

"That's because *she* got rid of everything else. His paints, his brushes, his palettes...everything!"

"Is the studio a special place for you, Susannah? I'm sorry if I intruded."

"Oh...I don't mind. Just so long as Karen and Weatherling don't go in there. I don't mind if you go in, Andrew." She smiled sweetly at me.

"Andrew?"

"Yes?"

"You'll help me find it, won't you? Please?

"Yes," I answered decisively. We stared at each other as conspiratorial grins spread across our faces.

"Come on," she said, grabbing me by the hand.

SHE led me down a flight of creaky stairs that we accessed through a heavy door off the kitchen, explaining that, while she'd searched thoroughly for the painting in other parts of the house, she'd afforded the basement little more than a brief once-over, as it gave her "the willies" to be down there.

The basement was less damp than I had expected, but after we'd passed beyond the main room, we had to dodge cobwebs as we fumbled for light switches.

We came upon an old laundry with an aging mangle washing machine and a treadle-style sewing machine, but...were those my slacks, the pair Weatherling offered to mend after I'd snagged them on the dock yesterday? Was this where he did *all* my laundry? A closer look revealed that, while elderly, the appliances were clean and in good repair. I wondered why Miss Thorne hadn't replaced these relics with newer, more convenient models.

The next door I tried was stuck, but I applied some pressure to it with my shoulder and was surprised to discover a game room, complete with shooting gallery and two bowling lanes.

Room after room relinquished nary a painting, but I began to see something through the debris and detritus: the history of the house.

I saw evidence of what I assumed to be Karen's forebears and the early days of their residence on the island. Here was a penny-far-thing bicycle, though considering the rough terrain of the island, it could never have been of much use; there, a collapsing carton with "Christmas" chalked on its side, a few strands of tarnished tinsel scattered on the floor around it. Testaments to happier times.

I was caught off guard by the fierce visage staring at me from a daguerreotype hanging slightly askew in one room, an obvious ancestor of Miss Thorne. He had the same long nose and imperious mien.

"Do you know who this is, Susannah?"

"I don't know...Artemus Some-body." She was indifferent to it all and seemed irritated when I stopped to examine an object or peruse a document. She was inter-ested in only the painting and her father. David Saxon had begun to take on mythic proportions in these dusty cellars. It made me wonder how well he had fit into the Thorne household while he was still alive.

We finally came to the last of the doors. Behind and above us, I thought I heard a creak, but Susannah pulled me through the portal we'd approached and into the room beyond.

Some minutes later, buried under a mountain of cast-off clothing pulled from all manner of cranny and cuddy, our quest had taken on the tone of a party game as we tried on garments that

had not seen the light of day since the Gibson Girl was the American ideal. Despite the hijinks, however, I knew Susannah was adamant about finding that painting.

Opening a chifforobe we had yet to raid, Susannah squealed and sprang into my arms. I looked over her shoulder at the huge spider dangling there. We were laughing. And then we were kissing.

Instinctively I thrust the girl away. That was when I saw Weath-erling standing in the doorway.

We stared at each other for a long minute. Then he looked at my companion.

"You shouldn't be down here, Miss Susannah," he croaked. "I wonder what your sister would say about what I just seen." He glow-ered at me.

"She's not my sister! And I don't care what she says! I'm sick and tired of everyone telling me what I can and can't do! I am not a child!"

"Heh."

"Come on, Susannah," I said, leading the way to the door. I looked back at her, but her eyes were fixed on Weatherling. "Come on, Susannah," I repeated. She looked at me then and tried to smile.

"He's always spying on me," she said *sotto voce*. "He tells Karen about everything I do."

BREAKFAST was no more awkward than usual; in fact, the mood seemed almost light, until Weatherling made his appearance. I'd just dunked a last dry toast strip into my coffee when he came and stood in the doorway, his expression unreadable.

"Why, Curt," Miss Thorne said. "What's the matter?"

"Caught a nice snappin' turtle for supper this evenin'" he replied, "but I can't find my knife."

"Which knife?"

"My fillet knife." His eyes met mine. I nearly recoiled under their scrutiny.

"Well, where did you leave it?" his employer asked.

"Same place I always leave it! In my chest!"

Miss Thorne and I exchanged glances. A sidelong glimpse of Susannah rewarded me with a picture of perfect innocence.

"Well, I'm afraid I don't know where it is," said Miss Thorne. "Susannah?" The younger girl shook her head and attacked her porridge with renewed enthusiasm. Miss Thorne didn't bother asking me.

Weatherling merely grunted. Casting a final suspicious glance at Susannah he turned and stalked away.

"HOW about an example of the composer at his most humorous today? Let us try Op. 7, No. 5 in C Major. Susannah?"

"Did you enjoy last night as much as I did, Andrew? If only that damned old Weatherling—"

"Language, Susannah. What

happened last night must never happen again. And call me Mr. Conway."

"But—"

"I shall find it necessary to leave the island if you don't start behaving as a young lady should. Now, play."

She sight-read the piece passably well and smiled at me in smug self-satisfaction.

"Do you happen to know anything about Weatherling's missing knife, Susannah?"

"Mr. Conway!" the girl exclaimed, popping up from the stool. She spun on her heel and bolted from the room.

MY student was playing "Liebestraum No. 3" with sublime fluidity. But we hadn't worked on Liszt. Could she have accomplished this before my arrival? My eyes opened. A dream. No, I still heard the piano. I rolled out of bed and padded softly to the music room.

Remembering the squeaky right door, I eased open the left and peered inside. I stood transfixed as the melody surged then trickled away.

"That was lovely."

"Oh!" came the startled reply.

"What other secrets are you keeping?"

"None that concern you, Mr. Conway. Excuse me."

"Karen, wait," I said as she stalked past. She froze.

"Good night, *Mr.* Conway," she

answered without turning. Her voice was icy.

KAREN did not appear at the breakfast table, and Susannah, who did, was sullen, so I gulped my coffee and made my way to the music room.

I sat at the piano, allowing my fingers to move of their own volition over the keys, improvising on the theme Karen had played so hauntingly in the night. It became entangled with a snippet of melody I'd been building, and I wondered how audacious it would be to borrow from Liszt for my symphony.

I'd been lost in the music for nearly an hour before realizing that Susannah was late for her lesson. I played exercises for the next fifteen minutes, waiting, and, when she still hadn't shown up, I went looking for her.

I knocked on the door to her room.

"Susannah?" No reply. Nor was she in her father's studio.

I climbed the narrow staircase to the third-floor servants' quarters. I'd never been up here before. Aside from myself, Weatherling was currently the only household retainer, and he stayed in a cottage separate from the main house, so the tiny rooms were empty, but I assumed, correctly, that there would be an entrance to the attics here.

"Susannah?" I called thru the hatch. No answer.

Heading back to the first floor, I went into the kitchen and shouted down the basement steps.

"Susannah!" Nothing. I sighed in exasperation and pulled on my jacket to go outdoors.

The cold air was bracing and felt good. I walked briskly at first, slowing only when I got to the shore. I avoided the lapping wavelets and detoured around a bobbing piece of driftwood. Following the western edge of the island, I decided to investigate some strange rock formations to the north.

On my approach I spotted a figure, too tall and slim to be either Susannah or Weatherling. Karen. Just the person I wanted to see.

Her gaze was directed lakeward; I followed her line of sight and saw a passing ferry and, even more distantly, a freighter. As I came closer, I noted that she was wearing a shabby pea coat and, incongruously, a brightly colored headscarf. The latter did little to protect her from the strong breeze, as several strands of dark hair had escaped it and were fluttering around her face. It was the first instance of frivolity I'd detected in the lady since I'd been on the island.

She became aware of me then and seemed surprised, but only momentarily, composing her features so quickly that I wondered if I'd imagined the carefree, almost gay, expression of seconds before.

"I'm searching for a recalcitrant student," I proclaimed over the sound of the wind. "You wouldn't happen to know where I might find one, would you?" She clicked her tongue, let out a long breath, and cast her eyes downward.

"Was she not present for her lesson?" she asked finally.

"Haven't seen her since breakfast."

"Oh, dear."

"Why didn't you tell me you played before?"

"It didn't seem important."

Not important? I thought. *For me it's difficult to see music as anything* but *important.*

"Besides, I don't have Susannah's technical skill."

"True, but Susannah could benefit from a little of your expressiveness.

"Karen, why did you hire me?"

"She shows promise, doesn't she?"

"She has talent, but she has no love of music," I answered bluntly. She slumped at this, took a few paces toward the weird formations.

"Tell me about those rocks."

"Glacial grooves." The smile transformed her face. "They were formed during the Ice Age." I smiled back.

"She's so restless. I thought it might help."

"I know you probably didn't really have the money to bring me out here." She looked at me sharply. "It's fairly obvious that times have been better."

"David squandered my mother's money after she died. We manage."

"Why didn't you sell the piano?" I asked carefully. "A Steinway Square in that condition must be worth a small fortune."

Karen stared into the lowering sky as if searching for something. "It was my mother's. I could never sell it."

Just then a powerful gust whisked her scarf off her head. I snatched at it, lost my footing on the loose gravel, and went skittering down the side of the groove, landing on my keister.

I craned my head around and saw her above, hands clamped over her mouth, stifling laughter.

"Well, at least I caught your scarf." She clambered down and helped me to my feet.

By unspoken consent we started slowly toward the house.

"So, this painting," I said, feeling emboldened. "The 'lost' work of David Saxon. If you—"

And just like that our conversation was over. There was so much hurt in her eyes when she looked at me that I could have kicked myself. She rushed ahead of me to the house. I watched her go.

THE clouds were roiling and so was my mood. I closed my eyes and let the wind buffet me. When I opened them, I saw a squall moving in from the northwest. Still I stood there. Sleet hit me like needles, stinging my face. I waited til I was numb before heading back to the house. By this time it was snowing, heavily enough to diminish visibility, and I tripped over the same piece of driftwood I'd skirted earlier. I reached the door thoroughly drenched, and thoroughly disgusted, after trudging thru the sloppy, slushy mess.

Hanging up my jacket and kicking off my shoes, I made for the music room where I started banging out my frustrations on the piano. What had I gotten myself into in this house? Sisterly discord...a skulking lackey....

Images of Karen Thorne and Susannah Saxon danced before me as I played. The younger Susannah was a cute kid, adorable, even, but her childish peevishness was as off-putting as her youthful exuberance was appealing. The elder Karen...she was an enigma.

The smirking face from the portrait upstairs materialized before me then. David Saxon. He was the mastermind behind this muddle. I had a mind to go up there right now and have it out with him. By golly, I would.

I entered the dead man's studio and closed the door behind me. Flicking the light switch I was stunned to see not the self-portrait I had expected, but—

A stick of dynamite went off in my head.

I blinked two or three times, willing my eyes to focus. She was kneeling on the scarred wood floor beside me.

"Poor Andrew. Did you hurt yourself when you fell?"

"Susannah?" She brought her simpering face close to mine. Her little white teeth reminded me of shoepeg corn.

"There it is, Andrew. Look!" She gazed rapturously at the wall. The pain when I moved my head was sickening, and I groaned.

"Oh, Andrew. Does it hurt very much?"

"Susannah. Where's Karen?"

"Who cares?"

"Susannah. Help me sit up."

"So you can hurt me again? Like you've hurt me before?"

"Susannah. H-help me sit up so I can see the painting."

"Oh. Well, in that case..." She wrapped her arms around my waist and pulled me up right. Her strength was prodigious.

"Look, Andrew! It was right there all along!"

Nausea washed over me, and I closed my eyes, steadied my breathing.

"Andrew, open your eyes!" Her voice was percussive in the nearly empty chamber. "Now, look!"

The orientation of the painting was vertical. The subject, a young woman in the lower right foreground, seemed to be fleeing the shaded mansion behind her. The style was impressionistic, moonlight and shadows utilized to spectacular effect.

"It was the last thing Daddy ever painted. It was a message to me. It was his way of telling me to leave this house."

I looked from the picture to Susannah and back again. The

brunette beauty was dressed in filmy, pale garments. The moonbeams shining on her tricked the viewer into believing initially that she was fair. But she was not. She was dark. This was not Susannah. It was Karen.

This, then, was the lost painting of David Saxon. I'd had occasion to see other of the artist's works in the past. The canvas in front of me was a masterpiece among them.

"Know how I found it?"

"Huh?"

"The painting. Do you know how I found it?"

"No." God, my head hurt.

"Well, I was very angry. You see, I'd just spotted you and *her* on the glacial grooves. I can see the whole island from the attic windows. I was up there when you called me earlier." She giggled.

"Oh, Andrew, how could you? I thought you loved me." She slapped my face resoundingly. I struggled not to vomit.

"I threw the decanter, Andrew. The empty decanter that she can't afford to fill. I keep it here, in this cupboard. Daddy always lets me mix his drinks. I used it to crown you, too." She grinned broadly.

"Oh, Daddy! I'm sorry I hit you with the decanter! I'm sorry for those things I said! I don't really hate you!"

Susannah Saxon was insane.

She seemed to forget about me as she sat sobbing by her parent's portrait. Now would be as good a time as any to make my escape. I inched my way toward the door. Rising quickly I grabbed its crystal knob. I turned it in vain.

The decanter crashed against the wall beside me.

"The door's locked, Andrew." She held up a brass skeleton key for me to see.

"Give me the key, Susannah." She smiled ruefully. "Susannah, give me the key."

"I can't do that. I'm going to kill you, Andrew," she explained in a sad little voice. "And then I'll kill Karen. And the two of you can be together forever."

From somewhere in the folds of her frock she produced a nine-inch blade: Weatherling's missing fillet knife. She lunged at me; I sidestepped, but just barely.

"Put down the knife, Susannah."

There was pounding at the door. It was Karen.

"Open the door! Susannah, open this door!"

"Karen, she's got a knife!" I bellowed. My head was killing me.

Susannah came at me a second time, weapon held high. I ducked. The movement was too abrupt. A wave of dizziness knocked me off-balance; the blade grazed my cheek.

"Susannah, please!" screamed Karen. She was throwing herself against the outside of the door. I heard Weatherling's voice in the hallway.

"Hurry, Curt, unlock it," pleaded Karen. The door swung inward;

Weatherling held a large ring of keys.

"Susannah. Darling. Please give me the knife."

"No, Karen! Stay back!" I ordered.

"Susannah, don't you remember when we were friends? We still are! Remember what fun we had when you first came here? Before Mama died? Before those awful people—"

"You were jealous, Karen! You still are! Daddy's colleagues liked me. They laughed at you because you're homely!"

"I remember what them people done to you," Weatherling growled.

"Shut up, Weatherling, or I'll kill you, too!"

"Oh, God, they petted, and they pawed. She craved the attention. It was wrong and I knew it. I tried to save her from them. She needed to be protected. She was just a child!"

"So were you!" I yelled.

"That's not the way it was, Karen! Daddy loved me! He wouldn't let anyone harm me!"

"Your father was selfish and cruel! You think that's you in the painting? It's not! It's me! Your father tormented me! He wanted to drive me from my own house! He threatened to sell the island four generations of my family called home! Fortunately he died before he got the chance!"

Her words hung suspended like shrimps in aspic.

What started as a whimper grew into a wail. Susannah cried with the abandon of a baby, mouth gaping, face scarlet, eyes streaming. She backed herself into the corner and slid down the wall to the floor, still clutching Weatherling's fillet knife.

"Susannah. Darling—"

"Don't touch me!" She turned the weapon on her sister. And then she turned it on herself.

"Susannah, no..." Karen groaned.

"Susannah, won't you give us the knife?"

"No! I hate myself!"

Susannah plunged the knife into her breast.

WEATHERLING insisted on waiting till first light before crossing. The trip was treacherous, regardless. I was on pins and needles the entire way. Karen was oblivious. She was too busy rocking Susannah like an infant and crooning to her.

Docking was difficult, but Weatherling managed, then left to find a telephone booth to call for an ambulance. I carried Susannah ashore.

There, in the shelter of a clapboard lean-to, Susannah died in her sister's arms, but not before a final rally.

"Karen?"

"Yes, my darling."

"Hold me tighter."

"Of course, my darling. I love you, Susannah."

"I love you, too."

And that was that.

THE sale of David Saxon's self-portrait brought in a modest sum. It might have been more if not for the damage it sustained when his daughter struck it with the decanter.

Girl Running from House sold at a considerably higher price, sufficient to refurbish the mansion and buy a nice stone for Susannah's grave. We travel to the mainland every week to visit her.

Karen's decided to restore the neglected vineyard her great-grandfather Artemus planted on the island when he came over from France in the 1800s. She might even grow some cherry trees.

Lonely Island Symphony premieres at the conservatory this autumn. I'm only slightly trepidatious about it. Aw, who am I kidding? I'm scared to death. But Karen will be there with me. We're planning a quiet June wedding.

I'm learning to love the island nearly as much as Karen does. We've already gotten a dog and a cat, so it's not quite so lonely anymore.

Sometimes, when the waves are crashing, I almost imagine I hear Susannah laughing.

Trouble Came Walking Through My Door

By KATHLEEN O'SHEA DAVID

"**B**LOOD is so much more difficult than wine to get out of a linen table cloth. Did you know that Mr. Gillen?"

I watched as the dame in front of me very carefully uncross and cross her legs giving me the best view of those tight gams that seem to go on forever.

"No, Mrs. Renard, I did not," I said.

"Oh, honey," she said in an accent that seemed a bit affected, "Mrs. Renard is my mother-in-law. I still go by my maiden name in public: O'Toole, but you can call me Trouble. You can get it out but it takes a lot of muscle power and the right combination of cleaners. If you don't take care of it promptly then you will never get rid of the stain."

Trouble O'Toole was what we call a gold digger. She managed to latch onto Rex Renard who was one of the silent partners of a number of shady enterprises and rumored mob ties.

She had come to me to find her missing brother Lucky who never lived up to his name in his miserable life. She had last set eyes on him at the track when she was there with her husband. According to others he had last been seen at the Golden Hine talking to his bookie. Since then no one had seen him or admitted seeing him.

"It's fifty dollars a day plus expenses with a minimum of four hundred dollars as a retainer."

"Total discretion? You only report to me?"

I nodded.

She opened the impossibly small purse and pulled out a wad of cash. She carefully counted off the four hundred and placed it on the desk.

"Only to me, Mr. Gillen," she said placing a hand on the money before pushing it towards me.

"Yes Ma'am," I said.

She got up and made sure that I was watching her as she left the room. There was an extra wiggle as she walked that I think she put in for my benefit. She did have magnificent legs.

As soon as she was gone, I shouted, "Mrs. Richmond!"

Illustration by Peter Krause

My secretary came in with her steno pad. I saw her eyes light on the small pile of money in front of me. I took fifty dollars and put it in my pocket.

"Put this in the safe after you pay yourself for last week and this week.," I said.

"You took the case," she said with a bit of reproach in her voice.

"What was I supposed to do?" I said, "Not like we have clients pouring out of our ears."

"But *her*? Her name was well chosen by her parents. And considering what happened last time you had to deal with Rex Renard, I will assume you have taken leave of your senses."

"Money is money," I said leaning back carefully in my wooden desk chair. It had been repaired after I had to use it as a weapon the last time, I dealt with Mr. Renard's associates.

She gave me a look that I remembered too well from my teachers in school and picked up the cash on the desk then swept out of the room.

I figured precinct would be first on the list in case Lucky was incarcerated and had used his phone call already.

I walked in to the police station and saw that the desk sergeant was a friendly.

"Officer Matthew Wang!" I said, "How are the wife and kids? John is in high school by, now right?"

"Laurence, what the hell are you doing on this side of town?

I thought you were peeping for some rich client to give them the goods on their cheating spouse. And thanks, Sean's on the high school basketball team and it looks good for them going to state."

"Wow," I said.

"Okay, Laurence, now that we got the niceties out of the way, what the hell do you want? And how did you get the guts to walk in here like you own the place?"

Matthew was right. It was pretty ballsy for me to come to my old station considering how I had been drummed out of the force. I figured about half the people here hated my guts and the other half respected what I did with a couple agreeing with it.

"I need to find out if someone is in the system or lost in the system," I said carefully putting the fifty I had in my pocket on the desk. It discretely vanished until the Sergeant's desk.

"Who?"

"Lucky O'Toole," I said.

Matthew responded with a barking laugh, "Really?"

"Yes," I said.

"He was here. He was brought in on a public indecency charge. Renard's goons came and collected him a couple of days ago. I don't know if they let him go or took him to Rex to answer for his 'crimes'. I overheard one of them saying that Lucky had run out of luck."

I nodded and said aloud, "Well

hug Peg for me and I hope things go better."

He nodded, "Thanks, Laurence, and best of luck on your case. Sorry I couldn't help you."

We shook hands and I left with a little more information.

Next was the racetrack to see if anyone had seen Lucky since his sister saw him there.

I could see the Rolls that belonged to Rex in the owners' lot as I walked towards the stables.

There were a couple of goons hanging around the stables that I pointedly ignored while entering the stables. I headed right for the trainer's room to find my brother-in-law Will.

I walked in on Rex reading the riot act to the men in the room.

"What were you thinking!? This is the most important race of the season! This is my ticket to an invite to the Triple Crown! I hired you to take care and train my horses not cause them to come up lame because you aren't doing your job!"

"She's the best exercise rider we have. Also she is the same weight as Todd," said Will, the barn manager, as he stretched his bad leg out. Will had been on his way to becoming the top jockey in the United States until a freak accident and a horse falling on top of him ended those hopes.

"Where is Todd?" asked Rex running his hands through what was left of his red hair. Rex was not sliding into middle age gracefully.

The trainers looked at each other.

"What?" said Rex with a tone in his voice that held warning within.

"We don't know," said Will, "He hasn't been here in a week. We sent one of the kids around to his apartment and his landlord said he hadn't seen him for at least that long."

Rex looked like he was going to spit tacks but he pulled himself back together and said in a very measured tone, "Find him."

He saw me leaning on the doorframe, "Hell, hire that loser to find him. I don't care but I want my jockey and my horse ready to go in two days at the Barnard sweepstakes."

He stormed out of the room making it a point to bump into me on his way out.

Will covered his face and sighed, "Okay everyone, back to work."

The other men filed out leaving Will and me in the office alone.

"What do you want this time Laurence? I don't have any betting tips or information for you and your sister is in good health thanks for asking as is your new niece that you haven't bothered to come by and see."

"I have a new niece?"

"Elizabeth Anne. Six pounds 12 ounces. She was born two weeks ago. We told Mrs. Richmond since we couldn't get in touch with you. You will be happy to know that she sent us a very nice baptismal set for her in your name. I swear you are the worst brother on the planet at times."

"I have been busy," I said as I sat down in one of the two chairs in front of his desk.

"Sure you have," he said, "but you are not here for that news. Why are you darkening my door?"

"Lucky O'Toole," I said.

Will snorted, "That loser. Why are you looking for him?"

"His sister asked me to…nicely."

"You mean she paid you well to make sure her husband doesn't know she is looking for him."

I shrugged, "She said the last place she saw him was here."

"Yeah, he was here doing a run for Rex. Or so he said. Seemed a little startled when Rex and Trouble showed up."

"Why do you think he was here?"

"I think he is sweet on our new exercise rider, Molly Lemont. He has been hanging around her since she got here a couple of months ago. I know they went out on a date."

"Is Molly around? Maybe she has seen him."

"I got her out of here when Captain came up lame."

"Sea-legs?"

Captain Sea-legs was *the* horse in Rex's stables. This one had winner written all over it. It was considered Rex's ticket to the elite club of horseracing that has been just out of his grasp.

"What happened?"

"It was a bit of a freak accident.

He got a stone in his shoe and pulled up lame. She recognized that his gait had changed and quickly got him back to the stable to Doc. He removed the stone but the damage was done. He'll be ready by race time but the rumors aren't helping. And of course Rex is not in the best of moods right now."

"So where is Molly?"

"Might try the Golden Hine. She hung out there with Lucky a lot."

"Thanks, Will," I said, standing up and getting ready to go then I stopped, "Is there anything Molly knew that might help Lucky get a big score?"

Will thought for a moment and said, "Other than what happened to the horse, which is pretty much public knowledge due to the rumor mill, I can't think of anything."

I nodded and started walking to the door.

"Oh and Laurence, please come by and see your sister. She actually misses you."

I laughed a hoarse laugh, "Pull the other one, Will. She wants nothing to do with me after I got drummed out of the force."

"She knows you had your reasons for what you did."

"Doesn't mean she has forgiven me," I said, "Look, I'll stop by this weekend after the race for dinner."

"Good. Don't disappoint her," he said.

"You mean don't disappoint her more, Will."

And with that I left and hopped back into my car. I felt the hairs on the back of my neck rise and knew I was being followed. I did what I could to ditch them on the way to the Golden Hine.

The Golden Hine was one of those bars that could only be found on word of mouth. They were very particular about who came through their doors not because they ran numbers and a number of bookies worked out of the place but most of their clientele were breaking the law by their choice of partners. Anonymity was the watchword of the place. What happened here stayed here and no one who visited it was ever really there and the bartender would swear to it.

I had participated in several raids on the place during my time with the force and had become friendly with the owner as I managed to get a number of the charges dropped against their employees. After I had found myself at loose ends with no idea what I was going to do next, it was Maxine who had given me my first case and a direction in my life and made sure I didn't just crawl into a bottle and give up.

The shows were legendary with Maxine being both the emcee and the headliner of the place. Maxine knew all the best comedians, singers, and magicians in the city. Many got their start at the Golden Hine.

I walked through the door and past Bryan the bouncer, a very large man named Cedric who had been a heavyweight contender until he was found in bed with his boyfriend and spent some time in the clink for that—and beating two paparazzi near to death for taking pictures.

He rumbled, "Maxine is in the back booth. You better behave yourself. I don't want to have to toss you out again."

I raised my hands palms out and said, "Not here to cause trouble,"

"Good," he said and went back to his position near the door.

I nodded to the bartender Phil on my way to see Maxine.

By the time I sat down, there was a scotch neat at my elbow.

Maxine was done to the nines. Her red wig set off the lovely caramel-colored skin which was accented with just enough make-up to make women wish they had half her skills and beauty. The tightly fitted blue sequin dress hugged her curves creating yet other bomb shell look that was envied by all who saw her. At her left elbow was an ashtray with cigarette butts with colorful lip-marks on most of them. On her right was a glass of white wine which also had lip prints on the rim. In front of her was a stack of papers and a notepad with scribbling. She looked up and saw me sitting across from her in the booth.

"Laurence darling," Maxine said, "to what do I owe the pleasure?

Not another raid on the horizon?"

"Not that I know of Maxine. I am here on a case."

"Oh how dull," she said lighting up another cigarette from the glowing butt of her previous one, "And why, my dear, are you here?"

"Lucky O'Toole is missing." I knew better than to couch my words with her. The direct approach worked best.

She stabbed out the cigarette in the ashtray, "That motherf.... Okay, I am going to tell you what I told Trouble and Rex's men and half a dozen other people who have come in looking for him here. He hasn't been here in over two weeks. He came by to see his bookie and then ran out like his tail was on fire. Neither my staff or I have seen him since."

I put my hands up, "Ok, ok you don't know where he is. I get it. I am not here about Lucky."

"Oh?"

"I am trying to find Molly Lemont," I said.

"That poor girl," said Maxine lighting another cigarette, "I felt so bad for her the way that Lucky was leading her on until I figure out that he wasn't and she wasn't interested in him. More interested in his sister. They had some sort of business thing going but I think it went south considering the amount of arguing there was last time they were here."

"Which was?"

"Same night Lucky talked to his bookie and left."

"Have you seen her since?"

"She came by about week ago looking for Lucky just like everyone else."

"Did she leave you a way to contact her? A number or a friend or something?"

Maxine looked over my shoulder. "Well, you can ask her your questions yourself."

I turned to see what she was looking at. There was a young woman at the bar wearing dungarees, a blue denim shirt with a red bandana tied around her neck. Her hair was in one long braid down her back. She was wearing a slouch cap low on her head to keep her face from being seen. She glanced towards us and started to bolt when Maxine gestured to her to join us. She picked up her drink and I slide over to the middle of the round bench seat giving her a place to sit.

"Molly, this is Laurence. Laurence, this is Molly,"

I held out my hand and said, "Nice to meet you. Will had some very nice things to say about your horsemanship."

"How do you know Will?" asked the quivering voice, which told me that this girl was terrified of something.

"He's my brother-in-law," I said, "His wife just had a baby girl they named Elizabeth Ann who I hope takes after my sister's looks rather than Will's."

I have no idea why I talked about the baby but it had been the right move as I watched Molly relax quite a bit and take off her hat.

"I thought you were another one of Rex's 'employees' looking for me," she said, "I didn't hurt the Captain. I pulled up as soon as I felt his gait change. Rex has some fool idea that I was trying to ruin his horse. Ever since then I have been looking over my shoulder and having to run like a rabbit. Did Will ask you to find me?"

"He is worried about you, Molly, but that is not why I was trying to find you. I am looking for Lucky."

Apparently, that was the wrong thing to say because the hat went back on and she started to pull her way out of the seat.

"Sit!" came the command from Maxine.

Molly froze for a second and then returned her butt to the bench.

"Now I have no idea what was going on with Lucky and you but Laurence here is a good man who will not screw you over but you got to be straight with him."

"His sister hired me to find him."

"If he is missing then I am dead," said Molly moving to get up again, "Everything he told me was horseshit. He probably ran away leaving me with the bag."

I pulled a card out of my wallet and handed it to her, "Look I know you are scared. Here's my number and address. You can call collect and I will take the call. I want to help you Molly."

She took the card and shoved it in her pocket, "If you want to help me, find that rat bastard and make him give you the page." She ran out of the bar like her tail was on fire.

"Well, that was intriguing. Thank you, Laurence, for an entertaining afternoon," said Maxine as she started to stack up all her papers and straighten them out.

I knew I was being dismissed or let go so I might follow Molly.

I left the club and allowed for my eyes to adjust to light. I looked around and saw a quick movement down the alley across the street from the Golden Hine. I found Molly squatting behind the garbage cans looking like a trapped animal.

"Molly, what did Lucky get you mixed up into?"

"He said that he had an easy score but he needed the page to prove that what he knew was true. Gave me fifty bucks in earnest money with promises of hundreds if I would help. Should have known that he was just playing me like he has so many others."

"What page?" I asked.

"From the breeder's book. The one that I stole for him," she said.

We heard the noise at the same time. I looked up to see a man coming down the alley and he didn't look friendly. I looked back and Molly had already scampered off and was out of the alley running for her life.

I stepped in front of the man, "Can I help you?"

"Get out of my way before you get hurt flatfoot," he rumbled showing me the brass knuckles on his left hand.

I smiled and opened my coat a bit to show him my gun. I wasn't going to show him the knife I had strapped to the back of my belt.

"Now there are several ways this can go. You can go back to Rex and tell him you lost the girl. I can give you a sound thrashing and you can go back to Rex and complain that I beat the tar out of you. Or I could shoot you where you stand and take my chances on which cops show up and which hospital Rex will be visiting you in."

He rushed me, going low for a tackle that I braced myself for. He knocked me into the garbage cans behind me. I got a grip on the hair on the back of his head and pulled his face up to connect with a right to the jaw. I kept punching until I felt him go limp. I pulled myself out from under his body and gave him a couple of kicks to the ribs for good measure. I picked him up and put him in a slumped sitting position with an empty liquor bottle in his hand. Just another rummy sleeping in the alley.

I took off my coat and hung it up on the coat rack behind the door. After taking off my shoes, I flopped down on the couch and covered up with the afghan that my mother had knitted me and shut my eyes for what seemed a minute when I was awoken by the phone ringing.

I picked it up and heard screaming for help and some sort of struggle. Then the line went dead. I couldn't tell if the screams were male or female, just that they sounded desperate.

I felt so helpless because I had no idea where the call came from. But it sure as hell woke me up. I looked to see that the sun was rising so I knew it was about six or so.

The insistent knock on my office door woke me from the light doze I had fallen into. I opened the door to see two men one in a cheap trench coat who's back was to me and the other in his police uniform.

The detective turned around and it was not one of my fans. Detective Michael Niosi blamed what I did for the loss of his partner, which was true if you looked at what happened sideways and squinted. His partner had screwed himself over all on his own.

"You need to come with us," said Niosi with a predatory grin.

"Why? Am I under arrest?" I asked, "Do I need to leave Mrs. Richardson a note to call my lawyer for me?"

The officer who I didn't know said, "No. Nothing like that. We need to see if you can identify a body."

"Whose body?"

"Like he said, we need you to tell us and I hope you have a strong stomach," said Niosi.

They put me in the back of the black and white and we drove with the siren on to the river that ran next to the town. This was one of the things I missed the most about being a cop, being able to get places very quickly.

We joined a swarm of police officers and homicide folks at the banks of the river where the less fortune of our society had made themselves a shantytown that the cops tended to turn a blind eye towards as long as there was no trouble.

I followed Niosi and Barker, as I learned in the car was the new kid's name, to what I could barely call a shed. It was made of discarded wood and had a door which had been scavenged from Lord knows where. The door had been kicked in. I was surprised that the shack hadn't fallen from that as rickety as it was.

Inside was what was left of someone and I knew who it was from the clothing and the braid wrapped her throat. Their face had been smashed in with a heavy object with the blood decorating the walls of the shed.

"Molly Lemont," I said after finding my voice again, "She's an exercise rider at the track, works for my brother-in-law Will."

"Any idea why she was clutching your business card so hard?"

"She was someone I talked to about a case I am working on."

"Did you decide that she wasn't being truthful?" said Niosi

"Excuse me? You don't think I did this?"

"Why not? You have been known to get your hands dirty," said Barker, "I have heard stories."

"I talked to her yesterday afternoon at the Golden Hine. You can ask Maxine about it. I gave her my card…How did you find out about this?" I asked.

"Someone phoned in a noise disturbance and the beat cop found this," said Barker.

"I had a call to my office early this morning. All I could hear was some screaming and then the line went dead. Is there a payphone near here?"

"Just up the block in front of Murphy's"

I went out and looked at the path leading that direction carefully walking along the side of the path until I found what I was looking for.

"Niosi, look here. Look at the struggle in the dirt. Someone was dragged to that shack and they didn't go willingly."

"Rather convenient you finding that," said Barker.

"No, this was the sort of stuff that Gillem was the best in the business at. It is why he made detective so early in his career. So why were you talking to Molly?"

"Um, my brother-in-law was worried when she didn't show up for work," I said hoping that the half-truth would hold and Will would cover my ass if they called him.

"If you don't have any other questions, I should probably tell Will what happened," I said figuring this would tell me how they were going to play this.

"Okay, but don't leave town," said Barker.

I nodded and left. The shantytown was not too far from the racetrack so I hoofed it to the stables to find Will going through the order of the day since this afternoon was the biggest race of the year.

He sent everyone off and said, "Well it's not good news."

"Molly is dead. Cops found her this morning beaten to death in shantytown. I think Renard had a hand in it. But I have a question for you. Molly told me that she stole a page out of a breeder's book to give to Lucky. Any reason you can think why Lucky wanted the page?"

"Probably to get a leg up on betting, but that is a damn strange thing to steal. Did she say which book?"

"No, but five will get you ten it was out of Renard's stable. What sort of information would it contain?"

"Sire, Dam, time and date of birth. Most of the horse's family tree for breeding purposes. Each trainer keeps their books differently. Most of it looks like code that only makes sense to the stable master."

"Thanks, Will. And the cops are probably going to be calling you so you asked me to check up on Molly."

Will groaned, "Why me? What did you do?"

"Nothing. I talked to Molly and then she ended up dead. That doesn't sit well with me."

"Losing one of my best riders doesn't sit well with me either. Find out who did this."

I nodded and walked out only to almost run into Trouble who was walking on Rex's arm. He was surrounded by reporters talking about Captain Sea-legs who was the best three-year-old that he has ever had the pleasure to own.

Trouble looked at me and shook her head slightly.

I stepped out of the way and walked out of the stable with more questions than answers.

I hailed a cab and had it take me to the Golden Hine.

I knocked on the door and was very surprised it was opened by a bleary-eyed Cedric."What could you possibly want at this hour?" he said with a groan.

"Is Lucky's bookie still here?"

"Ask Maxine," he said letting me through the door and quickly shutting it behind him.

I walked in and saw that the cleaning crew was finishing up picking up the mess from the night before.

Maxine was at her table in a dressing gown. Her wig was on a stand next to her. Her make-up was not ready for company and almost worn off. She looked like rough road.

"What?" she said in a low voice of too many cigarettes and singing the night before.

"I need to talk to Lucky's bookie. I think I know why Molly was killed but I need to talk to them before the running of the race today."

"Molly's dead?"

"Strangled with her own braid and her face beaten to a pulp," I said. "Poor kid. Damn Lucky for getting her mixed up in who knows what. That boy is bad news start to finish,"

Maxine motioned to Phil and the bartender came over to her table.

"Is Lou still in?" she asked.

"Yeah and still taking bets for some reason. I thought he would have closed out by this point."

"You think he might have a hot tip," I said.

Both of them looked at me.

"Go get Lou," said Maxine, "And accept no excuse Phil."

In short order Phil returned with Lou who was definitely not happy about being summoned.

If you looked up bookie in the dictionary, I swear you would find a picture of Lou. He was short and dumpy with thinning hair being made to look fuller with a lot of citrus scented pomade. He had ink stained fingers. His face was rat like with very beady eyes that kept shifting back and forth. He had a permanent hunch from his years as a bookie only adding to his rat like qualities. I will give him this: he has never been caught by the cops all the years he has been taking numbers. In fact, I know he was the go-to bookie for a number of cops and city officials.

"What!?" he said. "This is probably the busiest day of business for me and you summon me? What the hell? I give you your cut. I am losing money just standing here."

"Where is Lucky O'Toole?"

"How the hell should I know where that loser is and why should I even care?"

"Because he passed on some valuable information to you," I said, "Now one person is dead and Lucky is missing. How soon before he gives you up to whoever has him and they come looking for you?" I said.

"I swear on my mother's grave that I don't know what you are talking about," said Lou.

"Your mother is alive and you visit her every Sunday," said Maxine, "Now I strongly suggest you come clean on it."

"I wasn't lying. My mother's grave is right next to my dead departed father's grave. It's a family plot."

"What did Lucky tell you?" I said in a very measured tone.

"He's told me a lot of things over the years. Some of it was good and some of it was worthless."

"About today's race," I said knowing that he was going to

weasel his way through this whole conversation.

"He said he had proof that there was an illegal horse in the race."

"Illegal horse? How the hell can you have an illegal horse use a llama instead?" asked Phil.

"There are some races that are reserved for horses of a certain age. The triple crown is only opened to three-year olds as is the Barnard Sweepstakes, which is one of the entry races to run in for a chance to run in the Kentucky Derby," I said.

"Rex has been trying to do that for years. Although his horses have won, they haven't been picked to go for one reason or another," said Maxine.

"But this year he has a horse that has a lot of buzz in Captain Sea-legs. If his horse wins, he is a shoe-in for the Derby," said Phil.

"What's wrong with the horse?" I asked.

"I don't know. Lucky came to me all excited because he said he could prove Rex was cheating which would invalidate the race results. He called me saying he had proof but he never showed up," said Lou.

"You're betting against Sea-legs aren't you? Once the race is invalidated you get to keep all those bets," I said.

Lou smiled and I really wish he hadn't. Not an image I want to keep in my mind.

"You trusted Lucky?" said Maxine.

"Nope. But considering the extent that some people are going to stop the information from getting out, I would say it's a pretty safe bet," he said with a giggle.

"Get him out of my sight, Phil. And Lou, I would start looking for another office like yesterday," said Maxine.

"Wait. I want to see his books for today," I said.

"No way," said Lou, "I have a duty to my clients."

Phil pulled Lou's arm up behind his back, convincing him to give up the book.

Of course, it was in code but I recognized a phone number instantly.

I ran out and grabbed a cab back to the racetrack.

I WENT into Will's office to find him drinking a nice pull of scotch.

"Tell me that you aren't mix up in this," I said.

"What are you talking about, Laurence?"

"I found Lucky's bookie and had a look at his current list of numbers. I recognized your office number right off the bat."

"So I placed some bets," he said.

I slammed my hand down on his desk hard, "No! People have died over this. This is not just making a score. You are an accessory to murder unless you can explain to me why your number was on Lou's list."

"I let Lucky make his bets from

my phone. He would give me a cut of his winnings. I had nothing to do with whatever hair brain scheme got Molly killed. I am heartbroken over that."

"Do you know what Lucky found?"

"No. And I never asked. I didn't want Rex's eye to land on me."

"So, where is he?"

"Sorry?"

"Unless you have been making a series of bets today. Where is Lucky?"

He sighed, "Okay. he's hiding in the stable boy's quarters actually in a hidden room behind the quarters."

"Take me to him."

Will pulled a set of keys out of the desk and said, "Come on."

"Hold on, "I said picking up the phone and calling the precinct getting Sean.

"I believe I have information of illegal activity at the racetrack," I said, "and possibly the murder of Molly Lemont. Have Williamson meet me at the racetrack in about an hour."

Will took me to the stable boy's quarters and unlocked the door. He relocked it behind him and said, "Help me with this bunk."

We moved the bunk and Will opened the hidden door and there sleeping on a cot was the missing rather rumpled Lucky O'Toole.

I walked in and kicked the cot, "Get up, you jerk."

"What?"

"Do you know how much trouble you are in? Your sister is worried sick."

"I told her I was going to be gone for a while," he said after sitting up and rubbing his eyes.

"Where's the page?"

"Sorry?"

I grabbed him by the collar and hauled him to his feet, "The page you got from Molly that got her killed."

All the color went out of his face, "Molly's dead?"

"And I am betting your brother-in-law is the instigator. Now where is that goddamn page?"

He reached into his pocket and handed me an envelope.

"Now we are going to talk to the police or to Rex."

"Oh hell no. I have no wish to be a dead man which will happen either way."

"Will, can you go find Trouble and Rex and bring them to your office? We have half an hour before the cops arrive for their murderer,"

I grabbed Lucky to keep him from running and marched him up to Will's office.

I pulled a set of handcuffs out of my pocket and cuffed him to one of the stout oak chair.

"You got to let me go! He'll kill me if he knew what I was doing."

"He did know. He just couldn't find you. Tried to use your sister to find you and she failed so then she came to me."

Rex entered with Trouble. They both stopped short when they saw Lucky.

Rex took two steps towards Lucky with his hand raised and I stopped him.

"No Rex. This is not how this is going to play out. I am giving you a chance here to make this all right. If you don't, I think even your lawyers are going to have a hard time keeping you from jail time."

"What do you mean?"

I held up the paper that Lucky stole, "Too many people now know or suspect what is on this piece of paper. Captain was born a year earlier than your current papers on him state. He's a four-year-old and therefore ineligible for this race."

Rex's face turned a dangerous shade of red and stammered a bit before Trouble got him to sit down and take a drink of water.

"Here's how this is going to play out. This is easy. Captain Sea-legs came up lame while training. He's not ready to run today. You are going to give me your associate who killed Molly so I can pass him onto the police."

"Why should I do that?"

"To retain your reputation among the racing horse owners, of course. If it comes out that you tried to fudge his age, you will be blackballed. No track will accept your horses to run. That source of your income will dry up entirely. Oh, I know you have other rackets going so you won't be a pauper but this would put a serious dent in your social standing within the community which is a little shaky

right now anyway."

"Also you will let Lucky leave the city alive and unmolested. Give him a sum of money to compensate him for his hard work. And he agrees never to come back here again."

Trouble said, "No! You can't do that."

"Would you rather your brother be alive out in the world or dead in prison here? Rex can press charges for the theft of his property and then there is the matter of his sport bets which would definitely be of great interest to the police and the prosecutors not to mention the bettors who would be losing money on the race."

She knelt next to her brother and said, "I guess I can't protect you from everything, baby brother."

She kissed his temple and said, "Rex would you mind if I left? I am not feeling well."

"Sure doll, have Sydney take you home and could you have Seamus come up here?"

She kissed him and nodded.

She turned to me before she left the room and said, "Job well done, Mr. Ginnell. I will have the rest of your payment sent to your office. I hope we never see each other again."

Then Trouble walked through the door and out of my life.

The rest was pretty much textbook.

Will pulled the Captain out of the race due to an injury that had not healed yet.

Seamus, who was the guy in the alley, confessed to the murder of Molly.

Lucky vanished from the city never to be seen again but rumor had it that he had met his end on the wrong side of a gun after a bad bet.

And I found myself at loose ends in my office, cleaning my gun, wondering if it was all worth a tinker's damn.

Hate Hop

By LESTER DENT

"WHAT'S the idea, bud?" A hand flung out of the darkness, clamped on big Clack Waters' arm.

Not looking around, Clack wrenched, got free. He knew the strikingly pretty blonde he was leaving the dance with belonged to some other fellow. He didn't know who. He didn't care. But this was probably the man.

Clack, final training tests at Issoudun passed, was en route to the Ninetieth Observation Squadron at the front, and he intended this one night in Paris to be a celebration that *was* a celebration. That the captivating blonde was a necessity in the festivities, he had firmly decided, and she seemed to agree. Holding her arm, he dived for the deeper darkness further down the garden walk.

But the man behind kicked Clack's left foot sharply and it flew over, hooking his other leg so that he sprawled ignominiously to the gravel walk. He jerked erect, bony fingers made into big, square fists.

The man who had tripped him was scrawny, thin of face. His eyes stuck out in an angry glare and a snarl held his lips skinned off big teeth. He had the strappings of a lieutenant and, over his left breast, the half a wing of an observer, Air Service, A. E. F.

Clack blinked, incredulity on his homely face, then snorted his contempt.

"Runt Lee!" he gritted. "And you haven't changed a bit since you went to high school. Tripping kids was your idea of fun. Trip 'em and run. Remember how I licked you once for it?"

Runt Lee sneered through his teeth. "Clack Waters, the boy hero of the factory toughs! Yeah, I remember—and it's my girl you've got!"

He shot forward, right arm out rigid before him. His fist hit a little above the buckle of Clack's Sam Browne belt. Breath went out of Clack's lungs in a hoarse roar. He upset into the shrubbery beside the path, his big frame winding into a ball of agony.

The blonde clapped both shapely hands over her open mouth, but did not scream.

Face greenish, Clack untied himself, came upright.

"You dirty little rat!" he croaked.

He threw his left fist at Runt Lee's head. Runt ducked—ducked into Clack's other fist as it whistled up from a start close to his heels. Runt squawked and fell down.

Clack lunged, seized his collar, gritted: "Get up and take the rest!

Illustration by Tom Mandrake

You got my old man fired from your dad's factory the last fight we had! I'll take that out of your hide, too!"

Runt embraced Clack's legs, threw him. They rolled in the gravel, swapping blows. Runt got fingers into Clack's eyes, gouged. Clack used a knee. Runt squealed.

Off the walk, they flailed, into shrubbery. But the scrap was too unequal to last. Clack was a head taller, forty pounds heavier, with muscles tremendously larger. He landed a half dozen terrific blows with one hand, then the other. Runt Lee subsided, breath bubbling through his shredded lips and mashed nose.

Clack came out of the shrubbery grinning with all his homely face, pulling down the front of his coat, straightening his Sam Browne. The sobbing dance music inside the chateau—the Paris home of some American whose name Clack didn't even know—seemed to have covered the conflict sounds.

The blonde had not moved and her hands were still over her mouth. Clack took her arm, rushed her bodily down the walk to the exit.

"That's a swell start for one night!" he chuckled. "I've been aching to do that for seven years—ever since I last saw the little whistlepants. Who'd have thought I'd find him here in France, even a half-wing buzzard."

The blonde twisted, hissed: "You beast!" Her open hand, driven with all her strength, popped against Clack's mouth.

Clack grunted explosively, peered at her in the dim light of the street, demanded: "Now, is that any way to act, sister?"

"You brute!" she clipped. "Mr. Lee and I are engaged and we had a quarrel tonight and I only went with you to make him angry. And you—you beat him! You big ape!"

She slapped at him again. Clack, expecting something like that, dodged successfully. The blonde, sobbing loudly, pivoted, ran into the street, stopped a taxi and got aboard.

Clack, big fists jammed against his hips, glared at her departing taxi.

"Hell's bells!" he gritted. "These women!"

THE tarmac of the Ninetieth Observation Squadron, A. E. F., was a former French beet field between Chateau Thierry and Soissons. A wall of trees fenced the west side of the field and four hangars, splotched with green camouflage, squatted close to the trees. Deeper in the woods, also green-splotched, sprawled wooden Adrian huts used for barracks and offices and photo darkrooms.

War-sack over his shoulder, walking toward the operations office, Clack Waters took in the—to him—new scene with the avidness of a ten-year-old at his first circus. He was in the Zone of Advance at last. At the front!

A De Havilland two-seater, Liberty motored, was taxying around the field, a mechanic in the cockpit blooping the engine, testing it. In the shade of a hangar, an observer was dropping cartridges into the dismounted breech of a machine gun, testing them for size, then feeding them into a hand-operated belt-filling machine.

The *crump* of an occasional big gun came from the direction of the front; where two orange observation balloons were visible, hanging in the sky like fat grub worms.

A man came out of a darkroom hut ahead of Clack. He saw Clack, stiffened belligerently.

"You—again!" Clack grated.

Runt Lee sneered with swollen lips. "HQ must be hard up when they send us the likes of you!"

Clack made a gargling noise in his throat, dropped his war-sack. Fists raised, he hesitated. He knew a fight would mean time in the guardhouse. That didn't deter him. But he was at the critical stage of a flier's training, the stage where his every move was watched to determine whether he was fit for his wings. And Clack had left Issoudun with less than the usual number of hours upstairs. Getting off on the wrong foot might mean this squadron CO would shoot him back to school, or even ask his transfer to another branch of the service. Things like that had been known to happen. And Runt Lee was the kind of a fellow who would have a stand-in with those in authority. A teacher's pet. He had always been that.

Clack jammed his teeth together until they ached. He hated Runt Lee, hated him with more malice than was good for the soul of any man. He wracked his brain for some verbal barrage that would hurt Runt as badly as the blows he ached to land. He had it!

"That blonde of yours," he smirked. "She's got a nice body!" He grinned lewdly, added: "We had a hell of a night."

Blood drained out of Runt Lee's face until it was gray, corpse-like. He trembled so that his fists, held close in front of him, beat against his chest. Still shaking, he gritted, "I'm not through with you! No, I'm not."

He wheeled, stumbled blindly away.

Clack Waters, staring after him, licked his lips, mumbled, "Maybe I laid that on a little thick." Then his face bulged with angrily drawn muscles. "Damned if I did! The crummy rat got my dad fired from his old man's factory because I licked him when we were kids!"

He went to the operations office, found Major Maske, the CO.

Major Maske was a big man, solid looking, with a big nose, a big mouth and pale brown eyes as hard and brassy as the rumps of Vickers cartridges under his shaggy, sand-colored brows. He looked at Clack's papers, frowned, tossed the logbook back across the field desk.

"That does not show enough time upstairs!" he crisped. "They don't feed the pursuit squadrons men with as little training as that. Why should we be the goats?"

Clack grinned, said: "I'm sure I'll make it all right, sir."

"You would! They all think so." Major Maske picked up the chewed stub of a cigar, lit it, coughed out gray smoke. "The last four men they've sent us have been undertrained. Two of those have already lost us good ships and better observers. And all of the four had more time upstairs than your log shows. I told HQ explicitly that this squadron was no place for men with no front-line experience. And they send me you with none at all and only a few hours solo. Damned if I haven't got a notion to send you back!"

Clack changed feet uneasily. "But—don't I get a chance?"

Major Maske growled, threw his cigar through the door. "If I send you back, I'll get another one like you, probably." He grinned sheepishly. "No reflection on you, Waters. I boil over this way regularly when I see you young chaps sent up here raw with a dozen hours in the air, sometimes less. We've been having hell lately. The Boche have twice as many pursuit ships here as we have. The protection our pursuit squadrons are able to give us don't amount to a damn. We—" He stopped abruptly.

THE exhaust roar of planes dropping out of the sky throbbed across the tarmac outside, and a Klaxon hooter moaned. An Archie barked gruffly.

Machine guns opened a bedlam rattle.

"Now what the hell!?" Major Maske charged for the door.

Clack flung out of the operations office, treading his heels. At the tarmac edge, a machine gun on a wheel mount was swallowing an ammo belt and spewing smoking brass cartridge cases.

A De Havilland two-seater swooped, wobbling, for the tarmac. Hounding its tail, spewing Spandau lead, came a moaning wedge of gaudily painted Boche Fokkers. The observer huddled, not moving, in the D.H. rear cockpit. His pilot obviously was wounded, fighting the controls with last ebbings of strength.

The D.H. came down too hard, bounced. The undercarriage did an accordion. The D.H. skewered, wings losing shape. Came a great popping and tearing and dust enveloped the crack-up.

The Boche pursuits exploded out of formation and swirled over the Ninetieth dome like gaudy fall leaves in a whirlwind. The bawl of motors, the howl of flying wires, the clatter of rapid-firers, was deafening. Lead hammered hangars, traveled back and forth across the tarmac with angry spattings. Clack flattened precipitously as metal squealed in his ears. Through the thick of it, a crash and fire bus scooted clanging for the cracked D.H.

As suddenly as they had arrived, the German brood boiled away, flying low, carrying with them a stormy roar of following ground fire.

The crash bus clanged away with both occupants of the D.H. before Clack and Major Maske reached the washed-out ship. Major Maske asked a question.

"Shot up bad, sir," an armorer answered. "But they've both got a chance to pull through, the pill pusher said."

After a bit, Major Maske caught Clack's eye and gestured at the operations office with his chin.

"In a way, they're lucky—they got back," he said as they walked. "You see who we're up against, Waters. The Boche have enough ships to gang us. They split, some engaging the pursuit ships up to protect us, the others jumping our observation crates. The Germans must be cooking up an offensive, for they're taking unusual measures to keep our observation busses out of the air. This is no place for a raw man to pile up his first hundred hours."

Clack wiped sweat off his face, said nothing. He had just found a pair of small holes in the skirts of his uniform coat—holes that hadn't been there a few minutes before. He had known one of those squealing Spandau bursts had come close, but not that close.

"Well?" Major Maske demanded sharply.

Clack grinned faintly, said: "It's something like I expected."

Major Maske frowned. "I'll let you go over the lines in the morning and I'll go along in another bus and see how you make it. The first time usually tells the tale. This business seems to take a particular brand of guts. Either a man has them, or he hasn't."

Clack's grin widened. "Thank you, sir! Thank you!"

"Lieutenant Lee will be your observer."

The grin went off Clack's face. He gulped explosively: "But—!"

Major Maske, after waiting for him to go on, asked harshly, "But—what?"

"I—well, I know Runt—Lieutenant Lee. We're not exactly friends. Couldn't I have a different observer?"

"Nonsense!" snapped Major Maske. "Lee is the best observer in the squadron. He already has six Boche planes and some remarkable work directing gunfire to his credit. You couldn't have a better man with you. And if there's bad feeling between you two, forget it! Forget it, see! I won't have friction among the members of my squadron."

Clack nodded, said: "Yes, sir."

DAWN. Gray fog swirling with the morning breeze. Smoke columns oozing upward from cook shacks on both sides of the lines. The sun, fresh and warm in D.H. cockpits.

Flying at eight thousand, Clack Waters hung his chin over the padded cockpit rim, getting his first look at the lines; long scratches in the brown earth that were the trenches, water-filled shell holes that were like spilled pearls. Whatever enchantment the view might have held was dispelled by a lone Boche anti-aircraft gun that was opening successive wooly bears below and ahead.

"Getting our range!" Clack growled. "That gun has probably got brothers that'll give us hell when they have us located."

To the right, sunlight glanced a silver sheen from the wings of the D.H. in which Major Maske and his observer rode. Overhead, at near sixteen thousand, a flight of Yank pursuit ships jockeyed the stringy fringes of a cirrus cloud, watching for Hun falcons.

Major Maske threw an arm above his head, stirred with it. Obediently, Clack banked a lazy circle. He glanced into the rear cockpit; saw Runt Lee's right shoulder shaking as he pounded the radio key.

Looking down, Clack made out the location of the battery they were to direct fire for. The battery had a ground panel staked out. Clack consulted his panel chart. They were displaying the "ready to fire" signal.

The target would be that Archie battery pegging high explosive upstairs. Major Maske had told him that. It was a big battery, a constant source of trouble. Watching, Clack could see the stabbing red tongue of the one firing gun.

"This ought to be simple," Clack decided. He relaxed, gave his attention to keeping the D.H. level and circling. He saw the Yank battery whisk out the "battery has fired" panel, saw their burst explode to the left and beyond the flame-stabbing Boche gun.

Clack grinned. "This is a pipe!"

Wham! Sky fell out from under his D.H. The ship wallowed crazily, sank over on one wing. Overhead, a great wad of citrous smoke swelled outward.

Wham! Another Archie opened ahead. *Wham! Wham! Wham!* They were on the sides, behind. The Jerries had them boxed, were squeezing in the sides of the box.

What to do? Clack had learned the answer to that one in school. Dive! That was the quickest way out of the box, and the Boche could not correct their range downward as easily. Major Maske was already diving. Clack hit the instrument board with the stick.

Wires shrieking, the D.H. pitched down through hot, acrid cordite stink. Clack pulled up, safely below the Archie bursts, and swung on the tail of Major Maske's ship.

He lifted his gaze. At the sixteen thousand level, winged specks now swirled in the stringy vapor of the cirrus, darting, stabbing.

Part of a Boche circus had jumped the guarding Yank pursuits. There should be another flight of Hun falcons somewhere. Clack scanned the sky, searching anxiously.

He saw them abruptly, and the sight brought a grin. The Boche were to the north, a plunging duck-flight line of them. But dropping to meet them were more Yank buzzards who had been hanging around for exactly that.

"It's not going to work this time!" Clack chuckled.

HE swung as an Archibald opened close to them, swung deeper into Germany.

Then—the Liberty missed!

Listening, Clack knew two or more cylinders had stopped functioning. The tach needle was retreating as the engine lost speed.

Clack goosed the throttle frantically. That did not help. The sick engine did not have power enough to keep them upstairs. That meant only one thing—hoick for home. He eyed the instrument panel. Fuel okay. Oil the same. It must be in the ignition, wires cut by a shell fragment, perhaps.

He banked for France.

Came a pounding of fists on the camelback. Clack twisted. Runt Lee was standing, gesturing to remain in Germany.

"The engine!" Clack yelled. "It's half conked! Listen to it miss!"

Runt Lee waved his arms, squawked: "The engine is okay, damn you! Go back! There's no Boche near! There's nothing wrong with the engine. Go back!"

Clack eyed the tach. It showed bare idling speed. He shook his head.

"The hell there's nothing wrong! It's barely turning over!"

Wham! A wooly bear opened under them, heaved them over in the sky. Clack turned in the bucket, leveled the sodden D.H. facing the rear cockpit again; he noted Major Maske's ship alongside, the major eyeing them wonderingly.

Runt Lee was still standing, gesturing to go back. And now he had a flat, black automatic in his hand.

"You dirty, yellow coward!" he shrieked. "You're running for home. Go back!"

The other D.H. swung in, almost locking wings with them. And Major Maske was standing in his cockpit, staring.

Clack, eyes on the major, jerked his left hand at the sick motor. With his right hand he fumbled for the fire extinguisher, wrenched the canister out of its clips.

He twisted suddenly, threw the fire extinguisher at Runt Lee. It hit the flat automatic, knocked it back into Runt's face. Automatic and fire extinguisher fell overboard. Runt screeched, shook his fists, blood stringing from the reopened cuts in his lips.

Clack, grim-faced, headed the wobbling D.H. for the Ninetieth tarmac.

Major Maske followed him, crouched in his cockpit, staring

about alertly, often upward at the two dogfights in progress.

They crossed the lines. Boche Archie ceased to burst around them. Looking back, Clack saw the two gangs of Hun falcons scattering back into Germany.

Below, an orange kite balloon was being inflated behind a canvas windscreen, sand bags sticking to it like clusters of brown fruit. Clack frowned at the kite, ground his teeth.

"Damn this motor!" he croaked.

The plane was losing altitude steadily. He kept the throttle against the pin, nursing the ship along. The Ninetieth tarmac swung beneath.

Clack nosed down—and the Liberty suddenly started firing in all cans!

Incredulous, Clack sawed the throttle. The engine was working perfectly now! The tach needle rapidly climbed to where it should be. He banked to return.

But Major Maske swung in ahead, waggling his wings, ordering a descent.

Clack went down, three-pointed perfectly on the tarmac. The other D.H. rolled alongside and its motor sobbed dead. Major Maske swung out, walked over, stiff-legged.

"Well?" he asked shortly. "Why'd you come back? There wasn't an enemy ship near you and you were clear of that Archie."

"The motor, sir," Clack said. "It began missing badly, almost stopped. It came okay up there when I started to turn back."

Major Maske stared him up and down. Clack reddened. The Major said, "Lieutenant Lee, why did he hit you?"

Runt Lee, holding a handkerchief against his mouth, took it away to say "There was nothing wrong with the motor, sir. He showed yellow and ran. I was trying to make him turn back, and he hit me with that pyrene."

"You lying rat!" Clack roared. He lunged. His big fist, hitting, covered all the lower part of Runt Lee's face. Runt bounced from the blow, hit the fuselage of the D.H. with a hollow boom of taut fabric, flopped forward loosely on his face and did not get up.

Major Maske ripped an order. Half a dozen greaseballs rushed Clack. He knocked the first one rolling with a fist in the pit of the stomach. Then some of his red rage evaporated and he allowed himself to be pinioned.

"Lee lied!" he grated. "'Member I told you we don't like each other. Well, he's trying to get me in a jam."

Major Maske said, "Shut up!"

"The engine went bad, I tell you—"

"Shut up!" Major Maske's face was purple, his shoulders great knots of muscle, his voice a roar. "Somebody look at that motor!"

A man cut the ignition, uncowled the Liberty, inspected the gleaming cylinder banks. Climbing onto the wings, he doubled under the oil-pan belly of the engine. He stepped back at last.

"There's no loose wires, sir," he said positively. "It seems to be in perfect condition."

Clack opened his mouth, began: "But—"

"Shut up, damn you!" Major Maske bellowed. "Is there any evidence that the engine was hit by an Archie burst?"

"No," said the man who had looked. "There is not a single hole in the cowling."

Major Maske came over, hard-footed, and stood in front of Clack.

"You're under arrest, Waters. You will be transferred to another branch of the service as soon as possible. In the meantime, you will remain in your quarters. You are—"

His face bloodless, Clack objected: "That engine almost stopped. That's the truth."

Major Maske continued coldly, as if he had not heard. "You are getting off easily. There have been instances of men being shot for cowardice. You will take your meals in your quarters. I am sure the men of this squadron will not care for your presence."

CLACK crashed the door shut after he was inside his Adrian hut, sat on the edge of the cot, took his head in both hands.

"The dirty, stinking louse!" he gritted. "He's sure played hell with my playhouse!" In a hoarse, rage-cracked voice, he cursed Runt Lee roundly, blasphemously, with everything he could think of, taking up Runt's ancestors, accusing them of every foul vice that came to his tongue, only stopping when his throat was sore, his voice a guttering whisper. Then he lay back on the cot and smoked rapidly, lighting one cigarette off another.

The pile of discarded butts grew. Noon came and nobody brought him food and he made no effort to have any brought. The afternoon dragged. Planes came and went on the tarmac.

Several times armorers fired test bursts from machine guns. A mechanic hammered a stubborn bolt, cursed. There was some laughter and bantering as mail was distributed. Always, there was an undertone of distant thumping and rumbling from the front.

Clack slept some, to awake in darkness and comparative quiet. Through the one window, he could see splotches of moon-silvered night sky. It was nine o'clock, long past the hour of the evening meal. Somewhere down the line of barracks huts men were singing to a banjo.

He opened the door, sat on the threshold. The night was warm, with the slightest of breezes. The tang of gasoline came faintly from the direction of the tarmac. When the telephone rang in the operations office, he plainly heard the jangle.

The words of the man who answered it were an unintelligible murmur, but mounting in excitement. Then the Klaxon hooter honked out. Barracks huts spewed men. They charged past, headed for the operations office. Clack got up, hesitated, sat down again.

He heard Major Maske shout: "Boche ships are strafing the pursuit drome to the south of us. Another flight has been sighted, two-seaters, headed this way. HQ says for us to get ships upstairs. They've got an idea this strafing is meant to keep everybody out of the air while a Gotha flight goes over, headed for Paris."

Clack stood up suddenly. From the direction of the front, planes were coming. And over the motor sound he could hear the rattle of Maxims, the thumping of Archies.

"Here they come!" Major Maske bawled. "Upstairs, you monkeys!"

Clack hesitated, gritted, "To hell with this arrest business!" and sprinted for the tarmac edge.

He reached it in time to see a camouflage-gaudied Albatross come sliding down through the moonlight at a hangar and glance upward, followed by a great, spreading toadstool of black smoke full of shattered wood and metal which floated and fell down.

More German ships trailed it. Ground machine guns bayed out deafeningly. The earth jerked with the concussion of more bombs exploding. Maltese-crossed wings seemed to fill the sky. They were all two-seaters, ships for which the De Havillands, once they were in the air, would be more than a match.

Clack ran to a hangar, helped trundle out a D.H. He was back in the hangar after another when a bomb let loose outside and part of the hangar fell in on him. There was a cursing uproar, but nobody seemed badly hurt. Bruised some, bleeding from a skinned nose, Clack waded out in the open again.

He saw Major Maske vault into a warming D.H. and, with nobody in the rear cockpit, successfully take off. Another ship followed him. Another. Two Boche Albatrosses pounced on the fourth, hosing it with lead, and the crate went a flamer half way across the tarmac, stopping, a great, waving scarlet plume, among the trees that edged the drome.

Clack helped roll more ships out of the remaining hangars. Once, pushing beside the rear cockpit, he seized the twin Lewis guns, swung them on the tourelle mount and drove a long burst at a diving Jerry. The Hun sheered off, wobbling and streaked for home, evidently hit.

Another D.H. scooted across the tarmac. A Boche dived on it, Spandaus cackling. The D.H. bogged to a stop, the motor slowing to idling speed. The pilot threshed, fell over the cockpit rim, flopped about on the ground. The man in the rear jumped out, hunkered beside him.

Clack sprinted for the ship. A backward glance showed no other pilot near. He flung past the kneeling man and the flopping one on the ground and plugged his bulk into the forward cockpit.

A man yelled at him as he batted the throttle. He paid no attention. The D.H. leaped, gathered speed. As the trees slapped at him, Clack dragged the ship up, got it over. He banked as soon as he dared; grabbing altitude then turned his head.

A man was in the rear cockpit—the man who had been kneeling beside the wounded pilot.

Undersized Runt Lee!

"**T**HE little stinker!" Clack ground savagely. "Ran for home this morning, did I? I'll show him some running that is!"

He knocked the D.H. at a Kraut Albatross bus, squeezing out lead. The Boche waltzed to get away. Clack ringed him again—again. The German ship pitched, suddenly flailed downward to a certain crash.

Clack twisted, squawled: "You can tell 'em that one committed suicide, you lying rat!"

He flung the D.H. for the dogfight melee over the Ninetieth tarmac. Lewis guns hammered behind him. He rolled his head around, saw Runt Lee screwing slowly in the cockpit, his twin Lewis guns smoking at the breech, empties rattling in the canvas catch bags.

Moonlight flashed on the dot-and-circles cockades of a D.H. looping tightly to get on the tail of a pursuing black-crossed bus. Another Boche dived on the D.H.; Clack drove for that one, guns a-chatter. The German flailed away from the deadly hail and Clack chased him into the thick of the bird battle before the fellow got away.

Lead suddenly stormed about him. The left-wing bank became spottily ragged in the moon glimmer. He banked. Lead gnashed the fuselage frame somewhere.

Runt Lee's Lewis pair hammered successive ten and fifteen shot bursts that sounded like a kid jabbing a pencil into an electric fan. Head turned, Clack saw one of the Hun pack who had jumped them climb straight up for five hundred feet, then tail-slip down, gas tanks belching great flame sheets.

Runt Lee looked at Clack, sneered: "His engine went bad, didn't it, you yellow ape?"

Clack squawked a curse, rose up in the cockpit, fists doubled. But a D.H. got in front of them and Clack was forced to grab the controls to avoid a head-on smash. Only one of the other D.H. cockpits was occupied. The man in it—Major Maske. He glared at them as he went past, missing them by yards.

"Damn the luck!" Clack bit off.

He pitched their bus at a German, lost him. The sky scrap was drifting away from the Ninetieth tarmac, toward Germany. A Yank spiraled out of the melee, motor dead. A Boche followed him in short order, out of control.

It was an even scrap, about as matched as such affairs ever are. The Jerries had the edge in numbers, the Yanks a little less in their faster sky wagons. They were all two-seaters, for the Boche had apparently sent their observation busses to strafe observation squadrons.

Clack rushed another Hun, Vickers shuttling. The German crate fell out of the sky. Clack started down after him, to make certain the kill.

"Got enough of it, have you?" came Runt Lee's shrilled insult.

Clack cursed, oaths so harsh they tore throat tissue. He yanked the D.H. up, never seeing whether the Boche crashed. Back into the bat fight he piled.

Clouds hung low in Germany, cauliflower clouds, beginning almost over the lines, their upper surface less than a mile up. The Boche, openly retreating now, slowly climbed above the level of the clouds.

An Albatross, side-slipping, skidded in front of Clack's eyes. His fingers lightened on the Bowden trips. His feet sawed the rudder. Both Huns sagged in their cockpits and the Albatross cartwheeled dizzily.

Clack snarled: "Well?"

Runt Lee jerked a fist at the D.H. from which the Albatross had been side-slipping. "Trying to hog somebody else's credit, eh?"

Clack drove a fist at Runt Lee. Runt dodged, sat back where he could not be reached. Then the D.H. wallowed, took the loose controls and Clack had his hands full.

They were over the front now, above the clouds, from a Yank ship, a Very stitched colored fireballs. The signal—"Enemy ships near!"

Clack grinned thinly. Irony, that. Enemy ships near! They were everywhere! Then, abruptly, he saw what the rocket was meant to indicate. Great, winged monsters sweeping over the cloud carpet toward them. Gothas! The German bombers headed for Paris!

DE Havillands of the Yank squadron spilled through the moonlight toward the string of ponderous, multi-motored Gothas. And swarming over them, harrying them, pursued the surviving Boche two-seaters. No even odds, this! The German ships outnumbered Yank buggies three to one.

Clack whipped headlong at a multi-motored giant. Spandau lead shrieked about him, splintered a strut, clipped a flying wire, dug long rips in the wing fabric. Thorny customers, these Gothas. They had guns in front and behind, almost no blind spots. Another D.H. helped him gang the bomber. It blew up in the sky, a great cloud of smoke and splinters, one of its bombs lead-tapped. The D.H. heaved in the disturbed air. Clack leveled.

At his back, Runt Lee suddenly screeched. Spandau iron shocked the fuselage. Clack kicked left rudder—and the leg with which he kicked raised up almost in front of his face. His pants leg got mysteriously ragged. Something invisible tore holes in his left boot. Glass, metal, splinters from the instrument panel beat his chest and face. Then came pain, ghastly agony that wracked through his body, tied him in cramped knots.

The D.H., uncontrolled, fell out of the deadly Spandau lead stream. Clack lurched forward, forehead ramming the crash pad, both hands pincered about his bullet-riddled leg, eyelids pushed tightly shut. Torturous curtains of red swam in his eyeballs.

The rush of air against the side of his head told of a slip. Then the insane pound of more Spandau lead brought him back to reality. He straightened. A Gotha was floating past, fore and aft guns tipped with hungry crimson tongues. Above the Gotha, a D.H. dived, squirting tracer, one man hunched in the cockpit. Major Maske was still upstairs!

Clack rammed the stick ahead, booted the rudder with the one of his legs he could move. His two-seater heaved down. But smoke squeezed out of the cowl vents, black, foul wriggling yarns of the stuff. A gush of hot red jumped through the smoke yarns. Another.

They were afire!

Clack cut the ignition, twisted up, squawled: "My leg—shot to hell! See if you can get up here and help me with this rudder!"

But Runt Lee did not answer. He was loose in the rear bucket, head tipped back, eyes rolling madly, and the whole front of his coat was ragged and redly besodden.

Clack sat down again, booting first one rudder stirrup then the other with his good leg. He got the D.H. slipping steeply. They plunged into the clouds and, after several minutes of rushing, welcome dampness, out again below the vapor blanket.

Clack stared down. Another burning ship was falling a thousand feet below. A Gotha. It made a tremendous blaze, spreading fitful light over the German countryside. A field lay to the right, a field large enough to land several squadrons in. It was encircled by timbered country, the timber pocked with small clearings.

Clack gritted: "If this gas tank don't go!"

The fire was in the engine, probably where Spandau lead had ruptured the carburetors. But it was spreading steadily, jagged sheets squirming out of the cowl and licking hungrily around the firewall. Blackened fabric, curling, fell off the fuselage, off the lower wing banks close in and off the upper wing center-section. The heat was searing, the stink of burning dope gagging.

Clack, slipping steeply and hoping to make the field, saw he wasn't going to succeed. He leveled a little, trying to glide, but flame sheeted against his face, cooking, melting the soft rubber rims of his goggles. He tilted the ship into the slip again, the side-rush of air drawing the flame and heat away from him.

The field came nearer. Five hundred feet, three hundred, two. Then the D.H. dropped into the trees. Both wing banks folded back with the first rending impact. The undercarriage stuck in the ground, stayed there. The fuselage glanced off a tree, junking itself.

Clack pitched forward with the shock. The safety belt snapped. His head rammed the crash pad—blackness drenched his brain.

HE was out only an instant, for the burning plane was all about him, his clothing smoking, his body slowly baking, when he opened his eyes. Somebody, an arm under his chin, was laboriously dragging him out of the cracked and burning D.H. Feebly, by pushing with his hands, by kicking with his good leg, he helped a little.

The man who dragged him fell down. Clack rolled away from the blaze. The other man got up and staggered beside him, but a dozen yards from the flames, he moaned

and sat down. Clack stared at him incredulously.

"Runt Lee!"

Runt Lee's left arm hung string-limber. His left shoulder was lower than the right, and did not have exactly the shape of a shoulder.

"You dragged me out!" Clack muttered.

Runt Lee glared, red-eyed, said in a pain-cracked voice: "Go to hell!"

Clack shut his eyes, opened them quickly. He could hear a plane—landing in the field he had failed to make. He heard the rattle of trucks, then the blooping of the motor as the ship was taxied.

From high overhead, out of the black innards of the cloud-blanketed sky, drifted the bedlam of the bat fight, still in progress.

Clack swallowed. "I couldn't have gotten out by myself. You saved my life, Runt."

Runt, bitter-voiced, said: "You're welcome to it."

Clack listened. The blooping of the plane that had landed in the field had stopped and the motor was idling, the dull clanking of the rocker arms audible.

"That Boche landed to make sure we didn't get away. He'll find us in a minute. Before he does, I want to tell you I wasn't with your girl that night, Runt. I lied about that—to get your goat."

"You—did?" Runt's voice was hoarse.

"Yeah. She gave me a bust in the face and ran off crying a minute after I kayoed you. I kinda think—I'm damn sure she loves you."

Runt said nothing. But after a minute, Clack looked at him, and in the glare from the burning plane, Runt's face was twisted with emotion.

"Aw, hell!" Clack said ruefully. "It was a dirty stunt, Runt. I guess I've kinda misjudged you for a long time."

Runt, his lips hardly moving, jerked out: "No, you haven't. I—well, when our engine started missing upstairs this morning, I was the cause of it. During the night, after I learned I was going over the lines with you, I ran insulated wires from three of the spark plugs back under the fuselage to my cockpit, I put the ends of the wires together, shorted the plugs, to make the engine miss. Just before we landed, I pulled the wires loose, rolled them up and put them in my pocket. I—I wanted to get you kicked out of the Air Service for showing yellow."

Clack's face had turned into a hard, ugly mask as he listened. Then the hardness went away. "I had it coming, I guess. It don't matter much now, anyway, and I'd probably have done the same thing. We've been a couple of suckers, Runt. We sure have."

Runt opened and shut his mouth several times, finally managed to say: "Yeah—yeah, we have, at that. For a long time, Clack."

Clack looked at Runt, grinning. Then his jaw fell. "Hey—you've got a gun! Maybe we can pot-shot that damned Boche when he comes after us and get his plane!"

From out of the timber, a voice barked: "Shoot what Boche?"

Major Maske came striding into the light of the burning plane.

"You!" Clack yelped. "I thought that was a Boche plane come down!"

"Hell!" Major Maske snorted. "I landed to haul you two back to France, providing you had gotten down alive. There wasn't a Kraut in sight around this field." He stared at Clack, pride in his eyes. "I been watching you tonight, and I must say that I was about to kick a damned good buzzard out of the Air Service. Can you walk?"

Clack got up on one leg, said: "I can hop." He reached down a hand to help Runt Lee. "Come on, guy. We got a war ahead of us. Let's show 'em what a pilot-observer team really is!"

The Last Gunslinger

BY MARY FAN

WHENEVER people ask where I'm from, I say "nowhere." Somehow, our little town missed the spider web of telegraph poles and railroad tracks that entangled much of the West, as well as the new-fangled contraptions they might have brought. Beyond the horizon, the rest of the country was shrinking, with automobiles bringing cities closer together, telephones erasing the distance between folks, and electric lights blurring day into night. But, where we were, amid sprawling acres of desert, the sky still felt endless. So few papers reached us that tales of airships dropping bombs on the other side of the world felt as fantastical as stories about men journeying to the center of the earth. I dare say Silver Creek was the last of its kind—a remnant from those heady days of gold prospecting and frontier homesteading.

You won't find it on a map. And if you went there now, all you'll find are a few desiccated shells of buildings.

Most everyone in Silver Creek wasn't really from anywhere, so they didn't ask much when Ma arrived with nothing but a sack of clothes and baby me. Just told her that if she was looking for work, she should talk to Sunset Sam at the inn. Ten years before that, they hadn't asked much when Sam turned up with two bags of gold tied to his saddle.

For the first eight years of my life, all I remember is quiet. Even the folks who came into the saloon had this lazy haze around them, as if they'd just gotten up from a nap.

We were so used to strangers that we wouldn't have paid any attention to Warren Fields' stuck-up, blond-bearded face if he and his friends hadn't come riding in whooping like idiots and firing their pistols in the air.

I was helping Ma out at the inn, where we lived in a small basement room, when I heard people screaming and wood splintering.

Ms. Terry Lynn Shull, an older lady with silver-blond hair and steely brown eyes who owned the general store, looked up from her card game. "Damn hooligans making trouble again."

"Sure sounds like it." Ma waved one honey-brown hand at me. "Go downstairs, Abigale." She rushed out from behind the bar, her gray skirt whipping around her ankles and her curly brown hair bouncing by her shoulders.

I started to obey but paused when a black hat with a gaudy

band of silver and turquoise appeared over the swinging double doors. A pair of garish snakeskin boots struck the scuffed floor, silver spurs spinning behind the sharp black heels.

"Well, finally. A proper watering hole." Thin lips curled beneath the narrow nose of a blue-eyed man in a blood red shirt with a black vest.

I was so busy staring at his fancy clothes that I almost didn't notice the three men who trailed in after him.

Hands clutched gleaming new revolvers—with fair skin too unblemished to have seen a real day's work. Even my tiny, pudgy baby hands were rougher.

"Y'all look like a pack of fools," Ms. Shull muttered under her breath, so quiet I don't think anyone but me heard.

Ma walked up to the fancy man. "We don't want any trouble. So I'd thank you to leave my establishment."

Technically, it was still Sunset Sam's, but he'd as good as handed control over to Ma a few years back so he could spend more time camping or whatever it was he did when he rode off alone into the desert.

Fancy Man drew himself up to his full height. Though he was a good foot taller than Ma, she didn't look any smaller.

One of his friends stepped up to her with a scowl. "This here's the Last Gunslinger—the last *true* man of the West. Show some respect."

I may have been a little girl, but even I knew that was horseshit. A giggle escaped me.

Fancy Man's gaze landed on me, and he scooped me up before I could run. "This your brat, little lady?"

Anyone could tell at a glance that I was my Ma's. I looked just like her, except miniature and plump.

"Let her go!" Ma rushed forward, but Fancy Man's friend seized her arms.

Fancy Man's stinking tobacco breath blew into my cheek. "What are you, anyway? Mexican? Mulatto?"

I squirmed and hollered like a wild animal.

"I think the mutt needs something to chill her out!" One of his friends grabbed a flask and splashed a foul-smelling liquid onto my face. It burned my eyes and tongue, and I screamed even louder.

It was then that Frank Baxter, who'd been sitting frozen stiff at a table with his two brothers, did something profoundly stupid: He tried to be noble.

"Enough!" He stood, one hand on the pistol in his holster. "Release them, or else!"

He should've just drawn the damn thing.

Neither Fancy Man nor his friends so much as blinked before shooting him—all at once.

Screams followed—mine, Ma's, the other terrified customers. But one soul-shattering howl nearly drowned them all out—that of Frank's youngest brother, Ned, who couldn't have been more than nineteen.

Fortunately, the middle Baxter had some sense. Ned's fingers grasped desperately for his weapon, but Bill had him in some kind of wrestler's hold.

Frank's face hit the floor, his eyes empty as the sky.

"No one threatens the Last Gunslinger." Fancy Man, who'd freed one hand to shoot but still held me by the wrist, smirked. "Anyone else—"

Four gunshots pierced my ears. Four was all it took to send all their pistols tumbling to the ground.

The sinking sun nearly silhouetted Sunset Sam's tall, slim figure, and its shadows exaggerated the crevices of his weathered dark brown face. A white beard accented his powerful jaw. His worn brown hat looked shabby compared to Fancy Man's, but every inch of him spoke of an experience Fancy Man could only have dreamed of.

He walked up to Fancy Man, calm as a pool on a windless day. "Get out."

One of Fancy Man's friends moved his hand, reaching for a second weapon. A gunshot—two of his fingers fell clean off.

Sam didn't have to do anything else.

After the hooligans were gone, Ma rushed to me and held me close.

Sam walked up to the bar. "Jessamine."

Ma inhaled sharply and fetched him a glass of whiskey, as if it were no different from any other afternoon.

Ms. Shull, who'd wisely remained still as a mouse during the whole encounter, arched her dark brows at Sam. "Always in the nick of time, aren't you?"

Sam grunted in response.

"Why'd you let them go?" Ned looked ready to explode.

Sam shrugged. "That was Warren Fields. His daddy's got a lot of money. Don't need that kind of trouble."

"That bastard killed my brother! You expect me to let that go?"

"You want lawmen here?"

Now, the Baxter Boys claimed they did ranch work, but whatever else they got up to, neither Ned nor Bill wanted lawmen around.

"Rather kill him myself anyway," Ned grumbled. "If you won't do what needs doing, I will."

"Don't bother him, Ned." Bill shook his head of shaggy brown hair, which was near identical to Ned's. "It's just who Sam is."

With those words, Bill summed up how everyone thought about Sunset Sam, which is what folks started calling him when he bought the old Sunset Inn. Everyone had their own theory as to who he was. Some said he'd been with the rodeo. Some, a retired sheriff. Still others, a former outlaw.

Whoever he was, his skills were his secrets—until she showed up.

T HE moon had just peaked through the saloon's front window when the doors swung open. Worn boots tracked in a small cloud of tawny dust. Sam's gray, pointy-eared dog, Bonnie, trotted in beside him. In his arms, limp as a rag doll, lay a young woman with a long black braid. Maybe "woman" was too generous. She didn't look much bigger than me, though her figure was definitely more mature. Her cheeks were almost as round as mine, though a few shades lighter. Her small, full-lipped mouth looked as cracked as dry wood. Something about her struck me as... different. And it wasn't only because she wore trousers like a boy.

Eyes flicked up from drinks and cards, fixing on the sleeping stranger.

Ned Baxter cocked his head. "Where'd you find that Chinadoll, Sam?"

China? I gasped.

Ms. Shull gave Ned a chastising look. "Don't be rude, boy."

Ma turned to Sam. "Who's that?"

Sam shrugged. "Bonnie found her half dead in the desert. Figured I shouldn't leave her there."

"Put her in the empty room upstairs." Ma rushed to the wooden staircase. "I'll get her cleaned up.

Abigale, keep an eye on things."

"Yes, Ma," I said.

Gazes lingered on the stranger. As Sam moved past the Baxter boys' table, Ned peered at the girl. "I'd like to know your story, Chinadoll."

Her eyes fluttered—just enough for me to see that they were hooded like mine, though closer to black than my warm brown— and fixed on Ned. "Don't call me Chinadoll."

E VERY time a new book wound up in Silver Creek, Ma found ways to borrow it for me. Thanks to Ms. Shull, who'd always been liberal about stocking books in her store even though few bought them, I'd recently gotten *A Princess of Mars* into my hands, and so I was overjoyed when Ma tasked me with keeping an eye on our sleeping stranger because it meant I got to sit by her bedside and read to my heart's content.

I was so wrapped up in John Carter's adventures that I almost didn't hear her raspy voice.

"Get away from me!" She thrashed against the worn quilt. "Don't touch me!"

I hopped up, leaving the book on the chair, and grabbed her shoulder. "Wake up!"

One of her fists shot toward me. I ducked. "Whoa!"

Her inky eyes popped open. "Who're you?"

I stood a little taller. "Abigale Belle, daughter of Jessamine Belle, who's the co-proprietor of this inn. Who're you?"

She shook her head.

Thinking she was too dried out to talk, I rushed over to the small table in the corner, my long brown skirt swishing around my ankles, and fetched her a cup of water. "Here."

She gulped down the whole thing in maybe half a second.

"What's your name?" I asked.

"K—" She paused. "Kate."

Another stranger with a fake name. I knew better than to press her. "Nice to meet you, Kate."

"Where am I?"

"Silver Creek. Sam found you in the desert."

"Your grandfather?"

"No, though sometimes I pretend he is. Are you from China?"

"No."

"Where are you from, then?"

"Doesn't matter."

"Have you ever been to China?"

"You ask a lot of questions."

"Just curious." I shrugged. "People keep talking about you, but nothing they say is true."

Her lips twitched. "I've never been to China. Not really an option for me." Her hand moved to her collar, where something silver glinted at the edge of her shirt.

"What's that?"

She tugged at it, revealing a metal charm shaped like a serpent with two horns, four clawed legs, and a long snout. "A dragon. Probably the most Chinese thing about me, other than my face."

"Aren't dragons evil?"

"Not in my parents' culture."

I leaned in for a closer look. "Well, Kate, it sounds like there's a lot I could learn from you."

I DON'T recall Ma actually asking for Kate's help around the inn; Kate just started doing things that needed doing. I think it was her way of thanking Ma and Sam. It was obvious she had no place to go, so Ma said she could stay in exchange for work.

"But we don't need help," I said later that night.

"Neither did Sam when I showed up here." Ma unbound my hair from its tight braid. "He gave me a chance, and now, it's my turn to do the same for Kate."

I was pretty happy about Kate staying because that meant I got to learn about the legends and traditions of faraway China—her parents' world.

As the days rolled on, she still got lots of stares and rude comments from men who called her "Chinadoll," despite all the times she grumbled for them to stop.

The doors swung open. Smoke curled from the cigars hanging from between the Baxter Boys' teeth. It'd been three weeks since they were last here. Judging by Bill's spotless boots, Ned's shiny pistol—which he kept pulling out just to whip about—and their self-satisfied swaggers, they'd had a lucrative adventure.

"Jessamine!" Bill sauntered up

to the bar. "Pour us your best."

"Be right there, Bill." Ma, who was clearing a table on the other side of the room, handed me a stack of cups.

Ms. Shull briefly glanced up from her usual card game to give the Baxter boys an appraising look. She'd just finished cleaning out the local butcher, Blair Learn, who was cursing liberally as he shook his head of graying brown hair. "Seems y'all've done well for yourselves. Care to join us?" She gestured at the table.

Bill grinned. "Nah, Ms. Shull. I'd like to hang on to my fortune a little while longer."

Kate descended the stairs, dressed in trousers like always. Her brow was furrowed, and her mouth tight. It was her usual expression—a look that said she had an eternal ember of rage glowing in her heart.

"Well, look who's still here." Ned's lips quirked. That shiny new pistol swung like a propeller in one hand. "How're you doing, Chinadoll?"

Kate's eyes fixed on him, and I could practically see the sparks from that ember jumping out of them. "Name's Kate."

"That's no Chinese name."

"I'm no Chinese girl." Kate moved to pass him, but he blocked her.

An uncomfortable feeling rumbled in my gut.

Bill glanced at his brother. "Let her go, Ned."

"I'm only asking questions." Ned widened his green eyes in an exaggerated look of innocence.

Kate tried to get around him, but he stepped in closer—too close.

The pistol flicked around his finger. "What's your real name, Chinadoll?"

All I recall is a sudden gunshot, followed by the sound of shattering glass—I was so startled I dropped the cups. A smoking hole pierced the floor—and Ned's pistol was in Kate's hand.

Ned reached for it. "Why you—"

Sam clapped Ned's shoulder. He had a way of slipping in like that. "She doesn't like it when people call her that."

Ned scowled but nodded.

Sam's eyes flicked to Kate. "Give it back."

Her expression darkened, but she, too, obeyed. The pistol moved from one disgruntled grip to another, then reentered Ned's holster.

The rest of the saloon bustled on as if nothing had happened. Matches lit cigars. Cards flicked between fingers. Whisky slid out of glasses. At the table in the corner, Ms. Shull dealt another hand while Blair drained his cup.

"You've got a lot of anger, don't you, girl?" Sam examined Kate's face. "If you're gonna shoot, you'd better shoot straight. Come. I'll show you how." He walked across the room in slow, weary steps.

A strange expression flickered

across Kate's face—maybe excitement, maybe nervousness. She didn't look at Ned Baxter as she passed him, and he didn't look at her.

That was the last time anyone called her "Chinadoll."

SAM lived in a little house behind the inn, which had a wide yard. Every day, he'd set up empty bottles for Kate to shoot. And every day, she got a little better at hitting them.

I like to think that had I not been so little, Sam would've taught me too. Though I was more interested in the escapades of Tarzan or the Daring Twins than real-world adventures.

I leaned against the frame of the back door, watching. Enough weeks had passed that everyone in and around town knew that Sam was teaching Kate, and there was much grumbling about it. Some was about propriety, and some was about jealousy, since Sam had refused to train anyone else.

Ma approached and gave me a chastising look. "Stop idling, Abigale."

I crinkled my nose. "Kate's not doing any chores."

"Yes, she is. Take a good look."

It was then that I noticed how many times Sam made Kate do the same things over and over, until she looked ready to snap that revolver in half. Her face spoke all the words her voice didn't—the frustration, the determination.

Black brows, glistening with sweat, low over narrowed eyes. Jaw so tight, it seemed she might break her own teeth.

I glanced at Ma. "Why's Sam spending so much time with Kate?"

"He sees something in her, maybe something that reminds him of himself."

"But they're so different."

"Are they?" Ma crouched so that she was eye level with me. "Just because Sam and Kate look different doesn't mean they don't have similar souls. Look harder. What do you see?"

I thought for a moment. "Two people who're always strangers, no matter where they go. And who're tougher than they look and kinder than they like people to know."

Ma smiled.

A RUMBLING noise pounded outside, almost like an earthquake. Whooping and hollering thundered through the streets, punctuated by gunshots.

Standing in the middle of the street, where I was returning from delivering a package to Ms. Shull for Ma, I froze stiff. Months had passed since Warren Fields and his gang tucked their yellow tails between their legs and ran away, and I'd thought they'd never return.

Dust swirled under the hooves of a dozen horses, all of which carried a man in a gaudy outfit. Elaborate silver-and-turquoise ornaments, excessive patterns painted on leather, glittering boots that had barely been walked in—it was an ignorant rich boy's idea of what a tough cowboy might wear.

Our town was probably the last place where Fields and his gang could live out their outlaw fantasies, and they had a grand time of it, shooting through store signs, breaking windows, and taking whatever knickknacks suited their fancy. Panic rose up my throat. Sam was on another of his solo rides, and it was too much to hope that anyone else could scare them off. Even the Baxter boys were out of town.

The whirlwind of hooves drew closer. I raced back to the inn, burst through the doors, and crashed right into Kate.

She caught me, then looked past me at Fields. The color drained from her face, and her eyes filled with rage. Then she vanished so quickly, I didn't see where she ran to.

Ma rushed down the stairs, holding her pistol. "Abigale! Hide!"

The doors swung open before I could take a step.

Fields grabbed my arm as I tried to run. A new scar, long and thin, gleamed across his cheek. "Well, if it ain't the mutt."

I screamed.

Ma cocked her pistol. "I'll thank you kindly to release my daughter and get the hell out."

A flurry of guns shot up from holsters, gripped in the soft, lily-white hands of Fields' companions.

Fields swung me toward one man, who gripped my arms. "Hold this." He swaggered up to Ma. "I'd be happy to oblige, little lady, just as soon as I have a word with Sunset Sam."

Ma glowered. "He ain't here. What do you want?"

"To teach him some respect."

A muscle in her jaw twitched, and her glare remained steady.

"You wondering how I got my scar?" Fields spat. "Some whores in Chinatown got uppity with me. I shot the old one dead on the spot. The young one was slippery, but I chased her into the desert. She's probably a bleached pile of bones by now. And if she ain't, I'll kill her the next time I see her. That's what happens to people who cross me."

I don't know what it says about me that I immediately thought of Kate.

Elaborately carved boots scurried through the door. "Sunset Sam ain't here, boss. But I learned something interesting."

Fields glanced at the man. "What?"

"There's a Chinagirl working at this inn. Might be the one who gave you that scar."

Fields' lip twisted. "Well, little lady? Where's the Chinagirl?"

"With Sam." Ma's lie tumbled out a little too quickly. "They left town a few days ago. Don't know when they'll be back." She lowered her gun. "I don't want any trouble.

Just give me my daughter."

"Sure, ma'am." Fields nodded at the man holding me, who shoved me toward Ma. I yelped as I went tumbling.

Ma rushed to help me up.

Fields' eyes sparked. "If you really don't want trouble, you'll stay out of my way." He fired at the bar, breaking bottles. "Have fun, boys!"

Whoops and cheers rang out. Bullets pierced the furniture, and chairs flew across the room. The few customers fled, most without some item or another they'd possessed. One of Fields' men tried to snatch Ms. Shull's straw hat as she rushed out but received an elbow to the face instead.

"Sam'll get you for this!" I hollered.

"Hush now." Ma steered me downstairs, silent and stony.

THERE wasn't much left of the saloon by the time Fields and his gang were finished.

I sullenly swept up the splintered wood and shattered glass lying strewn across the hole-riddled floor. I'd never seen the inn so quiet before dark, with only the scrape of my broom and the clinking of shards disturbing the air.

Kate entered, her lips pressed into a thin line. Without a word, she grabbed a second broom from downstairs and began sweeping alongside me.

I'm not proud of what happened next.

"Was it you?" My muscles were still quivering even though Fields had been gone for about an hour. "The Chinatown whore Fields chased into the desert."

"Abigale!" Ma marched up to me.

"It's true, isn't it?" I threw down my broom and pointed one accusing finger at Kate. "You have to get out! It's bad enough that Fields is after Sam—if he finds out you're here too, he'll kill us all! Just like he killed Frank Baxter!"

"That's enough!" Ma seized my shoulder.

I collapsed against her and sobbed. "He'll keep coming back, won't he?"

Ma stroked my head. "We'll sort this out."

Moments slid by, and eventually, I stopped crying.

Kate had been standing stone still since my outburst. "I'm no whore," she said finally. "But as far as he's concerned, all women and girls from Chinatown are."

I stared at her. That was the most words she'd spoken about her past since she got here.

"He thought I was his for the taking." Anger simmered in her voice. "Wouldn't back off even after I drew a knife. My mother tried to intervene. He killed her. He was aiming for me." A tear slipped from her eye. "I would've kept fighting, but she told me to run."

Ma put an arm around Kate and gave her a squeeze.

"I'm sorry," I mumbled.

"No, I'm sorry." Kate balled her fists. "I should've confronted Fields instead of running. I'll leave before he finds out I'm here."

"And go where?" Sam's gruff voice shot toward us from the door. "You gonna return to the desert so you can wind up all the way dead this time?"

Kate looked away.

Ma turned to Sam. "I know you don't like getting lawmen involved, but I think it's time."

Deep lines formed between Sam's brows. "Thought you had more sense than that, Jessamine. Lawmen always side with people like Fields over people like us."

He could've meant because Fields was rich where we were poor or because Fields was white where we were not, but either way, he would've been right.

Quick footsteps scurried past the broken doors, which barely clung to their creaking hinges. "Where's Fields?" Ned Baxter's pistol gleamed under what remained of the day. "Heard he was heading this way."

Ma put her hands on her hips. "You missed him."

Ned cursed.

Bill, standing outside with their horses, jerked his head at the road. "Told you we should've kept riding. Let's go."

"You two wanna join your brother?" Sam gave them a stern look. "You're outmatched."

"I don't care." Ned spoke between gritted teeth. "One of us will be the one to put Fields in the ground. We have the most reason to want him dead."

"I have just as much reason." Kate's voice shook. "He killed my mother. Forced me to leave my home."

Ned's expression sobered. "Sorry to hear that. Before we kill him, we'll be sure to give him your regards. Bill, let's go."

The two rode off.

Sam shook his head. "Fools."

MA thought she could keep me away from the brewing storm by taking me down to Ms. Shull's store on the other side of town and asking her to watch me until after the whole mess with Fields blew over. Locking a little girl in the office with a new novel to read might have seemed like a good way to keep her from leaving. But Ms. Shull didn't know me well enough.

I'm not sure what I thought I was going to do, but my blood was screaming to do *something*. So, I fiddled with the lock until I got it open.

I arrived in time to see the cloud of dust kicked up by the arriving gang's horses. It looked large enough to swallow our little inn.

Riders dismounted, and boots pounded the dirt. The usual whooping and hollering was mixed with cruel laughter. I recognized Fields' turquoise-and-silver-banded hat. *Guess the Baxter boys didn't get their revenge.*

Gunfire peppered the air, and smoke curled from barrels aimed at the sky. I froze, suddenly realizing how stupidly I was acting. Fields marched up to the saloon's door while his gang waited in the street. He hurled something inside and ran.

An explosion ripped apart the walls, and fire climbed up its splintered remains.

Horror seized me. Ma, Sam, and Kate were inside—how could they have survived that?

"Abigale!" A hand seized my shoulder.

I spun and met Kate's eyes. "You—You're—"

Kate grabbed my hand. "You can't be here!"

"Where's Ma and Sam?"

Before Kate could answer, a powerful wind blew a hole in the smoke, revealing Ma and Sam standing armed in the middle of the street.

Later, I would realize that Sam had his own code of honor that meant giving even the likes of Fields a second chance. If that no-good swaggering fool had been content to destroy the inn, he could've ridden off and gone on living his fantasy of being "The Last Gunslinger."

But he turned his gun on Sam.

Sam's hand became a blur of motion.

One man down. Two. Three. *Bang. Bang. Bang.*

Had Fields not been blocked by his horse, he would've been the first to fall. But Sam refused to shoot horses unless they needed shooting.

Ma took a few shots too. She was Sam's partner in business, and she was determined to be his partner in defending what was theirs.

Kate dragged me out of the street. I didn't see where she was taking me since I was too busy watching.

Fields may've talked big, but the man was yellower than a sunflower. He must've noticed Sam's thing about not shooting horses, because he slithered behind them like a snake. Bullets whizzed.

Fourth man down. Fifth. Sixth. *Bang. Bang. Bang.*

Like a striking cobra, Fields sprung out and seized Ma. She clocked him in the face but wasn't strong enough to keep him from ripping the gun out of her hand. My legs instinctively tried to carry me to Ma, but Kate held me tight.

"Drop your gun!" Fields grinned at Sam, his gun pointed at Ma's head.

Tears of panic spilled from my eyes. I'm not sure when Kate dragged us behind the front porch of the store next door to the inn, but I was suddenly aware of the grayish-brown wood latticing my view.

The gun fell from Sam's hand and clattered onto the street.

Fields nodded with a self-satisfied smirk. "And the rest of your weapons. Set them down nice and slow."

Ma shook her head, but her jaw trembled.

Sam calmly lay down the second pistol that was tucked into his belt, as well as a knife he'd had in his boot.

Fields licked his lips and looked around for his companions. Four of them remained standing while a fifth examined the fallen men. "Get over here and hold this little lady for me. I've got some business to finish."

Sam stood still as a statue. He could've taken down the rest of them with a few flicks of his fingers, but he might've gotten Ma killed in the process, and he wasn't about to do that.

I stood trembling in Kate's grasp.

She crouched slightly to look me in the eye. "Stay here."

I was too scared to do anything else anyway.

Kate grabbed the gun from her belt, stepped out, and aimed at Fields. "Let them go!"

Fields glanced at her. "Who're you?"

"Just a girl from Chinatown."

Fields twisted his face, contorting his scar. "It's you!"

The barrel of his gun twisted away from Ma and toward Kate. Ma shoved her way free and leaped for one of Sam's weapons. A man whipped his gun toward her. Sam's pistol was back in his hand and aimed at the man.

Gunfire went off. I ducked and squeezed my eyes.

Bang. Bang. Bang.

Then, an explosion.

A scream escaped me. I peered around the porch—I had to see what had happened.

Swirling smoke filled the air, and I coughed.

A gust blew away the haze.

All of Fields' companions lay prone in the street, and I knew at once that they were dead. Sam was on the ground too, his dark blood staining the dirt. But he was still breathing, his chest heaving from the labor. Ma was sprawled several feet away with her eyes closed, but I didn't see any blood. I wanted to run to her at once, but it wasn't over yet.

Two remained standing.

Fields and Kate.

My gaze fell to their hands. They were empty.

Kate now stood a few steps away from Sam. Dirt streaked her face, accentuating her scowl. Fields' gun lay at his feet. His fingers twitched.

"Kate!" Sam flung his pistol at her.

Fields dove for his own.

He never reached it.

Crimson bloomed across his white shirt, and he toppled to the ground, lifeless eyes staring at the sky. Kate glared down at his body.

With the danger gone, I ran to Ma. She groaned, and relief cascaded down my chest.

"Abigale." Even though she was still blinking back into consciousness, she managed to give me a stern look. "I told you to stay away."

I threw my arms around her, tears streaming down my face.

She embraced me. "I'm okay. Got thrown by the dynamite, that's all." She took in our surroundings. "Sam!"

She rushed toward him, with me trailing her skirt.

Kate knelt by Sam, cradling his head. Her eyes glistened. A cry escaped Ma, and she collapsed to her knees. I crouched beside her, sobbing.

"No tears from any of you." Sam's rasping voice could barely be heard. "Always knew I'd go out like this. When the lawmen ask, say it was me who killed them all, got it? Don't need you girls going to the gallows."

Kate nodded, and Ma said, "Whatever you want, Sam."

A faint smile ghosted across Sam's lips—the first I'd seen in a long while. He turned to Kate. "Take care of my horse, my dog, and that pistol, got it?"

Kate nodded again.

Sam's gaze shifted to Ma. "There's a bag of gold buried beneath my bed. Build a new business. Make it something better."

"Yes, Sam." Ma's voice was choked.

I couldn't help the tears pouring from my eyes. "What about me?"

With frail fingers, Sam took the hat from his head and put it on mine. "Just remember me."

I didn't get a chance to reply

before the light left his gaze. For the first time in my life, I saw what pure contentment looked like on a person's face.

Ma closed his eyes with one trembling hand.

Townsfolk peeked out of doorways and windows. Hoof beats sounded behind us. I jumped up.

To my surprise, it was the Baxter Boys. Bill had his arm in a makeshift sling, and Ned's face was covered in cuts and bruises.

"You're not dead!" I exclaimed.

Ned jumped off his horse, glanced at Fields' corpse, and cursed. "Damn ravine made a good hiding spot but took too long to get out of. Who did this?" He looked at Sam, then at Kate.

She gave him a steady look.

A strange look crossed his face. I thought he was about to rage about not getting his revenge, but all he did was tip his hat to her.

THE Baxter Boys stuck around to help clean up the mess. Since the lawmen would've found their way to Silver Creek eventually, the town decided it'd be less suspicious to send a respectable man to fetch them and found a volunteer in Blair Learn, the butcher. When the lawmen arrived, Ma told them what Sam had wanted her to say. They didn't believe her at first, but when the Baxter Boys claimed they'd been there and seen Sam take down Fields and his gang by himself, the lawmen took their word for it. And none of the townsfolk contradicted them.

Kate stayed out of sight the entire time the lawmen were in town. Even after they finally left, she still seemed jittery.

Both Ma and I knew she wouldn't stay in Silver Creek for much longer. So neither of us were surprised when we woke up one morning to find that she'd run off with Sam's horse, dog, and pistol. I can only imagine where she might have gone. Even though gunslingers have become myths of Hollywood, I like to picture her riding wild and free across the untamed desert, bringing justice where she can, as Sunset Sam must have once. Every so often, I'll see a newspaper story about a mysterious woman who rescued someone or caught a dangerous fugitive. In my mind, it's her every time.

She left one thing behind: Her dragon pendant with a note that said, *Jessamine & Abigale—Thank you.*

Decades have passed since I found it on her empty bed. Women—well, white women—gained the right to vote, the country survived another world war, and there's talk of putting a man on the moon.

But I still have that pendant. Sam's hat too.

They sit in the living room of my suburban house. Many who know me only as the polished lawyer who defied all odds to gain a job white men with half my brains take for granted are surprised when I tell them I was a girl from nowhere.

The world's changed a lot. Yet much remains the same. Men like Fields still think that because they're rich and privileged, they can play outlaw and get away with murder. And I've dedicated my life to making sure they don't.

Last night, I received a parcel. All it contained was Sam's pistol. All the note said was, *Take care of this. I don't need it anymore.*

I placed it on the shelf beside Kate's dragon.

And then I sat down to tell her story—what little I know of it.

WHY AM I STARING OUT THE WINDOW INSTEAD OF ADVANCING THE STORY?

I WILL TELL YOU MY ENTIRE TALE AS A FLASHBACK, GENTLE READER, IN AN SNEAKY ATTEMPT TO BUILD EXTRA SUSPENSE! ∹OOH, SCARY!∹

IT ALL STARTED AT A SECRET OUPOST...

FLORA'S BRIDAL SHOPPE

YOU *SENT* FOR ME?

YES, AGENT 49... WE HAVE FINALLY GOTTEN ORDERS AT LAST! OUR PLAN COMMENCES ON *FRILBSDAY!*

BUT WAIT! OUR LEADER ADDRESSES US...!

HEED, AGENTS! WE ARE READY TO START "OPERATION SADIE HAWKINS!"

DIRK WAS SO *EASY* TO MANIPULATE...HE WOULD DO ANY LITTLE THING I ASKED HIM TO DO, SO GETTING HIM TO DO BIG THINGS WOULD BE EASY!

ALL I DID WAS KEEP HIM FOCUSED ON MY...*ASSETS*... AND HE WAS MINE!

IT WAS ALMOST LIKE TRAINING A *PUPPY DOG!*

DRUSILLA, I'M *SO* GLAD I'VE DECIDED TO DO WHAT YOU *TELL* ME TO! IT'S SO MUCH *EASIER!*

AND I WAS *TRAINING* HIM, ALL RIGHT!

SWEETIE, *WHY* DID WE BREAK UP IN THE FIRST PLACE? I *HONESTLY* CAN'T RECALL!

BECAUSE YOU HADN'T LEARNED TO GET ME FLOWERS, *DUMMY!*

HE DOESN'T SUSPECT A *THING*, FEARLESS LEADER! HIS HEART AND MIND ARE FOLLOWING MY COMMANDS TO *PERFECTION!*

EXCELLENT! ONWARD TO STAGE *2!*

DIRK, SWEETIE? THE *BROOKLYN DODGERS* ARE HOME TONIGHT--AND *I* WANT TO SEE YOU *TIED* AT THE BOTTOM OF THE 9TH!

THE NEXT MORNING...

8 AM? I WAS *SURE* THAT HE WOULDN'T UNTIE HIMSELF TIL *10!*

DIRK, DEAR! YOU'RE ALIVE AFTER THAT INCREDIBLY TIGHT GAME LAST NIGHT?

BARELY, MA'AM! I WANTED TO REMIND YOU THAT WE HAVE PROMISED THE KANIFFS WE'D CHECK ON THEIR BOY IN THE SANITARIUM!

OH...THE NUT HOUSE! THE KANIFFS HAD SOME TROUBLE WITH THEIR BOY AND HAD ENROLLED HIM IN *ART THERAPY!* BEING NICE TO THE LAD NOW MIGHT PAY OFF LATER!

AND WHAT ARE YOU DOING HERE, YOU RAGAMUFFIN REMBRANDT?

KARL IS SHOWING ME HOW HE DRAWS *SUPERBOY,* DARLING!

YEAH! I'M GIVING HIM A *JAMES DEAN* JACKET SO HE LOOKS REAL *COOL!*

FOR SHAME, KARL! HOW DARE YOU DRESS A HERO LIKE A JUVENILE DELINQUENT??

DIRK! DON'T GO TOO HARD ON HIM! CLEARLY THAT "ROCK AND ROLL" MUSIC DAMAGED HIS MIND!

YOU'LL SEE! I'LL KILL OFF SUPERMAN AND *MY* VERSION WILL BE THE REAL ONE!

WE'D BEST GO. THE NURSES WILL GIVE HIM SOME *HEALTHY* ELECTRO-SHOCKS...

THE *DOCTORS* GAVE KARL A NICE WHITE JACKET WITH VERY LONG SLEEVES SO HE COULD HUG HIMSELF *ALL DAY LONG!* WE TOOK THE KANIFFS OUT TO DINNER TO TELL THEM THAT HE WAS UNDER THE BEST CARE... AND THEN *I* COULD STEAL THE CODES!

RUSS, MARIE... WE SAW KARL TODAY AT THE SANITARIUM, AND I THINK I NEED TO WARN YOU THAT IT'S NOT LOOKING GOOD FOR HIM...

WHAT DO YOU MEAN, DIRK? HE SEEMS SO CHARGED UP IN THERE!

I'M SORRY, BUT KARL'S...DRAWING COMIC BOOKS!

GOOD LORD! ÷CHOKE÷

NOW, DIRK, *ANY* READING IS GOOD FOR A BOY, NO?

HOW *DARE* YOU, DRUSILLA? DR. WERTHAM IS *RIGHT!* MY BOY IS FOREVER LOST TO SOCIAL EYE-INJURING *DEPRAVITY!*

WHY COULDN'T HE BE MORE LIKE *IKE?*

COME, DRU, LET'S THROW SOME COMICS *ROMANTICALLY* ON THE FIRE!

OH, DIRK... THE WARMTH FROM THAT *ACTION #1* IS ALMOST AS WARM AS YOUR LOVE!

NICE TRY...TO *COVER UP!*

BUT *I* KNOW THE TRUTH, DRU...YOU'RE PART OF A COVERT NETWORK THAT'S TRYING TO STEAL OUR NATION'S SECRET *DEFENSE PLANS!*

÷GASP!÷ *YOU* FIGURED IT OUT?

THE EVER-CLANKIN' END!

Alien Invasion of Earth!

By KEITH R.A. DeCANDIDO

"THE general will see you now, Dr. Philipps."

Phillip P. Philipps, PhD, got up from the guest chair where he was reading a copy of *Life* full of photographs of the UN forces in Korea. Pipe clenched between his teeth, he set down the magazine and walked past the girl in uniform who'd spoken and opened the wooden door with the nameplate that read GENERAL MAXIMILLIAN BLUNT.

The general tapped out a cigar into an ashtray and then stood up from behind his handsome oak desk as the scientist entered the windowless office.

"Welcome to the Pentagon, Dr. Philipps," the general said.

"Thank you, General Blunt, though I have to admit to being surprised to be invited," Philipps said as he sat down in the general's guest chair.

Blunt re-took his seat in the leather chair. "Well, I'm surprised that you're surprised, Doctor. After all, you're the one who warned us—and it's a damn good thing, too, I'll tell you that for free. That object you found is heading right for Earth, and we need to be ready for it."

"Ah." Philipps puffed on his pipe. "Well, of course, General, my surprise is due to your taking my communication seriously. My experience with the military is that you prefer to tell scientists what to do. When the words go the other way, we're often ignored."

Blunt retrieved his cigar from the ashtray. "Not this time, Doctor, not this time. The object is definitely artificial, as you indicated in your report—it's changed course four times, and it's coming well outside the plane of the solar system. Our telescopes weren't even looking there, so it's a damn good thing yours was."

"Well, yes." Philipps took another puff of his pipe. "So what's the plan of attack for this rogue object?"

"That's what you're here for, Doctor. We need you to lead a think-tank of some of our top men to find out what this thing is. And we need to hurry. As you said in your report, it'll be right on top of us in a couple of days."

"Right. Well, the first thing I'll need is a lab. My two assistants will need to come with me to that lab, as they'll be bringing my notes, my specialized equipment, and such."

"We have all the equipment you'll need, Doctor, including access to the Hale Telescope at Palomar."

Philipps's mouth fell open, and he barely caught his pipe. The Hale Telescope was the most powerful telescope in the world. "I still will need my notes—plus my assistants are well versed in my methods and it will be easier for them to aid me than for me to bring one of your people up to speed."

"Very well, if you insist." Blunt stubbed his cigar out and got to his feet. "Let me show you the lab we've set up."

AFTER getting a tour of the underground laboratory where he'd be working to study the unidentified object hurtling toward Earth, Dr. Philipps returned to his own lab, located in Glen Burnie.

His two graduate assistants, Lamont Johnson from Howard University and Maria Chen from George Washington University, were waiting for him.

Before they could say anything, the scientist said, "I thought I told the two of you that your observations were nonsense and that you shouldn't bother the authorities with your idiocy!"

"Yeah, you did," Lamont said, sticking his chin out defiantly. "Except we were right, weren't we? That's why they called you in?"

Philipps shook his head. "I knew it was a mistake agreeing to

let a Negro be one of my graduate assistants. You people have no conception of—"

"But I was right, wasn't I?"

"That's not the point!"

Maria finally spoke. "What did they say to you at the Pentagon, Dr. Philipps?"

Philipps lit his pipe angrily. "They said that you were right. Well, no, they said that *I* was right, since apparently you wrote the letter on *my* stationery and forged *my* signature."

"Actually," Maria said, "we didn't have to forge your signature. You signed it when I gave you those requisitions last week. It was just part of the pile."

Lamont added, "Maybe if you ever paid attention to things, you might've noticed. Then again, if you paid attention, you might've seen the UFO."

Philipps winced. "Please don't call it that. It makes it sound like we're crackpots."

"Why not? It's unidentified, it's flying, and it's an object. What more you want?"

"The *point* is," Philipps said, puffing on his pipe, "that we need to gather up all the notes you took on your observations. We're going to be working at the Pentagon for the foreseeable future. We'll have access to Hale, also, so one of you may need to fly to California."

Lamont's already-wide eyes widened further. "I get to go to Palomar?"

Philipps sneered. "*Maybe.* I may

send Miss Chen, since she actually *knows* her place."

The doctor knew that Lamont had always dreamed of seeing the Hale Telescope. But he was the one who went over his head to General Blunt, and Philipps didn't think the uppity young man should be rewarded for such behavior. If he was going to rise above his station to become a scientist, he needed to stop giving in to his baser instincts.

"

*O*UR *top story tonight: what appears to be an alien spacecraft has crash-landed in South Mountain State Park, right on the Appalachian Trail! The White House has confirmed that Pentagon scientists are studying the craft, but no other details are forthcoming. Speculation has been running rampant, however, and President Eisenhower has authorized the National Advisory Committee for Aeronautics to begin work on an aircraft that can launch into space right away. Further bulletins as more details come in..."*

"**T**HANK you, Dr. Walker for that autopsy report on the alien corpse. Now then, Dr. Philipps has been studying the craft. What can you tell us, Doctor?"

At that prompt from General Blunt, Eamon Walker, a wizened old pathologist, slowly sat back down in the small auditorium, and Philipps got up. "I'm still continuing my investigation into the

machinery. The alien beings seem to have revolutionary technology. The amount of information they can compress into a tiny electronic device is like nothing we've ever seen before. However, I'm very close to a breakthrough in deciphering their language as well as their technology. It's only a matter of time."

"Let's hope so," Blunt said, "since Palomar is now confirming three more objects headed toward us, and I doubt that these three are going to crash the way this first one did."

PHILIPPS returned to the lab where Maria and Lamont were examining the wreckage of the spacecraft that had crashed in South Mountain State Park.

"Find anything?"

"Nothing new," Maria said, "I'm sorry."

Lamont asked, "You told them about all the data I found on those chips of theirs, right?"

Philipps rolled his eyes as he lit his pipe. "Of course I told them that. Well, about the data, I didn't bother about the chips. The general doesn't care about technical details."

Lamont sighed. "You forgot about the chips, didn't you?"

"It doesn't matter."

"How does it not matter? These chips could revolutionize electronic storage!"

"Who would ever want to store anything electronically? I keep telling you, that whole notion is absurd. Oh, and I told them we're close to deciphering their language."

"Goddammit, Doc, we're not linguists! We've got no idea *what* their language is or how to figure it out. Why would you tell them that?"

"First of all, young man, I don't want to hear you taking the Lord's name in vain in my presence again, all right? There'll be no blasphemy in my lab. And secondly, I just told the general that to let him know we're making progress. It's not like he cares about the specifics, as long as we get results. So you had better sure as shooting get some, understood?"

Maria said, "I may have something, Doctor. That machine they found implanted in the alien's head?"

Frowning, Philipps said, "There was a machine implanted in its head?"

Lamont stared at him. "Didn't you read the autopsy report? Godda—" He cleared his throat. "Didn't you just *hear* the autopsy report?"

Waving a hand, Philipps said, "Walker's a doddering old idiot, I can't stand listening to him. And besides, that's biology. I'm an astronomer."

Before Lamont could make another snotty remark, Maria said, "Dr. Walker's people sent over the machine, and it seems to be some kind of two-way radio.

It broadcasts on a frequency, but I haven't been able to isolate it. Thing is, the equipment in the wreckage also seems to broadcast on the same frequency."

"Good," Philipps said, "keep working on that. Oh, and write up a report on all this, including those chips. I'll sign it in the morning. I'm gonna go take a nap."

Lamont watched as Philipps went into the side room where they kept the cot, then looked at Maria. "Think he'll read it before he signs it?"

Maria shrugged. "Don't worry about it. Let's just get to work on this."

"*We interrupt this program for a special news bulletin. Three more alien spaceships have entered Earth's atmosphere and taken up position over the White House in Washington, the Kremlin in Moscow, and Chung Nan Hai in Peking. We now go live to Per Stalby in Washington.*"

"*Al, I'm standing on Pennsylvania Avenue, and the spaceship is just hovering over the White House. The U.S. Army has mobilized, and I'm told that the Air Force is also readying its planes. Oh, wait, it looks like something is happening. A hatch is opening—something is coming out of the hatch, it looks like some kind of nozzle.*

"*Oh my God! Al, some kind of lightning has shot out of the nozzle and hit the White House! But— that's odd. Nothing has happened to the structure.*"

"Sorry to interrupt, Per, but we're now getting reports that the ships in Moscow and Peking have done the same. There is no damage noticeable to the buildings, however."

"Al, the nozzle is changing position now, and it's—oh God, it's aimed at the street! I—"

"Per? Per? I'm sorry, ladies and gentlemen, but we seem to have lost Per's signal."

BLUNT stormed into the auditorium, a cloud of cigar smoke hovering over his head. "You'd better have some good news for me, gentlemen, or I'll by *God* know the reason why! These monsters have killed everyone in the White House, and everyone standing *near* the White House! Thank God that Vice President Nixon was in California. He's flying back now to take command, but still, we need to do *something* to stop these creatures!"

Walker said, "I heard that they also killed Stalin and Mao."

"I don't give a good goddamn about what they did to the Commies, Doctor," Blunt snapped. "I want a way to stop these godless heathens before they kill any more red-blooded Americans! Now, Dr. Philipps—my God, man, you look like hell."

Philipps put the pipe in his mouth with one hand, the other placed over his chest, which was feeling a bit tight. "Just having some trouble sleeping, General."

"You sent a report about the frequencies that these monsters use. Have you found it yet?"

"Well, actually, General, I—" Philipps cut himself off, feeling a great pain in his left arm.

He collapsed a second later.

Walker cried out, "Call an ambulance!"

"This is the Pentagon, you idiot, ambulances don't come here!" Blunt cried. "Besides, you're a doctor, aren't you?"

"Of course." Walker limped over to Philipps's prone form, but there was nothing to be done. His heart had stopped beating, he wasn't breathing, and he had no pulse. "I'm sorry, General, I'm afraid he's gone."

"Dammit. There goes our last, best hope."

One of the general's aides said, "Perhaps he left some notes. We could ask his assistants."

Blunt nodded. "I'll do it, Major. You take care of the doctor here. Notify family, take care of the body, all that nonsense."

"Yes, sir."

MARIA looked up from her work on the radio frequencies when a man wearing an Army uniform and a hat with three stars on it entered. She assumed it to be General Blunt.

"Excuse me, I'm looking for Dr. Philipps's lab assistants."

"Graduate assistants, actually," Lamont said, entering from the dark room where he'd been blowing up the latest pictures that came from Hale. "We're them."

"No, I need his actual assistants, not a secretary and an errand boy."

Lamont stepped forward and held out a hand. "Hi, I'm Lamont Johnson, currently working on my PhD in theoretical astronomy at Howard University."

The general stared at Lamont's hand for several seconds, then shook it. "General Max Blunt, and I have some bad news for you and your secretary. I'm afraid Dr. Philipps is dead."

Lamont dropped the envelope filled with negatives he'd been holding.

Maria put her hand to her mouth. "D-dead?" she stammered.

"I'm afraid so. We'll have time to mourn later, but right now, I need you to try to find Dr. Philipps's notes. I know that we'll have a devil of a time figuring them out. He was supposedly on his way to a breakthrough about the radio signals or some such bunk, but he croaked before we could find out what it was."

Wincing at the general's callous attitude toward Dr. Philipps's death, Maria said, "I believe he was going to tell you about the frequency the aliens are using."

Blunt snapped his fingers. "Yes, that's it! You wouldn't happen to have any notes or anything about that?"

"Of course. We've isolated the frequency, and I can—"

The general suddenly stepped forward and grabbed her shoulders.

"You mean to tell me that that egg-head actually doped out how these monsters talk to each other?"

"Um, you're hurting me," Maria said in a small voice.

Quickly, Blunt removed his hands. "Sorry, girlie, but these are difficult times. Any chance you can type up his notes into something us civilians can follow?"

Before Maria could respond, Lamont said, "Of course she can, sir. We'll have the full report for you in triplicate within the hour."

"I just need it toot sweet, savvy? These monsters are kicking our tails, and we need to turn the tide before we're all pushing up daisies."

With that, the general left.

"*The top story tonight is the sudden exodus of all the aliens who had invaded our planet and killed hundreds in Washington, as well as the capitals of China and Russia. Our nation—our world—is in mourning for those losses, but at least the perpetrators have been sent away. We now go to one of the few surviving members of the Eisenhower Administration, Press Secretary Michael Murphy.*

"*Good evening. Vice P—Excuse me, President Nixon has asked me to extend my thanks to all those who stood fast in this country's darkest hour. In particular, the president wanted to thank General Maximillian Blunt, who commanded our noble military forces during this crisis, and who implemented Operation*

Feedback. General Blunt will be receiving the Congressional Medal of Honor for his strong leadership. In addition, President Nixon will be posthumously awarding another Medal of Honor to Dr. Phillip P. Philipps. I am told by General Blunt that Dr. Philipps was the one who initially discovered the alien ship that first crash-landed on Earth, and that it was his diligent work that led to the scientific breakthrough that was the centerpiece of Operation Feedback. Dr. Philipps's designs were used in the weapons that drove the aliens away from the planet, using a radio frequency that caused the aliens great pain. These forty-eight United States of America owe Dr. Philipps and his brilliant mind a debt we can never repay. Rest in peace, Doctor. You served your country well."

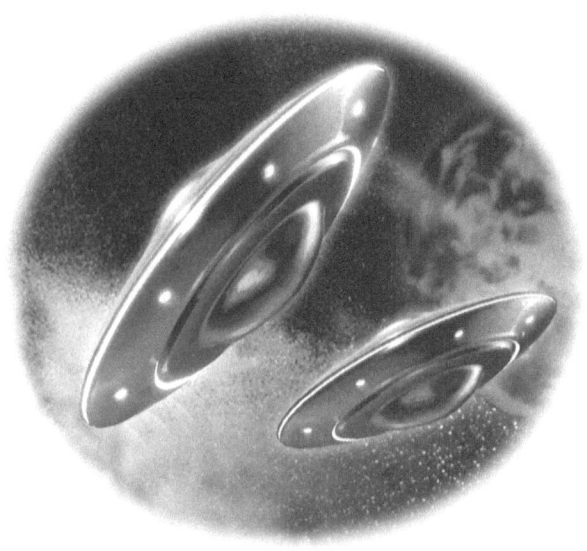

The Third Law

By Derek Tyler Attico

THE detective aimed for what should have been center mass and fired twice. Two bullets passed through the presence and slammed into the floorboard. A voice from the darkness chuckled, "You're going to have to do better than that."

Four hours earlier.
The box was a favorite among detectives in the 43rd precinct. Smaller than the standard interview room but slightly larger than a cell, the only thing that helped being in such a naturally confined space was which side of the table you were on.

Detective Omisha Monroe thumbed through the folder in her hands that gave her little insight into the pale man sitting handcuffed across from her. The brilliance of his blue eyes was set against tight and smooth skin. Tattooed numbers snaked up one arm around his neck and down the other arm, and his clothes were drenched in the arid stink of what he'd done. The foul air in the small space didn't leave much room to breathe, and even less for lies.

The detective looked up from the folder, "state your name for the record."

The suspect's only response to Monroe's request was the sound of the chain from his cuffed hand sliding through the metal ring embedded in the table as he folded his hands.

Monroe glanced over at her partner leaning against the wall, seemingly paying more attention to his coffee than the interview. Graying hair at Chappel's temples belied the powerful build stuffed into his blazer and tie. The senior detective said he wasn't much for words in the box, but after a few of these now, Monroe suspected he was just using his female partner to get a reaction out of the perps or testing her ability.

Probably both.

She understood being a cop came with tests, but it took so much more to be on the job. Ignoring the suspect's silence, Monroe continued. "No ID, no hits on fingerprints, DNA or social media, and the only thing found on you was this."

The detective took the small plastic zip lock bag marked EVIDENCE out of the folder and tossed it onto the table. Inside the bag was a worn movie stub with the word KENT faded at the top, beneath that, the words TER-2 11 p.m.

Monroe locked eyes with the man across the table, searching for

Illustration by Tom Mandrake

anything she could use. "The Kent closed back in 1991; *Terminator 2* was the last film to play there. There's a 99-cent store there now." The young woman leaned forward and into the suspect's face. "The Sound View apartments aren't even on the same side of the Bronx where the Kent used to be. I don't know what the connection is and honestly, I don't give a damn. Eight people died in that fire tonight." Monroe paused, then leaned back in her metal chair. "You can only play this game for so long, it's a small world."

Detective John Chappel watched as the John Doe chuckled softly at his partner's words. The numbers on this man's skin were visually striking, but they were only part of the story. On the job, he'd seen detachment before from criminals and cops, but not from an arsonist. He was used to them being excited, even aroused, but never this apathetic. Chappel peeled back the plastic lid on his blue and white cardboard cup, the steam from the hot coffee rose quickly, escaping the confines of its small world. The senior officer glanced over at Monroe, he'd been observing his partner almost as much as the perp. She'd been making an effort not to make any gesture that seemed overly "feminine" in the box. After her first month in the 43rd, she'd cut her hair down to almost nothing. Most likely trying to fit in with the boys, but all it really did was accentuate hazel

eyes set against flawless brown skin that didn't need makeup to be beautiful. For the NYPD Omisha Monroe checked all the boxes. The first female detective and person of color in a Bronx precinct—check, check, and check.

Chappel took a sip of his coffee, needing the caffeine at two in the morning. "I get it," the detective said to John Doe. "Deeds not words right? You're a man of action, that's why you chained all the exits and let the building burn." Chappel flicked the discarded coffee lid onto the desk. "But here's the thing, you picked the wrong borough, the Bronx hasn't gentrified yet. Brooklyn or Manhattan and sure people would care; even want to know who you are." This time Chappel took a long sip of his coffee letting his words settle in the small room before continuing. "Hell, anywhere else you could even feel like you'd done something, but you chose the Bronx, just like this cup of coffee, no one's gonna remember you tomorrow."

Keeping his gaze on the table, the smile on Doe's face slowly faded away.

Picking up on the cue, Monroe reached into her leather jacket and pulled out a lighter and pack of Newports. She shook out a cigarette and extended it across the desk. "Why the numbers?" she said as her eyes swept across the intricate tattoos.

Chappel watched Doe look at Monroe's lighter and then almost unconsciously rub the wrist that was handcuffed to the table. *Well, that did something* the senior detective thought.

Following up on the assist from his partner, Chappel interjected. "Are they...equations?

John Doe's hand moved slowly towards the extended cigarette but instead stopped at the small Ziploc evidence bag on the table. Slowly, almost hesitantly, Doe ran his fingers across the ticket encased in plastic. "So much death and destruction, so much... fire." For the first time, John Doe looked up into the faces of the two detectives, first Monroe and then Chappel. "But it doesn't matter, none of it's real."

For a split-second Monroe's eyes widened at Doe's words before she regained her composure. "Is that why you chained the doors, because you don't think it's real?"

John Doe opened his mouth to answer but began choking, detective Monroe shot a concerned look to her partner who was already heading for the door. Uncontrollably gaging, Doe reflexively began reaching for his throat only to have his hand stopped because it was handcuffed to the table, thrown off balance, he flailed about like a drowning man at sea, going down for the last time. Monroe leaped over the table, but as she reached the other side, Doe took his last, strained breath.

THE metal table was nearly identical to the one inside the box, but this one didn't have a handcuff ring, there was no need. John Doe's lifeless body lay on it unaware of the group standing around him.

"Subject is a John Doe, approximately thirty to thirty-five years of age; cause of death appears to be delayed asphyxia as a result of smoke inhalation." The eyes of the man that spoke into the microcassette recorder seemed empty, and as drained of life as the corpse he stood over.

"Wait a sec." Monroe looked down at the pinkish blue body on the slab and back up at the Medical Examiner and her partner. "Asphyxia...that can't be right."

David Chamberlain, the M.E., sighed and then turned his attention towards Chappel and began to speak again into the recorder. "Over eighty percent of the subject's body is covered in tattoos, vaccine and other scars are not apparent, most likely obscured by tattoo ink."

Now that the body was naked, Monroe could see there was some kind of pattern to the layout of the numerical tattoos, how certain areas of skin were completely covered while other patches were bare. Trying a different approach, she spoke again. "Why would some arsonist tattoo equations onto his body?"

Chappel walked around the table, looking at the tattoos from different angles. "The equations, they don't look finished."

The M.E. and young detective looked at Chappel, and Monroe asked the obvious question. "How do you know that?"

For the first time, Chappel seemed annoyed, even reluctant to answer the question.

Monroe waited for more to the explanation, but when it was apparent it wasn't coming, she continued. "Okay...so we have a dead arsonist that's bad at math?"

The M.E. looked over the body with years of disinterest. "Wasn't he caught chaining the exits, what else do you need?"

A voice from the entrance to the morgue answered. "Absolutely nothing."

The trio turned to see Lieutenant Shane Moroz filling up the doorway. Chappel couldn't remember the last time he'd seen his superior in the morgue. With boyish good looks and the frame of a linebacker, the only thing that hinted at Moroz's age was the shaved head that accentuated the imposing visage.

"Lieutenant? What are you doing down here?" Chappel asked.

Moroz walked up to the group, took a moment to look over the body before answering. "We got a hit from the missing person database. Our John Doe is firefighter Ben Stevenson of Sacramento, California. Two years ago, the Sacramento Fire Department reported him missing while fighting wildfires."

Monroe looked around the room. "Wait, he was a firefighter, and now he turns up an arsonist in the Bronx?

Moroz put on a smile that cracked the imposing image without revealing much else. "After twenty-five years on the job detective, there are just some things you can't explain."

Chappel walked over to the lieutenant. "You didn't come all the way down here to tell us that."

Lieutenant Moroz stared at the senior detective for a moment before answering, "No. We're honoring the next of kin request to cremate the body and send his ashes back to California."

Monroe looked down at the body and the evidence. "Shouldn't we at least —"

The lieutenant put up his hand. "Jesus, Monroe, learn how to take the win." Moroz started walking out of the morgue. "This one is done. I'm taking it off the board. Both of you go home, get some sleep...let it go."

AT 4 a.m. the South Bronx was wide awake and open for business. As the unmarked sedan moved through traffic, Omisha Monroe watched transactions take place that were too small to be officially noticed. "I don't understand what the hell happened," the detective said more to the streets than her partner.

John Chappel shot a glance over to the young woman as he moved in tight behind a delivery van that was just starting its day. "Word of advice, that's not something anyone wants to hear a detective say."

Monroe turned away from the view and towards her partner "I'm serious. Smoke inhalation? Cremation? First, he's a firefighter, now he's a dead arsonist? The young woman turned back to the window, defeat in her voice. "It's all upside down."

At a red light, Chappel slid up next to an empty city bus, he was eye level with an ad on the side of the bus promoting the exploits of the Bronx Bombers. Chappel stared at the advertisement until the light turned green. "A multi-billion-dollar baseball team has a stadium in one of the poorest places in America. The whole goddamn world is upside down."

In the weeks since she'd started, the only conversation with Chappel had been about the job, this was the first time she'd ever seen a glimpse of anything else from the man. "In the morgue, why didn't you answer me?"

For a long time, they rode in silence, Monroe thought he wasn't going to say anything again, and then Chappel just started talking. "I never gave a damn about people, numbers are what I was good at, what mattered. I only became a cop for the resume on my way to analyst for the Agency, money and power. Shit, the Bronx was just a

rung on the ladder, a place you went so you could say you cared. I didn't look at the people here, didn't even think about them; they were invisible to me. Then one day we get a call, this kid was playing on the tracks and gets clipped by a train. I'm holding his hand while we wait for EMT and he's bleeding all over the place, and now he's not so invisible anymore." He stopped, his voice back in the past. "Kid died, but he wasn't alone, and the numbers, all my plans... they just weren't that important anymore."

Chappel slipped into a space between two parked cars and turned off the engine. Monroe let her silence tell her partner how she felt.

About a minute later the young woman looked around, the street sign read 167th, they were just off the Grand Concourse. Security gates that would roll up and out of sight in the light of day were now walls of graffitied metal, guarding every storefront. Few people were on the street in the predawn night, but that would soon change as the diurnal world began to wake. "What are we doing over here?"

The detective chuckled. "Doing what Moroz said, letting go." Chappel nudged with his chin. "Across the street."

Monroe followed Chappel's gesture to a store with a marquee above it that read 99¢ Spot in bold red letters; it wasn't hard for Monroe to imagine in another time the same marquee read Kent Theatre. "So what do we do, wait for them to open up?" she said.

John Chappel smiled. "Not exactly."

THE young detective noticed an old woman looking down into the side street alley from her bathroom, Monroe took out her badge and held it up. As she did so, the old woman receded from view. Dawn was about to break, and in a few minutes, the two detectives wouldn't have the cover of night. "Are you sure this is even the right door?"

Chappel spoke softly as he picked the lock. "We're in the right place, the 99-cent shop is in the front where the ticket booth and concession stand used to be." The detective paused as the locked clicked. "This door is the fire exit by the movie screen," he said as he stood up and pulled out his 9 mm automatic and a small flashlight before stepping inside.

Following suit, Monroe pulled out her Glock, thumbed on her mini flashlight and followed her partner into the darkness.

THE silver screen that both detectives walked under was no longer the canvas of joy and excitement it had once been, but now it was just a tattered remnant of the past. Chappel moved slowly towards the left side of the theatre while Monroe stayed on the right. The older detective's flashlight stretched over three sections of rotted seats, a large main center section and two thinner sections on either side—decomposing spectators from a coliseum long forgotten. "I thought this would've been used for storage but looks like they just locked it off, cheaper not to renovate I guess."

Monroe aimed her flashlight up the aisle. "I thought we'd find squatters to question, but it looks empty."

Chappel didn't know what to expect, but it wasn't this. "There's got to be something here." The detective pointed his flashlight at what he wanted Monroe to do. "Check the projection booth, I'm gonna keep looking down here."

The young woman looked at her partner; even in the dim light, he could see the concern on her face. "Copy that," was all she said.

Halfway up the aisle, Chappel didn't see it as much as feel it. He'd been walking on the theatre's rotted carpet, but now he was standing on something solid and smooth. Pointing the flashlight to his feet, Chappel could see that he was standing on a large metal plate.

With equations carved into it.

Suddenly Chappel found himself unable to breathe and his mind reeled back to the look on the arsonist's face, and he understood. Somehow, the arsonist hadn't been choking, he had been strangled. From behind, a voice whispered into John Chappel's ear, "Ticket please."

Chappel could feel the cord around his neck, but could neither see it, nor his assailant. Instinctively, he reached backward dropping the flashlight while still gripping his 9 mm, only to clutch air. He could feel his heart jackhammering out of his chest, his lungs on fire, life slipping away from him. On the floor somewhere behind him, his flashlight stretched his shadow onto the wall in front of him, a macabre image of a man struggling, with perhaps death itself. As Chappel, watched his own shadow, another shadow appeared behind him as the cord tightened. "No one's gonna remember you tomorrow," the shadow whispered.

Passing her flashlight over the staircase, Monroe noticed them etched into the wall and stairs leading up to the projection booth.

Equations.

The young woman crouched down to inspect them when she heard her partner gasp for air. She turned to see his body arching backward unnaturally, a puppet, dancing on invisible strings.

As she moved toward Chappel, a presence lifted her by her throat off her feet, and slammed her into the wall next to the staircase. Like a lover's sweet caress, the presence whispered softly in front of her, "You should worry about yourself."

The detective aimed for what should have been center mass and fired twice. Two bullets passed through the presence and slammed into the floorboard. A voice from the darkness chuckled, "You're going to have to do better than that."

Ignoring the tightening vise around her neck, Monroe fired three more times in front of her, only to tear apart the far wall. As the edges of her vision began to darken and fade the young woman dropped her weapon and flashlight, choosing instead to claw at her throat for life. Somewhere in the recesses of her brain, she realized she was mimicking the last action of the arsonist and began to struggle even harder. As Monroe kicked and scratched, the unseen presence began to coalesce, first into a shadow and then solidified into a man with both of his hands around her neck, squeezing. Now, finally with someone to see, feel, and touch, Monroe grabbed both of his wrists, but no longer had the strength for anything else.

The man was easily over six feet, bald, wearing some sort of semitransparent latex suit. His green eyes were aflame with excitement. The muscular body underneath covered in tattooed unfinished equations. With his hands still around the throat of his prey, he moved toward the staircase, the tattoos on his body and the etchings on the stairs began to glow, the two sides of the equations coming together.

Too weak to pull away, Monroe's

eyes widened as a sphere of energy began to form around the man, and the staircase, pulsing like a heartbeat as it illuminated the darkened theatre, turning night into day.

Her assailant kept her on the threshold of the sphere as if she were on the edge of a universal precipice. His biceps stiffened as he squeezed harder, laughing. "Please keep your arms and legs inside the ride at all times."

Darkness pushed in on Monroe as the theatre erupted into a frenzy of light and energy. Her skin began to blister and burn, she opened her mouth to scream, but the hands around her throat denied her even that final release. The detective's eyes fluttered and then closed as she felt a force shove her toward the man and into the void of eternity.

AN echo of sound. A flash of light. An inhalation of life. Pain. Like the newborn emerging from the womb into the new world, Omisha Monroe opened her eyes—to see her partner, staring blankly.

"Chappel?" Monroe didn't understand what was wrong with her partner until her eyes began to look him over, and then she understood. Chappel had shoved her, and when he did, took her place on the edge of the sphere, the energy had sliced him in half.

Monroe lurched backward unable to break her partner's stare until her hands touched latex and muscle; she looked down to see the bisected body of her would-be assassin. When Chappel shoved her, he pushed the tattooed lunatic out the other end of the sphere. The detective stood up and stared at the broken pieces of both friend and foe. "What the fuck is going on?"

Monroe reached into her leather jacket and pulled out her cell phone, the face of the device informed her there was no service. Putting the phone away, she looked down the aisle of the theatre and immediately realized she was no longer in darkness, the theatre's lights along the walls were on and the movie screen was intact.

The seats, walls and even the rugs, everything looked like a normal movie theatre. Monroe quickly scanned the floor for her Glock, unable to find it, she crouched beside the body of her partner, gently taking his 9 mm automatic out of his hand and placing it in her shoulder holster. "Thank you for saving me," the young woman said as she closed Chappel's eyes.

The door that was supposed to lead to the renovated 99 cent store opened into the movie theatre lobby, concession stand and ticket booth. What should be there, wasn't. The tattoos, the energy field, Monroe didn't know where it was all leading, and there was really only one way to get real answers.

The detective unlocked the front door of the theater and stepped outside.

Terminator 2: Judgment Day. Monroe stared at the marquee above the Kent movie theatre that changed everything, but it was only the beginning. There were no cars outside, no shops on the street except for a bookstore and the theatre. There weren't even sidewalks, just pedestrian walkways, bike paths, and trees. The Grand Concourse, looked more like a park than a main roadway. Monroe watched people laughing and talking on their way to work or school or wherever they went here, in the place that was the Bronx, but wasn't.

A passerby in a suit glanced at her as he was walking by, noticing something about her, he suddenly stopped. "Are you alright, miss?"

The detective looked over the man, a thin metal nametag on his suit lapel said Joe Snyder, the relaxed body language and smile that reached eyes behind bifocals said he wasn't a threat. Monroe opened her mouth to answer the question, but then closed it when she realized she had no idea how to answer.

Snyder pointed to the right side of his own face and neck as he spoke while looking at hers. "Those are some pretty nasty burns, are you sure you're—"

Monroe touched the side of her face, the burns must've been bad from the look on the Samaritan's face, but there was only one thing she could think of. "What year is this?"

Snyder stepped closer as a nervous smile attempted to mask his concern. "Uhh you seem a little disoriented, why don't you let me take care of those burns."

Monroe looked at the unexpected Samaritan suspiciously. "Joe, is it, you're a doctor?"

Snyder's face broke out in confusion at the mention of his name, then he smiled as he looked down at his nametag. Reaching into his suit he took out what looked to be a smartphone. "No...of course not, just let me download the med app." After tapping a few buttons, the device chimed, and Snyder looked up as he turned the face of the phone towards the detective. Caduceus, the universal Greek symbol for medicine was flashing on the screen and just above it was the information that answered at least one question: May 7, 2019 06:24 a.m. "This'll only take a sec," he said, smiling.

Monroe was about to ask how his phone could help her when she felt a cooling sensation on her skin, a moment later Snyder pulled the device away. "All done," he said.

The detective felt her skin and returned the smile, but Snyder's grin had disappeared as he looked over her shoulder.

"Citizen, please step away from the suspect."

Snyder backed off with his arms raised as the detective turned to see a man and a woman wearing leather jackets with the words NYPD across them, they were standing in front of what looked like a blue and white version of a patrol car, except it had no wheels and was hovering about a foot off the ground.

Both policemen were brandishing nightsticks, with a blue tinge at the tips of the metal batons. The officer closest to Monroe, the woman, took a step forward as she spoke. "Ma'am my name is officer Gina DeSimone, this is my partner Gerry Ford, we'd like you to come with us please."

Without hesitating, Monroe pulled out her weapon and pointed it at the officer. "I don't think so."

The second officer, Ford scoffed when he saw the gun. "Barbaric," he said.

Officer DeSimone took another step forward. 'Ma'am, please lower the weapon, the use of firearms is expressly prohibited."

Monroe frowned, *what the hell where they talking about? Cops not using guns?* Wherever this was, it wasn't any place she was used to. "Last time I checked, a gun beats a stick, put them down, and I won't have to —"

Without warning, DeSimone fired her baton, a wave of energy struck the detective, knocking her unconscious. Officer Ford double tapped the thin radio headset attached to his ear. "Yeah, this is Ford, we've got a package for pickup."

"

STATE your name for the record."

It wasn't the words that pulled Monroe back to consciousness; it was the comfort of a familiar voice.

Her own.

Omisha Monroe looked up to see Omisha Monroe, identical and yet different. This other woman also wore short hair, but had a very different fashion sense. The pants suit accentuated this Omisha Monroe's beauty in every way her own jeans and leather jacket took it away.

Monroe could see that this woman, this Omisha had an elegance and confidence that she lacked.

The handcuff chained to the metal table and a quick glance around told Monroe where she was.

No two-way mirror, no cameras. A box.

She looked up at her doppelganger who stood against the wall sipping coffee out of a white and blue cardboard cup. "I think you know my name," Monroe said.

Omisha smiled, as she walked over to the table and sat down. "Your identification says you're a detective."

Monroe looked puzzled at her newfound twin. "You're not?"

Omisha smiled again. "No... Special Agent." The reflection casually crossed her legs before continuing. "Do you understand where you are, detective?"

Monroe nodded. "I've put together enough to know you have no intention on sending me back to where I come from."

Omisha looked up, genuinely surprised, "Excuse me?"

Now Monroe crossed her legs, mirroring her new twin. "C'mon, a special agent questioning a detective in the box, that's not professional courtesy." Monroe leaned forward. "I never had the stomach for bullshit, but I can see you don't have a problem with it."

Omisha leaned back in her chair and took in her counterpart, searching for something of herself in this other woman, after a long pause she reached into her suit and pulled out the 9 mm from Monroe's holster that she was now wearing. "These were outlawed before I was even born." Omisha looked over the weapon with disgust and then slid it back into the holster. "We're nothing like you people."

Monroe smiled. "Clearly, that's why you're sending nut jobs over to my world."

For a split second, Omisha's eyes widened from Monroe's words before she regained her composure. "You work in a slum, don't you detective? The idea of dumping everything unwanted into one place for the betterment of others shouldn't be new to you. We just do it on a different scale."

The air of detachment and privilege in the voice that sounded exactly like her own frightened Monroe. "That's insane," she whispered.

Agent Omisha laughed. "No, it's not. We haven't had a major war since the crossover equation was proven. When we started using your side as a dumping ground so we could make our world a better, safer place, things really started to come together."

Monroe wanted to lunge across the table, but knew handcuffed she wouldn't get very far.

Omisha stood up and took a smartphone out of her suit pocket. The special agent began tapping the face of the device as she spoke to her double. "You're being sent to a Pit, and trust me when I say that's not a metaphor. But before you go, I need to know everything about your investigation with Chappel on the other side." Omisha flipped the phone over so the strobing lights on the screen were facing Monroe. "This is going to hurt, but it's okay, you can scream all you want."

THE Director viewed the images of the dead cop and his Kharon agents with disgust. A Kharon with phasing tech didn't come cheap, and he'd lost two. The Kent Theatre would have to be closed down for clean-up, perhaps indefinitely. Crossover points into slums were valuable; he hated to lose this one. The arsonist they'd sent over cost them a lot, but like all the others, he belonged on that world, not this one.

And then there was detective John Chappel.

Seeing the cop's dead body made the director think about the day he changed the world after he saved a kid from bleeding out. Saving that life made him think about Newton's Third Law—how everything has an equal and opposite reaction. That was when he saw it in his mind's eye, the crossover equation that proved his theory.

Everywhere.

A knock interrupted the director's trip to the past, but when he saw who it was, he was thankful all over again he'd been able to save that kid all those years ago. The Director was proud of the woman she'd become. "Was it difficult Omisha, meeting that other you?" Director Chappel asked the Special Agent.

Monroe thought about everything she'd been through today, losing her partner, meeting her dark reflection, taking her place in front of this man that wore a familiar face but was a stranger, and how it was now up to her to change two worlds.

Monroe sighed, "just part of the job."

Not Just an Intern

By Amy Lewanski

ANNE'S long search for a journalism internship for her sophomore year of college was running dry. Her plain name, her simple resume, her wide blue eyes that made her look too innocent at interviews, all seemed to scare away potential employers. She felt like her classmates had always been one step ahead of her, especially Justine Jenkins, who had a cool journalist-styled name and sharp gray eyes, and had cut her teeth as a teenager helping at her brother's magazine. Justine claimed that by 17 she'd been interviewing local musicians and her brother had promoted her to head of personal ads.

Anne believed none of this, but still felt the jealousy crashing against her chest as she got yet another rejection, this time from one of the more minor papers in the city. She had heard from Emerson Kasak, Justine's sometimes-boyfriend who was also in their program, that Justine had been brought on at the Union as their production intern, and even dizzy Liza Sacks got an internship at the Fashion Institute magazine. But still nothing for Anne. Sitting in the campus cafe, staring at the impersonal email —" thanks, but no thanks" —she fought back tears, loathe to cry in public, refusing to run away to somewhere more private before she'd finished her salted caramel iced coffee. She kept her eyes on the pockmarked and stained dark wood table gathering condensation from her plastic cup. A chair scraped against the floor beside her. Justine sat down.

"Hi girl!" her chipper, pretentious voice cut through Anne like a saw. "Do you have an internship yet? I just got mine settled, what a thrill when the Union called me! Oh my god, but of course you have something lined up, you're one of the best in our class!"

Anne's breath shook like the unbalanced chair she was sitting on. "No, still nothing. It's been a hard summer," she admitted quietly, then took a stalwart sip of her coffee. The last thing she wanted was to deal with Justine's pity. And indeed, Justine's lovely face crumpled at Anne's words, and while on any other girl the expression would mar her face, Justine's beauty only lifted. Justine was so beautiful, and so qualified. Anne couldn't stand it.

"Anne, my dear, how unfair. You are better than so many in our cohort. Did you hear that Liza Sacks actually got an internship? How is she even still in the

Illustration by Peter Krause

journalism program? She isn't half as smart as you." Justine reached across the table and touched Anne's cool hand. Anne managed a half-hearted shrug.

"I know!" Justine cried suddenly. "My brother Ethan needs a TA for his journalism course at City College downtown! I can't believe I didn't think of this before, you're perfect! You're smart, the students will like you, and of course you can write anything."

"Justine..." Anne said, feeling steamrolled. Justine almost always wandered into Anne's life to make sweeping declarations and then change her life. "The program says specifically we needed an internship."

"You can argue anything you want, Anne, you should know this by now!" Justine laughed a light, tinkling laugh. "We'll just stop by the office right now, get the Dean and Professor Owens on board with the paperwork and then get you over to City College to meet Ethan."

"Oh Justine, I really couldn't impose like that," Anne tried to push against Justine's kind offer once again. "I'm sure your brother can find someone more qualified than I am to be a TA."

"Absolutely not! Anne, I won't take no for an answer. Come on, we've no time to lose, it's almost three, and we know that the staff leave early on Wednesdays." Justine stood, a bustling ball of excitement, and took Anne's arm,

pulling her onto her feet. Justine lead the way, gliding majestically through empty summer hallways.

And so, Anne found herself in some sort of dream fog, beholden to her occasional GPA nemesis for a job. Anne followed Justine to Professor Owen's office where Anne argued that a TA position at City College would fill the internship role, as she would be learning about publishing and journalism standards from an industry professional. The dream fog didn't lift as her professor signed the paperwork for her to use a TA position as her internship requirement, and then the dean also agreed, and as Anne thanked both profusely, the secretary began speaking with the journalism department at City College, setting up her interview.

Shaking, Anne stepped outside the program offices and leaned against the wall. She breathed deeply. Only an hour earlier, she had felt tapped out and at her wit's ends, without a way to complete her semester. Now, thanks to Justine yet again, she had an interview, the program on her side, and probably a steady, if small, income for the semester. She straightened her sweater and left for her interview with the department before meeting Ethan the following day.

The next morning, while she ironed her smartest blouse—white, long sleeved, collared, no pattern at all—she tried to recall everything she knew about Ethan Jenkins. He was in his mid-thirties, and was as handsome as Justine was beautiful. He had started *The Eagle* while in his senior year of university, and through his sheer willpower, charisma, and head for business, had quickly turned it into one of the city's best small magazines. It was noted for its excellent reporting of local issues, and it's strong ties to the community college.

Her phone buzzed; Justine was waiting in front of Anne's apartment building to pick her up. Anne buttoned her blouse, rushed downstairs, and off the two young ladies went. Little did either of them know that Justine was taking Anne to meet her destiny.

Justine left Anne in the anteroom before the department staff room and offices, confidently sweeping past the middle-aged receptionist and into the twisting hallways, looking for Ethan. The brunette receptionist shot Anne a critical look before returning to her work at several computer screens and answered the phone. After a few silent moments, the door flew open and Justine floated out like a sunbeam. She clasped Anne's hands in her own slim pair.

"Dear Anne, Ethan is so excited to meet you. I made sure to tell him all about you! That you're the top of our cohort, what a wonderful writer you are, and that you were shortlisted last year for the Leslie Anderson Award even though it's usually only given to sophomores and seniors. He was

very impressed, and so happy to have you be his TA. The department already told him that you were, of course, but the personal touch means so much." Justine's gray eyes looked deep into Anne's blue ones. Anne thought for half a moment that she heard the secretary huffing behind them. Then Justine urged her, "Well, what are you waiting for? Go on in and say hello!"

She pushed Anne bodily into the hallway and through an unmarked door to the staffroom where Ethan Jenkins was waiting for her. Anne stumbled at the force, but as soon as she was inside, she stopped dead in her tracks. Behind a cheap veneer topped table sat a pure, fine specimen of masculinity. Ethan Jenkins had broad shoulders that gave way to gently muscled arms and large hands. He shared Justine's cool gray eyes, but his hair was sable dark compared to Justine's chestnut, and graying just a little at the temples. Anne's heart jumped uncomfortably in her chest. The rumors about Ethan Jenkins's striking good looks, the pictures in the social pages—none of it had done him justice.

"Anne, it's a pleasure to meet you," he said in a deep baritone as he stood and walked to her, taking her hand in his with a firm shake. Anne gasped as their hands connected. "My sister has told me so much about you. Sounds as though you're a very impressive woman."

Anne felt herself blush. She pulled her hand back and nervously pushed her straw-colored hair behind her ears. She had never been in the presence of such a handsome and powerful man before. The wall behind Ethan had a bookcase full of instructional books on journalism, standards, and a crooked poster detailing the different editing marks. Anne inspected the book titles and poster, finding the institutional reminder of school a calming presence. She was here to work, not be overwhelmed by Ethan's attractiveness. "Thank you, Mr. Jenkins," she said. "It's a pleasure to meet you too."

"Please, call me Ethan," he said with a grimace. "*Mr. Jenkins* sounds so elderly, and I already feel old enough." He chuckled a bit and touched the gray at his temples, a little self-consciously. Anne felt the heat in her cheeks flare hotter.

"Oh, no, Mr. Jenkins—I mean, Ethan—you aren't old! You look so distinguished!" she blurted out. Her new boss looked at her with surprise. Anne ducked her head and stared at her feet, in shock that she had said anything so embarrassing. She couldn't understand how she could blush any more, yet somehow her face was growing even hotter, until she felt as though she were glowing like a lamp. She mentally began packing up her things and moving to a foreign country so she never

had to see Ethan Jenkins or his sister or anyone ever again. But then he reached for her hand again. The warmth of his palm was a comforting heat against the high flush of her embarrassment. She looked up at him.

"I'm glad you've signed on to be my TA, Anne. Teaching is hard, but rewarding, especially this semester: our course is Introduction to Reporting and Newswriting so we'll have a mix of experience in the classroom." He dropped her hand and moved to the door. "Let me show you where the TA lounge is, you can hold office hours there if you'd like, and my office is around the corner. I should also show you where the class will meet, since Justine did say you haven't been to City College before." Mr. Jenkins held the door and lead Anne around the confusing maze inside the Journalism and Media building. Anne was sure she would be lost for at least a month.

Ethan described the course and her role as they stopped their walk near Justine's car. Anne felt momentarily overwhelmed, but the paycheck steadied Anne. Ethan took her hand in his again for a genial shake, and Anne could not suppress the small shiver that ran down her spine from his touch. Her mouth felt suddenly dry and she looked into Mr. Jenkins' gray eyes. There was a deep, silent pause as the two met gazes and kept their hands locked.

"It was wonderful meeting you today, Anne," Mr. Jenkins said, his voice huskily deeper. He let go of her hand. "I'm looking forward to working with you." He turned quickly and walked back towards his building. Justine yelled that their mother expected him home for dinner that evening and he lifted a hand in acknowledgment.

Back in the small office he had to share with another journalism adjunct, Ethan settled into the worn-out desk chair and began going through his to do list before the semester started in a few days. But on this particular morning, he could barely pay attention to his own syllabus and book list. He kept thinking about Anne. He could not stop thinking about how her dark lashes framed her eyes and how her pale blonde hair brought out a sweet pink in her cheeks. Justine had always had good taste in friends; she had been the reason he had met and hired his managing editor Rachel Turner as well. Ethan had a funny, squiggly feeling in the pit of his stomach as he thought about Anne.

ETHAN'S phone rang in the middle of a lecture. He didn't allow his students to check their phones during a lecture, but he checked the screen briefly—it was *The Eagle*, and Rachel and the secretary had specific instructions to not call unless it was an emergency.

"Anne, could you take over for a few minutes please. This shouldn't take too long..." he trailed off as he rushed from the room. Ethan was confident in Anne, as he had been in the middle of a PowerPoint with excellent notes.

Nothing had been actually wrong, just an unpaid invoice from, and once he'd reassured Rachel and Daniel the accountant that he'd personally call the next day to sort out payment, he was free to return to the classroom. Ethan slipped back into the room and stood against the door, watching Anne teach. She had put her pale hair up in a ponytail and it swung heavily as she turned her head, caressing her neck and shoulder where it touched. Anne's voice was firm but light as she lectured the class on the different commas accepted by current publishing standards. Ethan found himself transfixed by her small hands fluttering around the dusty old chalkboard as she drew a second example for the students and he couldn't help but stare at her perfect bow of an upper lip as her tongue peeked between her parted mouth as she spoke. Not even the harsh light of the projector seemed to mar her lovely face, as the light sparkled off her crystal blue eyes. Ethan swallowed as he watched her teach, then shook his head as if to clear it and walked back up to the lectern.

Once Ethan had returned to his office after class, he collapsed into the creaking desk chair and buried his face in his hands. *Ethan, you lecherous old man,* he chastised himself. *How could you even look at Anne that way? She is your TA and just far too young for you. Don't be such a dirty old man.* He pulled a stack of essays toward him that Anne had graded earlier in the week, and began perusing the comments and grades she had written on them. Her handwriting scrawled across the pages in small, tight loops of purple and green ink and every comment was supportive in its criticism. He could tell that Anne took her job seriously and after watching her teach on the spot, Ethan knew she had the bones of a good teacher.

ANNE had settled into the routine of being a TA—show up to lecture, take attendance for Ethan, run discussion and critique groups during the "lab" section of the course, and assist students in editing and improving their work— and had opened her office hours for the week in the TA lounge. She had papers spread on a small table and was grading while waiting for students when Ethan stopped by the TA lounge to speak with her.

"Anne, I want you to interview at *The Eagle*. We need another copyeditor and you certainly have the skills to join our team. My managing editor Rachel Turner agreed to interview you tomorrow morning at our offices. I'm hoping you will become an important member of my magazine's team."

Anne worked to not drop her

mouth open in surprise. Mr. Jenkins—Ethan, she corrected herself—was offering her a job.

ANNE walked into *The Eagle*'s small lobby area and took a steadying breath. The doorway she stood at faced a glass door open to the bullpen; Anne could see the hustling writers and editors at laptops, desktops, or on their tablets and phones, while other employees ran purposefully from desk to desk. A low hum came through the door. The idea of sitting at a desk in that room calmed her nerves almost instantly. The noise and bustle called to her, deep within her soul. She knew that she belonged there.

Almost directly across from where she stood, Anne could see a small conference room set up as an office, and a plaque on the door that Anne could just make the words "managing editor" stamped on. A tall, brunette woman was writing notes on an easel in the corner. Her long chestnut colored hair was piled neatly in a bun, and Anne fidgeted while waiting for Rachel Turner to greet her. The young man in reception pressed a button on his phone to tell Rachel her next interview was in. When Rachel finally greeted her, Anne was struck by Rachel's firm gaze from brown eyes perfectly framed by wire-rimmed glasses. Anne could tell that Rachel was a woman who missed little and would be critical of anything—or anyone—that didn't measure up to her standards.

"Nice to meet you, Anne. Ethan's told me about your skills and we're glad to have you in for an interview," she said, shaking Anne's hand firmly. "I've had a chance to look at your resume and read some of your portfolio, and I'm impressed with your skills, especially your editing." Anne tried not to smile too broadly— her academic rivalry with Justine had resulted in Anne's excellently honed editing skills—and followed Rachel through the door through the bullpen and towards Rachel's office. The buzz of the room filled Anne's head. She itched to pull out her laptop and start working immediately. "Take a seat, please," Rachel said once the they entered her office. Anne took one of the simple white office chairs. Rachel sat behind her desk, crossing her long legs under her seat.

"I'm so excited to be here," Anne said, hoping this was what Rachel wanted to hear. "This is such a great magazine, and I've heard really good things about working here."

When their interview concluded, Anne offered to see herself out as Rachel's phone rang. Anne paused near the door to the lobby and inhaled a long breath through her nose. The noise and the energy of the employees fed the hum in her soul and she turned to push the door open and crashed into Ethan Jenkins.

Ethan had come in for his weekly staff meeting as editor-in-chief and was hoping to run into Anne while she was there for her interview, and his wish was granted when she turned and walked bodily into him. Anne stumbled back a step and Ethan caught her, his hands gripping her arm and her waist.

"Oh, I'm sorry, Mr. Jenkins!" Anne said, blushing a hot red. The corner of Ethan's mouth twitched. "Ethan, I didn't mean to bump into you!" He quickly dropped his hands from her waist.

"How was your interview?" he asked her, and though Anne heard his words, her mind was stuck on the fading warmth of his hand on her waist and the concerned look in his eyes as he steadied her. She took in his corporate look—crisp white button down with sleeves rolled to the elbow, revealing muscled forearms, a slim blue tie that enhanced his dark eyes—and Anne's breath came shallow in her throat and her knees threatened to give out on her. She liked his business look much more than his lumpy sweater-and-jeans adjunct professor look.

"Oh, really good," she managed to say as she steadied herself. "Thank you so much for asking Rachel to interview me." She stepped past Ethan's handsome frame, hoping he would touch her arm or her hand again. "I have to go—class soon." She left feeling as though Ethan was watching her and she liked that feeling. Her cheeks still flamed hotly as she left the office building.

Anne you idiot, he is your employer and professor, you cannot even dream of thinking he's handsome. Where is your professionalism. Do you want to be a stereotype? Anne thought viciously as she drove back to campus for her ethics in the workplace lecture. Her blush crept down her neck as embarrassment over her physical feelings for Ethan warred with her desire to remain employed.

Ethan ran the weekly staff meeting almost robotically, his mind was still with Anne. He could not get her shocked but pleased expression when she realized she had bumped into him out of his mind. Ethan let his small staff discuss the agenda and brainstorm holiday party themes while he contemplated Anne's bright blue eyes and the feeling of her in his arms. He had Rachel's notes from her interview, and her review was extremely positive—he was glad she liked Anne as much as he did. It wouldn't feel right to push hiring Anne if Rachel hadn't thought she could do the job. He didn't want to set a precedence for having women he found attractive in his employ.

Rachel was also a handsome woman, and much closer in age to Ethan, and she had been a driving force behind him for years, but their affair had flamed out years before. He hadn't thought of Rachel romantically since they grew apart, and he now trusted her completely as his managing editor. Ethan realized he would have many more opportunities to interact with Anne once she also worked at his magazine. There was a heavy, warm feeling in the pit of his stomach at the prospect of time with Anne.

"**E**THAN," Anne said, poking her head into his shared office. "When do you need these essays graded by?" She knew he needed them graded by the next day, but she had been finding excuses to visit his office on campus almost daily—either with a question, or to show a particularly great (or awful) piece of student work. She had the stack of mostly graded essays in her hands, her tight, tidy scrawl shimmering across the paper in still-damp purple ink.

"Tomorrow, Anne," Ethan said, fighting a smile. Her frequent visits distracted him nicely from lesson planning and approving budgets and writing arts and education proposals for grants and state funding. He just couldn't manage sitting alone in his shared office, or fighting for desk space with the other adjunct, Jim, on a consistent basis. Before Anne was hired as his TA, he only came to campus when he had to, but now he kept finding excuses to run into her on campus and at *The Eagle*'s office. "How are you doing, balancing your classes with TAing?"

"It's harder than I thought it

would be," Anne said, walking into the office and perching lightly on the sagging couch squished into the corner. "Ethan, I can't thank you enough for recommending me for an interview at *The Eagle*. It was such good experience to be interviewed."

"Rachel hasn't called you yet?" Ethan said, confused. Rachel was supposed to offer the job to Anne—the two had discussed it days before.

"Oh! She did, but I told her I would have to think about it because of my work here with you and my class schedule."

"Anne," Ethan said firmly, "you can do this job and the copyeditor job Rachel offered you. You are incredibly capable, I've seen that in your work here. We trust you to do both."

Anne felt yet another blush flare across her cheeks. She looked at her feet briefly, wondering if anyone had ever blushed this many times in front of anybody. Anne was convinced that with each flush of her cheeks, Ethan thought of her as younger and more incompetent. "Thank you," she managed to breathe out after a few seconds. "I'll call her back right now."

She left the essays and escaped to the hall to make her phone call, and when she returned, she was fighting a smile. Anne sat back down and began her grading in earnest. The small office filled with a companionable silence as Ethan continued writing his grant proposal for linking his classes and *The Eagle* together.

The semester continued, and while Anne did struggle occasionally with two jobs and her classes, she discovered she was able to do all her work, even if it meant she occasionally flaked on weekend plans with Justine. Anne decided to give *The Eagle* as much priority as she could, and she found herself working around when she knew Ethan would also be in the office. At staff meetings, she caught herself casting lingering glances in his direction, and she often realized she would sit near enough that she could look at him covertly. Sometimes she thought that Ethan's gaze also landed on her more than he looked at his other employees, but she didn't dare check.

With her small paychecks, Anne's bank balance inched higher, and she started buying nicer clothes to fit in with the older and more established employees at *The Eagle*, and to differentiate herself from her students—thrifted silken blouses, a dark pencil skirt, heeled shoes that lifted her another inch or two. With her new clothes, Anne felt her confidence leaping upwards. While editing at *The Eagle*, she often felt eyes on her especially when she came dressed up in something new, and a tiny, heart-thudding wish deep within her body hoped that the eyes belonged to Ethan.

"Anne, would you stay behind for a minute?" Ethan said one

Friday after a particularly long meeting at *The Eagle*. She swallowed, suddenly feeling shaky in her arms and legs like she had run a marathon. As the rest of the team dispersed, worry floated around her head like little flies; her coworkers' low conversations hummed in her ears. Rachel was the last to walk out. Ethan moved to the chair next to Anne and leaned towards her.

"You've been here over a month now, and I just wanted to check in. Are you managing? Do you like working here?" His deep voice had a husky quality Anne hadn't heard before.

"Oh, Ethan, yes" she said. "I love working here! It really is so much fun, and Rachel has become a wonderful mentor. I feel like she's really teaching me a lot..." Her voice bubbled out of her in an excited and energetic stream that, when she heard herself, made her feel very young. Especially given how seriously Ethan was regarding her with his intense gray eyes. Anne had never noticed his cologne before, but now the woodsy smell coiled down her nose and touched her somewhere deep as his dark eyes bored into hers. She stopped talking and swallowed hard.

"Rachel tells me she sees a lot of potential. Can I buy you a coffee? I remember my time at school, you must need a pick-me-up. We can talk about the next class project, too, while out."

"Ah, yes, okay," Anne stumbled over her words and yet another embarrassed flush flared across her cheeks.

Ethan's breath caught like he was suppressing a cough. Anne's flush had brought a gentle pink to her cheeks and made her pale eyes brighter than ever. Their gazes locked together, and—just for a moment—neither of them moved.

"I'll get my coat," Anne said finally, quickly smoothing her skirt and rushing to the little desk just outside the conference room where she did most of her work. She took her jacket off the back of her chair and whirled around, suddenly feeling as though her tiny table was a full city block, her purse, though it was just where she'd left it, somehow impossible to find. In fact, the entire bullpen's size seemed to have doubled. As she turned to leave, she realized she had to pass every single desk and every single coworker to meet Ethan at the main doors of the building. She walked with her head down, certain she would never, ever stop blushing while in *The Eagle*'s offices.

Ethan had no idea why he was taking Anne out anywhere. He didn't take any other employees, new or otherwise, for coffee just between them. He hadn't even taken Rachel out to lunch during work hours when they were dating, in order to prevent accusations of favoritism. But he found himself transfixed by Anne's simple and kind demeanor and her open face, how pretty and confident she was, the brightness and lightness she'd somehow brought to his offices. At every meeting, he spent half his time watching her, watching her reactions, like the way she would chew on her bottom lip or almost imperceptibly shrug her shoulders when she disagreed with an idea. He couldn't explain it beyond that he simply wanted to know her better. And then she was rushing down the middle of the bullpen towards him, coyly ducking her head, her face still prettily flushed, her wool peacoat hanging open over her lovely outfit. Ethan smiled.

Ethan took Anne to one of the more upscale cafes in the neighborhood, and gave a familiar nod to a barista, who blushed a bit herself. The pair sat in a secluded corner, below one of the large windows that looked out onto the street. When the light fell across Anne's pale face, Ethan could see a brush of freckles across her delicate nose, and her blue eyes sparkled like cloudless ice. He smiled at her—it was all he could do to keep from reaching across the table to brush her cheek with his hand. But his smile turned to a frown when she asked him for tea.

"Anne, you are my guest today. You can order whatever you like— and I mean anything at all." He glanced at her over his coffee, and his gray eyes held her gaze. Anne's heart stuttered in her chest and her cheeks flushed yet again, and she added a croissant to their bill.

As they sipped their drinks, they chatted amiably about their childhoods, their schooling, the birth of his magazine and Anne's own journalistic dreams. She couldn't help but notice how gently his large hands moved and how passionately they gestured as he spoke about the things he loved. Anne noticed their conversation stayed neatly away from the project they were assigning the next time their class met, but she realized she preferred this instead.

The wind had picked up quite a bit during the time they were at lunch, and as they left the cafe, it blew Anne fiercely into Ethan's side.

"Come now, Anne," he teased. "I can't have my best junior editor blowing down the street like all these fall leaves!" He laughed kindly and took her arm, tucking it firmly into the crook of his elbow. Anne's heart rate jumped to a painful staccato; she had to chew the inside of her cheek to keep herself from emitting an unbidden happy little squeal. He escorted Anne the entire way back to the office, keeping her close to his side for protection from the harsh autumn wind. And once within the safety of the walls, he helped her take off her coat and hung it up for her on the rack in the entryway. Anne's shoulders tingled lightly in the wake of his touch.

Back in his office, Ethan sat with his head in his hands. Anne Wilson was a great TA and employee; his sister had been perfectly correct in connecting her to him. Her copy-editing skills were excellent, and Rachel had nothing but praise for her quick and clear edits. She was the perfect addition to his company: professional, driven, smart. Yet earlier when she'd knocked into him on the street and looked at him innocently with her bright blue eyes, his heart had lurched in his chest. All he'd wanted to do was wrap his arms around her slim waist and make sure she was safe. But he was her boss; it wouldn't have been appropriate. So he'd settled for taking her arm in his—still, he agonized, it hadn't been enough.

How could one young woman bewitch his heart so suddenly? Ethan had no idea what to do except to call Justine. She always knew when to tell him to get over himself; surely, she would be able to talk some sense into him now. He was halfway done dialing when he paused, considering, and then hung up. What was he doing? Did he really want to get over himself? Or did he, on some level, want to see this Anne thing through, even if it ended in disaster? He turned a little in his chair and watched Anne typing something on her computer. Then she picked up her desk phone and her head popped up. Ethan quickly ducked away and turned back to his desk. It wouldn't do for Anne to catch him staring.

E VEN when dealing with gru-eling assignments of her own, and the grumblings of unhappy and equally stressed students, Anne felt her semester moving smoothly towards midterms and winter break. She sometimes wasn't sure if she could handle everything, but at the end of each day, she felt proud her work, her editing, and her growing teaching skills. As the weeks wore on, Anne and Ethan continued to go for coffees from any cafe around *The Eagle* and on City College's campus. What seemed strange to Anne was that they never spoke of work—and yet there was never a lull in the conversation and she never felt unproductive afterwards. They had more in common than Anne ever could have thought: the same favorite children's book, the same opinion on salad greens. Soon Anne began to look forward to their weekly coffee meetings more than anything else she did during the week.

Then one day, deep in the throes of midwinter, while Anne was struggling to balance her workload with midterms and the unfair amount of self-reflection essays she'd been assigned at school, she had just picked up her parka for her weekly coffee when Rachel walked up with a sheaf of papers in her arms. She set the papers on Anne's desk. Anne, her face drawn and sleepless, was struggling with one of the buttons on her coat.

"Off to another lunch date with Ethan?" Rachel asked, a grin playing around her full lips. Her brown eyes sparkled behind her glasses, and she winked.

"Date!? Rachel, of course not. We're just having a meeting." Anne felt her cheeks flush. A date! How absurd. She shook her head slowly, trying to shake the pink out of her cheeks. She had lost count of the number of times she had blushed in the office, and she hated how often she did.

Rachel leaned in towards her. "I think he's in love with you," she whispered, her voice conspiratorial. Anne felt her flush deepen. Her heart lurched against her ribs.

"Don't be silly! I'm much younger than he is, and besides, it's inappropriate as an employee and his TA." But her heart kept thumping loudly in her chest. Love?

"Sure. Maybe in the beginning. But I haven't seen him look at anyone like how he looks at you in a long time." Rachel shook her head a little sadly and left. Anne had heard the office rumors about how Rachel and Ethan had been in a serious relationship back at the very beginning of the paper's life. The office had been shocked when they split up instead of announcing their engagement. Even now, five years later, the office gossips still whispered of their lingering affection for one another.

Anne's face must have been drawn and pale when she reached the doorway where Ethan was standing, filling the space between them as he always did, with his confidence and his gut-wrenching smile. Anne swallowed dryly and attempted a smile in return.

Ethan took one look at her—her white face, her wide, sleepless blue eyes—and without saying a word, offered his arm. It was the first time they had touched since their first coffee together, when he had used the same gesture to guide her back to the office through the biting wind. But now everyone at *The Eagle* could see them. Suddenly, Anne didn't care. She clung to Ethan Jenkins. The pair walked in silence to their favorite sandwich shop, Anne all the while trying to push Rachel's comments out of her mind and focus instead on the feel of Ethan's muscular arm beneath her fingers.

Ethan was in the middle of telling her how he'd just secured an advertising deal with Last Whistle Aleworks, the city's most popular microbrewery. Ethan claimed that the promotions rep from Aleworks was a character, who had insisted that Ethan try every beer they brewed, and then, after he'd drank all 16 four-ounce tasters, had immediately challenged him to a race. Anne looked up from her turkey sandwich.

"Ethan," she said, her blue eyes boring into his. Her teacher's look was well trained by now. "Why didn't you marry Rachel?"

Ethan stared at her in surprise. The way she'd said 'Ethan' had sent a shiver through him and jolted his heart. What's more, he had had no idea that Anne even knew about his relationship with Rachel. Clearly, he needed to have

HR send the entire office a memo about the impropriety of gossiping.

"She and I... we met in college, Anne. Justine introduced us—I don't remember how... I still don't understand how Justine even knew Rachel, actually. But Rachel and I were really intense together, she is basically the reason why *The Eagle* is as successful it is. She made me go for all the funding, and she helped me find our first writers, and she found the deal on this office too, but as the business built up around us, it just... became more of a business partnership. And then we reached that part of the relationship where you think you might get married, and we talked about it, and... it just didn't feel right. Maybe it was me. Maybe I just wasn't ready for marriage yet five years ago." Ethan had never told anyone this much about his relationship with Rachel, and he could barely meet Anne's eyes as he spoke.

Anne reached across the table and took his large, warm hand in her slim, small one. He looked up and met her gaze and held it as though trying to finish his speech with just his eyes. But what was the rest? He hadn't been ready for a serious relationship five years ago... But now? Anne's pulse thudded in her chest and skittered through her veins.

Anne breathed slowly, all her focus on her nerves in her fingers and palm where Ethan's fingers brushed against her own. She realized she had been jealous of Rachel, just a little, for her past with Ethan. But now Rachel was back at the office while Ethan was sitting in a sandwich shop with her, holding hands with her. Surely that meant something.

Then Ethan stood, keeping his hand firmly around Anne's, and pulled her to her feet. They left the shop hand-in-hand, which made Anne feel almost scandalous. Would anyone notice the infamous Ethan Jenkins holding hands with such a young nobody? Her breath came shallow in her throat. Anne kept trying to tell herself, as they walked to the corner, that it wasn't the twenties anymore; in this modern age, an unwed woman could walk with an unwed man without it meaning anything.

But Anne wanted it to mean something. Anything. She knew, deeply, suddenly, when she asked Ethan over lunch about his relationship with Rachel, that she had fallen in love with him. That was the real scandal. Cliché, even, falling in love with her professor and boss. She couldn't ask for a better job, and she felt like she could become financially secure for the first time—no, she was not going to mess up her future. She couldn't let that happen. She decided she would take Justine out for dinner as another thanks soon, for the job and to make up for every time they had fought during lectures and competed over workloads in group projects, and somehow that dinner would solidify that she and Justine were friends and Ethan was her boss, and that would be that.

She was so consumed with her own thoughts that she hadn't noticed that Ethan wasn't talking either. A small frown creased his handsome face. At the corner that would return them to the office, he stopped. Anne took a few more steps, but when Ethan didn't follow, she turned, still holding his hand.

"Ethan?" she asked. He still said nothing, but released her hand, and her stomach dropped to her knees like a broken elevator. She knew it had been too good to be true. Anne might be in love with Ethan, but clearly Ethan was not in love with Anne. As soon as they rounded this corner, they would once again be boss and employee. After her impertinence in asking about Rachel, maybe even the lunches would stop. Anne felt heavy with disappointment. She swallowed and counted backwards from ten to keep herself from crying. She would not cry in front of Ethan, especially not about something so stupid as her feelings for him.

Ethan looked at her, his gray eyes burning brightly in the winter air. Then, suddenly, his hand moved to her lower back and pulled her towards him. Anne felt her breath catch in her throat and the now common flame of a blush crept up her neck. Then Ethan's other hand was touching her hot cheek, cooling her skin. Then Ethan was kissing her.

Anne melted into Ethan's arms. She relaxed, gripping his shoulders as he drew her closer still. The winter breeze whipped around them. Anne shivered but she didn't feel cold. She held Ethan tightly. Her thoughts and wild fears were lost in Ethan's kiss.

When they finally pulled apart, Anne kept her hands on his shoulders and looked up at him, smiling, as their breath mingled between lips still just inches away. Ethan's eyes seemed to have darkened while they were kissing, and now his gaze was so intense, it made Anne shudder. He cupped her face in his large, warm hands and kissed her gently once more.

"It's too bad we have to go back to the office," he said, the honeyed regret in his deep voice warming Anne from the inside out. "But we must." He drew his hand again along her cheek. "Anne, my dear, make me the happiest man alive and say you'll love me just as much as I love you."

Anne took his hand in both of hers. The sun burst through the clouds, as though it knew that only its brightness could match her joy. Ethan exhaled slowly. The fingers of his free hand tapped a nervous pattern against his thigh. Was he really worried she'd say no? Anne nearly laughed, but instead she arched up onto her toes and pressed her lips warmly against his for a moment before she said,

"Ethan, there is no easier promise you could ask me to make."

The Green Lady and the Rogue

By KARISSA LAUREL

THE folks of New Hanover county, particularly the men-folk, had been known to say that Tamsyn Gruene's figure was like the Cape Fear river after a heavy rain—curving and swelling in all the right places. While not ashamed of her feminine attributes, Tamsyn took great pains to conceal her allure, along with her identity. She often wore a drab green cape that aided her ability to blend into shadows and camouflaged her hour-glass shape. An emerald scarf cut with eyeholes covered her hair, nose, and brow, leaving only her full lips on display. But if her disguise wasn't enough to deter unwanted attention, the pair of flintlock pistols strapped to hips usually did the trick.

On this particularly warm evening, Tamsyn left her cape's hood down, and her lantern drew cinnamon highlights from the braid draped over her shoulder as she crept through the woods beyond her grandfather's farm. Her neighbor, a mousy woman named Sarah Walker, accompanied her. Sarah's protruding belly gave her the illusion of late pregnancy, but closer inspection would reveal only a bundle of rags stuffed under her threadbare dress. Together the two women prowled like a pair of she-cats over a loamy forest floor toward the banks of the Cape Fear.

Sugar, bacon, cornmeal. Flour, too, I hope. Silently, Tamsyn reviewed her mental wish list, compiling an inventory of the items that had become scarce. Her community was starving, nearly quartered and rationed to death by King George's troops. Combined with the loss of sons and husbands to the war effort, few strong bodies remained to work the fields and collect harvests. Tamsyn's community was desperate, and she couldn't bear to stand by and do nothing. *Boot leather, a new plow blade or axe, and gunpowder if God is feeling especially benevolent tonight.*

The river's dark waters caught the moonlight and spat it out in silver ripples and boiling foam. Its soft roar muffled Tamsyn's breath and the thump of her anxious heartbeat. She and Sarah hurried along the bank, heading south and east, following the Cape Fear toward Wilmington—a strategic port town crucial to British and Colonial forces alike. Several yards ahead at a bend in the river, a pale light flashed once, twice. After a pause,

Illustration by Caio Cacau

it flashed twice again, completing the secret code that confirmed the lantern holders' identities.

Tamsyn and Sarah rushed to greet the pair of women awaiting them: Prudie and Cora Bisette, twin sisters from the neighboring village of Spring Garden. The two girls towered over and outweighed most grown men. In a fight, they were like a pair of wild she-bears protecting their cubs. They wore broad brimmed hats and dressed as men to better conceal their identities. "Tamsyn," Prudie whispered. "You're late. We feared you'd been caught."

Tamsyn gave Prudie's thick biceps a reassuring squeeze. "John Brady stopped by. I could barely get rid of him, not without raising suspicion."

"Doesn't like taking no for an answer, does he?" Prudie fell into step beside Tamsyn as the group proceeded through the woods, drawing away from the river's swampy banks. Tamsyn understood the risk of taking their party closer to the road, but if she were going to face her death, she'd rather be taken by a bullet or saber on firm, dry ground as opposed to disappearing into some bottomless mudhole.

"Thanks to this war, pickings are slim," Tamsyn admitted, "but they'll never be so slim that I'd accept a proposal from John Brady."

Prudie snickered. "Even Paw's old mule is better looking and has more teeth."

"Maybe I should marry your pa's mule, instead."

The young women giggled until Sarah shushed them. She raised a knife, one of the half dozen she carried in strategic locations all over her body. Tamsyn's lantern light gleamed along its sharp edge. "You'll bring the militia right to us, and we'll never hear 'em coming."

Remembering where they were, what they were about to do, and the inherent danger that came with it, the women fell silent. They lightened their footsteps and focused on their surroundings, searching each shadow for a sign of pursuit. The redcoats and Tory militias had increased their patrols, as if anticipating trouble. Tamsyn wondered if that trouble was her band of merry highway robbers. Their reputation had grown to almost mythic proportions, and she liked hearing her alias whispered between neighbors after she'd dropped off packages of desperately needed provisions on their doorsteps.

The Green Lady...

Shuttering all but Tamsyn's lantern, the crew crept forward, relying on moonlight and weak candle glow. Spanish moss drooped like the webs of a monstrous spider—lending the forest a perpetually eerie mood. The group walked countless miles, swatting at mosquitos and grumbling under their breaths about bugs, heat, and empty bellies.

They'd prowled this same stretch of road the previous three nights and had encountered nothing worthwhile, but Tamsyn's nerves tingled in a way that convinced her tonight was going to be different.

Her instincts had never been wrong before.

Nearly another hour ticked away before the clatter of horse tack and wagon wheels played like a siren song in the night, drawing the women's instant attention. Tamsyn drew up her hood. She slipped one pistol free from its holster while the rest of her gang scrambled into position. Sarah wound her shawl over her head and charged into the road, limping and moaning, clutching her padded belly. "Oh, merciful Father. Please, God, help me."

The clip-clop of horse hooves slowed. The creak of wagon wheels softened. Clinging to the shadows, Tamsyn sneaked closer.

"Oh, please, sir," Sarah cried. "It's my baby. Something's wrong—there's blood. Help me, please."

A light flared as the wagon driver, a hunched figure in a dark cloak, repositioned his lantern. He replied to Sarah's pleas, but his words were too quiet for Tamsyn to hear.

Sarah's dark silhouette limped nearer.

The driver leaned toward her.

Tamsyn didn't have to watch to know what would happen next. They had practiced this routine with military precision until they could perform it blindfolded.

Next, Sarah would latch onto the driver, whip out her knife, and hold it to his throat. Prudie and Cora would emerge from either side of the road, clubs drawn as they awaited Tamsyn's appearance, which she would make with a flourish of her cape and the brandishing of her pistol. As Sarah held the driver hostage, Prudie and Cora would make a quick search for other passengers and deal with them accordingly. Meanwhile, Tamsyn would encourage the driver to give up his wagon peacefully. If he resisted—and, oh, how she loved when they resisted—she'd use her guns and Sarah's knives to make their demands more convincing.

But that was not what happened.

Instead, the driver yelled and lunged for Sarah.

Lantern light erupted from the wagon as figures boiled from beneath the oiled tarp covering the cargo.

Before Tamsyn could cock her pistol and fire, Sarah, Prudie, and Cora were surrounded by men armed to their teeth—guns, knives, even a few short-swords. They launched into a fight, swinging fists and clubs. Grunts and groans filled the air. Sarah and the wagon driver struggled for control of her knife.

Tamsyn's heart leapt into her throat. She swallowed a scream as she stepped forward and raised her pistol, aiming at the sky, but a strong arm cinched around her throat, tugging her off her feet. She stumbled back, falling against a rock-hard body that smelled of sea salt and expensive cologne. Her captor wrapped long fingers around her wrist and twisted, disarming her. Her pistol dropped to the ground. He removed her second gun from the holster at her hip and pressed the barrel to her temple.

"No one move a muscle," her captor shouted, his accent as French as a bottle of Merlot. "I have your lady at my mercy."

The fight stumbled to a halt, and Tamsyn analyzed the scene by the light of several lanterns hanging from the wagon. Cora had fallen to her knees and was still armed but bleeding from a fierce cut on her brow. Prudie was standing but had lost her club, and the two men on either side of her had the rare honor of exceeding her in both size and brawn. The wagon driver had locked Sarah in his arms. He tugged her knife, and she released it without resistance.

Tamsyn swallowed and cleared her throat, fighting back a rising tide of panic. She struggled against her captor, but his strength exceeded hers. "You're not British."

He snorted sardonically in her ear. "What gave me away?"

"Not local militia, either."

"My men outnumber you, and that is the only thing that need concern you, my green lady." He said the last bit with a sneer as he pushed her forward, stepped back, and raised his lantern, revealing the face of the most striking man Tamsyn had ever seen. High

cheekbones, hooded dark eyes, and sensuous lips that promised unimaginable, carnal pleasures. He raised the pistol he'd taken from her and leveled the barrel at her breast bone. He leered at her and winked.

On anyone else, that look of mockery would have earned Tamsyn's immediate repugnance, but this stranger, this… *scoundrel* wore acerbity like a king wears a crown, proudly and full of conceit. A conceit he had every right to possess, considering the breadth of his fine shoulders and the curtain of inky curls falling past his chin. Tamsyn's dread retreated, replaced by a warm sensation in the pit of her belly.

There were more treasures here than the contents of this rapscallion's wagon, and if she played her next moves carefully, she might have the pleasure of discovering them herself. Forward and unladylike thinking, perhaps, but while her neighbors might have assumed Tamsyn Gruene was a circumspect young woman, no one had ever mistaken the Green Lady for a wilting flower.

"Who are you?" she asked, setting her hands on her hips. She threw back her shoulders, proudly presenting her full bosom. The Frenchman's eyes dropped, taking in the dip and sway of each curve revealed by her clinging blouse and tight trousers.

Leaning forward, he swept off his cocked hat and dropped into a theatrical and graceful bow. "Gabriel Labeau, *mon chéri.*" His voice was as rich and seductive as hot coffee on a cold morning. "And you are the mysterious Green Lady. The image of you on the broadsheets fails to capture the true magnificence of your assets, though it's difficult to be certain while you're wearing that absurd disguise."

So, not only had he heard of her, but he'd presumably set this trap to catch her. Perhaps she should have feared his intentions, but instead she felt a deep satisfaction. Her grandfather was apt to quote Proverbs at her: *"Pride goeth before destruction, and a haughty spirit before a fall."* Maybe the Good Book was right, but if this clever rogue were the one to take her down, she wondered if she could bring herself to regret it.

His tongue briefly touched his bottom lip. "Take off your mask, *ma belle.*"

"And if I refuse?"

"Then it shall be my great pleasure to remove it for you."

A brief image of him removing more than merely her mask flashed through her mind, tempting her to rebuff his order. As if reading her thoughts, he twitched his hand and the gun barrel bobbed. "But only after you'd been properly bound and gagged, and I think you'd rather avoid such extreme measures."

"Oh, I would, would I?" Tamsyn offered a teasing smile. "Threats are meaningless without action, monsieur."

He arched a sleek black eyebrow and paused as if considering. Then he gestured to one of the large men at Prudie's side, beckoning him closer. "Take this gun. Point it at her. Shoot her if she attempts any trickery."

"You want me to *kill* her?" The big man asked.

Labeau's dark eyes slid over Tamsyn's figure again, appraising, appreciating. "It would be a tremendous waste, but her bounty will be paid regardless of the state of her mortality. 'Dead or alive', the broadsheets said. I prefer alive, but that depends on the actions of *la Dame Verte.*"

Highway robbery was not Tamsyn's only form of amusement. She enjoyed playing games of chance as well, and this encounter was no different than betting on a cock fight. She wagered that if she attempted any "trickery", Labeau's man would hesitate to shoot out of fear hitting his leader. It was upon that loyalty that she placed her bet as Labeau approached, having found a length of rope in the back of his wagon.

The instant he reached for her, she yanked his hand, headbutted his nose, threw her weight forward, and knocked them both to the ground.

Tamsyn rolled, reaching for the third pistol stashed in her boot.

Labeau's man fired.

Dirt grazed Tamsyn's cheek as

the bullet struck close enough to fling debris, but he had missed, and it would take him too long to reload to pose further threat.

Her attack had stunned Labeau, but barely. He shook off his surprise and turned his pistol on Tamsyn at the same moment she drew on him. He had lost his hat. Blood trickled from his nose, and based on the slight hump in its otherwise streamlined silhouette, she suspected this wasn't the first time he'd broken it. They locked gazes, each challenging the other to make a move.

"I underestimated you, it seems." Labeau tugged a lacy handkerchief from his coat pocket and dabbed his upper lip.

"You wouldn't be the first man to make that mistake." Tamsyn tightened her grip on her pistol. "Probably won't be the last."

"Then we're at an impasse."

"But in truth we are not."

That same black eyebrow arched again. "Oh?"

"I have a proposition. One I think you won't be able to resist."

"Go on." His grin turned sly like a barn cat spotting a vole in the grain bin.

"Let my ladies go. Release them, and I'll come with you willingly." Sarah gasped, but Tamsyn raised her hand, silencing further objections from her crew. "I'll come with you willingly, for one night, but *not* to the British. My neck is perfectly fine the way it is. I'd prefer not to lengthen it on the King's gallows."

Labeau pressed his lips together, smothering a smile. His eyes twinkled. "If I don't deliver you to the British, then where else should I take you?"

The corners of Tamsyn's mouth curled. "Have you ever heard of the Hopewell Inn?"

That eyebrow again. This time she noticed the slim scar bisecting its arch. "Your tastes run rich," he purred.

Tamsyn made an obvious show of her appraisal of him, from the fine leather of his tall boots to the elegant cut of his coat and the gold ring on his pinkie. He was no French aristocrat, though—she'd bet her life on it. His face was too hard, his knuckles too scarred, and his mannerisms too rough. She'd seen her share of French dandies sailing in and out of Wilmington and Labeau lacked their froggish ways. "It seems that yours may run richer, but the Hopewell is the best Wilmington has to offer."

"*Non.*" Labeau shook his head. "I suspect the best Wilmington has to offer is *you.*"

"Then you accept?"

He raised his chin. "You ask a great boon from me. It's only fair that I should know the full details of the deal I'm considering. Remove your mask."

She could've argued about who was asking a boon from whom but disputing the point would have been counterproductive. To the folks of New Hanover County, Tamsyn Gruene appeared to be nothing more than a sweet, mild-mannered farm girl. Only her crew knew the truth of the woman beneath the Green Lady's mask. Removing her façade for Labeau would be a gesture of supreme trust and submission. She wondered if he was worthy of such an honor, but for the safety of her crew she would give him the benefit of her doubt.

Keeping her pistol leveled on Labeau, she reached behind her head, grasped the knot of her scarf, and slipped off her mask. She raised her chin, boldly meeting Labeau's gaze. She knew the worth of her beauty and had never seen the value of modesty, particularly in a situation like this. If she were going to escape this encounter with her freedom, and the freedom of her friends, she'd have to spend every credit her exceptional looks afforded her.

Labeau's breath caught. His hooded eyes blazed. "*Three* nights," he countered in a voice that had gone rough and smoky. "The bounty on your head is worth at least three nights, and I intend to be paid, one way or another."

Tamsyn cupped her breasts briefly before sliding her hands over her trim waist and round hips. Labeau's gaze followed, looking like the proverbial man in the desert spotting an oasis when he was on the verge of thirsting to death. His tongue darted out, licking his lush bottom lip. "*One* night." She raised a hand, silencing his obvious

objection. "But I vow it shall be a night you'll never forget."

Labeau pointed at one of his men. "Bring me my horse. Release the women." He nodded at Tamsyn as his men dropped their weapons. The wagon driver set Sarah back on her feet although he did not return her knife. "A contract cannot be made without both parties giving their name. You know mine. Now I must know yours."

She tugged her cape and dropped into a short curtsy as her friends retreated into the shadows. "Tamsyn Gruene. It's a pleasure to do business with you, Monsieur Labeau."

"WHERE does a woman learn to fight like you do?" Labeau cinched his arm tighter around Tamsysn's waist as their horse side stepped a wide hole in the cobbled streets of Wilmington. Other than issuing a few terse orders to his crew, Labeau had remained mostly silent after accepting Tamsyn's proposal. He left her unbound, tied only by the strength of her honor and integrity. She could escape him, but her curiosity outweighed her desire to get away, and she suspected he knew it. Besides, he had her name now, and could easily report her. If she had to choose between a night with Labeau or a night in a British prison, her decision was easily made.

"From my brother. He's small for his age, always felt he had to fight to prove himself a man. He learned a thing or two over the years and taught them to me."

"Why would he do such a thing?" Labeau's grasp on her eased and his knuckles skimmed her breast as he adjusted the grip on his reins. His touch sent heat sizzling through her. In her experience, few men were as clever or appealing as this one. This contractual obligation was one she might actually enjoy satisfying.

"He made up his mind to join the Colonial Army. Wanted to march with General Washington. That left me alone with our grandfather, and he's in no state to defend our land or my honor. I had to learn to do that myself."

"But what about your father?"

"Dead. Fever took him and my mother when I was a baby. It's been only me, Jimmy, and our grandfather for the last twenty years."

Labeau clicked his tongue. "Those women you fight with. They are...*formidable*."

"A woman must be formidable to survive, especially in times like these. Desperation makes a potent motivator." Tamsyn thought of Sarah and her knives. She'd practiced with them for weeks before their first heist, stabbing and slicing targets made of straw, cotton, and wood that simulated bones. Sarah looked timid on the outside, but Tamsyn knew her friend's spine was made of the same iron as her blades. The Bissett sisters, however, were fighters by birth.

All Tamsyn had to do was find a target and point them at it. They'd done the rest on their own.

"I'm sad to say I agree. These are the sorts of times that define who is a survivor and who is not."

"And you are certainly a survivor, aren't you Mr. Labeau? More than a survivor, if I had to guess."

"Please, call me Gabriel." He sniffed. "And what do you mean by that?"

"I'd wager that you're not only a bounty hunter but a profiteer." She inhaled his sea-salt and cologne scent again. "Maybe even a blockade runner, smuggling French finery past British patrol ships and selling it to the highest bidder?"

He neither confirmed nor denied but merely grunted. "It is as you say: 'desperation makes a potent motivator'."

The horse slowed as they approached the Hopewell Inn, and Gabriel brought their mount to a halt in the flagstone drive. He dismounted first then offered his hand to Tamsyn. She twined her fingers around his larger, rougher ones and slid from the saddle. He caught her before her feet hit the ground and held her close. His lips hovered mere centimeters from hers. Notes of desire hung in his warm breath. "Until dawn, *ma chérie*, you are mine, oui?"

Tamsyn nodded, anticipation licking at her like tongues of flame.

"Of your own consent?"

"If it were not so, I would've

escaped from you already."

He chuckled. "Perhaps. But I would have been a fool to let you get you get away."

GABRIEL arranged for their accommodations with the inn's proprietor and ordered wine to be brought to their room, an airy comfortable space with a large bed, a pitcher and ewer on a stand in one corner, and small vanity in the other. Tamsyn lit candles, and their soft glow filled the atmosphere with romance, possibility, and more than a little trepidation. Alone with a strange man in such an intimate space, Tamsysn's confidence faltered for the first time. Pure brazen instinct had carried her this far, but she supposed it would take more than that to satisfy a man like Gabriel Labeu. Or would it?

His nose had stopped bleeding long ago, and a suggestion of purple bruising shown under his eyes. That hint of vulnerability eased some of her misgivings. She caught his dark gaze following her as she poured wine into a pair of crystal goblets that probably cost more than all the furniture in her grandfather's old farm house. Swallowing a long fruity gulp, she sat at the foot of the bed and patted the empty space beside her. Gabriel joined her. He took the wine glass she offered and sniffed its contents.

"Meet your approval?" she asked.

"It should. The owner bought this wine from me, and I imported it straight from the vintner in Burgundy."

"Imported? Or smuggled?"

"You say potato, I say *patate*." He shrugged. "War is pain, hunger, horror. People want to be reminded of the finer things in life." His gaze captured hers. "Things worth fighting for."

"People fight for wine?"

"For the experiences that go along with sharing a bottle of wine." He toyed with the green ribbon at the end of her braid. "Experiences like this one."

He tugged, the ribbon came loose, and Tamsyn's thick hair, like fire captured in silk, unwound. It fell in luxuriant waves over her shoulder and breast. A low hungry noise rumbled in his throat. Tossing his goblet back, he guzzled the contents before setting his glass aside. He stood and shrugged off his dark coat, revealing an elegant white shirt that hugged his shoulders. He untied the cravat at his throat, and his collar fell open, exposing skin browned by the sun. Tamsyn's fingers itched to touch him there. Instead she finished the rest of her wine.

Gabriel took her empty glass and set it on the vanity. Slowly, carefully, he knelt, placing himself between her knees as she remained seated at the edge of the bed. He took her face in his broad, rough hands and gently, ever so gently, brought his lips near hers. "It's not only your cloak and mask— your eyes are green as well. Chips of peridot sparkling in a tumbler of whisky. I would like to kiss you now, *ma belle dame verte*, as I have wanted to do since the moment you drew your pistol on me."

He'd issued a statement, but she heard the question in his words. In reply, she leaned forward, pressing her mouth to his. He tasted of wine, salt, and desire. Her bones softened. She slumped against him, and his arms folded around her, accepting her weight. His tongue swept against hers, and she opened to him.

He pulled away first, displaying more self-control than Tamsyn could muster. Until he'd touched her, she hadn't realized she'd been starving for so much more than just food. "We have all night, *non?*" he asked.

She nodded. "But only this one."

"That is still no reason to hurry."

"Isn't it though?"

He groaned but it turned into a chuckle. He rose and stepped back from her, peering down. "One night to make a lasting memory. I think I know how we should begin."

Tamsyn was willing to defer to his wisdom, suspecting he had much more of it than she did in these matters. Her few hurried and incognito sensual encounters hardly counted as experience. "What do you suggest?"

He poured more wine and passed her glass. "Three questions each. If you refuse to answer, you must remove an article of clothing instead."

"You seem to me to be a man of no shame. What secrets could you possibly have to hide?"

He gave her a solemn look. "Ask the right question and you might find out. Everyone has secrets."

Tamsyn sipped her wine and waved toward him. "You've got a head start on me."

"Then remove your cloak and we shall be even."

She untied the knot at her throat and shed the outer layer that always made her feel safe and protected. Yet even without her cape, she felt no threat from Gabriel. If he meant to hurt her, he'd had dozens of chances to do so already. "Who goes first?"

"The honor belongs to the lady."

She drew her eyes up the length of his long, tall figure. "Who are you, Gabriel? Not a soldier, not an aristocrat, but certainly no pauper. A rich merchant hoping to get richer, perhaps?"

He crossed the room and stretched out on the bed with the animal grace of a wild cat lounging in the sun. He folded his hands behind his head and crossed his feet at his ankles, looking as relaxed as a man could be. "I am nobody, mademoiselle. My mother was a prostitute in Paris. My father was one of her, what should we call him? ...*Un mécène?* A patron. A man whose name I've never known. I am self-made."

Pity twanged in her heart, but she doubted he wanted her sympathy, so she schooled her face, showing him nothing but cool interest. "And now here you are, running British blockades and accosting women in the night."

"Only when they throw themselves at me."

"I didn't throw myself. We attacked you."

"Is that what you were doing?" Tamsyn snatched a pillow and chucked it at him.

He caught it and stuffed it behind his head, chuckling. "You're much too young and innocent to be a hardened criminal. What inspired you to turn to a life of highway robbery?"

"The war, obviously." Tamsyn rolled to her knees and crawled toward the headboard. "It's cost me and my neighbors everything. We were starving to death. Somebody had to do something."

"And that someone was you?"

"Who else? Everyone in my village is either too old, too sick, too young, or too broken to manage." Turning over, she flopped onto her back beside him and stared at the ceiling.

"So brave of you."

"Maybe. Or monumentally stupid. You could've just as easily turned me over to the British, and I'd be swinging before the week was through."

Gabriel raised up on one elbow and leaned over her. "Then I'm pleased we could come to this alternative arrangement."

"You would've made a nice profit from it."

"I prefer profiting from things, rather than people."

"I thought you were a bounty hunter."

"Your bounty was my first and my last. The Green Lady's exploits are legendary. I had to know if you deserved your notoriety."

"And do I?" On impulse she brushed her knuckles across the dark stubble on his jaw.

He caught her hand and pressed a hot kiss to her palm. "That remains to be seen. The next question is yours. We are tied, one-to-one."

"Have you no woman of your own? No wife. No... fiancée?"

Gabriel stiffened. A dark shadow crossed his face. For a moment she thought he would refuse, but then he smiled. "You'll not get rid of my clothes so easily. I was married. I'm not anymore, and that's all I will say about that. Same question for you, *ma belle*. No husband? No betrothed?"

"The war has taken the best men. There's nothing much to choose from, really. Not unless I'm willing to lower my standards. Which I'm not."

"I shall take your words as a compliment, then." His eyes sparkled, all trace of his earlier seriousness gone.

"You should." Tamsyn touched Gabriel's shirt collar. "This game isn't going so well. Neither of us has lost any clothing."

"Then I suggest you make your questions more personal."

"Questions like that can cause pain."

"I can take it if there's the promise of pleasure in the end. Can you?"

Tamsyn furrowed her brow, regretting her next blow as she made it. "What was her name? Your wife."

Gabriel flinched as if she had struck him. He sat up and tugged his shirt over his head, saying nothing. But Tamsyn figured he revealed as much information in his silence as he would have with his words. Whoever his wife had been, he had obviously loved her, and her loss had wounded him. It was another of his vulnerabilities revealed, another wall that crumbled between them. She touched a puckered scar near his ribs that looked like a bullet wound. She'd ask about that later.

His eyes slipped closed. His voice was a low growl when he spoke again. "Is this the first time you've been with a man?"

Tamsyn might have plainly admitted the truth; she wasn't ashamed of her past, but she thought Gabriel would appreciate mystery more. Besides, she was losing her patience with this game. Sitting up, she untied her laces and pulled her shirt over her head, leaving her in a thin chemise that hid nothing. As his gaze slid over her, his pupils dilated, turning already dark eyes to deep pools of black. She climbed to her knees, unfastened the buckle at her waist, and pulled her belt loose. "Your game was clever, but not clever enough. We're out of questions, yet here we are, still in our clothes. We can play another round if you like, but the dawn will be here before we know it. We have no time to waste."

He sat up, ridges of abdominal muscles flexing. He kicked off his boots and stripped off his stockings. "I only wanted us not to be such strangers."

"I took off my mask for you, in more ways than one. You know who I am." Her fingers trailed over his own belt buckle as she met his gaze and held it. "I know you, too, Gabriel. I know you, and I want you. Does anything else really matter?"

With a groan, he buried his fingers in her thick hair and brought his lips hard against hers. In a flurry of eagerness and lingering touches, they shed the last of their clothes, and flesh met flesh. Mouths and tongues explored until Tamsyn's body ached to be filled by his.

She stroked the dusting of dark hairs across his chest, and her touch drifted lower, wrapping around his length and guiding him to the warm cleft between her legs. He throbbed against her, hot, hard, and as smooth as silk, and her body echoed his desire. He growled, a hungry sound that set her skin aflame, before dipping his head to tease her breasts, one at a time. Arching her back, she voiced her pleasure in a raw gasp.

Pausing, he pulled away to capture

her gaze once more. The heat in his eyes burned her to ash.

"Don't stop, now," Tamsyn urged. "*Please.*"

She wrapped her legs around his hips, and gently, slowly, he sheathed himself in her warmth. When he moaned her name, she raised her hips, drawing him in deeper. Again and again she met his thrusts until their passion found its rhythm, composing the kind of night commemorated in songs and myths. Memories to keep them warm through the approaching frigid winter. As they surrendered to each other fully, Tamsyn wondered who had actually captured whom.

We captured each other, she decided, *and that's the only answer there is.*

WHEN Tamsyn awoke at dawn, she was not surprised to find herself alone, and for a moment she felt disappointed. The sun was rising, and Gabriel Labeau had kept his word. One night—no more and no less. For a scoundrel smuggler, he apparently had a strong sense of honor.

As she hurried to pull on her clothes and braid her hair, she discovered a slip of paper on the vanity beside the empty wine carafe. Gabriel had written her name on it in an elegant scrawl. Unfolding the note, she held a breath filled with anticipation, and then she read.

Ma Belle Dame Verte,

I would never have given you to the British, even if the bounty on your head had been ten times as much. They would squander a treasure such as you, and I could never abide wastefulness, especially not in these desperate days. King George has never known how to appreciate a good thing when he had it, and this war is the grandest proof of his improvidence.

Take care, mon chéri, that your spark is not snuffed prematurely. I have many more blockades to run, and many more late-night roads to travel before this war is through, and I will require a light as bright as yours to be the Northern Star that guides me. Without you, I might lose my way.

Yours most humbly and devoted,
G. Labeau

Tamsyn folded the note, stuffed it in her trouser pocket, and sneaked away from the inn, humming a bright tune under her breath. As soon as she had a chance, she'd burn Gabriel's letter. Its contents were far too incriminating if the wrong person discovered it. But before she set it aflame, she'd read his words once more and hold them in her heart until she saw him again.

One way or another, she *would* see him again. Even if she had to rob every wagon in Wilmington to find him. She was his Northern Star, and every Northern Star needed her voyager.

Outsider

By Jenifer Purcell Rosenberg

Historic home near waterfront available for short-term rental. Inquire within.

ANGELA stared at the image printed on the flyer, a beautiful Victorian painted lady in shades of rose and cream, with a view of the ocean visible from the back. She'd seen this home frequently as a child, while visiting her grandparents for the summer. By "near waterfront," they meant on the cliff overlooking the beach, steep downward steps carved into the stone of the cliff itself. Although the Burghley House had not been regularly inhabited in decades, it was frequently let from April through November, as tourists trickled through town in search of history and the ambience of a seaside village. The house was never leased by locals, but then Angela had only been one of the seasonal residents. She didn't count as local.

Starting over after leaving Greg seemed almost impossible. She had never thought she would find herself without him, but then that poseur had arrived on the local art scene back home, and suddenly Greg was always working late or on a trip to acquire new art for the gallery. Angela knew none of

Ruby's art was selling, and wondered why Greg insisted on keeping her signed at the gallery. Then she'd been contacted by an old classmate who had seen Greg while on a cruise to the Bahamas, hand in hand with Ruby. What was the appeal, Angela wondered. Ruby could paint about as well as a petulant toddler, leaving bright, gloppy streaks of paint on a cheap canvas and charging more than most people pay for two months rent. Be that as it may, it had been time to move on, and Angela didn't want to be found. Everything about Ruby screamed grifter, and Angela wasn't willing to pick up the pieces when Greg finally realized the mistake he had made. If she went inside and paid in cash, Greg would never know where she had gone. Being in a place where renting without a paper trail was possible provided the added security she was seeking. She took a deep breath and went in to ask about the house.

Local woman's granddaughter missing. The white glare of the computer screen lit the room with a harsh glow. This disappearance was at least the sixth in a series over the past decade. The small town locals always seemed

Illustration by Mike Collins

surprised, and eventually assumed the missing persons had moved on, had stopped in Wallings Village on their way up north and off the grid. Not much care was given to those who disappeared, and even the disappearance of a nanogenarian's granddaughter wouldn't hold attention for very long. It was as if the knowledge that people went missing in the town just slid out of people's minds and landed like pudding onto the floor. Nigella opened up a search window to look for driving directions, guessing she could be there by late morning if she got up with the dawn.

Nigella glanced at the corkboard on the wall beside her computer, where a printed screencap from the webcast that had put the quiet coastal town on her radar was tacked. In the image, an amateur ghost hunter and blogger named Amber Blaine stood facing her camera, unaware that an odd light disturbance was taking place behind her. She'd disappeared shortly afterward, over two months ago. "Thanks for the tip," Nigella said, lightly tapping the image. It would be the first time since Layla and Kiaan had died that Nigella would be going on a hunt, but sitting around pining wouldn't bring her fiancée and soon-to-be brother-in-law back. She knew the risks, of course. They had met their fate on the last hunt, right after Nigella had moved to the United States to live with Layla.

THE air in the shop smelled like cheap wood polish and vinyl upholstery. Most of the merchandise consisted of overpriced replicas of tacky antiques, though they also had a section of "Locally Made!" items at extreme mark-ups. The woman behind the worn laminate counter feigned distraction, as many of the townsfolk so far seemed to do when presented with strangers. "Good afternoon," Nigella began, knowing her English accent often helped to break the proverbial ice. It did the trick, and the shop woman smiled at her, revealing small, even teeth that had clearly known braces.

"Oh, hello!" she said, "How can I help you, miss?"

"I've come to your lovely town in search of a quiet place to compose a book," Nigella said.

This clearly piqued the woman's interest, and she leaned forward, her pale pink sweater catching slightly on the counter in the process and pulling the v-neck lower. Nigella wasn't certain if this was deliberate or accidental, and decided it was best to pretend she hadn't noticed. "What're you writing about?" the woman asked.

"Grand American families at the dawn of the Twentieth century. Some romance, some intrigue. You know how it goes. A thriller set in a quaint town such as this."

The young woman snapped her chewing gum and beamed, wide-eyed, at the foreign visitor. "Cool! You staying at the Vanguard or the Mermaid Hotel?"

Nigella smiled and winked. It was a bit sleazy, but she had a feeling that it would work to her favor. The shop clerk blushed and sat up straight, laying perfectly manicured fingers on the counter, the nails extra short and pale-pink to match her jumper. Nigella raised her eyebrows and smiled. "So, miss..."

"Call me Kelly!"

"Kelly. I was curious about the rental listings in the window of this fine establishment."

Kelly looked surprised, her pastel pink lipstick forming a perfect O. "It said to inquire within," Nigella coaxed.

Kelly nodded. "Yes! The owner manages a few properties. Were you interested in the ranch on Haye Street, or the colonial on Willow Drive?"

Nigella put her hand over the younger woman's still-displayed ones, and Kelly gasped in delight. "I was hoping the lovely Victorian overlooking the beach would be available," Nigella said.

Kelly frowned and looked away, though she did not withdraw her hands. "I see, it must have already been let," said Nigella.

"What's been let?"

Nigella turned around as Kelly quickly pulled back, and saw an unusually tall, slim man with close-cropped hair and fashionable glasses. He regarded Nigella with keen, appraising eyes.

"Ah! I was interested in the property on Sealine Drive. It's posted in the window."

The man beamed and extended his hand. "How are you? I'm Alan J. Brava. I own this shop, and manage some real estate on the side. The Burghley house is absolutely available to let! How long of a stay are you looking for?"

Nigella shook the proffered hand and smiled. "Pleased to meet you, Mr. Brava. My name is Nigella Scott. I'm looking for a few months to write a book, and that house seems a lovely location." As Nigella followed Alan back to his office, she noticed Kelly staring wistfully after her.

THE rental agreement signed, Nigella drove about the town to get the lay of the land. She stopped by the village library and historical society to find out some of the local history.

The Burghley House had been built by Wilmington Burghley, a man who had made his fortune in shipping in the late 19th century. It seemed that his wife, Elizabeth, had also disappeared without a trace. In fact, a few searches in the library database of the local newspaper turned up over eighty disappearances over the decades. This definitely warranted further investigation.

Nigella was denied a library card since she was not actually a local resident, but she was granted permission to spend $132 in copying fees to bring home printouts of the information she wanted to study further, as well as photos of some of the missing people.

The historical society was slightly more helpful, since she had told them she was writing a book about the town's founding families. They gave her access to some books with genealogies and town timelines. They also gave her some pamphlets and some new printouts free of charge, and welcomed her to come again.

Nigella had been assured that the Burghley house would have all of the modern amenities she needed: Wi-Fi, central heat and air (she was told heat would be the only one she needed in November), refurbished bathrooms, an exercise room, and a modern kitchen. Apparently, other than this, the house was untouched. Nigella found a local mercantile market, and stocked up on necessities, including some groceries. The house was furnished and had dishes and cookware, Mr. Brava had said, so it would be a great opportunity to eat well while on her investigative holiday. She also found a small hardware store and bought some extension cords, batteries, extra flashlights, and fishing line. She was ready to see the house.

The front veranda was wide, and wrapped around to the right of the house. Nigella noted some rocking chairs strategically placed for an optimal view of the neighborhood. The heavy oaken front door was carved with intricate vines and petals, and painted to match the rest of the house in shades of dusty rose, pink, and cream, with the vines done in a gentle sage.

While the door was original to the house, it had clearly been fitted with more modern locks—three, in fact. Nigella fumbled over which of the identical-seeming brass keys opened which lock for a moment, and finally pushed the heavy door open into a beautiful reception hall. She pulled her luggage inside and took out her phone to record the initial layout.

A quick look around the first floor showed a front parlor, a library, a grand formal dining room, a hall with servant's stairs, a pantry, a kitchen, and a small porch that led to the back yard overlooking the ocean from atop the cliff. There was a narrow porch through the parlor that led to the flower garden, and a petite stairway to an elevated powder room that was nestled under the main stairs up. Had she been in the market for a house outside of New York, this beautiful specimen would have been at the top of her list. As long as it proved to not be haunted, of course.

Taking the main stairs up to the second level, Nigella heard a hint of distant laughter, like a tinkling bell, from somewhere further up. She paused, recalling that there had been phantom laughter shortly before Layla and Kiaan had met their fate at the old asylum down

South. She shuddered, and continued up the stairs. It was best not to let fear show when investigating a haunted premises.

There were five bedrooms on the second level, and Nigella wished she still had a team, so that several people could sleep in separate rooms. She knew there would be servant's quarters on the top level as well, but she chose what was clearly the master bedroom, which had a side turret as well as a front-facing bay window. It was connected to the second bedroom by a modern bath that had likely once served as a dressing room. This was the room that renters were most likely to have taken when staying here. Nigella made a mental note to try staying in different rooms on different nights, while keeping the master as her base of operation.

She then climbed up to the third level, where she found additional bedrooms, which had likely served as servant's dormitories, a small sewing room, and a room lined with bookcases and slate boards that was likely where children had been home schooled. The school room felt particularly cold, and she thought she saw movement just out of her line of sight. This room would have to be documented as well.

Nigella went back downstairs to retrieve her equipment and begin setup. It would take longer on her own, and she wanted everything in place before she began. She also needed to designate a safe room, which she could rim in salt and other protective elements, for when she needed to safely rest.

As she was taking some gear from her case on the main floor, she began to hear a banging, slow at first, and then increasing in intensity. She thought she heard her name as well. Nigella stood and walked toward the kitchen, EMF detector in hand. She had planned to wait until sunset for this part, but this banging was clearly an immediate concern. As she went through the dining room into the servant's hall, she realized the banging was coming from the small porch off of the kitchen. She rushed to the door.

Standing on the porch at the window was the young woman from the shop downtown. Kelly looked as if she were in a panic, and had tears streaming down her face. Nigella opened the door to let her in, and Kelly crept in apprehensively.

"Are you quite all right, Kelly? How can I help you?"

Kelly gulped. "I...You don't want to be here!" she cried, "I know this sounds crazy, but this house is..."

"Haunted?" Nigella asked.

Kelly nodded. Nigella patted her guest on the shoulder. "Come sit down and have a cup of tea. I've been to the grocery, and can make us a spot of supper as well." Kelly blinked, confused, and Nigella ushered her to one of the hand-carved antique chairs at the kitchen table. "It's all right, Kelly. I'm a paranormal investigator. This is what I do."

Kelly's eyes widened, "Shouldn't you have a team?" she asked.

Nigella nodded. "It would certainly help, but I can manage," she said. "Tell me a bit about the house's history. Does everyone know it's haunted? Are they aware of the missing persons who have stayed here?"

"That's why I didn't want you to rent this place," Kelly said. "They always disappear.

Nigella put the kettle on and brewed some tea for them to drink while she made a light meal. Kelly told Nigella about how the house hadn't been regularly inhabited since the last of the Burghleys passed away in the 1960's. The first few families who had tried to purchase the house had met tragic ends, so Alan Brava's father had bought it to rent out to tourists instead, only several of the tourists had disappeared. There was a town superstition that if the house wasn't rented, bad things would happen to the townsfolk, so they had an unspoken agreement to overlook the disappearances of strangers, and they tried not to get too close to anyone new.

"But some of us think that's wrong," said Kelly, "we have a secret group that's been wanting to find a way to stop the disappearances. Problem is, every time we get someone to come out to look, they disappear, too! You're in danger!" Nigella regarded Kelly calmly, and realized she could get some help preparing for the night ahead.

"Kelly, how many people are in your group?" she asked. Kelly considered for a moment, and said she thought there were about fifteen. "If you can get them here soon, we can do something about the house," Nigella said. "We have about an hour forty-five till the sun sets. If all your friends can help to set up monitoring equipment and prep the rooms, it will go a long way toward securing everything and finding out where the disturbance originates."

The younger woman looked frightened.

"Don't worry, Kelly. We can get you all safely out of here before the sun sets, though I'm not sure whatever entity resides in this house would attack a local. Has your family been here long?"

Kelly sat up straight, a hint of pride in her smile. "The Ouelette family has been here for over 200 years," she said.

"Is everyone in your group from a family that predates this house?"

Kelly shook her head, "No, Destiny's family moved here in the '80s."

"Probably best for Destiny to stay home then," Nigella said.

WITHIN fifteen minutes, six of Kelly's friends, all ranging from their mid-twenties, like Kelly, to closer to Nigella's thirty-two, arrived to help set up motion detectors, cameras, EMF sensors, and audio recorders. Nigella had everyone pair off in order to be certain nobody was alone.

An initial run-through with a handheld EMF reader showed the front reception hall as having the least potential for activity. Since there was also a powder room just off that room, and it was right by the front door, it was an ideal base of operations. Nigella set up the monitors for all of the cameras and equipment by the built-in bench, and had Kelly help her salt the border of the room, the small stairway up, and the powder room.

The sun was growing heavy behind the clouds and getting ready to dissolve in the distance by the time they had finished. She offered everyone the opportunity to stay. Only Kelly and two of her friends chose to do so. She let the others out with instructions to come back late the next morning when the sun was nearly overhead to make sure everyone was still standing. She touched up the salt border after they left.

The two friends who had stayed behind were brothers, though they didn't strike Nigella as looking alike. Jason Pickering was tall and spindly with bright ginger hair and hazel eyes, and his brother Tim was average height and muscular with dark chestnut hair and brown eyes. Nigella wondered briefly which features they received from which parent, and imagined a tall ginger woman with a much shorter husband.

Kelly had pulled her golden hair up into a loose topknot and was wearing an oversized red hoodie that one of her friends had dropped off. Nigella reminded herself to not get attached to, or distracted by, these volunteers. The image of Layla dying in anguish would be forever seared in to her brain, and she did not need more souls weighing on her conscience. There would be plenty of time to find out more about Kelly when this was all over. She'd signed a three-month lease, after all.

Nigella knew she had to go through the house alone. Jason seemed adept with computers, so she gave him the task of monitoring the various readouts on the laptop that was collecting temperature samples from the different locations in the house. She asked Kelly to put on headphones and click through the different audio feeds, writing down what she heard, even if it seemed insignificant. Tim was tasked with keeping watch on the monitors for visuals, and for relaying information back to Nigella about which rooms seemed to be experiencing unusual phenomena.

She was armed with an EVP wrist recorder, a head-mounted full-spectrum camera, a handheld trifield meter for detecting magnetic, electrical, and radio wave fluctuations, a directional non-touch thermometer, salt, a lighter and smudge stick, a first aid kit, extra batteries, and some bottled water and nutrition bars, a pack of tissues, as well as a handheld communication radio, and the earpiece she was wearing to keep in contact with her makeshift team. Most of the non-active items were in a backpack, which also held a Mylar emergency blanket in case she found any survivors. Although she had set up variations of these things throughout the house, she wanted to have active ones on her person, in case she encountered an angle that had not been covered, or in case the recording of events malfunctioned in the control room. With a nod to the team, she stepped over the salt barrier and entered the parlor.

They had only left minimal light on in the house, to allow for the equipment to pick up more spectrums, and so as to not alert any curious neighbors to the fact that something was afoot. Nigella crept through the parlor, walking the perimeter slowly in case of activity.

When she passed the large French doors that led to a small, closed in section under the left-side turret, and then to the front side porch and flower garden, she thought she glimpsed a woman, soaking wet, with layers of white rendered almost translucent, staring back at her. When she blinked the woman was gone, but the digital read on the tri-field meter began to jump.

Nigella felt a chill in the air as her skin turned to gooseflesh. A soft whisper seemed to float out of nowhere, saying "please go." There were no sounds from the next room, so she wondered if they hadn't seen this happen, or if they were too frightened to respond. She knew better than to look back, however, and pushed open the French doors, careful not to step into the vestibule, lest she become trapped. Malevolent spirits would attempt to lure out anyone in the protected zone, and even the protective talismans she had given her three assistants couldn't keep them completely safe if they left the salt. Nigella noted that the presence of the woman had moved onto the porch, beyond the bay windows of the turret, and was gesturing toward the garden. That was an investigation for another time—in daylight, with a shovel and witnesses—so she backed up and moved slowly toward the library.

As she crossed the threshold into the library, movement to her right caught her eye. Across the hall, on the stairway to the upper floor, stood a young child in clothing from a bygone era. He looked perfectly clean and healthy, as if a young boy in costume were standing there, rosy-cheeked, ready for his Halloween portrait.

He beckoned for Nigella to come toward him. "Upstairs," he said, but his voice seemed somehow hollow, distant, like a child's game of telephone with tin cans and waxed twine. The boy was standing just out of the line of vision of the investigation team, behind a small dividing wall. Nigella stepped toward the child, and he began to back up the stairs slowly.

"What is your name?" Nigella asked. "Where are you leading me?"

The boy pointed upward. "To her."

Nigella touched her headset button. "Team, there is a spectral male child, aged roughly seven, leading me up the stairs. Please record the readings for the route and report back."

Tim's voice came back, "We have activity in the basement and kitchen, too. Where should we focus?"

Nigella sighed, hoping nobody would forget their instructions and do something careless. "Follow my movements. Oh, and please remember that you will all need to stay in the safe room. I'm afraid there is activity on the exterior of the property. It won't be safe to leave until morning."

As they reached the second floor, Nigella heard laughter again, and turned just in time to see a crystal candy dish hurtling toward her. She rushed up the next flight of steps toward the third floor, and stumbled through the apparition of the young boy. Her body felt as if it was being pierced with millions of tiny ice shards, and the boy backed up quickly, looking utterly horrified and slightly translucent now.

What few lights were on began to flicker, and Nigella heard shouting from the control room downstairs, though there was only broken static on her earpiece. Ahead of her, a second child had appeared with the boy. This one was far less solid, and had the ethereal glow usually associated with ghosts. It appeared to be a girl of about ten years of age.

"Quickly!" the new apparition pleaded, and Nigella scrambled up the stairs after the children, making a point of not looking back. When spirits seemed frightened, one did not want to encounter what was scaring them! Nigella's earpiece crackled, and she could now hear Kelly sobbing "Nonon-onono!" Aware that this could be a trick, she pressed on. The children led her to the school room, which was two stories directly above the control room.

Upon entering the room, Nigella noticed that the temperature had plummeted. Despite the fact that it was a mild 52 degrees outside, this room was decidedly below freezing. Nigella could see her breath puffing out into the room as she sought to calm her breathing after the rushed ascension to this level.

Inside the room, the spectral children began to waver, flickering in and out, their voices growing fainter. They were both standing by the slate board against one wall. As if written by an invisible piece of chalk, the word HELP took form on the slate. The children seemed urgent, the boy trying to clap his hand against the slate. Nigella stepped forward and gently pushed on the wooden frame, surprised when it clicked and dipped inward before opening out. Apparently, the slate board had also served as a supply closet, as it opened up into a small shelf-lined alcove about the same size as the bathroom in Nigella's tiny NYC apartment. There was something in the middle of the alcove, but the light was too low to see it, so she took out her small flashlight and shone it into the space.

Lying in the middle of the space was a woman who appeared to be sleeping or unconscious. Nigella glanced back toward the apparitions, but they had vanished. This woman did not appear to be a ghost, but looks could be deceiving, and entering the space could lead to being trapped. Could she trust her earpieces at this point? The interference was extreme. Her trifield meter was stuck on maximum, and her directional thermometer was reading the room as a frigid 22 degrees. "Hello?" she called.

The figure on the floor stirred, slowly turning its head. Nigella braced herself for the worst, and let out a sigh of relief when the light from her flashlight touched on the face, and cold evaporating breath, of Angela McNally, the woman whose grandmother was missing her. Wild-eyed and gaunt, the woman frantically crawled forward toward Nigella.

"Help me!" she pleaded.

As Nigella was reaching to help the injured woman to her feet, there was a horrible keening sound accompanied by a mad clambering. Kelly and Jason burst into the room, gasping for air. Nigella finished helping Angela up, and handed her a bottle of water and the Mylar blanket. "We need to leave this room," she said.

The second they left the room, the temperature in the house was noticeably warmer. The two children had not reappeared. Nigella knew there was violent activity on the second floor, but was apprehensive about what could have driven two of her three volunteers up the stairs. While they were helping Angela down the stairs, Nigella turned to Kelly. "Where's Tim?"

Kelly bit her lower lip and looked away.

"He left," said Jason, "and we think something got him on the front porch."

"The sound was horrible, Nigella!" Kelly cried, "we had to get away from it!"

Nigella nodded, then asked, "Jason, I thought your family was from town. You all should have been safe."

Jason gasped. "Tim's adopted," he said.

Nigella realized she should have asked when she realized the brothers looked so dissimilar. "Angela needs to be taken to a hospital right away, and it would be safest for the two of you to take her, though I do understand that none of the exits are ideal. The back porch might be our best bet if there's a presence on the front, because the side porch is absolutely occupied. But you'll have to be careful, take the walkway along the South side of the house, away from the gardens, and be sure to stay well away from the edge of the cliff!"

The small group scrambled to the back of the house, going through the pantry to the kitchen so as to avoid the stairway in the service hall that led to the basement. The porch was on the wrong side of the house for an easy escape, of course, so they would need to make quick work of it.

As they reached the back porch, Nigella shut the door behind the other three and locked it. Kelly looked alarmed "Why aren't you coming with us? Come help us and return to this tomorrow!" she pleaded.

Nigella knew there was sense in that action, but had to see this through. The basement had showed higher activity readings on the initial scan than the schoolroom had done, and she wanted to make sure that none of the missing persons were sequestered down there as Angela had been upstairs—though she suspected the children may have hidden Angela from something else more sinister. "I have to make sure there aren't other living people trapped here," she said,

"Please, get Angela to the hospital. I will see you in the morning."

As Jason and Kelly rushed Angela away, Nigella withdrew a small paper list from her pocket and walked around to the service hall.

The heavy wooden door squealed on its hinges as Nigella pushed it open. The air in the service hall was thick with the smell of decay, despite having been perfectly clean that afternoon. She wasn't surprised to see Tim standing there, at the top of the stairway leading down. His clothes were torn, and his eyes rimmed in red. His mouth twisted into a grotesque yawn as a deep, guttural voice escaped him, not matching his movements.

"Leave. This. House."

Nigella had been prepared for a confrontation, and threw a handful of salt at the inhabited man. She hadn't mentioned to the volunteers earlier that the salt had been blessed.

"Leave this man's body! His is not yours to take!" she shouted.

The voice began to laugh, thrusting a hand forward, and propelling Nigella against the wall without touching her. The sharpness in the back of her head was dulled by the sudden anxiety she felt for not having checked to be certain that Kelly and Jason were themselves before entrusting Angela to them. As she tried to recall whether she had seen their breath freeze up in the school room, the images of the service hall slid out of her vision and she lost consciousness.

NIGELLA awoke, heaving as a wave of nausea overtook her. The smell around her was unbearable. She fumbled for her backpack, only to realize it was gone. The floor beneath her was cold and damp, and seemed gritty.

She remembered that she'd put a couple of chemical glow sticks in the cargo pocket of the pants she was wearing. She tugged at the Velcro closure, cringing at the overwhelmingly loud sound it seemed to make. She held her breath and listened. There was a panting sound, and something else. Slide, shuffle. Slide, shuffle. She managed to fumble out a glow stick, cracking the plastic tube and shaking it to allow some light.

As the bluish glow gently illuminated the space around her, she heard the shuffling pause. Nigella's eyes were taking a moment to adjust to the light, and she felt that her vision might have been blurry if she had been able to see anything. Slowly, her eyes began to focus on her surroundings. She immediately regretted having light.

She was in a low space, with a dirt floor. At a guess, a sub-basement of some sort, possibly where coal had been kept once, perhaps a root cellar. Her head still splitting, Nigella rolled onto her side and dry heaved uncontrollably.

All around her, there were bodies in various states of decay. Some still had features, clothing, hair. Others were hardly more than skeletal remains. She remembered Tim Pickering, possessed, and wondered if he would be able to escape and survive. She had lost her list in the turmoil, but felt it was important to recite the names of the dead, remind them that they could cross over and be free from this place. So often, those slaughtered by the supernatural didn't know they could leave. From what she could see in the light of the stick, however, Nigella didn't know all of the names. She recited what she could recall, and the names of some missing persons she had acquired from her research.

"Elizabeth Burghley, Harrison Burghley, Rodger Samuel, Sadie Hempstead, Drake Smith, Michael Wade, Carol and Roger Oakes, Amber Blaine…"

"Present," said a weak voice, and the slide, shuffle resumed.

Nigella gulped to hold back more heaving, and shifted the glow stick toward the sound. An utterly emaciated woman was desperately trying to reach her, arms outstretched, fingers digging into the dirt. Her eyes looked haunted, sunken. With every shuffle the stench in the room got closer. With every pull, the tightness in Nigella's stomach increased. Amber Blaine had disappeared ten weeks ago. The likelihood of her surviving all this time seemed impossible.

Nigella realized that it was important to finish what she had been saying before Amber managed to drag herself across the darkened room. Taking a deep breath, and trying to resist the nausea, Nigella made a concentrated effort to speak forcefully. "All who have met a wrongful death in this place! You are free to leave! Go! You need not be tied to your physical remains, and no entity here is entitled to you! Move on! Flee!"

"They cannot hear you," croaked Angela, still clawing her way toward Nigella.

Slide, shuffle. Despite this declaration, there was a sudden chill in the air, and a sound similar to the opening of a pressure-sealed jar, a sucking pop! Then another, and another. With each of these pops, one of the bodies in the room crumbled, skin and bone falling away into dust, fluttering into nothingness. Not every body dissipated, but there had been at least half a dozen pops.

Nigella tried to push herself up on her hands and knees, to find a way out, to survive. Slide, shuffle. Amber was advancing, but Nigella was too overcome with dizziness and nausea to be able to lift herself fully. She put her hand to her aching head and thought she might have felt some splinters amid the hair and blood. She tried to claw her way to the side of the room opposite from the skeletal woman's approach, but felt a sharp pain in her side and realized she had broken ribs.

As Amber approached, Nigella realized her fear was correct.

This was no woman but a decaying corpse clawing its way toward her. The rancid flesh was peeling further from the bones with every slide and shuffle. Amber Blaine had been gone for some time. As the corpse pulled level to Nigella, it stared into her face, empty eye sockets puckering around nothingness, yet still staring, boring into Nigella's mind.

"You have destroyed my home," the voice rasped.

Nigella pulled together her last ounces of strength. "Wilmington Burghley," she coughed, "you are commanded to leave. This house is no longer your own, and your time has passed. It is time for you to transition beyond the veil and stop inhabiting this plane. You must..."

Her words were cut short by a filthy, decaying hand closing around her neck. Nigella struggled for air, determined to complete what she needed to say.

"You must leave. Go now."

Nigella could feel herself slipping out of consciousness. She willed herself to open her eyes, and gulped in air when the corpse released her throat. As the body that had once belonged to Amber Blaine began to disintegrate, Nigella allowed the exhaustion she had been fighting to take hold. She had set the spirits free.

"I'm coming back to you, Layla," she said, and closed her heavy eyes.

Chaos at Feast

By DAVID MACK

THE voice haunts me. It's followed me from one side of the world to the other. When I'm awake it echoes in my thoughts, feeds on my darkest desires. When I sleep it lords over my nightmares. Sometimes it whispers, issues curses on foul breezes; sometimes it sinks into manic laughter. I don't know what it wants, but its hatred needs no translation.

Fog blankets the moor, envelops me like a cloak. Overhead the moon is full, its cold glow dulled and dispersed by the uncanny vapor. The path underfoot is narrow and stone-paved.

I can't remember when last I ate. Has it been days? Weeks?

My legs shudder with each step I take. My hands tremble as if with palsy. I wonder if I'll be able to draw my Colt when the time comes. Will I even be able to see, let alone aim? To come all this way and miss the mark—that would be a waste. I would never forgive myself.

A great shadow takes shape ahead of me, looms large beyond the veils of mist: an old English manor on the edge of the moor, Gothic in design. The gauzy mists unravel as I draw near, and moonlight splashes the manor's moldering walls of dark grey stone, rendering it both gloomy and sublime. Silent and alone, it seems to frown in defiance of my approach.

All its windows are dark save one, in the front corner on the main floor. The curtains there are drawn, preserving the mystery of what lies beyond.

My boots scrape across gritty paving stones as I walk to the front entrance. I stop in front of the double doors and confront the startling specters in their windows. Is that my reflection? I don't recognize myself. My face has been rendered gaunt, my skin sallow. And my eyes—I can see through them, as if they were windows into my deepest fears, and I hear the jabbering cries of the living and the dead, a clamor swallowing up my mind, where darkness is shoveled over my dreams like cold earth flung into a grave.

I try to expunge the horror from my stare, but my unblinking eyes won't obey. They gleam at me, and like my rictus of a smile, they are too wide and too empty. I've worn this mask of madness for so long that I can no longer cast it off. This wild visage has become my true face, and it mocks every mad ambition I'd ever dared to hold.

How did I not see the peril that

Illustration by Daniele Sera

came to me in plain sight?

Christ, what a fool I was.

I rest my right hand on my Colt revolver and cock the hammer.

With my shaking left hand, I open the front door and go inside.

"**I** CAN pay you half now," the stranger says. "The rest when you bring me the idol."

I poke the brim of my fedora upward. Take a good look at her. Everything about this woman—burgundy dress, exquisitely styled sable hair, pale young flesh over cheekbones that could cut glass, upper lip shaped like a longbow pulled to its limit, toff London accent, and a brown-skinned young Asian man in olive drab hovering at her shoulder awaiting instructions—tells me she's richer than Croesus. I'd bet America's great depression hasn't even touched her.

I take an instant dislike to her.

"Won't lie to you, lady. That's more money than I've seen in years."

"So, you'll take the job?"

"Didn't say that. Borneo ain't what I'd call a dream vacation."

Her servant glares at me with dark eyes. "The natives call it *Kalimantan.*"

"They can call it Saint-Tropez, I ain't goin'. And who's talkin' to *you*?"

Other conversations in the bar go quiet. Life is cheap everywhere these days, but nowhere more so than in Bangkok. Under the table,

my hand hovers above my Colt. The Asian fellow wants to reach for the knife on his belt, but he knows he'll eat lead before he can draw steel.

His lady puts on a phony smile, plays peacemaker. "Gentlemen, please."

I wait until her retainer backs off, then I meet the stranger's gaze. "So. This idol?"

"The monkey god of the Urok Malay. A gold statue about two fists tall."

Her green eyes gleam with avarice. As if she sold her soul to the god of greed and hasn't missed it even once. But who am I to throw stones? What am I in this for if not the money?

"The Urok Malay. I've heard of them. Not keen on visitors."

The Stranger tilts her head, as if in concession. "True."

"Also heard they're cannibals."

"A distinct possibility." She lifts one elegantly arched eyebrow and smirks. "So? What say you, Mister Havelock? Do you accept my commission or not?"

This feels wrong. My hand wants to reach for the Colt again. I glance at her man, and then I look back at her, searching for anything that might hint at the truth. "Why me?"

"Because your reputation precedes you. The Lance of Longinus. The Scarab of Anubis. The Menorah from the Second Temple. You've recovered more lost artifacts than anyone else in history, and all since the end of the Great War. Quite a résumé for just fourteen years of work." She leans forward. Her countenance takes on a conspiratorial air. "Is it true you recovered the Oak Island treasure and then reset the original traps to conceal your success?"

"I don't know where you could've heard such an outrageous tale."

I have to give her credit: she's done her homework. It'll be a shame to disappoint her. "Tempting offer, but it could take me years to find the Urok Malay, never mind the idol."

She gestures toward the brown man in the olive fatigues. "That's where Tjilik comes in."

Tjilik stares at me like he's picturing my spleen in a skillet.

"No. No fucking way."

"He knows the jungles, the rivers, and the languages. He can take you to within a day's walk of the Urok Malay, and give you a map to the cave."

"Why not just send him?"

"Because he lacks your courage, Mister Havelock. Also, unlike you, he's woefully inept with a firearm, and as superstitious as they come."

"So, what's in this for him?"

Tjilik answers for himself. "Revenge. Urok Malay kill my tribe. My family. Want them to suffer. Lose their god. Lose hope the way I did. Hurt like I did."

I lip a cigarette from my half-empty pack, strike a wooden match against the edge of the table. Light my coffin nail with a few quick puffs. "You got the map?"

Tjilik pats a chest pocket of his shirt.

"All right." I shake the lady's hand. "You got yourself a treasure hunter."

Fortune and glory, here I come.

TJILIK isn't one for small talk. We've traded barely a dozen words since we left Bangkok a week ago. I could tell he disliked sea travel though he refused to admit it. Maybe it was the seasickness. Maybe it was being cooped up in a tin can. Either way, his cold confidence returned once we'd landed in Borneo—or, as he insists on correcting me, Kalimantan.

I didn't need his help to buy a motorized shallow-bottom riverboat, but I let him help provision it. When we set off yesterday, our boat's tiny motor struggling against the current, I asked the name of the river we were following into the rainforest.

"River has no name," Tjilik said, squinting into the sun. "And no memory."

Now, less than a day inland, I fear I've made a grave mistake. Traveling up this river is like going backward in time, to an age when the world had no use for people, when wild plants owned the land. I once knew a professor who said people have lived on Borneo for fifty thousand years, but looking out at this impenetrable forest, you'd never know it.

The stream beneath our boat is muddy. I've caught no fish so far, but I'm not fool enough to think this water is empty. Falling out of the boat here would be a death sentence.

Going ashore won't bring safety, either. The big trees echo with the sounds of animal hungers, and keen eyes shimmer in the darkness. Always watching. Waiting for us. For me.

The air on the river is thick, sluggish, leaden. By late afternoon it grows so heavy that even tropical sunlight loses its brilliance, and at night there's no joy in the moonlight.

Before sundown I spy a python three times longer than our boat, coiled around a branch overhanging the river. Tjilik ignores it, but I steer wide of the beast all the same.

At night we tie up the boat to some long branches. An eerie stillness surrounds us. It's not a peaceful quiet; it's the hush of a pitiless force brooding with inscrutable intention. It's the jungle regarding us with a will to vengeance.

I sink into a fitful sleep, hoping but not hopeful that come daylight, the labor of piloting the river will ground me in dull reality and help me turn a blind eye to these terrors primeval.

*K*nowing it's a nightmare doesn't *help me. I can't break free—I'm caught, swimming in some kind of gelatinous mass, and I'm surrounded*

by mouths. They're horrid, insatiable, packed with jagged, bloody teeth, all of them gibbering nonsense or chittering madly. And the eyes! Millions of them, filled with a hate older than this world, older than the cosmos, looking through me.

I'm being devoured, digested, torn apart one bit at a time—

I jolt awake in the skiff, enveloped in the sawsong of jungle insects.

Tjilik crouches over me, his machete in hand.

I freeze, my face a mask of panic as Tjilik raises his blade.

My hand fumbles toward the Colt as the blade falls—

—and slashes off the head of a fanged serpent that had been dangling from the branch above my head, the one we'd used to anchor the boat mid-stream this night. The snake's head lands on my chest as its warm blood spurts into my face, into my eyes. I yelp and flail for a second until I recover my wits. I toss the head overboard. Fling the body in after it.

Just a snake. I've killed a few dozen myself over the years.

Tjilik wipes the snake's blood off his blade, onto the leg of his pants. He settles back into the skiff's bow. Wraps his hat's mosquito netting over his face and head. Goes back to sleep with his blade in his hand.

I sink back into the stern and try to do the same. But I can't stop hearing the voice from my nightmare, that inchoate gibbering, and when I close my eyes, all I can see is a color I can't name and can't describe, except to say that in my heart I know it is the color of true evil.

THE old woman sits alone in the manor's study. A banked fire in the hearth paints her with a ruddy glow. In her gnarled, age-spotted hand she holds a snifter of golden liquor. On the table beside her chair stands a nearly empty bottle of brandy. Past that rests a well-stocked liquor cart.

A small lamp on the desk provides the room's only other light. As I cross the study, I feel the promise of evil in the shadows around me. My Colt quakes in my hand, which is filthy with caked dirt and dried blood. I do my best to keep it aimed at the crone while I ease myself into the seat on the other side of the hearth. "Where is she?"

Her smirk is equal parts malice and mischief. "Who?"

"Your granddaughter. Lisa Sullivan."

Her left eyebrow creeps upward. The smirk opens into a smile, revealing her mouthful of yellowed, broken teeth. "I have no children, much less a granddaughter."

I've seen that expression before. In Bangkok, six months ago.

I look closer. Her hair is gray, her cheeks gaunt, her eyes sunken into their sockets...but it's her. I'd stake my life on it. "You. You're the one who hired me."

"Yes." She sips her brandy and gazes at the smoldering embers in the fireplace.

I can't help but stare at her wrinkled visage and recall the heartbreaker who just half a year ago promised me riches beyond compare. "But...how?"

Bitterness colors her reply. "I think you know." Her emerald eyes blaze with anger as she looks at me. "You found the cave."

"Of course I did. Your map and your guide were both perfect. That was how I knew."

"Knew what?"

"That you'd sent me into a trap."

IT takes two days for the river to shrink to a stream, another for the stream to become a trickle.

I spend an hour watching the trickle evaporate into mud.

The skiff squelches to a halt. I climb out of the boat and try to get my bearings. With the sun directly overhead, I have no shadow and no sense of direction. The jungle is no help. Endless green dripping with danger and shadow.

Tjilik pulls the skiff to dry ground. He eyes me as I load up with gear for my trek into the unknown. It's clear he disapproves. "Too much. Better to travel light."

He has a point. It's hotter than hell out here, and the air is so thick I can barely breathe without feeling like I'm drowning. All I've done so far is pick up my things and my shirt is soaked with sweat.

But what can I live without for two days?

Two canteens of water? Essential. Compass? Gotta have it. My Colt? He can have that when he takes it from my dead hand—as long as he shoots himself in the process.

I leave the tent. If it rains, I have a poncho. That and three sticks makes a lean-to.

The cooking gear stays. Time to live off the land.

But I won't give up my lantern and its kerosene refill.

Tjilik still seems to think I'm crazy, but I don't give a shit. He sits on a rock and whittles a piece of deadwood with his machete, pays me no mind as I approach. "You'll guard the boat?"

He nods, keeps his eye on his blade.

"Can I have the map now?"

His eyes narrow. He stabs his machete into the dirt, takes the map from his shirt pocket. Pushes it into my palm. Points to get me started. "One day that way. Watch step. Many snakes."

"Gee, and I thought you didn't care." I start walking.

He doesn't wish me good luck, say good-bye, or even look up as I depart.

I'm pretty sure he's not following me, but as the forest envelops me in its trackless riot of green, I can't shake the feeling that I'm being watched by something merciless and inhuman.

Either way, there's no turning back now. From here my only way out is through.

DRUMS in the night. Their rhythms draw me forward, through the darkness, to the mouth of the cave. The percussion is primitive, powerful, relentless, an engine of desire and fear. I feel the beat like a siren's call, shaking in my bones and coursing in my blood.

At the cave's entrance I freeze, shocked immobile by the unholy cacophony from within. I've never heard anything like it. Groans and growls, shrieks and whooping hollers. I can't tell if its source is human, animal, or Something Else. An instinct deep inside of me tells me to run, fills me with a need to get away from this place. I remind myself of the mad fortune the stranger promised me in exchange for the idol of the Urok Malay. And I go inside.

Three steps into the cave, I regret my decision. The rocky ground is strewn with gnawed bones and wet with fresh excrement. I gag as the smell of piss engulfs me, followed by wafting odors of meat-eaters' spoor. Within a few more steps the coppery perfume of blood dominates the stale air inside the cave, and I realize I'm treading toward an abattoir.

I tell myself I can handle it. That I've seen the worst the world has to offer. That after Gallipoli and the Somme, I am beyond revulsion.

Then I reach the end of the tunnel and peek into the cavern beyond.

I'm lucky my stomach's empty, because my body's first urge is a dry heave. I avert my eyes in denial. Pray to a god I don't believe in that I'm seeing things, that my eyes are playing cruel tricks on me. I should turn back now. I know it. But I'm drawn to the nightmare.

I look again.

Small fire pits around the cavern's perimeter illuminate a grotesque orgy-as-feast. The floor of the small cavern is packed with bodies. Some are humans, all of them naked, their eyes gouged out. Coated in blood and filth, they wrestle with a troop of gibbons whose orange furs are flecked with blood and shit. Humans and apes lie together, violating each other, clawing at one another's backs. The gibbons bite chunks of flesh off the humans, who growl in pain and groan with ecstasy, while the apes shriek and hoot and gibber with psychotic excitement.

But they aren't what holds my gaze.

I am transfixed by the gelatinous mass that rests atop a mound of dirty bones in the center of this interspecies atrocity. Translucent, trembling, its surface is covered in fanged mouths dripping blood and spittle, and countless yellow eyes gleaming with a hatred that must have been ancient before our sun was born. Its mouths don't speak, but gazing upon it, I know it can't be of this world, or even this universe. This is no mere monster. No pagan deity.

This thing eats our puny gods and shits out darkness.

And as it plumbs my weak human brain with invisible tendrils of cold contempt, I realize that I'm the next thing on its menu.

THE crone swoons. I almost shoot her on principle. "Am I turning you on, grandma?"

She opens her eyes, and I see they are bright with madness.

"It's been almost a hundred years since I saw the cave," she says, her voice dreamy and reverent. "Since I witnessed the beauty in the terror…"

"Trust me, lady. There was nothing beautiful about that thing, or the shit-stained wretches tearing themselves apart beneath it."

"Oh, that's where you're wrong." She waggles a wrinkled, bony index finger. "The beauty is there, if only you have the courage to see it."

"See what?"

"The truth. That there's nothing special about any of us, or this world, or the universe." She leans in, her face contorted by a vacant smile of insanity. "That life is *malignantly useless.*"

I want to argue. To protest. But I have seen the insatiable hatred in the cave, and now its indescribable color of despair dwells within me…and that's how I know she speaks the truth.

Life is malignantly useless.
And death is the only mercy.

I BACK away from the cavern, into the tunnel that led here. This is a party I don't want to join.

I mind my step, taking care not to trip or kick loose something that will betray me to the bestial mob cavorting for the amusement of the nightmare of eyes. I've almost lost sight of the stomach-turning spectacle when I feel a point of cold steel against my back.

Tjilik's foul breath is hot on my neck: "No going back."

He prods me forward at the end of his machete.

So much for superstition keeping him at a distance. How do I reason with this maniac? How do I tell him this job isn't worth doing even for twice what the woman promised? I'd bet his revenge on the Urok Malay isn't worth his life, and I know it sure as shit isn't worth mine. I have to believe he'll see that for himself as we reach the edge of the cavern and he lays eyes on this carnal abomination.

Instead he lets out an ululating war cry that brings the orgy to a halt—and with a powerful shove he sends me sprawling into the scrum.

Hands human and simian, claw at me, pull me down, rip the ruck from my back. I'm buried in bodies, and I gag at their fetid reek. I thrash, try to break free, but their sheer weight is too much. One of the creatures—for none of these deserve to be called people, not any more—bludgeons my head with a rock. My vision goes purple and my limbs go limp. My mind cries out, refuses to accept what is coming, but my body betrays me, surrenders in spite of me.

The throng whoops and yammers, filling the firelit cavern with a din of pure savagery. They drag me across the stone floor. My boots cut a trail through their slick of mingled fluids.

Panic is my world now, a primal need to escape at any cost.

Cruel laughter spills from the hundred mouths of the fiend on its bone pile.

Its minions lift me. There are dozens of them, madmen with empty charred eye sockets, screeching apes with blood-soaked fangs. They slam me down onto a blood-stained altar of stone, pin my arms and legs, and pull my head backward to force my mouth open.

A wild woman, her face painted with streaks of blood and feces, chitters like an insect as she drifts toward me. She holds in both hands a bowl fashioned from a human skull. Black liquid sloshes out of it and spills across her feet as she raises the skull above my face.

I scream, a roar of fury and denial—

She pours the noxious brew down my throat. I gag, try to spit it out, but she keeps pouring, and the harder I fight to expel it, the more I swallow as I fight for breath. It tastes of dead things, damned things, of bitter roots and the ferric tang of human blood.

The beasts are ecstatic now, jumping and bouncing in place. For a moment I'm able to shift my hand, which finds the handle of my Colt, and then the trigger—

A deafening report. It echoes in the cavern like a dying peal of thunder.

The savages recoil, crying out in wordless alarm.

I roll off of the slab. Target the largest and nearest of the bastards. Blast the top of his head clean the fuck off. Blood and brains spatter the rest of the tribe, who retreat—

—as Tjilik charges at me, his machete held high, ready to cleave me in half.

No time for fancy. I aim at his torso and shoot twice, three times. It's the third bullet in his gut that brings him to his knees.

I put my last bullet into his forehead.

As he slumps to the floor, I take the machete from his hand.

The creatures sense that my hand cannon is empty, and I know there's no time to fumble through a reload. I'll have to do this the old-fashioned way.

They surge forward, a seething mass of atavistic rage.

I swing the machete in broad arcs, cutting throats, severing hands, hacking through clavicles, each blow painting the cavern in fresh sprays of crimson. I don't discriminate between men and apes—they're all animals in here. Wild beasts beyond redemption or pity.

None of them have the sense to retreat, even as their numbers dwindle.

I cut them down, one and all.

Only when the last of them lies dead at my feet does my blade rest in my hand.

The monster on its mountain of bones is still laughing. It's the voice of chaos incarnate. A god of blood and slaughter, an avatar of carnage. A thousand mouths and a thousand eyes, all of them mocking me.

I find my ruck amid the corpses. Retrieve my kerosene lamp and the refill canister. I pour fuel over the bodies, and then I splash the last generous portion onto the eldritch horror itself.

I retreat to the cavern's mouth and ignite the lantern.

With a lob I hurl it at the monster. The lantern shatters against its osseous pedestal. The flames spread fast, consuming the beast and its butchered congregation. I stand and feel the heat sear my face and singe my eyebrows as the fuckpile becomes a funeral pyre.

As the blaze devours the beast, I long to hear its mouths scream in agony.

Instead, it goes on laughing. As it boils away into froth and vapor, those yellow eyes continue to stare into my soul—or, I now realize, the void where I thought my soul would be.

At last the heat becomes too much to bear. I flee down the tunnel, and then out into the jungle. I run through the night, following a trail of notches I'd cut into trees on my way here, and just before dawn I reach the skiff, still beached in the mud. I launch it into the shallows, climb aboard, and collapse. I let the current bear me away, carry me downstream, back to the river and then to the coast, and then I flee as far from this accursed place as I can go.

I set to sea, desperate to escape this unholy laughter, but my commitment only makes the voice in my head laugh harder—because It knows there's nowhere I can go that It won't find me.

"THERE never was any idol, was there?"

My question amuses the old bitch. "No."

I let my finger curl around the Colt's trigger. "You sent me there to die."

"You were hardly the first."

"I made sure I was the *last*."

She lifts her hand, traces the deep lines in her face with her fingertips. "A pity." Her green eyes, still piercing in their intensity, look out from under white brows. "What now?"

"Now? You're gonna die."

"Silly boy. *Everything* dies. You. Me. The world. The sun. Even *time*. Can't you see it doesn't matter? That nothing ever did?"

I can't listen to another word. It's like she's channeling the beast.

I stand and fire. Put two slugs in her chest and one in her head.

From the rolling liquor cart beside her chair I grab a bottle of grappa. With my last full measure of defiance, I hurl it into the fireplace.

The bottle shatters. The alcohol ignites, engulfs the crone's body, and scatters across the room. The rug, the curtains, the furniture—it all goes up in flames.

Standing in the middle of the roaring inferno, all I can hear is the laughter.

Tongues of fire lick at my fingers. The hairs on my arms shrivel.

My clothes catch fire as I raise the Colt.

Praying for silence, I put its barrel in my mouth and pull the trigger.

My world turns white—

Darkness falls—

...but the laughter goes on...

...and on...

...and on...

Dreams of Kingdom

BY PAUL KUPPERBERG

E heard the distant twang of longbows and clash of swords filtered through the trees and left the road to follow them into the forest. Whatever the conflict, it was no concern of his. He was a free agent, bound to no monarch or cause, but he had long lost count of his days on the road and thought this would be, at least, a momentary distraction from the tedium. Perhaps even an opportunity for profit.

Battle cries and cries of the dying joined the clash and clatter of weapons as he guided his mount through the sparse, young forest. The black horse's nostrils flared at the scent of blood and his ears twitched in the direction of combat, but he made no sound. The stallion had been well trained for combat by his previous owner, a captain in the army of the City of the Mists, an armored giant of a man who carried the biggest broadsword Aculeus the Bastard had even seen. Had the giant trained half as well in the use of his weapon as he had his mount, Aculeus would not today be riding the great steed. The broadsword he left clutched in the captain's hands where he had fallen on the bloodied mud of the battlefield.

The wars were done. In this, the twenty-eighth year of the reign of Kalahos, peace had been declared between the principalities in the rich valleys of the Lower Kingdoms. The conflicts dividing them had been settled on the battlefields and across the tables of truce and the invading armies had withdrawn back behind borders both long held and newly redrawn by treaty. And with the peace came the release from service of thousands of mercenaries, free-lancers, and adventurers who had joined whichever cause offered the highest wages or best opportunity for loot. With no wars left to fight, many of the freebooters turned to other means of subsistence. They became highwaymen and pirates, assassins for hire, strong-arms and enforcers for the moneylenders, gamblers and way-layers, pimps and thieves.

To be sure, there were fortunes to be made in the Lower Kingdoms, but not for the likes of him. This knowledge had come to him at the cost of an eye, a finger, scars too numerous to count, and several small fortunes that had slipped through his fingers. Birth was destiny and Aculeus' birth had been in the backroom of a whorehouse in the City of the Scorpion. He did not have a name until he chose his

Illustration by Mike Collins

own as a youth. The whore who had birthed him had been strangled by the rich man whose seed contributed to his creation when she went to blackmail him with the news of their shared sin.

When he was thirteen, no longer a boy but barely a man, a deathbed rant by a whore whose mind had been ravaged by the diseases of her trade revealed the name of his mother's killer. He was a man of wealth and public piety, an advisor to princes, one not easily approached by a street urchin in filthy rags, but Aculeus found a way. And the moment the merchant saw his own features reflected in the snarling face of the boy who came towards him, his hand went for a jewel-handled dagger in his sash. But the boy was big for his age, strong and fast. He sliced open the whoremonger's throat with an old, rusty blade he had scavenged from the trash and honed against the cobblestones in the street, his manhood celebrated in the baptismal spray of his ancestral blood.

Birth was destiny, and Aculeus's birth had been a squalid bit of cheap commerce. He had no love for the mother he had never known, nor a hatred of the father who had killed her. He only knew that even in a deal driven by animal lust, there was the weak and the strong, and the one was always preyed upon by the other. It was time he learned which he was. Watching the last of the blood

pulse from the scarlet smile he had carved in his father's throat, the nameless child saw that wealth and power didn't amount to strength. He learned its true meaning in that alley: The strong were the first and the fastest to kill. And the last to fear dying.

He tugged gently on the reins, bringing his horse to a stop. He was close enough to hear the fast approaching thunder of multiple riders, along with another sound. A wagon, its wheels clattering as it raced over the rutted road, urged on by the frightened shouts of its driver and his whip.

Aculeus urged his mount on with a press of his heel to its flank. It nodded its great head as if in understanding and stepped on. Only a narrow stand of trees separated the lone rider from a road that curved through the forest and he kept to their shadows as the hoof beats and wagon wheels drew nearer. He dropped the reins and let the horse pick its own cautious way ahead. His sword was sheathed within easy reach at his side and both his rusty old knife and his father's dagger were tucked inside the folds of his wrappings. The precious gems that once decorated the handle had long since been sold or lost in games of chance, but a knife's true worth was judged by its other end, and this one was kept sharp so that it could always be counted on to cut deep. His only bit of preparation was to wrap his left forearm and hand, his dagger hand from which he had already sacrificed one finger, in a long, leather strap fitted with sharp iron studs across the knuckles.

The frightened whinny of horses pierced the air ahead of a loud crash and the sounds of splintering wood. Then came a confusion of pounding hooves and the screams of women, cut short by the harsh shouts and threatening growls of men.

The wagon had overturned taking a bend in the road at too fast a gallop. It was a fancy coach, enclosed and top heavy, and once it had started to tip to one side on its thin, carved wheels, the team of four horses could not hold the road. When Aculeus at last came to the scene, the dust had not yet settled around the wreckage and the men who had chased the wagon to ground were leaping down from their own horses, shouting commands to the dazed driver and two footmen who, despite being thrown from the coach, had survived, though not unbloodied.

Aculeus the Bastard did not recognize the faces of any of the attackers but he knew who they were. Soldiers of fortune, some still wearing remnants of the trappings of the royal units they once served. This batch had put their talents to use as highwaymen or kidnappers. Selling human beings back to their own people could be a lucrative trade and from the looks of the ruined coach and the fine horseflesh pulling it, these victims came from wealth.

The leader was a small, dark haired wiry man wearing the sash of a sergeant in the army of the Prince of Paran. He was the last man off his horse, and as he stalked towards the coach, he made an angry slashing motion with his arm. Some of his men stepped in and ran the startled driver and footmen through with their swords, dropping them where they stood.

Three more highwaymen were struggling to drag the occupants from the upended coach and the sergeant yelled for them to be quick about it. They finally succeeded in pulling two squirming women from inside and threw them to the ground.

Eight of them, Aculeus noted. Each a veteran armed with well-worn weapons and scars to attest to their lives on the field.

The men encircled the women, laughing and jeering. One was young with fiery hair the color of the sunset and dressed in a rainbow of fine silks and satins. She clung as though her life depended on it to her traveling companion, a sturdy older woman wrapped in plainer garb, her head demurely covered. A merchant's daughter and her nanny, he thought.

The sergeant pushed through the ring of men and make a mock bow.

"Dear princess," he growled in a northern accent.

The older woman stepped in front of her shivering charge and stared at the brute with indignation. "Don't touch her, you scum," she announced in a strong if slightly quivering voice.

"I wouldn't dream of it, lady. It's hands off the princess if we wants full price for her return. But you, little mother," he said, taking her chin in his hand and bringing his face in close to hers, "you ain't worth a thin copper to nobody, broken or whole. What say I throw you to my men and let them take what value they can from you?"

The nanny refused to look away from the little man. She stared him straight in the eye when she spit in his face. With a growl, he slapped her across the cheek, spinning her around. She stumbled back into one of the men who shoved her again towards his leader with a hearty laugh.

The sergeant caught a fistful of the dazed woman's wrap at her throat and held her dangling before him. He laughed, her saliva still dripping down his cruel face. "We likes it rough too, lady," he said, drawing back his other fist.

But the nanny was less of a lady than the sergeant believed, and she was first to land a blow, a right foot to his balls. Likely more surprised than hurt, the sergeant yelled, dropping her to grab his injured parts. But his look had turned angry and he was no longer of a mind to merely toy with her. His hand went to the hilt of his sword.

"What man needs so much blade for so small a woman?" Aculeus called in challenge as he stepped from the cover of the forest.

Every head turned his way and, for a moment, no one moved.

Aculeus knew the sight he made. He was large, his shoulders and chest broad and his arms knotted with muscle from a lifetime of combat wielding heavy weapons. The last he had bothered to look at himself in a reflecting glass, he had seen a hard face with the decades of experience chiseled into his flesh. His one eye stared back, black like coal. Over where the other once had been was a mass of scars and an empty socket covered by a black leather patch. His head was shaved clean, except for the topknot that reached down to his shoulders, a ceremonial scorpion's tail. He wore only a wrap around his waist and legs, with a sash from which to hang his scabbard and secure his knives, and no protection except for his leather wrapped left hand.

The sergeant was the first to recover his senses and he completed drawing his sword, only now it was to menace the newcomer.

"This ain't no business of yours, rider. Move on and let us be about ours."

"The business of ransom."

"What matter to you? You expectin' to be made a partner?" He thrust his sword at Aculeus.

"'Cause this is the only cuttin' in you'll be getting here." The highwaymen laughed heartily with their leader, almost at ease. They were eight to his one, with little to fear from him.

Aculeus was in no hurry to correct that impression. He kept his sword lowered at his side as he walked to the knot of thieves.

"I wasn't thinking of a piece, little sergeant. I thought I'd take the whole pie," Aculeus said. He looked at the nanny. She was watching him with narrowed, weary eyes. "A true princess is she?"

"Aye, sir."

"Wealthy?"

"Very, sir."

"And her daddy? Does he think her worth a ransom?"

The sergeant stepped in front of Aculeus and shouted indignantly, "Hey now!"

The nanny threw the man a withering glance and said to Aculeus, "He does, sir. He dotes upon the child and spoils her to meanness. His reward to her rescuer would be more generous than any ransom to her abductors."

Aculeus said, "I like you, little mother," and then sidestepped the bellowing sergeant, impaling the dark little man on his sword.

The nanny's laughter was drowned out by the angry shouts of the highwaymen. They swarmed the one-eyed soldier like angry bees, stabbing and feinting and getting in one another's way with all the skill of washerwomen. Aculeus

might have felt sorry for them, but he wasn't to blame for their having chosen dangerous work for which they were so ill-suited. The only fields some of these fools belonged on were ones in which they were behind plows.

He pulled his double-edged sword from the man's gut, swinging it around as it came free in a fine spray of bloody fluids to take the sword hand off another man. A single blow from Aculeus' leather and studded fist crushed the throat of a third, and then that same hand reached into his sash and came out clutching the tip of his old knife.

The remaining highwaymen backed off and spread apart, encircling him on shuffling feet with swords at the ready. The attack would come from behind; the others would then pile on, taking him down by sheer weight of numbers.

Aculeus whirled, releasing the knife to spin through the air and thud into the chest of the heavily bearded man in mid lunge at his back. The man dropped to his knees with a stunned look. He wrapped both hands around the hilt and wrested the deep sunk blade from his body, releasing a gurgling sigh of relief before pitching face first into the spreading pool of blood pumping from the wound.

Two of the highwaymen approached, one from either side. And a third one, behind him and to his right, seeking to take advantage of his blind side. It was the first smart move any of them had made. Too bad it was executed so poorly, the man's sandals scuffing through the dirt loud enough to alert a dead man.

The men before him took turns, stepping in and feinting. But he did not take the bait or even flinch, maintaining an easy crouch, the tip of his sword circling the air slowly between them. The eyes of the swordsman to his left flickered briefly, a signal to the one behind him, before bellowing a battle cry and lunging. Aculeus went right, splitting the man behind him from crotch to sternum. He ducked below one blade, cutting the legs out from under its owner.

The two kidnappers still standing chose to remain that way and were already racing for their horses by the time he turned to challenge them. They galloped off into the forest without a look back, but Aculeus stood with raised sword and heaving chest, listening until the sounds of their horses faded to silence. Only then did he let loose a great, shuddering breath, willing his battle tensed body to relax, to loosen fingers aching from gripping his weapons, to clear his mind and vision of the red haze that seemed to slow down time and make his heart pound with bloodlust.

"Ya says ya likes it rough, aye, ya stinkin' bastard," he heard the nanny growl. She was kneeling next to the sergeant, holding his head up by the hair, her other hand gripping Aculeus' old knife over his chest. The impaling hadn't quite ended his life, but the way his guts spilled from the wound, he hadn't long to last. Just enough to know who it was who plunged the knife into his black heart that ended him for good.

Flushed and panting, the nanny rose and stood over her kill. She wiped the blade clean on her wrappings and as an afterthought spit on the body before returning the knife to Aculeus.

She barked a harsh laugh at his surprised expression. "What? *I* wasn't born a princess, you know."

FROM the high mountains of the City of the Sun, rivers and streams ran into the valleys of the Lower Kingdoms, emptying at last into the great Southern Sea. Some of those waters flowed with riches, carrying vast quantities of gold scrubbed from the earth by their rushing power. First among the cities of the valleys was the City of the Mists, rising at the convergence of the gold rich Trilos, Atlan, and Sun Rivers, ruled by Kalahos the Just, author of the treaties which had ended the latest round of wars.

The nanny was called Sister Kine, and the princess was named Taliss. Her father was Brunn, the second richest man in the kingdom, ruler of the small but powerful banking and commerce principality, Heavenskeep. If there was a seamy side to this scrubbed little kingdom Aculeus could find no of sign of it as Sister Kine led their horses through swept streets filled with finely garbed aristocracy, past opulent shops and ornate houses of commerce. Want did not seem to exist in Heavenskeep. Likely, it was barred entry through the city gates.

Taliss said nothing the entire ride to the city on the back of one of the highwaymen's horses, but the beautiful young woman with hair like flame never took her eyes off Aculeus. She wasn't afraid. She was curious. And something else. Aculeus wasn't sure he wished to know what. She rode snuggled against her nanny, who petted her and cooed gentle sounds when she wasn't chattering at him about the magnificence and munificence of her master and of the generosity of his household staff, of which she was a willing and giving member.

Unlike Taliss' mysterious stare, Sister Kine's eyes were easy to read. Why not? Upon closer inspection, she was not quite the matron her dress suggested. Her maiden years were firmly behind her, but she was a handsome woman still and he suspected he would not be disappointed by what was to be found beneath her wrappings. Besides, how often did he cross paths with a woman who handled a knife as well as this one?

Brunn was waiting for them on the palace steps, having been alerted to his daughter's return in the company of a one-eyed stranger by a runner from the gates. He was tall and thin, with a head too large for his slender frame capped by a cascade of fussily arranged red hair that flowed down his back to his waist over his multicolored silks. Footmen scurried past him from the entrance to help the princess from her mount and she flounced past him going into the palace, ignoring his outstretched arms and relieved words of concern. The spurned father's head dropped and when Aculeus looked over at Sister Kine, he found her watching him with a secret smile.

The nanny told her master of the mercenary's fortuitous arrival in time to save them from kidnapping and likely worse at the hands of the highwaymen. There were twenty opponents in her telling, none surviving Aculeus' blade. She also failed to mention her own role in dispatching the sergeant, but he decided not to correct her on either detail.

In his overwhelming gratitude, the master of Heavenskeep called upon all the gods to bless and keep Aculeus and all his ancestors who ever were and descendants who shall ever be. Brunn compared him to the heroes of myth and legend and offered that the name Aculeus the Bastard be inscribed forever in the scrolls of history so that it were never to be forgotten. Aculeus bore the gushing of flowery praise for as long as he could, then he snapped, "Screw history. I'll take my reward in *this* life."

"Name it, my friend. I am a wealthy man, but all my diamonds and gold would mean nothing to me without my Taliss."

"Well, you've got your Taliss, so I'll just take all the diamonds and gold."

Brunn's fingertips fluttered to his lips and he laughed nervously. "Oh. No, you misunderstand. I spoke hyperbolically, good sir. Surely you don't expect..."

Aculeus dismounted, handing the reins to a footman. "Relax, father. I wouldn't know what to do with your fortune if I had it."

"But I insist upon rewarding you for your gallantry in some way, no matter how modest," Brunn said hastily but in obvious relief.

"It won't be modest, I assure you," Aculeus said.

Sister Kine said, "Master Aculeus has traveled a long way, my prince, and I could not help but brag to him of the hospitality of the House of Brunn."

The master of the house clapped his hands together and said, "Yes, yes, what am I thinking? Please, good sir, you are welcome to my house and a seat of honor at my table." He bowed his head and swept his arm towards the door, bidding Aculeus enter.

WITHOUT a word spoken, a manservant appeared at Aculeus' side and led him through a maze of hushed marble corridors and up a grand stairway to a bedchamber that could have billeted a squad of soldiers. The vast room had a high ceiling and opened onto a terrace with space for another dozen to sleep that overlooked the perpetual curtain of mist that hung over the thundering falls where the three rivers met.

He had only ever seen luxury like this in one place, a high-class whorehouse in the City of the Serpent in which he had taken up several weeks residence until he drank and screwed his way through a sudden windfall of riches.

He told the manservant to bring him wine and then settled into a generously sized sunken marble tub fed by warm spring waters to consider his situation. He couldn't remember the last time he had slept in a proper bed, much less bathed in anything but cold rivers. Nor did he worry that the wine cellar and kitchens of the second richest man in the Lower Kingdoms would not far outstrip whatever grub he could kill and char over an open flame. He didn't think the foppish prince would begrudge the road weary traveler who had saved his daughter from abduction, and likely worse, a few weeks' stay as his guest. Anyway, a few weeks was all Aculeus could properly be expected to stand the constraints of polite society before he would have to get out among real men and hit someone.

And he was sure he would not be allowed ride off without something substantial weighing down his pouch.

But beyond the wine and food and even the gold was the question of another amenity. The women. Aculeus' could still warm himself on cold nights sleeping on hard ground with memories of those weeks in the City of the Serpent. Of course, he expected no professionally produced spectaculars here as were experienced there, but his needs were, at their core, simple.

It was just as his thoughts were turning to Sister Kine and what may be hidden beneath her wrappings that Aculeus heard the soft sigh of parting silk curtains and the pad of bare feet across the floor. He expected that would be the good nanny, come to make good with her body the promise of her eyes.

"No need to rise," said the princess Taliss, behind him.

"Did you bring my wine?" Aculeus said without turning his head.

"Don't be impertinent. What did you say you were called?"

"Aculeus the Bastard."

She was standing over him now, at the edge of the tub, looking down at him.

"Because you're so mean?" she said, but with no coyness in her voice.

"That, and because my mother was a nameless whore and I was sired by a father whose throat I'd one day cut."

The girl started to speak, but stopped when the manservant returned with a jug of wine and a golden drinking cup on a tray. Looking at neither Aculeus or Taliss, the man knelt to set the tray by the side of the tub and picked up the jug to pour. Aculeus grabbed the jug from the man's hand and said, "This will do. For now."

He filled the silence as the man bowed and scraped his way backwards out of the chamber with several long draughts of the cool, sweet wine. He smacked his lips and said, "By Wtcher, that is fine."

"We have our own vineyards. These are father's special grapes," Taliss said, staring impatiently at the departing servant. When he was at last gone from earshot, she said, "Did you really kill your father?"

He nodded.

The flame-haired young woman hesitated, then said, "What, what was it like?"

"What do you mean?" he asked her, smiling around the jug.

"Killing him. Your father. What did it feel like?" Her attempt to sound casual was betrayed by the quiver in her voice.

He shrugged. "What's it feel like to squash a bug?"

"Did you hate him?"

Aculeus finally turned his head. Her naturally pale skin was stark white now except for spots of pink on her cheeks. She met his eyes but the defiance was gone from them.

"I didn't know him. I just did

what needed to be done."

She nodded and the fear he saw on her face confirmed what he already guessed. She hadn't come to thank him for saving her life. A pampered child of royal breeding, she didn't understand gratitude much less feel a need to express it.

The motive for her visit was patricide.

"My father is a fool," she said.

"He's done alright for a fool," Aculeus said, glancing at their surroundings.

"The House of Brunn should rule the Lower Kingdoms, instead he settles for being Kalahos' puppet and purse."

"Kalahos has an army."

"Their loyalty wouldn't last long without father's gold to pay them." Aculeus settled back into the clear warm water.

"Pity then it's your father and not you who controls the purse strings."

"He won't hear reason. He's frightened King Elsgar of the First City would not let his withholding of funds to his cousin Kalahos stand."

Aculeus laughed. "Old Elsgar's got too much to worry about in the north to spare an army to come reprimand your daddy. Hells, girl, the king will need your family gold soon enough himself to prop up his own treasury if he can't get that under control."

"Even a one-eyed mercenary bastard can see what father will not."

She waited, watching him. Like everything else in her life, she expected even this lowest, darkest deed to be made easy for her. A servant would speak the words and she could dispatch him to the task with a nod. But in Aculeus' world, one spoke up to what they wanted or else they swallowed their anger or greed or jealousy and slunk away to let their weakness and failure devour them.

"Tell me what you want, girl," he said and swallowed more wine.

His words startled her. "Want? From you?"

"A little while ago you wanted my sword to save your royal ass. So unless you're planning to join me in my ablutions, I don't know what you want of me."

Indignation flashed across her features, but she caught herself before she erupted in regal rage. Whatever her father may be, this one was no fool. But she was young.

"I want you to kill my father," she sneered in the contemptuous tones of a child out to prove a smug adult wrong. "Kill him, make me head of the House of Brunn, and I'll give you a kingdom of your own."

Young, but learning fast.

"There, girl. Was that so hard to do?"

NO sooner had the princess' footsteps faded from hearing did Aculeus' next visitor appear, slipping in from the terrace like the breeze through the fluttering silk curtains.

"What did she want?" Sister Kine asked. The nanny had bathed and changed. With her head uncovered and in less austere wrappings, he saw he hadn't been incorrect in his assessment of her.

"She had a proposition," Aculeus said. He reached for the golden drinking cup and filled it from the jug.

"Don't tell me the child offered herself to you," she said with pretend shock.

"She never made any real sort of offer, but I think she left here believing we'd struck a bargain for my sword." He handed up the wine cup. Sister Kine came forward to accept it from him and take a swallow.

"Palace intrigue," she said with a sigh. She gazed down at him in the tub and smiled. "Are you sure that's all she wanted, Aculeus?"

"Aye, just my sword."

Sister Kine laughed, a deep, husky laugh, and with one hand, reached up to her shoulder and tugged at her wrapping. The soft fabric loosened and began to unwind from her body, shifting like sands washing down the length of her full, dark body to fall to her feet. She stepped down into the warm bath and sank beside him.

"What do you think I'm here for?" she said and reached for him.

MUCH later, after his visitor had left him exhausted, another manservant slipped discreetly into the chamber to bring Aculeus fresh garments and Brunn's invitation to a modest banquet in the hero's honor. The hero grunted his acceptance and was left to dress.

While they rested, Sister Kine filled the idle time with gossip about the House of Brunn. There were three heirs to the family fortune; Taliss, her older sister, Tulia, and their younger brother, Thar. Taliss, she told him, was by far the smartest of the lot, but baby brother Thar possessed a streak of ruthlessness that she thought more than made up for his lack of brains. Those two had declared open war on one another years ago and spent the days since jockeying for position with their father or scheming with the prince's enemies for alliances. Tulia cared for none of the intrigue. She would side with whoever promised to continue to provide her extravagant needs. Brunn's first chancellor, his brother Bhaliss, was a man of considerable ambition, as well as being the lover of Brunn's wife.

There were others as well, aunts and uncles and cousins, all swarming around court, all plotting and scheming, creating alliances of opportunity or convenience against the others, sneaking around in search of the most advantageous betrayals, all seeking a way to lay hands on the wealth of Heavenskeep.

"Stop, woman, you're making my head ache," Aculeus demanded. "Gods, if this is civilization, I'll stick to the battlefield. At least there you know who you can trust and who you're supposed to kill."

"Princess Taliss appears to know who to kill."

"But not the courage to do it herself."

Sister Kine shrugged. "She doesn't have to wipe her own ass if she doesn't wish to, my soldier. She has servants to do everything for her."

"I'm no servant."

"No, you are not, even if you have served *me* quite well," she said, rolling on top of him and changing the subject.

Aculeus was greeted at the entrance to the dining hall by Brunn. He was dressed in formal garb that sparkled and shimmered with little points of colorful light and his long cascade of red hair had been tied into dozens of strands and woven around his shoulders and down his back in an elaborate pattern.

"Welcome, welcome, Aculeus, hero of Heavenskeep, honored guest of the House of Brunn," he announced loudly with widespread arms and swept his visitor into the hall.

Brunn's modest banquet was more elaborate than some festivals to Dakkis the Dreamer Aculeus had seen. A full orchestra filled the chamber with music to entertain the hundreds of royals and their courtiers sprawled on cushions and furs around tables laden with meats, fish, fowl, and fruits while servants scurried among them cleaning up their messes or bent under the weight of tubs of wine, beer, and liquors to keep their goblets filled. The air was thick with the odor of sweet smoke, the same sticky little ball of narcotic oblivion familiar to him from slums and waterfronts across the empire, only here the drug was smoked from elaborate hookahs attended by servants instead of from rough wooden or clay pipes in dank cellars.

There were too many people with too much of everything. The merriment wasn't real. Their hilarity was forced, fueled by wine and sweet smoke. They were there to be seen and needed to be louder or more outrageously garbed than anyone else to make their mark, perhaps to be rewarded by a smile and nod from their prince, or the accolades of their peers for initiating a new fashion trend.

Aculeus was relieved when Brunn lead him across the dining hall and into a smaller dining area behind a thick wall of curtains. Servants swept them aside and the prince ushered his guest inside.

The room held merely dozens of diners, seated in proper chairs around tables, dining in awkward silence. From Sister Kine's descriptions, he could guess the identities of some. Sister Tulia, a slightly plumper version of Taliss, sat beside her mother, a hard-faced woman laden down with more gold and gems than the rest of the guests combined. The heavyset man in black and gray, his red hair cropped short around his too large head would be Bhaliss, Brunn's brother, chancellor, and cuckold. Taliss sat surrounded by her court maidens at a separate table, and the thin lad in silks and hair to rival Brunn's was doubtless the baby, Thar, a sullen faced boy who had inherited his father and uncle's oversized skulls. The rest were a selection of kin, none of whom Brunn bothered to introduce him to.

The prince spoke long and loudly of Aculeus' achievement and numerous toasts were raised to him. He didn't bother to listen to the praise, content to down Brunn's fine liquors and eat his food while he studied this nest of royal vipers.

None were listening to their lord and master and he seemed not to notice or care, happy to keep talking and having his goblet refilled for the endless toasts. Some of the others talked softly, some might say conspiratorially, among themselves, or they ate, fondled their mates, dozed, or sucked sweet smoke from hookahs. Taliss never took her eyes from Aculeus, while her sister and mother glanced only occasionally his way, their heads together in conversation. Bhaliss sprawled in his chair and stroked his chin, pretending to listen to his brother.

AS the night droned on, the royal family poise began to slip. Drink made tongues loose enough that some began to slip and little arguments erupted. The diners moved between tables now, some to find fresh companions, others to betray confidences just learned. The boys grew louder and chased the giggling girls. Early in the evening, he had received a steady flow of well-wishers, but his grunted replies made fast work of that line and discouraged further conversation. Concerned with his comfort and happiness, Brunn fluttered about him like a nervous nanny. Aculeus thought of going off in search of Sister Kine.

He was drunk, but pleasantly so. He wasn't expecting any trouble, but he was a stranger here and thought it best not to allow himself to become too dulled by drink.

The young prince approached with a polite bow of his head before drawing up a chair. He raised his cup to the mercenary and said, "I drink to your rescue of my dear sister."

Aculeus returned the salute with his own cup and downed a long draught.

"I don't know if you're aware that you're in a position to rescue Taliss a second time, this very night," the boy said, trying to sound like a man.

Aculeus took another drink. "How do I do that?"

"I know she was to see you, probably to buy your sword. Tell her to forget her plans and stay out of my way."

"How do you know she tried to buy me?"

"Because it's what I would do if I were in her position." Thar looked down into his cup, then back up with a sly smile. "Which, indeed, I am. I will give you double what she promised you."

"Careful, boy. She offered me a kingdom of my own," Aculeus said.

"To kill father, yes? And me as well, I suppose."

Aculeus shook his head and smiled. "Ask her what she plans."

"But I'm asking you. I place a high premium on loyalty, you know. My sister will use you and betray you."

"And you won't?"

"You have my pledge of honor as a prince of the House of Brunn, and as a man," the boy said with so much sincerity that Aculeus had to hold back his laughter.

"Well, then it's best you tell me what you have in mind, my prince," the soldier said.

A CULEUS thought the hour was late enough and the family sufficiently distracted that no one had seen him slip from the royal dining room, but Bhaliss was on his heels before he could pass through the banquet hall.

"I am glad we finally have a moment to speak," the large man said breathlessly, having had to run to catch up with him.

"Are you?"

"Yes, yes. It occurs to me that your arrival at this particular time is most fortuitous."

"Is it?"

"Oh, indeed. That is, do I understand? You are a professional swordsman, are you not?"

Aculeus nodded.

"Ah, then, I wish to hire you." His smile reminded Aculeus of every thief and liar he had ever met, full of warmth and delivered with the cold, dead eyes of a serpent.

"To do what?"

Bhaliss glanced furtively around the crowded hall, as if he might be heard over the music and raucous laughter.

"Well, it's a rather delicate situation, you see," he said. "It involves family."

"Your brother's wife, I wager."

The chancellor stopped in his tracks and looked sharply at Aculeus. A small smile to tug at the corner of his mouth.

"Yes. You are the man for the job. I won't underestimate you again, my friend. Now, tell me, how do you feel about fratricide?"

A CULEUS didn't know which he found more tiring, the late hour or the naked treachery of the House of Brunn. Together, they left him exhausted and he fell into his bed. Between them, they hadn't the honor of a horse thief or the courage of a pickpocket. In his world, a man did his own dirty work. It was one thing to rent out his sword as a soldier. Soldiering was an honorable profession, acted out on in the full light of day on battlefields for all to see. What these people wanted from him was an assassin's hand, slinking about in the shadows, murdering in cold blood women, children, and old men.

The tapers were burned down to a soft glow when Aculeus awoke with a start from a dream of chasing screaming children down an alley with his bloody knives.

"Hush, my soldier," Sister Kine whispered, sliding her warm, naked body against his under the furs. "You were having a nightmare."

Aculeus grunted, wiping the night sweat from his face. "It's this damned place. They all want one or more of the others dead and me to slay them."

"My poor Aculeus," she cooed, stroking his chest. "Beset by royal tomfoolery. The inbred fools. The only thing maintaining the House of Brunn's position is heredity and its ancestral hold on the rivers and their gold."

"Maybe I should just kill them all and proclaim myself prince of Heavenskeep," he said with a laugh.

In the darkness, Sister Kine laughed with him. She pressed closer to him and Aculeus heard something catch in her throat. Her hand began making longer strokes, down his belly.

"*Prince* Aculeus," she breathed. "That does sound grand." Her hand reached lower now and her lips traced the line of his neck. "You could do it, you know. A man like you, you could kill them all and take the crown."

"Just like that, eh?" He looked at her, but all he could see in the dying candlelight was a dark, featureless form. "I don't know much about court, but Heavenskeep's a principality. Doesn't rule need to stay in the bloodline?"

"Take one of the girls for a bride, one of the cousins. There's one or two among them you'll find pleasing and who are greedy enough to enter the bargain."

Her breath was coming faster now and he could feel the heat rising in her and himself as her hand move tantalizingly over his skin.

"Where would that leave you?"

"The prince's courtesan and most trusted advisor. Until the bitch of Brunn gives you legitimate heirs." Under the furs, her fingers closed around him. "Then I would wed the widower prince."

Aculeus roared with laughter and rolled over on top of her.

"You've given this much thought," he said.

"I have many thoughts, my soldier," Sister Kine said and enclosed him in her arms and legs just as the last of the candles sputtered out, leaving them in darkness.

HE awoke late the next morning, alone and thankful for it. Less than one day in the lap of the polite and civilized and his head was aching from more than just their wine. He wondered if they danced this dance of intrigue all the time or if his chance visit to court had ignited all this treachery.

Aculeus bathed and dressed, then took his morning meal on the terrace with a view of the thundering falls. After that, he left his chambers and wandered out into the lush royal gardens. They were carefully planted to look wild and untamed and were stocked with a variety of gentle game and fowl that wandered the grounds, unafraid.

He wasn't the only predator afoot in the gardens, but he was the only one not hiding his danger behind a pretty smile and flirtatious eyes. She was called Netel, the daughter of Bhaliss' eldest son. And she was, as Sister Kine had predicted, pleasing enough to look at, if one liked his women pale and virginal.

The mercenary let her flirt and flatter, touching his broad shoulders and muscular arms and brushing against him as they walked the garden paths. He said little and she prattled on, filling the time with family gossip and taking her time to make her offer.

"I saw grandfather Bhaliss leave the banquet with you last night," Netel said.

"I left. He followed me."

"What did he say?"

"He said a lot. I didn't really listen."

She nodded. "No one does anymore. He's old, his reason is going." The young woman glanced at him with wide, honest eyes. "Can I trust you, Aculeus?"

"As much as I trust you, girl," he said truthfully.

"The people have lost faith in Brunn," she said with a sad shake of her head. "Loathe as I am to say it, but he and his entire line are corrupt. The merchants and the lenders are held hostage to his usury rates and forced to pay him bribes for the privilege. Oh, it is all very difficult for one such as yourself to understand, I am sure."

Aculeus grunted.

"My father is too weak to intervene and grandfather too old and addled, but something must be done, for the sake of Heavenskeep and the empire."

"That's no business of mine."

Netel stepped in front of him, stopping him with both hands on his chest.

"We can make it your business," she said. "I am a smart woman, but a woman nonetheless. I need the strong arm of a man to help clear the way for me through the thicket." She raised up on her toes and kissed him. "And then to sit beside me on the throne."

THAT evening, Aculeus was accosted on his way to supper by Thar. The boy had a wild look in his eyes even as he tried to maintain his outer calm.

"Who have you been talking to?" he whispered in a strained voice.

"I'm a hero. Everyone wants to talk to me."

"You know what I mean," Thar said angrily. "Our conversation. I know you've been talking to my uncle and my cousin. What did you tell them?"

Aculeus squinted his one good eye at the boy. "I said nothing."

"Then how do they know?" Thar said through clenched teeth, raising his fists in frustration. "How the Seven Hells do they know what I'm planning if you didn't tell them?"

"Maybe they saw you, as you saw them with me. Maybe the servants are spying for and on all of you. Or maybe you're not as smart as you think you are."

Thar was no longer listening. His eyes shifted back and forth and he chewed on his lip. "No matter," he said to himself. "No matter. Before they've sorted out what I've planned, we can have their heads." He looked at the mercenary with narrowed eyes. "I have a diversion planned that will draw the guards away from the living quarters and give you time to do what needs doing."

"Clever."

"Yes. I said you'd not be sorry if you backed me, and I meant it.

I've still arrangements to make, but keep yourself handy, Aculeus. Wait for my signal."

As the day progressed, Aculeus found himself at the heart of many fast-moving palace intrigues. Wherever he went, he would encounter a co-conspirator, come with whispered updates of their progressing plots, the urgency of their messages increasing with each passing hour.

From Taliss: "My brother is up to something. It must be done tonight or I fear the opportunity will be lost. Tonight, my father and brother must die."

From Thar: "I've had agents stirring up public sentiment against father for weeks. Tonight, they will foment a riot and direct a mob to storm the palace. This will draw the guards from the residence, clearing the way for you to kill him and Taliss. And whoever else fails to fall into step behind their new prince."

From Bhaliss: "You will strike in the dead of night, slaying my brother and his whelps in their sleep...but no harm must come to his wife. Otherwise, trust no one else, not even those of my direct bloodline, do you understand? I've evidence prepared proving the assassinations were ordered by a coterie of his ministers. As Brunn's chancellor I will naturally assume emergency powers and my first act will be to have the entire cabinet arrested for treason."

From Netel: "There is no time

to waste. The palace is buzzing with secrets and everyone looks frightened. It must be now, before one of my spineless kin stumbles across some courage. The first family of the House of Brunn must be wiped out. You can leave my grandfather to me. Once the bloodshed begins, he'll lose his stomach for killing his own flesh."

From Sister Kine: "The lambs have invited the lion into their yard. Why, they're offering you their necks on the block and are practically begging you to chop them off. Then frail little Netel will hand you the kingdom. *Our* kingdom, my prince."

IN the dark of night, Aculeus the Bastard sat and waited. He wore the garb and battered leather boots he had rode in with. His scabbard and sword hung at his side, and tucked into the folds of his sash were his rusty old knife and his father's dagger. His left hand and forearm were wrapped in leather and iron studs.

Aculeus waited and listened. He imagined he could hear the furtive scurrying of treacherous feet all around him in the darkened chamber, out in the courtyard and in the corridors. He knew it was all in his mind, his nerves filling the silence with imagined sounds.

Clouds drifted in to hide the scant light of the crescent moon, joining in the conspiracies.

And then, dimmed candle light,

wafting like a spirit past his doorway.

"Aculeus," the light whispered. "My master bids you now."

"Who is your master?"

"My *young* master," whispered the light as it drifted from his door. "It is his command."

Aculeus rose and strode out onto the terrace. Had the pup Thar actually done it? Outside, he heard it. From a distance, on the far side of the palace from where he stood, came the echoes of angry shouts and cries from the little princess' whipped up mob of malcontents.

The mercenary went back inside and crossed the room to the door. He paused, again to listen, and was rewarded this time with the receding slap of soldiers boots on marble as they raced to reinforce the guard on the other side of the palace. With a touch for luck to his scorpion tail topknot, he slipped from his bedchambers and into the night.

THE corridors of the royal quarters were empty, the guards having gone off to help bar the doors against the mob, leaving their charges unattended and vulnerable.

He found Bhaliss standing in his doorway, confused and trembling, a dagger gripped tight in both hands.

"What is it? What is happening, Aculeus? My plan..."

The mercenary said, "This wasn't part of your plan?"

"No, no, you fool, I told you! I

wanted them executed quietly in the night, with blame to be laid at the feet of his...." The redheaded man stopped and his eyes went wide. "You. You betrayed me to the others, didn't you?"

"We had no bargain to betray, Bhaliss."

"How can you say that? You agreed to hire your sword to my cause."

Aculeus shook his head.

"But you did. You heard me out and... and... dear Dakkis!" Bhaliss sagged against the wall, the dagger in his trembling hands. "What have I done?" he whispered.

"Nothing that the rest of your mad clan hasn't also done."

"Grandfather!"

Netel emerged from her rooms and was running towards them. "I told you to leave him to me, you oaf," she yelled.

"Granddaughter?" Bhaliss looked back and forth at them without comprehension. "You cannot mean you've thrown in with this...this barbarian trash."

She laughed. "Why? What were your plans for me if *you* had been the victor?"

"No harm was to come to you, my child," Bhaliss said, shocked at the suggestion.

Aculeus laughed. "Aye, your grandfatherly concern was evident when you told me to trust none of your line."

The girl turned on Bhaliss with a snarl. "You lying old toad," she said and her hand came out of the

folds of her nightclothes with a knife clutched in it and she lunged at her father's father.

The old man cried out in surprise and plunged the blade in his hands into her stomach. Her face formed a momentary elegant mask of surprise that quickly crumpled into shock and then pain as she collapsed against Bhaliss. He cried out again, this time in horror and jumped back to let her body fall to the floor, staring in disbelief at the bloodied dagger he still clutched. He tossed it aside and went to his knees, whispering "Netel, my little Netel," over and over again, until he was close enough for her to drive her knife into his heart with her last breath.

Aculeus continued on his way to Prince Brunn's chambers.

OTHERS were stirring now, peeking into the corridor or stepping out to investigate. Aculeus heard screams and shouting behind him; Bhaliss and Netel had been discovered. Shouts went out for guards. The noise woke others, but there were those who, like Aculeus, had not yet been to bed.

The mercenary drew his sword and quickened his pace. Grand schemes were collapsing all around him and the perpetrators of these plots or their allies might wish to take him to task for their failures.

Arriving at the entry to Brunn's rooms, he found the corridor dark and deserted. Hefting his sword, he parted the heavy drapes over the portal and stepped inside.

"Welcome, Aculeus," Brunn said. "You're just in time to bid my children a goodnight."

The master of the House of Brunn was seat in the center of the torch-lit room, a line of palace guards at attention behind him. Before him, kneeling with bowed heads and manacled wrists, were Taliss and Thar. The boy looked up at Aculeus, his eyes blazing with hatred.

"You treacherous bastard," he hissed.

Brunn rose and stood over his son. "You are not one to speak of treason, boy." The foppish manner and uncertainty Aculeus had seen in his prior dealings with Brunn were gone. This was the true prince. A man as weak as Brunn had first appeared would never have been able to hold on to his power for this long. He turned his steely eyes on Taliss and, for an instant, the fire in them dimmed.

He reached down and took her chin in hand and lifted her face to him. "You disappoint me, Taliss," he said softly. "Or perhaps I am to blame. You were always my favorite child and I could never be stern with you."

She made her lip quiver and brought a tear to eye. "Daddy," she whimpered.

He released her and straightened up, shaking his head with sadness. "Your false tears have lost their power over me, Taliss. I'm afraid

you must be punished, my dear." He cleared his throat. "Harshly."

"You see her now for what she is, father," Thar cried. "Can't you also see that I was trying to stop her, to save you."

"Ah, Thar. You are so much like your mother; I'm surprised that brother of mine didn't try to bed you as well."

"Father, please, I beg of you...a chance."

"You had your chance, Thar. You failed."

Brunn made a gesture and two of the guards stepped forward and pulled the imprisoned children to their feet by their chains.

"You all failed, but I suppose I should be thankful for this night of treachery. It's revealed my enemies me and given me the opportunity to purge my house of those whose future loyalty I have come to question."

Brunn snapped his fingers and another soldier stepped forward, this one hefting two well-stuffed saddlebags that he held out to Aculeus.

"Your reward, good sir, and my thanks. Take your pick. Gold or gemstones."

"Both will do, if you don't mind," Aculeus said.

"Not at all. As I told you when you first came to me, your information is priceless. Indeed, I'd gladly give you more..."

"You betrayed me...for trifles?" Taliss screamed in stunned disbelief. "I offered you a kingdom, and you settle for a handful of coins and stones?"

Aculeus slung a bag over each shoulder.

"Aye," he said. "Dreams of kingdom were yours, child, not mine." He shrugged to adjust the bags on his shoulders. "I don't need any more than I can carry."

"You're a fool," Thar sneered. "You'll gamble, drink, and whore it all away in no time and be left with nothing."

"I'll find more. I always do," Aculeus said. He patted the bag of gold. "Look how easy it is."

Aftermath

BY ROBERT GREENBERGER

ELDRITCH energy melted the armor of the first soldier to enter the throne room. His screams were loud and echoed off the stonework, accompanied by the crackling of his roasting flesh. Queen Phaulius, her hands glowing a sickly yellow, readied another burst of her dread magic as three more soldiers clambered over their dead comrade in arms. They were met sword for sword by her sworn guardians, each bearing the talon sigil that marked her reign.

As she unleashed a fresh burst of the chaos magic that had helped her maintain control of the land for generations, the three attackers stood fast. They had prepared for this, knowing they were going to die but willing to give their lives for the kingdom they loved. The heat was intense, causing Phaulius' men to drop back towards the throne. Try as they might, the dying attackers could not hold back the screams.

The queen watched, glee in her wild eyes, as they stood melting like candles.

So intent was she on the dying men that she did not notice the shape in the doorway, covered head to foot in highly polished armor. When she did, she readied yet another magical fireball, but a swift flick of the right arm had already sent a long, keen-edged knife flying towards her. At the last moment, she twisted and the knife buried itself in her bicep, not the breast that had been its target.

Her left-hand flicked magic at the new attacker, but the weakened bolt splashed across the mirror-like armor. Her guards spring forward to fight, giving her time to scurry to a hidden recess behind the throne and enter the labyrinth that no map had ever revealed.

The mirror soldier was joined by four more comrades and the fight was fierce but mercifully brief, since the stench of burning flesh and melted steel made all gag.

In short order, the guardians were dead. The Queen had vanished.

MORE soldiers' metallic footfalls echoed in the throne room, occasionally muffled as they shifted from stone to tread instead on thick rugs. There were a score of them scattered around the grand chamber, necks craning to take in the sights of charred paintings that had once depicted great battles. Interspersed between the paintings were iron statues of men in armor from different eras, some covered head to toe, others

Illustration by Jerry Ordway

in cruder armaments. Several of the visitors held their noses to the stench as they stepped over the corpses. Both thrones were toppled over, one arm keeping a fragment of fabric as a souvenir. Braziers flickered as they grew low and men called for more fuel but no one knew where supplies were kept. To a man, it was their first visit to the great hall of Bortas.

As several men righted the chairs, removing the scrap in an effort to tidy things, the general strode in. All that separated him from the soldiers was the purple sigil of rank on each shoulder—that and how others deferred to his approach. Pausing before the throne's raised dais, he looked at it, up at the torn roof, at the damage done, emblematic of what had befallen most buildings in the capital. When he removed his helmet, thick, curling black hair tumbled from release and shrouded his shoulders. He took a sharp breath and coughed. The air was still thick with wood smoke, the fires having been quelled a mere quarter-hour before. Wisps of smoke still filled the air, rising through the wounded roof to join the darkening clouds.

"Clear the room of our honored dead," the leader said. Gingerly, the first burned man was lifted, bits of flesh, blood, and armor falling to the thick rugs, ruining them.

"It stinks worse than the latrines," a man muttered.

"Whatever we missed, the rains will get," another man in heavily dented armor said to the general's right.

"Patching the roof will become a priority to preserve what's left here," a second man said from behind. Both men sounded weary, as they should. The final battle against the queen's troops had taken all day, ending well past twilight, and that after a week-long siege. The toll on both sides had been heavy but the rebels were victorious. No one was celebrating yet, though—all were too tired, too hungry, or too sore to revel. There were dead to count and bury, prisoners to sort and try, a populace to calm and order to restore.

So many tasks.

"The throne is yours," the first speaker said.

The general, a man of six and thirty who a year earlier had been a blacksmith, stared at the throne, not moving. The others milled about, uncertain what to do, studying paintings and other finery, whatever had survived a final battle which involved using burning coal in ways meant to destroy, not build. The familiar odor of burning coal was welcome to the general, making him long for his own shop and wonder if it had survived the battle. He was unlikely ever to return to it, now that he was expected to lead the state. That made him sad.

"Bas...that is, General Basson," the man began anew. "What do we do now?"

Before Basson could answer, there were footsteps followed by the sound of steel being withdrawn from a dozen scabbards. The general raised a hand to forestall his men, recognizing his sister as she burst into the room surrounded by four soldiers, one with a limp, all with blood-stained armor.

"Bas!" she cried and hurried forward. They embraced for a long while and finally, breaking the hold, she slowly turned in a circle, taking in the throne room. She gazed at the torn ceiling, clouds now mostly obscuring the moon and casting fleeting shadows on the floor.

"The children?"

She smiled up at him, a finger tugging at his unkempt beard. "They are fine and sheltered, Basson."

"We must get that patched," she said, a dainty finger gesturing at the ceiling.

Basson laughed, a throaty sound cut off by a cough from the lingering smoke. "So I have been told."

"We need a list," she continued, but he cut her off.

"Always with lists," he said, and laughed once more. "Just as Father taught you. Where shall we begin, then? Try the queen in absentia for her crimes against her people or fix the roof so we don't get wet?"

Anahita theatrically put her finger to her chin, considering the question.

"Seriously, Basson, what do we do?" his comrade in arms, Ganthis, asked.

"No one thought we'd win," Basson mused aloud. That caught the meandering soldiers' attention. His voice was loud enough to echo and they stood in place, ready to act should an order be given. "Hell, I didn't expect to be a general, let alone survive this rebellion."

"But the odds were in our favor," Ganthis said.

"No, the gods took pity on us or are mocking us, letting us win and leaving us a mess to clean up," the general said. "There is so much evil to undo, so much to rebuild. I can rebuild better from my shop than from that chair." He gestured at the throne, still refusing to take his place there.

"But we swore you our allegiance," said a man whose name he could not recall.

He gave a bitter laugh at that, shrugged his shoulders, and replied, "Only because the real general died a month ago. You decided I was good enough to follow. More fool you."

"Wulfe trusted you," Anahita pointed out. "He said you were good enough to shoe his horse and lead men at the same time. He put his faith in you and when he died, so did we."

That was true enough. He had had the misfortune of standing beside Wulfe, who had led the rebellion a year earlier, when a giant boulder, fired from a trebuchet, had banked off a tower and unexpectedly crushed him. That Basson survived was declared by some a miracle, a sign of his worthiness, while he ascribed it to pure chance. Either way, he had been in the general's private council and knew all the plans and the variations on the plans. He had helped craft them and then the men had wanted him to execute them. Basson, weary and ready for the rebellion to come to an end, had felt that he'd had little choice. The queen and her warped inner circle had to be removed before the entire state crumbled to corruption or conquest. Neither was an appetizing option, so he had accepted the rebels' faith and gotten them to this point.

General Wulfe had hoped for a clean beginning, a new era for the people, but he had never considered the aftermath.

Anahita turned to the men and ordered, "Secure the keep. Sentries everywhere. Send a runner to the amphitheater. All prisoners should be fed and bedded for the night. A squad should gather the surviving priests and doctors. They have work to do."

Ganthis and the others nodded, then turned to her older brother. He chuckled and said, "You always were the bossy one. As she said, Ganthis. And have food and drink brought in, along with the Grand Priest."

The anticipated rain arrived, causing the throne room to begin steaming as hot stones cooled and the stench of the dead was washed away. All Basson wanted to do was sleep but runners arrived by the dozen, it seemed, and all brought news or asked for instructions. After the first two hours, members of the keep's household staff, those who had not fled with the queen or died in battle, finally made themselves known, ready to serve whoever commanded them. Still, Basson could not come up with a proper list of tasks—there were just too many.

Anahita caught his eye and he nodded toward her. She rattled off a list of instructions almost too fast for the staff to follow. Her and her lists, he mused. The men followed him now because Wulfe had believed in his goodness and honesty, but he was no leader. His sister, though, there was someone to bow before.

GRAND Priest Prytor IV and a small retinue arrived after Basson had fallen asleep leaning against a wall. Anahita shook him awake and he spat out grit that had accumulated in his slack mouth as he rested. The earthly leader of the primal gods appeared completely unscathed by the battles even though his spire-topped church was within striking distance of the final battle. The moon was peeking between clouds and its pale light made the jewels at his throat dance. His robes were pristine, his pale blue eyes bright, and the set of his mouth firm.

"Your grace," Basson said.

"Blessings, General Basson. I take it you won."

"You know damned well we won," Basson snapped, not caring that he sounded angry. He believed in the primal gods, less so in their human vessels.

"You are to be our king now." It was a statement.

"Does that suit the church?"

"If it suits the gods, we will abide," the priest answered solemnly. "Am I here to crown you?"

Basson hadn't even considered all that pomp and circumstance. He shook his head.

"Very well. Why have I been summoned?"

"We need to rebuild, we need to mourn the dead, we need to… carry on."

"I agree," the priest said, dipping his chin once in affirmation.

"I would have your council," Basson admitted softly. "I don't know where to begin. Join us."

Without hesitation, as if he had been thinking of little else, the priest began talking. He rattled off one set of priorities after another at almost the same rate as Basson's sister. He chuckled, which only earned him a reproving look down the priest's long nose. The tasks all sounded reasonable, all sounded necessary, and there were just so many of them. The priest wanted funeral pyres to whisk the dead on their way and to cleanse the capitol. He spoke of masses,

charitable works, and overseeing the investiture.

"Have you a wife?" he asked suddenly, interrupting a train of thought about reconstruction.

"He's never had time," Anahita said, elbowing her brother.

"First, there's work to be done," he grumbled. He knew he'd be pressured to wed and quickly so an heir could be produced, one who would sit the throne after him. At six and thirty, he was behind. Briefly, he considered formally adopting Anahita's two children, his niece and nephew. They had been fatherless since Owan died, a victim of the queen's policies towards the poor. Anahita had thrown in with the rebellion before him and had pleaded on Wulfe's behalf. Basson had truly felt he had little choice but to join so the children could have a better future.

He asked the priest to have the myriad projects, the many, many projects, put into writing for consideration. He'd convene a working council in the morning, summon whichever nobles and lords were still alive and willing to help rebuild. Prytor nodded in approval, held out his hand, and an acolyte handed over three scrolls.

"The last we finished before this evening's prayers," the priest explained.

"You were prepared for this?"

"The church takes no sides but does keep its eyes open. We saw the outcome, yes, and began preparing for whoever succeeded the queen. Her time was clearly at an end and we are here to serve." With that, he nodded once more and turned to leave.

The church might not choose sides, but Basson was suddenly aware of its invisible hand behind the throne. Clutching the three scrolls, he instructed a new group of runners to begin finding the nobles and lords he needed. After that, he found a stray cloak and wrapped himself in it to sleep, leaning against a wall.

THE council chamber was nicely full, a dozen and a half nobles having turned up at Basson's request, as had the Grand Priest. Anahita sat beside her brother, constantly reviewing scrolls thrust in his direction. Everyone, it seemed, had been prepared for the rebellion's success. A show of order was necessary in the clear light of day, despite the remaining haze and drizzle that proved an inauspicious start to the new regime.

Basson was tired and hungry, even though he had eaten at dawn. He could smell bread baking below and couldn't wait for the fresh loaves to arrive. At least the queen hadn't taken all the flour! The nobles, of course, wanted an accounting of what *had* been looted and if any of their holdings had been taken. They were all vying for influence without being the least bit helpful. Most were talking down to him, presuming the blacksmith turned general was illiterate or an idiot. At least one, a corpulent man with thick lips, was already suggesting that some form of election among the landholders be used to select a new king.

"No noble backed the rebellion and the townsfolk know it," Prytor commented. "We seat one of you and the fighting begins fresh. No, it must be the man they backed, who they followed." He reached out and laid a reassuring hand on Basson's forearm. It was as good as a blessing and no noble objected further.

"We fought for the people, who backed us at great risk. Now we must repay them with food and water. The wells need cleansing and we will share the larder with the neediest," Basson began.

"Your apologies, general," Prytor said, snatching the hand back. He kept calling him by rank, not by name, more an act of some subtle disapproval than actual respect. "Prayers for the dead should commence no later than sundown. We must divert available manpower to preparing the bodies."

"They can't wrap corpses while fainting from thirst," Basson countered.

"Do we even have a map of the wells so we can begin looking?" a noble asked.

The digression took them to bureaucratic matters, slowly angering Basson, his soul beginning to burn like his coals. Every time he brought up feeding the poor or cleaning up their sectors of the capitol, the conversation was always steered away to other state matters. Yes, their defenses needed shoring up and, yes, emissaries needed to be sent to neighboring kingdoms, but surely there was time for that. Hunger did not wait.

They were well into their fourth hour of talk when finally a half-score of young boys and girls marched into the chamber, each bearing pitchers filled with wine and trays laden with still-warm bread. The children served with practiced ease and were gone in a blink. Basson wanted to tear into the food, but of course, Prytor needed to bless it.

With care, he began handing out the wine, first to Basson, then to each noble. He gestured in the direction of the four winds, the stars, and the earth, praying in an echoing, stentorian voice. He added extra blessings for those who died for just causes, for those who died defending a wicked monarch, and for those now tasked with rebuilding the state. A final wave of his hands, and the prayers ended.

Basson ate with vigor, letting the nobles and Prytor slurp the red wine and speak with bursting jowls. He listened, his mood blackening, while Anahita continued to pore through the scrolls, beginning to make notes of things he couldn't see from his angle.

His bottom ached and he desperately wished for a bath. Prytor had earlier scoffed at the length of his hair and the fullness of his beard, as if the rebels had carried a working barber with them. Or as if there had been time for such things. Next time there was a rebellion, he'd bring the priesthood along to get a taste of what it meant to *fight* for a belief, not just *pray* for it. There'd be time enough for grooming, even if the nobles stuck with their plan to crown him within a fortnight.

He once more tried to steer the conversation back to the practical matters of the people, the ones who had needed the rebellion far more than the nobles had. Suddenly voices were raised, accusations hurled, and the spirit of togetherness that had greeted the hazy day faded like the mist. It was clear to Basson that the nobles were fine with the status quo and he could change whatever he wanted—after their riches and businesses were first secured. He was being patronized and he began to seethe.

Anahita saw it and interrupted a lengthy lecture about property values. "Excuse me, Lord Longstaff, but did you support the rebellion?"

"What business is it of yours? The rebellion won, the fighting is over," the far older man snarled.

"I was just wondering, because you act as if everything was fine in the state."

"Wasn't it?"

"I'm surprised you ask that, considering how many people took up arms against the queen. Clearly, there were grievances…"

"There are always grievances. I have many right now."

"…that were being ignored but needed to be addressed. Don't you think we're repeating that history right now?"

Basson chuckled at that, as it caused several to stop murmuring amongst themselves and pay attention to the exchange. Even so, he began to feel poorly, the hours and quarreling taking its toll on him.

"Are we, girl?"

"Girl!" Basson roared. "She may be my younger sister but she is a mother and a widow, not a girl. Anahita has endured much for freedom. What have you sacrificed? I daresay, not much."

He was ready to say more but slumped back in his chair, feeling beads of perspiration emerge across his forehead. He also felt ready to give back the bread and wine but clenched his teeth against anything so unseemly. Basson needed to act the part of leader, whether he was ready or not. Stealthily, his fingers crept to his ribs, probing to see if there was heat. He feared infection from a wound he had left poorly treated. The fabric was cool enough, although he was now sweating freely. His vision blurred and he blinked repeatedly, something a

noble mistook as a signal and tried to gesture back. Instead, the man grew blurry and the world faded from sight.

A NAHITA sat beside her brother's corpse, ignoring the squabbling she heard from the next chamber. They were alone and tears glistened on her prominent cheekbones but her mind drifted from her brother to her children. If he had died from a disease, then everyone he'd encountered of late would be at risk. She'd read Runciter's histories and there was always some plague that trailed after a campaign. Each was different yet all claimed countless lives, indiscriminate about which side of the fight the once-living had been on. Physicians had been summoned, the keep's doors blocked to all others to contain the potential scourge.

She'd placed so much hope in her brother, knowing how noble he was despite their lowly background. He had been the kind of leader the people had hungered for: one of them, not someone born to lands and riches. Opposing the queen and court had been a risk and one he'd deemed worth taking, and his words had carried, swaying others to the cause.

Prytor and the nobles were rumbling about who would take the throne. Already, talk of food and water for the masses was a fading echo within the keep, igniting her own ire.

The doctor had come but could do nothing for the dead. She sat, the numbness quickly shifting to anger.

Then Basson's leg twitched.

Anahita gave out a surprised yelp.

The dead body of her brother, the chest not registering a breath, began to move of its own accord, rising from the bed.

Trembling from fear, she still followed the shambling shape into the throne room. Upon seeing the dead general, the lords and Prytor stopped arguing. Most gaped at the corpse among them, while one or two—including Prytor—smiled.

"Well done," Lord Ramin murmured.

"Our studies have always involved understanding the ways of the dark, including necromancy. Going from comprehension to execution, well, it just takes practice," Prytor said, rising and walking toward Basson's body. He rested a hand on the still chest and added, "And I have had plenty of time to practice."

"You knew of this," Lord Longstaff of the fisheries declared. "This is an abomination!"

"No, my friend, it is actually an elegant solution to who could possibly follow Queen Phaulius and lead our country," Ramin replied.

"We had planned this for Wulfe, who we presumed would prevail. When he fell and everyone transferred their allegiance to our blacksmith here, well, it wasn't difficult to obtain some of his hair and mix a fresh potion. He died but now lives at our command. King Basson will rule from this throne, but we, his loyal council, will speak for him. He will appear now and then from a distance, wave when told to, and never once question us,' Prytor explained.

There was a creak and all heads swiveled to the doorway where Basson's sister stood.

"My dear Anahita," Prytor said, taking her hand. His own skin was soft, lotioned with a flowery scent, the fingernails perfectly kept. Her eyes studied the ring of office on his left index finger, the four elements represented with different jewels. Such a little bauble denoting such influence.

"Your grace," she automatically replied, meeting his gaze. His eyes were hard and unforgiving. "Obviously, this is a state secret and one you cannot be allowed to share." With a gesture, two of the lords gripped her arms. Prytor withdrew a stiletto from the folds of his robes and, with a few flicks, sliced the fastenings from her outfit. While she did not resist, her eyes burned, briefly flashing as if molten gold, something the priest missed as he ripped the garments from her, leaving her standing only in sandals.

"We may have use for her, take her to a cell and let us think on it," Prytor instructed. The two lords began to move her and as she passed by her brother, she tugged and forced them to pause. She rose on her toes, kissed the cold cheek, and, unbothered by her nakedness, walked from the throne room.

THE cell they placed her in had been swept out and restocked with fresh straw on the floor, a clean chamber pot, and a small pillow. There was nothing to cover her with so the lords left her, locking the door behind them.

Once their footfalls faded from hearing, she pursed her lips, and her long fingers reached up and withdrew some of her brother's hair. His stink still on her lips, she licked them, sat cross-legged on the floor, and got to work.

While Basson had been taught to work a fire and become an excellent blacksmith, she had been taken by the women of the family and taught secrets, the kind never spoken aloud, never written in a book. The lessons had been passed on from generation to generation, preparing the women for a day when they were needed. Fire and smoke seemed to run in Basson's blood, but her veins coursed with iron and magic.

Closing her eyes, she began to murmur a chant with a rising rhythm, one that matched her quickening pulse. At the appropriate moment, her well-maintained fingernails tore into her skin, bringing forth rivulets of blood. Running down her forearms, they pooled in her palms and were then carefully used to form a circle around the captured hair. As the blood made contact, green smoke rose from the floor. It caught an air current and flowed through the door's iron bars. The iron melted, dripping and scarring the thick wooden door.

Anahita did not notice. She was now swaying with the chant, sweat rising from her exposed skin despite the cooling night air. The woman was putting into practice that which she had studied her entire life, unsure if the lessons were not merely fairy tales.

As the moon peaked over the horizon, her eyes opened. The chant stopped and she calmly rose. With a gentle push, the locked door swung open.

Still naked, she walked back to the throne room, where the lords and Grand Priest Prytor were still making their plans. Plates of meat and cheese had been reduced to crumbs while the men drank from flagons. Her dead brother stood to the side, still frozen in the same pose.

As she entered, the conversation stopped. Eyes bulged or raked over her body, while Prytor audibly gasped.

"Promised someone your quim to gain freedom? It won't last," Longstaff snarled.

Prytor waved a hand in Basson's direction, then watched expectantly. The corpse began to move, but rather than attack its sister, it moved for the priest. The corpse's arms reached out and pinned the man in his seat.

"You seem confused," Anahita said. "Allow me to explain. You used necromancy to kill my brother then reanimate his corpse to make him your puppet. But you and that bitch queen aren't the only ones to know magic. I have control of my brother now. We are still connected by blood, giving me an advantage."

She met the priest's eyes, which showed her his anger and, behind that, a flicker of fear. It was something to be stoked.

"Let me show you what else I can do." With that, she resumed her chant, this time loud and clear, in a language no one else in the room knew.

The iron statues that ringed the throne room, still splatted in gore from the queen's final stand, groaned. Stone crumbled as they moved. The priest tried to say something, perhaps a counter spell, but she leaned in and kissed him, covering his lips with hers, her dead brother's stink still lingering.

As she held him in place, the iron statues did as they were bidden and surrounded the panicked lords, none of whom had dared move earlier and now were all no doubt regretting their inaction.

"Now," Anahita ordered as her lips left the priest's.

As one, the iron statues raised their arms and brought them swiftly down on the lords' heads. The sound of screams and cracking bone were sickening and they were joined soon after by the priest's own cries. The ring on his finger had grown hot enough to burn, then began to melt, searing into his skin.

He tried to rise, but Basson held him in place, a silent sentinel to the carnage his sister had wrought. Smoke rose from the mangled hand and Prytor screamed long after the lords had fallen silent.

She carefully wiped a finger through the pool of blood the priest had so kindly provided. Approaching her brother, she used the blood as paint, making symbols on his cheeks and wrists.

"Wh-what are you doing?" Prytor finally managed to croak.

"Ah, so there are some things you never learned," Anahita responded. "You took his life and turned him into a life-sized doll. Did you know there's a theory that this can be reversed if done quickly? No one I know has ever tried it, so this should be interesting."

Prytor, still in pain, sat and gaped. As he did so, warmth and color could be seen on Basson's face.

"It has to be started quickly but it takes time. It will need several coats, like a good paint, but with blood, of course. Specifically, the blood of his killer. After all, the universe is about balance. If I am to reclaim my brother from Death, he will expect a replacement."

She stopped gazing at her brother and crouched low near Prytor's now-pale face.

"Basson will live and rule. It just won't be tomorrow. You I need alive for a while, but I can't have you wandering free. Thankfully, this keep has many cells, many dungeons. I just have to find the deepest, darkest one, where no one will hear your screams. After all, draining you drop by drop will take time. And it will hurt."

"You can't..." he began, but Basson's hand, still rough from years at the forge, clapped him on the shoulder.

"I can. Once I put some clothes on, I will issue decrees in my brother's name and help him rule until he's better."

"Better..." Prytor repeated, his voice small.

"Iron and blood are very potent together, a new lesson for you to ponder as you are drained," she said. Then, with a thought, she asked her brother to kindly carry Prytor down to the dungeons. She'd follow soon enough. The iron soldiers fell into place ahead and behind the priest, giving him no chance to run.

Anahita lingered in the throne room, studying the carnage she had wrought. Outside, the morning sun was just beginning to show its face, and the first tendrils of its light added a touch of warmth to her bare flesh. She chose to take that as a sign, perhaps even a blessing.

Things would get better. She would see to that.

About Our Contributors

DEREK TYLER ATTICO is an author, photographer and former cable-TV production editor.

He is a two-time winner of the *Star Trek Strange New Worlds* anthology, and his essays have appeared in *Star Trek* magazine.

An avid reader, Derek enjoys exploring the possibilities of humanity's future while studying its past.

Derek lives in New York City where he has escaped the captivity of the corporate world and is now loose on the plains of imagination with his weapons of choice—a pen and a camera.

SINCE their days spent living together in an arts colony, Toledo natives JIM AND BECKY BEARD have collaborated on a variety of projects including writing for a local newspaper. In 2010, Becky contributed to *Gotham City 14 Miles*, a collection of essays about the 1960s *Batman* television series edited by Jim. Becky was associate editor on Jim's 2012 novel *Captain Action Riddle of the Glowing Men*, the first prose adventure of the classic toy. 2015 saw the publication of *Something Strange Is Going On!*, new tales set in the universe of comic book creator Fletcher Hanks, featuring Fantomah and Big Red McLane yarns spun by Jim and Becky respectively. In 2019, their text piece appeared in *Love Romances*, a one-shot celebrating eighty years of Marvel Comics. Jim has also directed a *Batman* reader's theatre production in which Becky voiced all the female characters. "Like" A Jim & Becky Team-Up on Facebook.

RUSS COLCHAMIRO is the author of the rollicking space adventure *Crossline*, the zany scifi backpacking comedy series *Finders Keepers*, *Genius de Milo*, and *Astropalooza*, and was editor of the scifi mystery anthology *Love, Murder & Mayhem*, all with Crazy 8 Press. He has contributed to several other anthologies including *Tales of the Crimson Keep*, *Pangaea*, *They Keep Killing Glenn*, *Altered States of the Union*, *Brave New Girls*, *Camelot 13*, and *TV Gods 2*. Russ is finalizing a noir anthology releasing October 2019 and is writing the first in an ongoing SFF mystery series featuring hard-boiled private eye Angela Hardwicke. Russ lives in New Jersey with his wife, twin ninjas, and crazy dog, Simon. For more on Russ' works, visit www.russcolchamiro.com, and follow him on Facebook, Twitter and Instagram @AuthorDudeRuss.

MIKE COLLINS has been working in comics, books and TV for over 25 years, producing graphics for publishers including Marvel, DC and Warners Comics in the USA, Rebellion, Panini and Eaglemoss in the UK. For TV, he contributed art to the *I'm In A Rock'n'Roll Band* and *Boy Band* series, also Planet Dinosaur; for *Doctor Who Confidential* and *Totally Doctor Who*. He has also been involved in set design for S4C. He is a storyboard artist for animation, including *Horrid Henry, Hana's Helpline, Cym Teg* and *Igam Ogam*, and produced illustrations for *The Daily Telegraph, Western Mail* and *The Daily Star*. He wrote and illustrated *Matthew Daemon* for *Weekly World News*. He has also worked extensively for Future Publications on a variety of titles, principally *SFX Magazine*. In advertising, Mike has worked on campaigns for Colmans and Coca-Cola. He has worked extensively in using comics as a way of promoting learning, in workshops and in publications, for various initiatives and educational plans, most prominently with Read A Million Words in Wales.

PAIGE DANIELS, aka Tina Closser, grew up in Northern Kentucky. After graduating Northern Kentucky University with a Bachelors of Science in Physics, she chose to get an Electrical Engineering degree at the University of Kentucky in Lexington. Armed with two science degrees, she went to work for the Navy in Indiana. She is currently a Science Technology Engineering and Math Coordinator, acting as a liaison to schools and getting kids excited about careers in science and technology.

Her first novel, *Non-Compliance: The Sector*, was published in 2012 by Kristell Ink. *Non-Compliance: The Transition* was published in 2013, and *Non Compliance: Equilibrium* in 2014.

She is also very active in her local chapter of Society of Women Engineers, doing outreach to inspire girls to consider a career in engineering. Part of her book proceeds go to fund a partial scholarship for a young woman to go to engineering school.

In her spare time she coaches a robotics team and attends various robotics competitions. She also fiddles with her viola and likes to pretend she knows how to be a farmer on her small hobby farm with her husband and two kids.

Cyberstalk her at:

http://www.goodreads.com/PaigeDaniels

www.facebook/paigedanielsauthor.com

www.twitter.com/TClosser

KATHLEEN O'SHEA DAVID is the author of the short story "On a Pedestal" in the Big Finish anthology *Doctor Who: Quality of Leadership*. With her husband Peter David, she adapted the first four issues of the Japanese Manga *Negima*, the *Ghostbusters* comic entitled What the Samhain just happened? and *Head Cases*. She has done numerous non-fiction essays for various publications. She was an assistant editor at Del Rey Books and worked on *Star Wars: New Jedi Order* along with the *Star Wars* non-fiction and work with many authors on original fiction. She was most recently an associate editor for *Time and Space* magazine.

PETER DAVID is a *New York Times* bestselling author with works ranging from science fiction to fantasy. His media tie-in works include his corner of the *Star Trek* universe, New Frontier, along with novelizations of *Hulk, Spider-Man,* and *The Rocketeer.* His original works include *Artful,* from Amazon, the now-back-in-print Sir Apropos trilogy (plus the new *Gypsies, Vamps & Thieves), The Camelot Papers,* and the *Hidden Earth* trilogy from Crazy 8 Press. He's also written for animated and live-action television as well as film. Follow Peter at www.peterdavid.net, @PeterDavid_PAD, and Facebook.

KEITH R.A. DeCANDIDO has written a ridiculous amount of fiction for the past twenty-five years. He's written extensively in media tie-in fiction, creating stories in more than thirty different licensed universes from *Alien* to *Zorro,* and receiving a Lifetime Achievement Award from the International Association of Media Tie-in Writers in 2009. In addition, he writes stories in places of his own creation, Cliff's End and Super City, as well as New York City and Key West. Recent and upcoming work includes the *Alien* novel *Isolation,* based on the hit videogame; *Mermaid Precinct,* the fifth novel in his acclaimed fantasy/police procedural series; *A Furnace Sealed,* the first book in a new urban fantasy series; fiction based on the game *Summoners War;* four new *Super City Cops* novellas; and stories in the prior Crazy 8 anthologies *Altered States of the Union* and *They Keep Killing Glenn,* as well as both *Baker Street Irregulars* anthologies, *Unearthed,* the latest *Brave New Girls* anthology, and *Release the Virgins!* Keith also writes about pop culture for Tor.com and on his own Patreon, is a third-degree black belt in karate (he both trains and teaches), is a musician (currently percussionist for the parody band Boogie Knights), and a professional editor of three decades' standing (working with both personal and corporate clients). Find out more at DeCandido.net.

BEFORE he created the seminal superhero Doc Savage in 1932, Missouri writer LESTER DENT (1904-1959) mastered most of the pulp-fiction genres popular at the dawn of the Great Depression. Breaking into the field with a string of aviation-centered adventure stories, Dent quickly branched out into other sub-genres, penning Westerns inspired by his upbringing in Wyoming and Oklahoma, acclaimed hardboiled detective mysteries, and briefly, several so-called "air-war" tales set during World War I. "Hate Hop" belongs to what its practitioners dubbed "yammering-gun" pulp yarns because they invariably centered around bloody aerial dogfights of the War to End All Wars.

MARY FAN is a YA and SFF author based in Jersey City. Her books include the Jane Colt space opera trilogy, comprising *Artificial Absolutes* (2013), *Synthetic Illusions* (2014), and *Virtual Shadows* (2015), and *Starswept* (2017), a YA sci-fi novel. Her latest book, *Flynn Nightsider and the Edge of Evil*, is a YA dark fantasy from Crazy 8 Press. In addition, she is the co-editor of the *Brave New Girls* YA sci-fi anthologies about girls in STEM, which aim to encourage more girls to explore STEM fields and raise money for the Society of Women Engineers scholarship fund.

MICHAEL JAN FRIEDMAN is the author of 78 books of fiction and non-fiction, nearly half of them set in the *Star Trek* universe. Eleven of his books, including the autobiography *Hollywood Hulk Hogan* and *Ghost Hunting* (written with SyFy's *Ghost Hunters*), have been *New York Times* bestsellers, and his novel adaptation of the *Batman & Robin* movie was the #1 bestselling book in Poland (really). Among his comic book credits is the *Darkstars* series from DC Comics, on which he collaborated with Mike Collins, and the *Outlaws* limited series, created with artist Luke McDonnell. He also co-wrote the story for the acclaimed second-season *Star Trek: Voyager* TV episode "Resistance," which guest-starred Joel Grey. In 2011, Friedman spearheaded the establishment of Crazy 8 Press, an imprint through which authors publish their purest and most passionate visions.

ROBERT GREENBERGER is a writer/editor/teacher with an extensive array of credits ranging from media tie-in fiction to adult non-fiction. He has worked for Starlog Press, DC Comics, Gist Communications, Marvel Comics, and *Weekly World News*. He was instrumental in relaunching Famous Monsters of Filmland as a brand and briefly served as News Editor at ComicMix.com. He is the co-creator of the *Latchkeys* and *ReDeus* series, and one of the founders of Crazy

8 Press. His novelization of *Hellboy II: The Golden Army* won the 2009 Scribe Award. He continues to work as a comic book historian when not writing original fiction. His more recent works include Chartwell Books' *100 Greatest Moments* series, celebrating milestones in DC Comics' history. Additionally, he is a high school English teacher in Maryland, where he resides with his wife, Deb. To learn more about Bob, visit his website at bobgreenberger. com and follow him on Twitter @ bobgreenberger and Goodreads.

G LENN HAUMAN, alternately known as "Da Big Guy", "G to the H", and "Party Of The First Part", made the mistake of asking his friends during a Cards Against Humanity game, "What's missing from my biographical blurb?" The responses included "Spectacular abs", "A low standard of living", "The secret formula for ultimate female satisfaction", "Pretty Pretty Princess Dress-Up Board Game", and "Some god-damn peace and quiet". You can find out more at http://www.glennhauman.com, @glennhauman, or at his day job at ComicMix.com.

R OBERT JESCHONEK is an Amazon-bestselling author whose action-packed, envelope-pushing fiction has made waves around the world. His stories have appeared in *Pulphouse*, *Fiction River*, *Galaxy's Edge*, *Tales from the Canyons of the Damned*, and many other publications. He has also written official *Doctor Who* and *Star Trek* fiction and Batman and Justice Society comics for DC Comics. Robert has won an International Book Award, a Scribe Award for Best Original Novel, and the grand prize in Pocket Books' Strange New Worlds contest. Hugo and Nebula Award-winning author Mike Resnick calls him "a towering talent." Visit Robert online at www.robertjeschonek.com. You can also find him on Facebook and follow him as @TheFictioneer on Twitter.

K ARL KESEL loves his job far more than he has any right to. He has written, inked, and occasionally penciled: *Superman*, *Superboy*, *Harley Quinn*, *Spider-Man*, *Suicide Squad*, *Fantastic Four*, *Captain America* and many others—although he has an inexplicable fondness for obscure characters no one else remembers. His current obsessions are his creator-owned comics with Tom Grummett—the Jack-Kirby-does-the-*X-Files*-esque *Section Zero* on Kickstarter now at sectionzero1959.com—and David Hahn—the grin-and-gritty *Impossible Jones* (coming soon)! He lives in Portland, Oregon with his wonderful wife Myrna, their joyful son Isaac, and cute-as-a-bug daughter Eliza. He really can't complain about much.

PETER KRAUSE is a graduate of the University of Minnesota, with a B.A. in both journalism and studio arts. For ten years, he was a full-time artist for DC Comics, New York. Peter drew Captain Marvel, Superman and other DC super-heroes. He was the artist for the series *Star Trek: The Next Generation*, *Metropolis: Special Crimes Unit*, and *The Power of Shazam!* Peter was also a guest artist on the series *Adventure of Superman, Superboy, Birds of Prey* and "*Secret Files*.

Since the mid-1990s, Peter has worked with a number of advertising agencies and production houses in North America. His work includes storyboards, print concepts, ad layouts, billboard designs, interior retail concepts and depictions of promotional events. The drawings are done with markers and Photoshop.

Peter lives in Minneapolis, Minnesota with his wife Lisa. They have three sons—Timothy, David and Nicholas.

PAUL KUPPERBERG is the author of *The Same Old Story* and *In My Shorts: Hitler's Bellhop and Other Stories* (both published by Crazy 8 Press), as well as the writer of, or a contributor to, dozens of other books of fiction and nonfiction for readers of all ages. He's is a forty-plus year veteran comic book writer who has scripted hundreds of characters from Archie to Zatanna in more than one thousand comic book stories. He has also been an editor for DC Comics, *Weekly World News*, and *WWE Kids Magazine*, and is currently publishing through Crazy 8 Press and Charlton Neo Comics (morttodd.com/ Charlton), publishers of *Paul Kupperberg's Guide to Writing Comic Books*. You can follow him on Facebook, Twitter, and Instagram, and at PaulKupperberg.com.

KARISSA LAUREL is a science fiction and fantasy author living in central North Carolina with her son, her husband, the occasional in-law, and a very hairy husky named Bonnie. Her favorite things are coffee, super heroes, and *Star Wars*. She can quote *Princess Bride* verbatim. Karissa's latest project is *Touch of Smoke*, a paranormal romance novel coming soon from Red Adept Publishing. She's also the author of *The Norse Chronicles*, an urban fantasy series, and *The Stormbourne Chronicles*, a young adult, epic steampunk fantasy series. Her short stories have appeared in various anthologies including *Wicked South: Secrets and Lies* (Blue Crow Publishing, 2018), *Magic at Midnight* (Snowy Wings Publishing, 2018), *Love Murder and Mayhem* (Crazy 8 Press, 2018), and *Brave New Girls; Stories of Girls who Science and Scheme* (Brave New Girls, 2017). Her short fiction has also appeared at *Daily Science Fiction, Luna Station Quarterly*, and *Cast of Wonders*.

AMY LEWANSKI lives in San Diego, California with her husband, and originally hails from Calgary, Canada. She received her Masters of Fine Arts in Creative Writing from Antioch University Los Angeles in 2016. Amy writes sci-fi fiction for adults and teens, and dabbles in lifestyle reporting when she isn't working on her novel. She has been published in *47-16: Collected Short Fiction and Poetry Inspired by David Bowie, They Keep Killing Glenn,* and the websites Prime+Set and DoSD Events. Find Amy on Twitter at @bibliovoracious.

DAVID MACK is the award-winning and *New York Times* bestselling author of 30+ novels and numerous short works of science-fiction, fantasy, and adventure, including the *Star Trek Destiny* and *Cold Equations* trilogies. Beyond prose, Mack's writing credits include television (for produced episodes of *Star Trek: Deep Space Nine*) and comic books. Mack's most recent novels are *The Midnight Front* and *The Iron Codex*, the first two books of his Dark Arts series from Tor Books. His upcoming works include the Dark Arts series finale *The Shadow Commission*, a 1960s-era urban fantasy conspiracy thriller, and the *Star Trek: The Next Generation* novel *Collateral Damage*. Mack resides in New York City with his wife, Kara. Find him at davidmack.pro or @DavidAlanMack.

TOM MANDRAKE has created and illustrated comic books and graphic novels for all the major publishers. Titles he has worked on include *Batman, Martian Manhunter, Firestorm, Shazam,* and his acclaimed five-year run on *The Spectre* (DC Comics); *The New Mutants, The Punisher, Weapon X, Wolverine,* and *The Hulk Unchained* (Marvel Comics); *Grimjack* (First Comics); *The X-Files* (IDW); *Sidekick* (Joe Comics); *Captain Kronos: Vampire Hunter* (Titan Comics); and many more. Tom's creator owned projects include *To Hell you Ride* with Lance Henriksen and Joe Maddrey (Dark Horse Comics), *Creeps* with Dan Mishkin (Image Comics), and *Kros: Hallowed Ground* with John Ostrander. Tom is the co-developer of the Horror Comics correspondence course for the Joe Kubert School of Cartoon and Graphic Art.

WILL MURRAY is the author of over 70 novels, including 20 posthumous Doc Savage collaborations with Lester Dent, and 40 books in the long-running Destroyer series. Other Murray novels star the Executioner, Pat Savage and the Mars Attacks characters. His year 2000 book, *Nick Fury, Agent of S.H.I.E.L.D.: Empyre,* reads like a blueprint for the 9/11 terrorist attacks.

Murray has penned several milestone crossover novels. He pitted Doc Savage against King Kong in *Skull Island,* and followed up with

King Kong Vs. Tarzan. His 2015 Doc Savage novel, *The Sinister Shadow,* revived the famous radio and pulp mystery man, and *Empire of Doom* reunited them. His first Spider novel, *The Doom Legion,* stars that classic crime buster, as well as James Christopher, AKA Operator 5, and the renowned G-8. His next novel, *Tarzan, Conqueror of Mars* (Altus Press), costars John Carter.

For anthologies, Murray has written such iconic characters as Superman, Batman, Wonder Woman, Spider-Man, Ant-Man, The Hulk, The Avenger, The Green Hornet, Honey West, Sherlock Holmes, Cthulhu, Dr. Herbert West, The Secret 6, and Lee Falk's immortal Ghost Who Walks, The Phantom. For Marvel Comics, he created the Unbeatable Squirrel Girl. Find him at adventuresinbronze.com.

JERRY ORDWAY studied at the Milwaukee Technical High School and worked as a water color painter in the mid-1970s. Around this time, he also began to contribute to comics fanzines. His first break in comics was in 1980 when he inked a Carmine Infantino-penciled story for *Mystery in Space.* Since then, Ordway has worked on a variety of titles, mostly published by DC including *Justice League of America, All-Star Squadron,* Infinity, Inc., and *The Power of Shazam!',* for which he also did script work. He also inked the majority of *Crisis on Infinite Earths.* He was a writer/artist

on *Adventures of Superman* and has done cover illustrations for Dark Horse and Charlton, and did minor assignments for other publishers, including Eclipse Enterprises, First Publishing and Image Comics.

ALEX RONALD is a British comics artist. He has illustrated *Rot & Ruin* (published by IDW), *Lady Death* (published by Coffin Comics) *Patriotika* (published by Mount Olympus Comics) and *2000 AD* as well as creating covers for Titan Comics' *Doctor Who* line. Ronald's sequential work for *2000 AD* includes Judge Dredd and Missionary Man. More recently, he has been providing painted covers for strips *Ulysses Sweet, Black Shuck,* and *Devlin Waugh,* all for 2000 AD. His own comic strip, *Vampire Vixens of the Wehrmacht* appeared in *Heavy Metal* in 2014.

AARON ROSENBERG is the author of the best-selling DuckBob SF comedy series, the *Dread Remora* space-opera series, the Relicant epic fantasy series, and (with David Niall Wilson) the O.C.L.T. occult thriller series. Aaron's tie-in work contains novels for *Star Trek, Warhammer, World of WarCraft, Shadowrun, Eureka, Mutants & Masterminds,* and more. He has written children's books (including the original series STEM Squad and Pete and Penny's Pizza Puzzles, the award-winning *Bandslam: The Junior Novel,* and the #1 best-selling *42: The Jackie Robinson Story*), educational books, and over seventy roleplaying games (such as the original games *Asylum*, *Spookshow*, and *Chosen*, work for White Wolf, Wizards of the Coast, Fantasy Flight, Pinnacle, and others, the Origins Award-winning *Gamemastering Secrets*, and the Gold ENnie-winning *Lure of the Lich Lord*). He is the co-creator of the *ReDeus* series, and a founding member of Crazy 8 Press. Aaron lives in New York with his family. You can follow him online at gryphonrose.com, on Facebook at facebook.com/gryphonrose, and on Twitter @gryphonrose.

J ENIFER ROSENBERG wrote her first story, a children's book, for her third grade Gifted and Talented teacher. She's been hooked on writing ever since. Jenifer wrote and illustrated the book *Alligator's Friends*, which is about a socially awkward reptile trying to make new pals in the animal world. Her short story credits include "The Power of Five" from the 2018 Brave New Girls anthology *Tales of Heroines Who Hack*, "Waking Things" from the Crazy 8 Press anthology *They Keep Killing Glenn*, "Night Path" from the upcoming anthology *The Nature of Cities*, and "Evening Sonnet" from an upcoming release by Nisaba Press. Jenifer has also written for online publications and for the tabletop RPG industry. When she isn't writing, Jenifer keeps busy

with excessive volunteering, organizing charitable events, teaching paint classes, getting involved with Pride events, and learning new languages. She also makes wine with her friends and loves to cook. Jenifer lives in New York City with her family. She is thrilled to be a part of this project, and plans to write more paranormal fiction in the future.

M ARK WHEATLEY, Overstreet Hall of Fame inductee, has been awarded the Eisner, Inkpot, Mucker, Gem, Speakeasy and nominations for the Harvey and the Ignatz. His work has appeared in *Spectrum*, the Library of Congress, The Norman Rockwell Museum, and other museums. He has designed for Lady Gaga, The Black Eyed Peas, ABC's *Beauty and the Beast*, and Square Roots, as well as *Super Clyde*, *The Millers*, and *2 Broke Girls* on CBS. His most recent print projects include *Doctor Cthulittle*, *Tarzan and the Dark Heart of Time*, *Swords Against the Moon Men*, *The Philip Jose Farmer Centennial Collection*, *Mine!* and *Wild Stars*. Past creations include *Breathtaker*, *Return of The Human*, *Ez Street*, *Lone Justice*, *Mars*, *Black Hood*, *Prince Nightmare*, *Hammer of The Gods*, *Blood of The Innocent*, *Frankenstein Mobster*, and *Skultar* as well as *Tarzan*, *Baron Munchausen*, *Jonny Quest*, *Dr. Strange*, *The Flash*, *Captain Action*, *Argus*, *The Spider*, *Stargate Atlantis*, *Torchwood* and *Doctor Who*.

Thanks to our Patrons

WHILE we had 400 backers for our Kickstarter campaign, we offered in-print acknowledgement to our Patrons who are listed below. Some are friends, none are blood relations, but all have Crazy 8 Press' undying gratitude for your support.

Michael A. Burstein
Ray Riethmeier
Tina Good
Anthony Rais
James Cherry-McDonough
Paul Milligan
Guest 893718708
Guest 10805067
Andy Pavlik
Dale Russell
Conor Carton
Dean Wesley Smith
John Nacinovich
Bill Thom
John Lancaster
Jeff Sigmund
Denzil Martinez
Don Walsh
Cato Vandrare
Zack Kruse
Guest 103133379
connerbooks@gmail.com
Heather Disco
Michael Bowker

Eric Greenberger
Gene Moyers
Tim Tucker
Judith Waidlich
Jeremy Gunter
Martin Stever
David Dierks
Matthew Rex
David A. Lloyd
Originalname5
Paul Renn
David Brun
John Koperwhats
Bill
Joe Rixman
Barbara Strell
CapnDon
Jim Bertrand
John Michael Huang
cubaed
Fidel Jiron Jr.
Julia Scott
Phil Menard
Terry Emery

Tales From The MAGICIAN'S SKULL

NO. 1

ALL-NEW SWORDS & SORCERY FICTION

STORIES BY ENGE, WILLRICH, HOCKING, & OTHERS

GOODMAN PUBLICATIONS

ALL-NEW FICTION:

James Enge

John C. Hocking

Howard Andrew Jones

Aeryn Rudel

Bill Ward

C. L. Werner

Chris Willrich

GOODMAN ·GAMES·

THE SKULL SPEAKS: *Hear this, mortal dogs. You hold in your hands a magazine the likes of which has not been seen for many suns. Once there were magicians whose weird tales could change the wormy earth. They infiltrated your waking world, bringing wonder and glory and imagination. Fantastic visions you dogs could barely grasp. But mortals they were, all of them. They're dust now. With their passing a Thing was gone, a Secret passed. Well, no more. Magicians of the word, the weird tale-tellers: they may be gone, but their vision lives on. I am the skull and soul of one such word-wizard, and I'll bring you Secrets that haven't walked the earth in this century. Stories they'll be, stories that make you bolt up and hunger for adventure. You'll remember what glory could be, you'll realize how you worms have lost sight of the sun. I am the Magician's Skull. Which magician? One you've never heard of: a peer of Howard and Lovecraft, Burroughs and Derleth, Dunsany and Leiber. A wizard who knew Merritt and St. Clair and Vance and Brackett and Wellman and Weinbaum, and Clark Ashton Smith and even grand Gygax himself. All the word-wizards wove wonder, and it matters not whose bones I rot with today. All you need to know is: I bring tales of great fantasy and wondrous adventure. Get ready, mortal dogs. Enjoy this first issue. Enjoy the adventure!* **www.goodman-games.com**

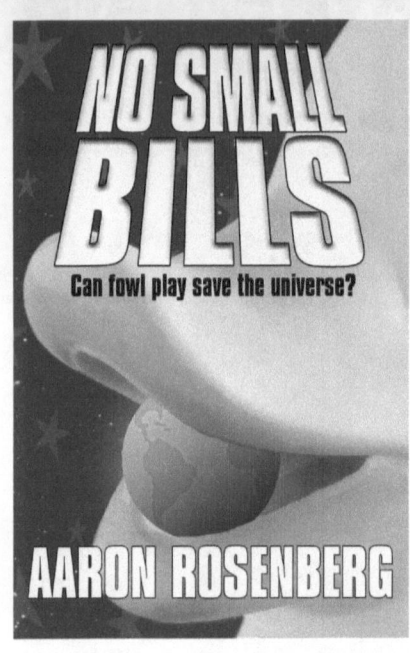

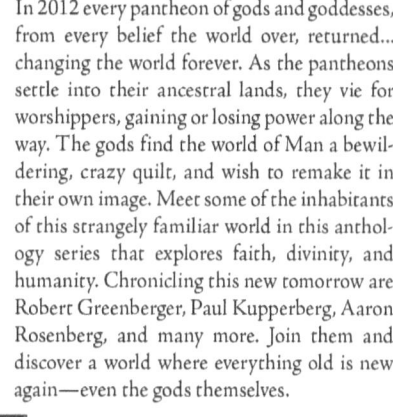

www.ingramcontent.com/pod-product-compliance
Lightning Source LLC
Chambersburg PA
CBHW052020240626
47153CB00006B/1890